Brownsmith's Boy
A Romance In A Garden

By

George Manville Fenn

Brownsmith's Boy
A Romance In A Garden
by George Manville Fenn

Copyright © 2023

All Rights reserved.

ISBN: 978-93-60463-86-1

Published by

DOUBLE 9 BOOKS

2/13-B, Ansari Road
Daryaganj, New Delhi – 110002
info@double9books.com
www.double9books.com
Tel. 011-40042856

This book is under public domain

ABOUT THE AUTHOR

George Manville Fenn was a very productive author of novels, a writer, an editor, and an educator from England. He was born on January 3, 1831, in Pimlico, London. He mostly learned on his own; he taught himself Italian, French, and German. During the years 1851–1854, he went to Battersea Training College for Teachers and then became the head of a state school in Alford, Lincolnshire. In the early 1850s, Fenn started to write short stories and pieces for newspapers and magazines. The Old Forest Ranger, his first book, came out in 1856. Afterward, he wrote more than 100 books, many of them for teenagers and young adults. He was one of the most famous writers of his time, and his books were well-liked and read by many people. He also worked as a reporter and writer for Fenn. Among the newspapers and magazines, he worked for was The Boy's Own Paper, which he ran from 1866 to 1874. He worked hard to make children's books better and was a strong supporter of education and reading. The Englishman Fenn passed away on August 26, 1909, in Isleworth.

CONTENTS

Chapter One
The Boy in the Garden

I always felt as if I should like to punch that boy's head, and then directly after I used to feel as if I shouldn't care to touch him, because he looked so dirty and ragged.

It was not dirty dirt, if you know what I mean by that, but dirt that he gathered up in his work—bits of hay and straw, and dust off a shed floor; mud over his boots and on his toes, for you could see that the big boots he wore seemed to be like a kind of coarse rough shell with a great open mouth in front, and his toes used to seem as if they lived in there as hermit-crabs do in whelk shells. They used to play about in there and waggle this side and that side when he was standing still looking at you; and I used to think that some day they would come a little way out and wait for prey like the different molluscs I had read about in my books.

But you should have seen his hands! I've seen them so coated with dirt that it hung on them in knobs, and at such times he used to hold them up to me with the thumbs and fingers spread out wide, and then down he would go again and continue his work, which, when he was in this state, would be pulling up the weeds from among the onions in the long beds.

I didn't want him to do it, but he used to see me at the window looking out; and I being one lonely boy in the big pond of life, and he being another lonely boy in the same big pond, and both floating about like bits of stick, he seemed as if he wanted to gravitate towards me as bits of stick do to each other, and in his uncouth way he would do all sorts of things to attract my attention.

Sometimes it seemed as if it was to frighten me, at others to show how clever he was; but of course I know now that it was all out of the superabundant energy he had in him, and the natural longing of a boy for a companion.

I'll just tell you what he'd do. After showing me his muddy fingers, and crawling along and digging them as hard as he could into the soil to tear out the weeds, all at once he would kick his heels up in the air like a donkey. Then he would go on weeding again, look to see if I was watching him, and leave his basket and run down between two onion beds on all-fours like a dog, run back, and go on with his work.

Every now and then he would pull up a young onion with the weeds and pick it out, give it a rub on his sleeve, put one end in his mouth, and eat it gradually, taking it in as I've seen a cow with a long strand of rye or grass.

Another time he would fall to punching the ground with his doubled fist, make a basin-like depression, put his head in, support himself by setting his hands on each side of the depression, and then, as easily as could be, throw up his heels and stand upon his head.

It seemed to be no trouble to him to keep his balance, and when up like that he would twist his legs about, open them wide, put them forwards and backwards, and end by insulting me with his feet, so it seemed to me, for he would spar at me with them and make believe to hit out.

All at once he would see one of the labourers in the distance, and then down he would go and continue his weeding.

Perhaps, when no one was looking, he would start up, look round, go down again on all-fours, and canter up to a pear-tree, raise himself up, and begin scratching the bark like one of the cats sharpening its claws; or perhaps trot to an apple-tree, climb up with wonderful activity, creep out along a horizontal branch, and pretend to fall, but save himself by catching with and hanging by one hand.

That done he would make a snatch with his other hand, swing about for a few moments, and then up would go his legs to be crossed over the branch, when he would swing to and fro head downwards, making derisive gestures at me with his hands.

So it was that I used to hate that boy, and think he was little better than a monkey; but somehow I felt envious of him too when the sun shone—I didn't so much mind when it was wet—for he seemed so free and independent, and he was so active and clever, while whenever I tried to stand on my head on the carpet I always tipped right over and hurt my back.

That was a wonderful place, that garden, and I used to gaze over the high wall with its bristle of young shoots of plum-trees growing over the coping, and see the chaffinches building in the spring-time among the green leaves and milky-white blossoms of the pear-trees; or, perhaps, it would be in a handy fork of an apple-tree, with the crimson and pink blossoms all around.

Those trees were planted in straight rows, so that, look which way I would, I could see straight down an avenue; and under them there were rows of gooseberry trees or red currants that the men used to cut so closely in the winter that they seemed to be complete skeletons.

Where there were no gooseberries or currants, the rows of rhubarb plants used to send up their red stems and great green leaves; and in other places there would be great patches of wallflowers, from which wafts of delicious scent would come in at the open window. In the spring there would be great rows of red and yellow tulips, and later on sweet-william and rockets, and purple and yellow pansies in great beds.

I used to wonder that such a boy was allowed to go loose in such a garden as that, among those flowers and strawberry beds, and, above all, apples, and pears, and plums, for in the autumn time the trees trained up against the high red-brick wall were covered with purple and yellow plums, and the rosy apples peeped from among the green leaves, and the pears would hang down till it seemed as if the branches must break.

But that boy went about just as he liked, and it often seemed very hard that such a shaggy-looking wild fellow in rags should have the run of such a beautiful garden, while I had none.

There was a little single opera-glass on the chimney-piece which I used to take down and focus, so that I could see the fruit that was ripe, and the fruit that was green, and the beauty of the flowers. I used to watch the birds building through that glass, and could almost see the eggs in one little mossy cup of a chaffinch's nest; but I could not quite. I did see the tips of the young birds' beaks, though, when they were hatched and the old ones came to feed them.

It was by means of that glass that I could see how the boy fastened up his trousers with one strap and a piece of string, for he had no braces, and there were no brace buttons. Those corduroy trousers had been made for somebody else, I should say for a man, and pieces of the legs had been cut off, and the upper part came well over his back and chest. He had no waistcoat, but he wore a jacket that must have belonged to a man. It was a jacket that was fustian behind, and had fustian sleeves, but the front was of purple plush with red and yellow flowers, softened down with dirt; and the sleeves of this jacket were tucked up very high, while the bottom came down to his knees.

He did not wear a hat, but the crown of an old straw bonnet, the top of which had come unsewed, and rose and fell like the lid of a round box with one hinge, and when the lid blew open you could see his shaggy hair, which seemed as if it had never been brushed since it first came up out of his skin.

The opera-glass was very useful to me, especially as the boy fascinated me so, for I used to watch him with it till I knew that he had two brass shank-buttons and three four-holes of bone on his jacket, that there were no buttons at all on his shirt, and that he had blue eyes, a snub-nose, and had lost one of his top front teeth.

I must have been quite as great an attraction to him as he was to me, but he showed it in a very different way. There would be threatening movements made with his fists. After an hour's hard work at weeding, without paying the slightest heed to my presence, he would suddenly jump up as if resenting my watching, catch up the basket, and make believe to hurl it at me. Perhaps he would pick up a great clod and pretend to throw that, but let it fall beside him; while one day, when I went to the window and looked out, I found him with a good-sized switch which had been the young shoot of a pear tree, and a lump of something of a yellowish brown tucked in the fork of a tree close by where he worked.

He had a basket by his side and was busily engaged as usual weeding, for there was a great battle for ever going on in that garden, where the weeds were always trying to master the flowers and vegetables, and that boy's duty seemed to be to tear up weeds by the roots, and nothing else.

But there by his side stuck in the ground was the switch, and as soon as he saw me at the window he gave a look round to see if he was watched, and then picked up the stick.

"I wonder what he is going to do!" I thought, as I twisted the glass a little and had a good look.

He was so near that the glass was not necessary, but I saw through it that he pinched off a bit of the yellowish-brown stuff, which was evidently clay, and, after rolling it between his hands, he stuck what seemed to be a bit as big as a large taw marble on the end of the switch, gave it a flourish, and the bit of clay flew off.

I could not see where it went, but I saw him watching it, as he quickly took another piece, kneaded it, and with another flourish away that flew.

That bit evidently went over our house; and the next time he tried— *flap!* the piece struck the wall somewhere under the window.

Five times more did he throw, the clay flying swiftly, till all at once *thud!* came a pellet and stuck on the window pane just above my head.

I looked up at the flattened clay, which was sticking fast, and then at that boy, who was down on his knees again weeding away as hard as he could weed, but taking no more notice of me, and I saw the reason: his master was coming down the garden.

Chapter Two
Old Brownsmith

I used to take a good deal of notice of that boy's master as I sat at the window, and it always seemed to me that he went up and down his garden because he was so fond of it.

Later on I knew that it was because he was a market-gardener, and was making his plans as to what was to be cut or picked, or what wanted doing in the place.

He was a pleasant-looking man, with white hair and whiskers, and a red face that always used to make me think of apples, and he was always dressed the same—in black, with a clean white shirt front, and a white cravat without any starch. Perhaps it was so that they might not get in the mud, but at any rate his black trousers were very tight, and his tail-coat was cut very broad and loose, with cross pockets like a shooting-jacket, and these pockets used to bulge.

Sometimes they bulged because he had bast matting for tying up plants, and a knife in one, and a lot of shreds and nails and a hammer in the other; sometimes it was because he had been picking up fruit, or vegetable marrows, or new potatoes, whatever was in season. They always made me think of the clown's breeches, because he used to put everything in, and very often a good deal would be sticking out.

I remember once seeing him go down the garden with a good-sized kitten in each pocket, for there were their heads looking over the sides, and they seemed to be quite contented, blinking away at the other cats which were running and skipping about.

For that boy's master, who was called Brownsmith, was a great man for cats; and whenever he went down his garden there were always six or eight blacks, and black and whites, and tabbies, and tortoise-shells running on before or behind him. When he stopped, first one and then another would have a rub against his leg, beginning with the point of its nose, and running itself along right to the end of its tail, crossing over and having a rub on the other side against the other leg.

So sure as one cat had a rub all the others that could get a chance had a rub as well. Then perhaps their master would stoop down with his knife in his teeth, and take a piece of bast from his pocket, to tie up a flower or a lettuce, when one of the cats was sure to jump on his back, and stop there till he rose, when sometimes it would go on and sit upon his shoulder, more often jump off.

It used to interest me a good deal to watch old Brownsmith and his cats, for I had never known that a cat would run after any one out of doors like a dog. Then, too, they were so full of fun, chasing each other through the bushes, crouching down with their tails writhing from side to side, ready to spring out at their master, or dash off again up the side of a big tree, and look down at him from high upon some branch.

I say all this used to interest me, for I had no companions, and went to no school, but spent my time with my poor mother, who was very ill; and I know now how greatly she must have suffered often and often, when, broken down in health and spirit, suffering from a great sorrow, she used to devote all her time to teaching me.

Our apartments, as you see, overlooked old Brownsmith's market-garden, and very often, as I sat there watching it, I used to wish that I could be as other boys were, running about free in the fields, playing cricket and football, and learning to swim, instead of being shut up there with my mother.

Perhaps I was a selfish boy, perhaps I was no worse than others of my age. I know I was very fond of my mother, for she was always so sweet, and gentle, and tender with me, making the most tedious lessons pleasant by the way she explained them, and helping me when I was worried over some arithmetical question about how many men would do so much work in such and such a number of days if so many men would do the same work in another number of days.

These sums always puzzled me, and do now; perhaps it is because I have an awkwardly shaped brain.

Sometimes, as we sat over the lessons, I used to see a curious pained look spread over my mother's face, and the tears would come in her eyes, but when I kissed her she would smile directly and call my attention to the beauty of the rime frost on the fruit-trees in Brownsmith's garden; or, if it was summer, to the sweet scent of the flowers; or to the ripening fruit in autumn.

Ah, if I had known then, I say to myself, how different I might have been; how much more patient and helpful to her! But I did not know, for I was a very thoughtless boy.

Now it came to pass one day that an idea entered my head as I saw my mother seated with her pale cheek resting upon her hand, looking out over old Brownsmith's garden, which was just then at its best. It was summer time, and wherever you looked there were flowers—not neat flower-beds, but great clumps and patches of roses, and sweet-williams and pinks, and carnations, that made the air thick with their sweet odours. Her eyes were half closed, and every now and then I saw her draw in a long breath, as if she were enjoying the sweet scent.

As I said, I had an idea, and the idea was that I would slip out quietly and go and spend that sixpence.

Which sixpence?

Why, that sixpence—that red-hot one that tried so hard to burn a hole through my pocket.

I had had it for two days, and it was still at the bottom along with my knife, a ball of string, and that piece of india-rubber I had chewed for hours to make a pop patch. I had nearly spent it twice—the first time on one of these large white neatly-sewn balls, with "Best Tennis" printed upon them in blue; the second time in a pewter squirt.

I had wanted a squirt for a long time, for those things had a great fascination for me, and I had actually entered the shop door to make my purchase when something seemed to stop me, and I ran home.

And now I thought I would go and spend that coin.

I slipped quietly to the other window, and had a good look round, but I could not see that boy, for if I had seen him I don't think I should have had the heart to go, feeling sure, as I did, that he had a spite against me. As I said, though, he was nowhere visible, so I slipped downstairs, ran along the lane to the big gate, and walked boldly in.

There were several people about, but they took no notice of me—stout hard-looking women, with coarse aprons tied tightly about their waists and legs; there were men too, but all were busy in the great sheds, where they seemed to be packing baskets, quite a mountain of which stood close at hand.

There were high oblong baskets big enough to hold me, but besides these there were piles upon piles of round flat baskets of two sizes, and hanging to the side of one of the sheds great bunches of white wood strawberry pottles, looking at a distance like some kind of giant flower, all in elongated buds.

Close by was a cart with its shafts sticking up in the air. Farther on a wagon with "Brownsmith" in yellow letters on a great red band; and this I passed to go up to the house. But the door was closed, and it was evident that every one was busy in the garden preparing the night's load for market.

I stood still for a minute, thinking that I could not be very wrong if I went down the garden, to see if I could find Mr Brownsmith, and my heart began to beat fast at the idea of penetrating what was to me a land of mystery, of which, just then, I held the silver pass-key in the shape of that sixpence.

"I'll go," I said. "He can't be very cross;" and, plucking up courage, but with the feeling upon me that I was trespassing, I went past the cart, and had gone half-way by the wagon, when there was a creaking, rattling noise of baskets, and something made a bound.

I started back, feeling sure that some huge dog was coming at me; but there in the wagon, and kneeling on the edge to gaze down at me with a fierce grin, was that boy.

I was dreadfully alarmed, and felt as if the next minute he and I would be having a big fight; but I wouldn't show my fear, and I stared up at him defiantly with my fists clenching, ready for his first attack.

He did not speak—I did not speak; but we stared at each other for some moments, before he took a small round turnip out of his pocket and began to munch it.

"Shock!" cried somebody just then; and the boy turned himself over the edge of the wagon, dropped on to the ground, and ran towards one of the sheds, while, greatly relieved, I looked about me, and could see Mr Brownsmith some distance off, down between two rows of trees that formed quite an avenue.

It seemed so beautiful after being shut up so much in our sitting-room, to walk down between clusters of white roses and moss roses, with Anne Boleyne pinks scenting the air, and far back in the shade bright orange double wallflowers blowing a little after their time.

I had not gone far when a blackbird flew out of a pear-tree, and I knew that there must be a nest somewhere close by. Sure enough I could see it in a fork, with a curious chirping noise coming from it, as another blackbird flew out, saw me, and darted back.

I would have given that sixpence for the right to climb that pear-tree, and I gave vent to a sigh as I saw the figure of old Brownsmith coming towards me, looking much more stern and sharp than he did at a distance, and with his side pockets bulging enormously.

"Hallo, young shaver! what's your business?" he said, in a quick authoritative way, as we drew near to each other.

I turned a little red, for it sounded insulting for a market gardener to speak to me like that, for I never forgot that my father had been a captain in an Indian regiment, and was killed fighting in the Sikh war.

I did not answer, but drew myself up a little, before saying rather consequentially:

"Sixpenn'orth of flowers and strawberries—good ones."

"Oh, get out!" he said gruffly, and he half turned away. "We've no time for picking sixpenn'orths, boy. Run up into the road to the greengrocer's shop."

My face grew scarlet, and the beautiful garden seemed as if it was under a cloud instead of the full blaze of sunshine, while I turned upon my heel and was walking straight back.

"Here!"

I walked on.

"Hi, boy!" shouted old Brownsmith.

I turned round, and he was signalling to me with the whole of his crooked arm.

"Come on," he shouted, and he thrust a hand and the greater part of his arm into one of his big pockets, and pulled out one of those curved buckhorn-handled knives, which he opened with his white teeth.

He did not look quite so grim now, as he said:

"Come o' purpose, eh?"

"Yes," I said.

"Ah! well, I won't send you back without 'em, only I don't keep a shop."

I looked rather haughty and consequential, I believe, but the looks of such a boy as I made no impression, and he began to cut here and there moss, and maiden's blush, and cabbage roses—simple old-fashioned flowers, for the great French growers had not filled England with their beautiful children, and a gardener in these days would not have believed in the possibility of a creamy *Gloire de Dijon* or that great hook-thorned golden beauty *Maréchal Niel*.

He cut and cut, long-stalked flowers with leaf and bud, and thrust them into his left hand, his knife cutting and his hand grasping the flower in one movement, while his eye selected the best blossom at a glance.

At last there were so many that I grew fidgety.

"I said sixpenn'orth, sir, flowers and strawberries," I ventured to remark.

"Not deaf, my lad," he replied with a grim smile. "Here, let's get some of these."

These were pinks and carnations, of which he cut a number, pushing one of the cats aside with his foot so that it should not be in his way.

"Here you are!" he cried. "Mind the thorns. My roses have got plenty to keep off pickers and stealers. Now, what next?"

"I did want some strawberries," I said, "but—"

"Where's your basket, my hearty?"

I replied that I had not brought one.

"You're a pretty fellow," he said. "I can't tie strawberries up in a bunch. Why didn't you bring a basket? Oh, I see; you want to carry 'em inside?"

"No," I said shortly, for he seemed now unpleasantly familiar, and the garden was not half so agreeable as I had expected.

However he seemed to be quite good-tempered now, and giving me a nod and a jerk of his head, which meant—"This way," he went down a path, cut a great rhubarb leaf, and turned to me.

"Here, catch hold," he cried; "here's one of nature's own baskets. Now let's see if there's any strawberries ripe."

I saw that he was noticing me a good deal as we went along another path towards where the garden was more open, but I kept on in an independent way, smelling the pinks from time to time, till we came to a great square bed, all straw, with the great tufts of the dark green strawberry plants standing out of it in rows. The leaves looked large, and glistened in the sunshine, and every here and there I could see the great scarlet berries shining as if they had been varnished, and waiting to be picked.

"Ah, thief!" shouted my guide, as a blackbird flew out of the bed, uttering its loud call. "Why, boys, boys, you ought to have caught him."

This was to the cats, one of which answered by giving itself a rub down his leg, while he clapped his hand upon my shoulder.

"There you are, my hearty. It isn't so far for you to stoop as it would be for me. Go and pick 'em."

"Pick them?" I said, looking at him wonderingly.

"To be sure. Go ahead. I'll hold your flowers. Only take the ripe ones, and see here—do you know how to pick strawberries?"

I felt so amused at such a silly question that I looked up at him and laughed.

"Oh, you do?" he said.

"Why, anybody could pick strawberries," I replied.

"Really, now! Well, let's see. There's a big flat fellow, pick him."

I handed him the flowers, and stepping between two rows of plants, stooped down, and picked the great strawberry he pointed out.

"Oh, you call that picking, do you?" he said.

"Yes, sir. Don't you?"

"No: I call it tearing my plants to pieces. Why, look here, if my pickers were to go to work like that, I should only get half a crop and my plants would be spoiled."

I looked at him helplessly, and wished he would pick the strawberries himself.

"Look here," he said, stooping over a plant, and letting a great scarlet berry specked with golden seeds fall over into his hand. "Now see: finger nail and thumb nail; turn 'em into scissors; draw one against the other, and the stalk's through. That's the way to do it, and the rest of the bunch not hurt. Now then, your back's younger than mine. Go ahead."

I felt hot and uncomfortable, but I took the rhubarb leaf, stepped in amongst the clean straw, and, using my nails as he had bid me, found that the strawberries came off wonderfully well.

"Only the ripe ones, boy; leave the others. Pick away. Poor old Tommy then!"

I looked up to see if he was speaking to me, but he had let one of the cats run up to his shoulder, and he was stroking the soft lithe creature as it rubbed itself against his head.

"That's the way, boy," he cried, as I scissored off two or three berries in the way he had taught me. "I like to see a chap with brains. Come, pick away."

I did pick away, till I had about twenty in the soft green leaf, and then I stopped, knowing that in flowers and fruit I had twice as much as I should have obtained at the shop.

"Oh, come, get on," he cried contemptuously. "You're not half a fellow. Don't stop. Does your back ache?"

"No, sir," I said; "but—"

"Oh, you wouldn't earn your salt as a picker," he cried. As he said this he came on to the bed, and, bending down, seemed to sweep a hand round the strawberry plant, gathering its leaves aside, and leaving the berries free to be snipped off by the right finger and thumb. He kept on bidding me pick away, but he sheared off three to my one, and at the end of a few minutes I was holding the rhubarb leaf against my breast to keep the fruit from falling over the side.

"There you are," he cried at last. "That do?"

"Oh, yes, sir," I said; "but—"

"That's enough," he cried sharply. "Here, hand over that sixpence. Money's money, and you can't get on without it, youngster."

I gave him the coin, and he took it, span it up in the air, caught it, and after dragging out a small wash-leather bag he dropped it in, gave me a comical look as he twisted a string about the neck, tucked it in, and replaced the bag in his pocket.

"There you are," he cried. "Small profits and quick returns. No credit given. Toddle; and don't you come and bother me again. I'm a market grower, my young shaver, and can't trade your fashion."

"I did not know, sir," I said, trying to look and speak with dignity, for it was very unpleasant to be addressed so off-handedly by this man, just as if I had been asking him a favour.

"I'm very much obliged to you," I added, for I had glanced at the bunch of roses; and as I looked at the fresh sweet-scented beauties I thought of how delighted my poor mother would be, and I could not help feeling that old Brownsmith had been very generous.

Then making him rather an awkward bow, I stalked off, feeling very small, and was some distance back towards the gate, wondering whether I should meet "Shock," when from behind there came a loud "Hi!"

I paid no heed and went on, for it was not pleasant to be shouted at like that by a market grower, and my dignity was a good deal touched by the treatment I had received; but all at once there came from behind me such a roar that I was compelled to stop, and on turning round there was old Brownsmith trotting after me, with his cats skipping about in all directions to avoid being trodden on and to keep up.

He was very much more red in the face now, for the colour went all down below his cheeks and about his temples, and he was shining very much.

"Why, I didn't know you with your cap on," he cried. "Take it off. No, you can't. I will."

To my great annoyance he snatched off my cap.

"To be sure! I'm right," he said, and then he put my cap on again, uncomfortably wrong, and all back: for no one can put your cap on for you as you do it yourself. "You live over yonder at the white house with the lady who is ill?"

I nodded.

"The widow lady?"

"I live with mamma," I said shortly.

"Been very ill, hasn't she?"

"Yes, sir."

"Ah! bad thing illness, I suppose. Never was ill, only when the wagon went over my leg."

"Yes, sir, she has been very bad."

I was fidgeting to go, but he took hold of one of the ends of my little check silk tie, and kept fiddling it about between his finger and thumb.

"What's the matter?"

"Dr Morrison told Mrs Beeton, our landlady, that it was decline, sir."

"And then Mrs Beeton told you?"

"No, sir, I heard the doctor tell her."

"And then you went and frightened the poor thing and made her worse by telling her?"

"No, I did not, sir," I said warmly.

"Why not?"

"Because I thought it might make her worse."

"Humph! Hah! Poor dear lady!" he said more softly. "Looked too ill to come to church last Sunday, boy. Flowers and fruit for her?"

I nodded.

"She send you to buy 'em?"

I shook my head, for I was so hurt by his abrupt way, his sharp cross-examination, and the thoughts of my mother's illness, that I could not speak.

"Who sent you then—Mrs Beeton?"

"No, sir."

"Who did?"

"Nobody, sir. I thought she would like some, and I came."

"For a surprise, eh?"

Yes, sir.

"Own money?"

I stared at him hard.

"I said, Own money? the sixpence? Where did you get it?"

"I have sixpence a week allowed me to spend."

"Hah! to be sure," he said, still holding on by my tie, and staring at me as he fumbled with one hand in his trousers pocket. "Get out, Dick, or I'll tread on you!" this to one of the cats, who seemed to think because he was black and covered with black fur that he was a blacking-brush, and he was using himself accordingly all over his master's boots.

"If you please, I want to go now," I said hurriedly.

"To be sure you do," he said, still holding on to the end of my tie—"to be sure you do. Hah! that's got him at last."

I stared in return, for there had been a great deal of screwing about going on in that pocket, as if he could not get out his big fist, but it came out at last with a snatch.

"Here, where are you?" he said. "Weskit? why, what a bit of a slit it is to call a pocket. Hold the sixpence though, won't it?"

"If you please I'd rather pay for the flowers," I cried, flushing as he held on by the tie with one hand, and thrust the sixpence back in my pocket with the other.

"Dessay you would," he replied; "but I told you before I'm market grower and dursen't take small sums. Not according to Cocker. Didn't know Cocker, I suppose, did you?"

"No, sir."

"Taught 'rithmetic. Didn't learn his 'rithmetic then?"

"No, sir," I replied, "Walkinghame's."

"Did you though? There, now, you play a walking game, and get home and count your strawberries."

"Yes, sir, but—"

"I say, what a fellow you are to but! Why, you're like Teddy, my goat, I once had. No, no! No money. Welcome to the fruit, ditto flowers, boy. This way."

He was leading me towards the gate now like a dog by a string, and it annoyed me that he would hold me by the end of my tie, the more so that I could see Shock with a basket turned over his head watching me from down amongst the trees.

"Come on again, my lad, often as you like. Lots growing—lots spoils."

"Thank you, sir," I said diffidently, "but—"

"Woa, Teddy," he cried, laughing. "There; that'll do. Look here, why don't you bring her for a walk round the garden—do her good? Glad to see her any time. Here, what a fellow you are, dropping your strawberries. Let it alone, Dick. Do for Shock."

I had let a great double strawberry roll off the top of my heap, and a cat darted at it to give it a sniff; but old Brownsmith picked it up and laid it on the top of a post formed of a cut-down tree.

"Now, then, let's get a basket. Look better for an invalid. One minute: some leaves."

He stooped and picked some strawberry leaves, and one or two very large ripe berries, which he told me were Myatt's.

Then taking me to a low cool shed that smelt strongly of cut flowers, he took down a large open strawberry basket from a nail, and deftly arranged the leaves and fruit therein, with the finest ripened fruit pointing upwards.

"That's the way to manage it, my lad," he said, giving me a queer look; "put all the bad ones at the bottom and the good ones at the top. That's what you'd better do with your qualities, only never let the bad ones get out."

"Now, your pinks and roses," he said; and, taking them, he shook them out loosely on the bench beneath a window, arranged them all very cleverly in a bunch, and tied it up with a piece of matting.

"I'm sure I'm very much obliged to you, sir," I said, warmly now, for it seemed to me that I had been making a mistake about Mr Brownsmith, and that he was a very good old fellow after all.

"That's right," he said, laughing. "So you ought to be. Good-bye. Come again soon. My dooty to your mamma, and I hope she'll be better. Shake hands."

I held out my hand and grasped his warmly as we reached the gate, seeing Shock watching me all the time. Then as I stood outside old Brownsmith laughed and nodded.

"Mind how you pack your strawberries," he said with a laugh; "bad 'uns at bottom, good 'uns at top. Good-bye, youngster, good-bye."

Chapter Three
Old Brownsmith's Visitor

The time glided on, but I did not go to the garden again, for my mother felt that we must not put ourselves under so great an obligation to a stranger. Neither did I take her over for a walk, but we sat at the window a great deal after lesson time; and whenever I was alone and Shock was within sight, he used to indulge in some monkey-like gesture, all of which seemed meant to show me what a very little he thought of me.

At the end of a fortnight, as I was sitting at the window talking to a boy who went to a neighbouring school, and telling him why I did not go, a great clod of earth came over the wall and hit the boy in the back.

"Who's that!" he cried sharply. "Did you shy that lump?"

"No," I said; and before I could say more, he cried:

"I know. It was Brownsmith's baboon shied that. Only let us get him out in the fields, we'll give it him. You know him, don't you?"

"Do you mean Shock?" I said.

"Yes, that ragged old dirty chap," he cried. "You can see him out of your window, can't you?"

"I can sometimes," I said; "but I can't now."

"That's because he's sneaking along under the wall. Never mind; we'll pay him some day if he only comes out."

"Doesn't he come out then?"

"No. He's nobody's boy, and sleeps in the sheds over there. One of Brownsmith's men picked him up in the road, and brought him home in one of the market carts. Brownsmith sent him to the workhouse, but he always runs away and comes back. He's just like a monkey, ain't he? Here, I must go; but I say, why don't you ask your ma to let you come and play with us; we have rare games down the meadows, bathing, and wading, and catching dace?"

"I should like to come," I said dolefully.

"Ah, there's no end of things to see down there—water-rats and frogs; and there's a swan's nest, with the old bird sitting; and don't the old cock come after you savage if you go near! Oh, we do have rare games there on half-holidays! I wish you'd come."

"I should like to," I said.

"Ain't too proud; are you?"

"Oh no!" I said, shaking my head.

"Because I was afraid you were. Well, I shall catch it if I stop any longer. I say, is your ma better?"

I shook my head.

"Ain't going to die, is she?"

"Oh no!" I said sharply.

"That's all right. Well, you get her to let you come. What's your name?"

"Grant," I said.

"Grant! Grant what?"

"Dennison."

"Oh, all right, Grant! I shall call for you next half-holiday; and mind you come."

"Stop a moment," I said. "What's your name?"

"George Day," he replied; and then my new friend trotted off, swinging half-a-dozen books at the end of a strap, and I sat at the window wishing that I too could go to school and have a strap to put round my books and swing them, for my life seemed very dull.

All at once I saw something amongst the bristly young shoots of the plum-trees along the wall, and on looking more attentively I made out that it was the top of Shock's straw head-piece with the lid gone, and the hair sticking out in the most comical way.

I watched him intently, fully expecting to see another great clod of earth come over, and wishing I had something to throw back at him; but I had nothing but a flower-pot with a geranium in it, and the shells upon the chimney-piece, and they were Mrs Beeton's, and I didn't like to take them.

The head came a little higher till the whole of the straw bonnet crown was visible, and I could just make out the boy's eyes.

Of course he was watching me, and I sat and watched him, feeling that he must have turned one of the trained plum-trees into a ladder, and climbed up; and I found myself wondering whether he had knocked off any of the young fruit.

Then, as he remained perfectly still, watching me, I began to wonder why he should be so fond of taking every opportunity he could find to stare at me; and then I wondered what old Brownsmith would say to him, or do, if he came slowly up behind him and caught him climbing up his beautifully trained trees.

Just then I heard a loud cough that I knew was old Brownsmith's, for I had heard it dozens of times, and Shock's head disappeared as if by magic.

I jumped up to see, for I felt sure that Shock was going to catch it, and then I saw that old Brownsmith was not in his garden, but in the lane on our side, and that he was close beneath the window looking up at me.

He nodded, and I had just made up my mind that I would not complain about Shock, when there was a loud thump of the knocker, and directly after I heard the door open, a heavy step in the passage, the door closed, and then the sound of old Brownsmith wiping his shoes on the big mat.

His shoes could not have wanted wiping, for it was a very dry day, but he kept on rub—rub—rub, till Mrs Beeton, who waited upon us as well as let us her apartments, came upstairs, knocked at my mother's door, and went down again.

Then there was old Brownsmith's heavy foot on the stair, and he was shown in to where I was waiting.

"Mrs Dennison will be here directly," said our landlady, and the old man smiled pleasantly at me.

I say old man, for he was in my eyes a very old man, though I don't suppose he was far beyond fifty; but he was very grey, and grey hairs in those days meant to me age.

"How do?" he said as soon as he saw me. "Being such a nigh neighbour I thought I'd come and pay my respects."

He had a basket in his hand, and just then my mother entered, and he turned and began backing before her on to me.

"Like taking a liberty," he said in his rough way, "but your son and me's old friends, ma'am, and I've brought you a few strawberries before they're over."

Before my mother could thank him he went on:

"Been no rain, you see, and the sun's ripening of 'em off so fast. A few flowers, too, not so good as they should be, ma'am, but he said you liked flowers."

I saw the tears stand in my mother's eyes as she thanked him warmly for his consideration, and begged him to sit down.

But no. He was too busy. Lot of people getting ready for market and he was wanted at home, he said, but he thought he would bring those few strawberries and flowers.

"I told him, you know, how welcome you'd be," he continued. "Garden's always open to you, ma'am. Come often. Him too."

He was at the door as he said this, and nodding and bowing he backed out, while I followed him downstairs to open the door.

"Look here," he said, offending me directly by catching hold of one end of my neckerchief, "you bring her over, and look here," he went on in a severe whisper, "you be a good boy to her, and try all you can to make her happy. Do you hear?"

"*Yes*, sir," I said. "I do try."

"That's right. Don't you worry her, because—because it's my opinion that she couldn't bear it, and boys are such fellows. Now you mind."

"Yes, sir," I said, "I'll mind;" and he went away, while, when I returned to the room where my mother was holding the flowers to her face, and seeming as if their beauty and sweetness were almost more than she could bear, I glanced towards the window, and there once more, with his head just above the wall, and peering through the thick bristling twigs, was that boy Shock, watching our window till old Brownsmith reached his gate.

Hardly a week had passed before the old man got hold of me as I was going by his gate, taking me as usual by the end of my tie and leading me down the garden to cut some more flowers.

"You haven't brought her yet," he said. "Look here, if you don't bring her I shall think you are too proud."

"He shall not think that," my mother said; and for the next week or two she went across for a short time every day, while I walked beside her, for her to lean upon my shoulder, and to carry the folding seat so that she might sit down from time to time.

Upon these occasions I never saw Shock, and old Brownsmith never came near us. It was as if he wanted us to have the garden to ourselves for these walks, and to a great extent we did.

Of course I used to notice how often I had to spread out that chair for her to sit down under the shady trees; but I thought very little more of it. She was weak. Well, I knew that; but some people were weak, I said, and some were strong, and she would be better when it was not so hot.

Chapter Four
A Lesson in Swimming

It was hot! One of those dry summers when the air seems to quiver with the heat, and one afternoon, as I was in my old place at the window watching Shock go to and fro, carrying baskets of what seemed to be beans, George Day came along.

"I say," he cried, "ask leave to come with us. We've got a half-holiday."

Just then I saw the bristling shoots on the wall shake, but I paid no heed, for I was too much interested in my new friend's words.

"Where are you going?" I asked.

"Oh, down the meadows! that's the best place, and there's no end of fun to be had. I'll take a fishing-rod." I went to where my mother was lying down and asked her consent, receiving a feeble *yes*, and her hand went up to my neck, to draw me down that she might kiss me.

"Be back in good time," she whispered. "George Day, you said?"

"Yes; his father is something in London, and he goes to the grammar-school."

"Be back in good time," she whispered again; and getting my cap, I just caught sight of Shock at the top of the wall as I ran by the window.

"Poor fellow!" I thought, "how he, too, would like a holiday!"

"Here I am," I cried; and feeling as if I had been just released from some long confinement, I set off with my companion at a sharp run.

We had to call at his house, a large red brick place just at the end of the village, close to Isleworth church, where the rod was obtained, with a basket to hold bait, lines, and the fish that we were going to catch; and soon after we were down where the sleek cows were contentedly lying about munching, and giving their heads an angry toss now and then to keep off the flies.

Rich grass, golden butter-cups, bushes and trees whose boughs swept down towards the ground, swallows and swifts darting here and there, and beneath the vividly blue sky there was the river like so much damascened silver, for in those days one never thought about the mud.

I cannot describe the joy I felt in running here and there with my companion, and a couple of his school-fellows who had preceded us, and who saluted us as we approached with a shout.

We ran about till we were tired, and then the fishing commenced from the bank, for the tide was well up, and according to my companion's account the fish were in plenty.

Perhaps they were, but though bait after bait was placed upon the hook, and the line thrown out to float along with the current, not a fish was caught, no vestige of that nerve-titillating tremble of the float—a bite—was seen.

Every now and then some one struck sharply, trying to make himself believe that roach or dace had taken the bait, but the movement of the float was always due to the line dragging the gravelly ground, or the bait touching one of the many weeds.

The sun was intensely hot, and scorched our backs, and burned our faces by flashing back from the water, which looked cool and tempting, as it ran past our feet.

We fished on, sometimes one handling the rod and sometimes the other—beginning by throwing in the line with whispered words, so as not to frighten the fish that were evidently not there, and ending by sending in bait and float with a splash, and with noise and joking.

"There's a big one," some one would cry, and a clod torn out from the bank, or a stone, would be thrown in amidst bursts of laughter.

"Oh it's not a jolly bit of good," cried one of the boys; "they won't bite to-day. I'm so thirsty, let's have a drink."

"No, no, don't drink the water," I said; "it isn't good enough."

"What shall we do then—run after the cows for a pen'orth of milk?"

"I say, look there," cried George Day; "the tide's turned. It's running down. We shall get plenty of fish now."

"Why, there's somebody bathing down below there," cried another of the boys.

"Yes, and can't he swim!"

"Let's all have a bathe," cried young Day.

"Ah, come on: it will be jolly here. Who's first in?"

I looked on half in amazement, for directly after catching sight of the head of some lad in the water about a couple of hundred yards below us, who seemed to be swimming about in the cool water with the greatest ease, my companions began to throw off caps and jackets, and to untie and kick off their boots.

"But we haven't got any towels," cried George Day.

"Towels!" cried one of the others; "why, the sun will dry us in five minutes; come on. What a day for a swim!"

It did look tempting there at the bottom of that green meadow, deep in grass and with the waving trees to hide us from observation, though there was not a house within a mile, nor, saving an occasional barge with a sleepy man hanging over the tiller, a boat to be seen, and as I watched the actions of my companions, I, for the first time in my life, felt the desire to imitate them come on me strongly.

They were not long undressing, one kicking off his things anyhow, another carefully folding them as he took them off, and tucking his socks inside his boots. But careful and careless alike, five minutes had not elapsed before to my delight George Day, who was a boy of about fourteen, ran back a dozen yards from the river's brink and threw up his arms.

"One, two, three, cock warning!" he shouted, ran by me swiftly, and plunged into the river with a tremendous splash.

I felt horrified, but the next moment his head reappeared bobbing about, and he swam along easily and well.

"Oh it's so lovely," he cried. "Come along."

"All right!" cried one of his friends, sitting down on the edge of the bank, and lowering himself in gently, to stand for a few moments up to his arm-pits, and then duck his head down twice, rubbing his eyes to get the water out, and then stooping down and beginning to swim slowly and laboriously, and with a great deal of puffing.

"Oh, what a cowardly way of getting in!" said the third, who stood on the bank, hesitating.

"Well, let's see you, then," cried George Day, who was swimming close at hand. "Jump in."

"Oh, I can't jump in like you do," said the other; "it gives me the headache."

"Why, you're afraid."

"No, I'm not."

"Yes, you are. Come in, or I'll pull you down."

"There!"

The boy jumped in feet first, and as soon as he came up he struggled to the bank, and puffed and panted and squeezed the water out of his hair.

"Oh my, isn't it jolly cold!" he cried. "It takes all my breath away."

"Cold!" cried the others; "it's lovely. Here you, Dennison, come in."

"I can't swim," I said, feeling a curious shrinking on the one side, quite a temptation on the other.

"And you never will," cried George Day, "if you don't try. It's so easy: look here!"

He swam a few yards with the greatest ease, turned round, and began swimming slowly back.

"Go on—faster," I cried, for I was interested.

"Can't," he cried, "tide runs so sharp. If I didn't mind I should be swept right away. Come in. I'll soon teach you."

I shook my head.

"Oh, you are a fellow. Come on."

"No, I sha'n't bathe," I said in a doubtful tone.

"Oh, here's a chap! I say isn't he a one! Always tied to his mother's apron-string: can't play cricket, or rounders, or football, and can't swim. I say, isn't he a molly."

The others laughed, and being now out of their misery, as they termed it, they were splashing about and enjoying the water, but neither of them went far from the bank.

"I say, why don't you come in?" cried the boy who jumped in feet first. "You will like it so."

"Yes: come along, and try to swim. I can take five strokes. Look here."

I watched while the boy went along puffing and panting, and making a great deal of splashing.

"Get out!" said the other; "he has got one leg on the ground. This is the way to learn to swim. Look here, Dennison, my father showed me."

I looked, and he waded out three or four yards, till the water was nearly over his shoulders.

"Oh, I say, isn't the tide strong!" he cried. "Now, then, look."

He threw up his arms, joined his hands as he stood facing me, made a sort of jump and turned right over, plunging down before me, his legs and feet coming right out, and then for some seconds there was a great deal of turmoil and splashing in the muddy water, and he came up close to the bank.

"That's the way," he cried, panting. "You have to try to get to the bottom, and that gives you confidence."

"I didn't learn that way," shouted George Day. "See me float!"

We all looked, and he turned over on his back, but splashed a good deal to keep himself up. Then all at once he went under, and my heart seemed to stand still, but he came up again directly, shaking his head and spitting.

"Tread water!" he cried; and he seemed to be wading about with difficulty.

"Is it deep there?" I shouted.

"Look," he cried; and raising his hands above his head he sank out of sight, his hands disappearing too, and then he was up again directly and swam to the bank.

"I wish I could swim like you do," I said, looking at him with admiration.

"Well, it's easy enough," he said. "Come along."

"Shall I?"

"Yes. Why, what are you afraid of? Nobody ever comes down here except us boys who want a bathe. Slip off your clothes and have a good dip. You're sure to like it."

"But I've never been used to it," I protested.

"Then get used to it," he cried. "I say, boys, he ought to learn, oughtn't he?"

"Yes," cried the others. "Let's get out and make him."

"Oh, I don't want any making," I said proudly. "But I say—is it dangerous?"

"Dangerous! Hark at him! Ha—ha—ha!" laughed Day. "Why, what are you afraid of? There, jump out of your jacket. I sha'n't stop in much longer, and I want to give you a lesson."

"He's afraid," shouted the other two boys.

"Am I! You'll see," I said sturdily; and, feeling as if I were going to do something very desperate, and with a curious sensation of dread coming all over me, even to the roots of my hair, I rapidly undressed and went to the edge.

"Hooray!" shouted Day. "Now, look here: you can jump in head first, which is the proper way, or sneak in toes first, like they do. Show 'em you aren't afraid. They daren't jump in head first. Come on; I'll take care you don't come up too far out, as you can't swim."

"Would it matter if I did?" I said excitedly.

"Get along with you! no," cried Day.

I hesitated, for the water looked very dreadful, and in spite of the burning sunshine it seemed cold. I felt so helpless too, and would gladly have run back to my clothes and dressed, instead of standing on the brink of the river.

"In with you," shouted Day, backing away from the bank, and the other two boys stood a little way off, with the water up to their chests, grinning and jeering.

"He daren't."

"He's afraid."

"I say, don't you jump in: you'll get wet."

"I say, young 'un, don't. You learn to swim in the washing-tub in warm water."

"Don't you take any notice of them," cried Day. "You jump in. Join your hands above your head and go in with a regular good leap. They can't."

I felt desperate. The water seemed to drive me back, but all the time the jeers of the boys pricked and stirred me on, and at last, obeying Day to the letter, I placed my hands above my head, diver fashion, and took the plunge down into the darkness of the chilly water, which seemed to roar and thunder in my ears, and then, before I knew where I was, I found myself standing up, spitting, half blind, with a curious burning sensation in my nostrils, and a horrible catching of the breath.

"Hooray!" shouted Day. "You've beat them hollow. Now you're out of your misery and can show them. I bet a penny you learn to swim before they can."

This was encouraging, and I began to feel a warm glow of satisfaction in my veins.

"Catch hold of my hand," cried Day.

"No, no," I cried excitedly. "You'll take me where it's deep."

"Get out!" he said. "I shouldn't be such a fool. There, go on then by yourself. Don't go where it's more than up to your chin."

"Oh, no!" I said, stooping and rising, and letting the water, as it ran swiftly, send a curious cold thrill all over me. And then, as I began cautiously to wade about, panting, and with my breath coming in an irregular manner, there was a very pleasurable sensation in it all. First I began to notice how firm and close and heavy the water felt, and how it pressed against me. Then I began to think of how hard it was to walk, the water keeping me back; and directly after, as I stepped suddenly in a soft place all mud, which seemed to ooze up between my toes, the water came to my shoulders, and I felt as if I were being lifted from my feet.

"I say how do you like it?" cried Day, who was swimming a few yards away.

"I don't know," I panted. "I think I like it."

"Oh, you'll soon think it glorious," he replied. "You'll love it as soon as you can swim."

The other two had waded on for some distance against the current, taking no further interest in me now I had made my plunge.

"I should like to swim," I said.

"Oh it's easy enough once you get used to it. That chap down below there swims twice as well as I can, but I don't know who he is."

"What shall I do first?" I asked.

"Oh, throw yourself flat on the water, and kick out your arms and legs like I do—like a frog. You'll soon learn. Now I'm going to swim up as far as they are, and then let myself float back. You'll see me come down. It's so easy. You watch."

"All right!" I said.

"You keep close in to the bank," he shouted; "the tide don't run there. Keep on trying to throw yourself down and kick out like a frog. You'll soon swim."

I nodded, and stood holding on by a tuft of coarse sedge, watching him as he threw himself on his side, and went off pretty close to the bank, where the water was eddying; and the next minute he was beyond a clump of sedge that projected into the river, and I was alone.

I felt no dread now, for the water seemed pleasantly cool, and I began to grow more confident. The buoyancy was delicious, and I found that by holding on with both hands to the long rushes I could float on the water, throwing myself down and keeping close to the surface, but with my legs gradually sinking, till I gave them a kick and rose again.

I amused myself this way for a minute or two, and then, leaving the tuft of rushes, I began to wade slowly along with the water up to my chest, and every now and then I stooped down, so that it came above my shoulders, and struck out with my hands; but I dare not throw myself flat with my legs off the bottom. That was too much to expect, and I had not recovered yet from the desperate plunge in, the recollection of which made me wonder at my temerity.

It was very nice, that first lesson in the water's buoyancy, and as I jumped up, or lowered myself down, or held on by the tufts by the brink, and let myself float, I could not help comparing myself to the soap in the bathtub at home, for that almost floated, but gradually settled down to the bottom, just as my body seemed to do.

"I shall soon swim," I thought to myself; but I felt no inclination to risk the first plunge and begin the struggle. It was far more pleasant to keep on wading there with the water up to my chest, and the delicious sensation of novelty, half fear, half pleasure, making me now venture out a few inches into deeper water, now shrink back towards the bank.

How beautiful it all seemed, with the mellow afternoon sunlight dancing on the water as a puff of warm wind came now and then along the river. The trees were so green and the sky so blue, and the barges, and horses that drew them by the towing-path on the other side, all seemed to add to my pleasure, for the barges seemed to glide along so easily, and they floated, and that was what I wanted to do.

I forgot all about my companions, who must have been a couple of hundred yards higher up the river, while I was wading down.

By degrees I found the water a little deeper, and I shrank from it at first, but I was close to the bank and had only to stretch out my hand to catch hold of a tuft of grass or sedge, and, after the shrinking sensation, it seemed pleasant to have the water higher up about my shoulders. It was so much harder to walk, and I could feel myself almost panting. Beside this there was a nice soft muddy bottom, pleasanter to the feet than the gravel where I had plunged in.

Yes: I thought it a much nicer place there, and I was slowly and cautiously wading on, while all at once I found the water seeming to come in the opposite direction, curving round towards me in a place where the bank was scooped out.

It looked so smooth that I pressed on, taking one step forward, so that the water might rush up against me, and—then I was floating, for my feet found no bottom, and with an excited thrill of delight I felt that I could swim.

Yes; there was no doubt about it. I could swim as easily as George Day, only I was not moving my hands, while the water was bearing me up and carrying me round as in a whirlpool just once, and then I was swept into the tide-way with the water thundering in my ears, a horrible strangling sensation in my nostrils, and a dimness coming over my aching eyes.

I could never remember much about it, only that it was all a confusion of thundering in my ears and rushing sounds. I kept on beating the water with my hands as I had seen a dog beat the surface when he could not swim, and I seemed to throw my head right back as I gasped for breath. But I do not remember that it was very horrible, or that I was drowning, as I surely was. Confusion is the best expression for explaining my sensations as I was swept rapidly down by the tide.

What do I remember next? I hardly know. Only a sensation of some one catching me by the wrist, from somewhere in the darkness that was closing me in. But the next thing after that is, I remember shutting my eyes, because the sun shone in them so fiercely as I lay on my back in the grass, with my head aching furiously, and a strange pain at the back of my neck, as if some one had been trying to break my head off, as a mischievous child would serve a doll.

Just then I heard some one sobbing and crying, and I felt as if I must be asleep and dreaming all this.

"Don't make that row. He's all right, I tell you. He isn't drowned. What's the good of making a row like that!"

It was George Day's voice, and opening my eyes I said hoarsely:

"What's the matter? Is he hurt?"

"No: it's only Harry Leggatt thought you were—you were hurt, you know. Can you get up, and run? All our clothes are two fields off. Come on. The sun will dry you."

I got up, feeling giddy and strange, and the aching at the back of my head was almost unbearable; but I began to walk with Day holding my hand, and after a time—he guiding me, for I felt very stupid—I began to trot; and at last, with my head throbbing and whirring, I found myself standing by my clothes, and my companions helped me to dress.

"You went out too far," Day said. "I told you not, you know."

I was shivering with cold and terribly uncomfortable with putting on my things over my wet chilled body. It had been a hard task too, especially with my socks, but I hardly spoke till we were walking home, and when I did it was during the time I was smoothing my wet hair with a pocket comb lent me by one of the boys.

"How was it I went too far?" I said at last, dolefully.

"I don't know," said Day. "I shouldn't have known anything if that chap Shock hadn't come shouting to us; and when we came, thinking he was going to steal our clothes, he brought us and showed us where he had dragged you out on to the bank. It was him we saw swimming when we first went in."

"Where is he now?" I said wearily. "Let's ask him all about it."

"I don't know," replied Day. "He ran off to dress himself, I suppose, and he didn't come back. But I say, you're better now."

"Oh yes!" I said, "I'm better now;" and by degrees the walk in the warm afternoon sunshine seemed to make me feel more myself; beside which I was dry when I got back home, but very low-spirited and dull.

I did not say anything, for my mother was lying down, and Mrs Beeton never invited my confidence; beside which I felt rather conscience-stricken, and after having my solitary tea I went to the window, feeling warmer, and less disposed to shiver.

And as I sat there about seven o'clock on that warm summer evening it almost seemed as if my afternoon's experience had been a dream, and that Shock had not swum out and saved me from drowning, for there he was under one of the pear-trees, with a switch and a piece of clay, throwing pellets at our house, one of which came right in at the open window close by my cheek, and struck against Mrs Beeton's cheffonier door.

Chapter Five
Beginning a New Life

I don't want to say much about a sad, sad time in my life, but old Brownsmith played so large a part in it then that I feel bound to set it all down.

I saw very little more of George Day, for just about that time he was sent off to another school; and I am glad to recollect that I went little away from the invalid who used to watch me with such wistful eyes.

I had no more lessons in swimming, but I saved up a shilling for a particular purpose, and that was to give to Shock; but though I tried to get near him time after time when I was in the big garden with my mother, no sooner did I seem to be going after him than the boy went off like some wild thing—diving in amongst the bushes, and, knowing the garden so well, he soon got out of sight.

I did not want to send the present by anybody, for that seemed to me like entering into explanations why I sent the money; and I knew that if the news reached my mother's ears that I had been half-drowned, it would come upon her like a terrible shock; and she was, I knew now, too ill to bear anything more.

So though I was most friendly in my disposition towards Shock, and wanted to pay him in my mild way for saving my life, he persisted in looking upon me as an enemy, and threw clay, clods, and, so to speak, derisive gestures, whenever we met at a distance.

"I won't run after him any more," I said to myself one day. "He's half a wild beast, and if he wants us to be enemies, we will."

I suppose I knew a good deal for my age, as far as education went. If I had been set to answer the questions in an examination paper I believe I should have failed; but all the same I had learned a great deal of French, German, and Latin, and I could write a fair hand and express myself decently on paper. But when I sat at our window watching Shock's wonderful activity, and recalled how splendidly he must be able to swim, I used to feel as if I were a very inferior being, and that he was a long way ahead of me.

As the time went on our visits to the garden used to grow less frequent; but whenever the weather was fine and my mother felt equal to the task, we used to go over; and towards the end old Brownsmith's big armed Windsor chair, with its cushions, used to be set under a big quince tree in the centre walk, just where there were most flowers, and as soon as we had reached it the old fellow used to come down with a piece of carpet to double up and put beneath my mother's feet.

"Used to be a bit of a spring here," he said with a nod to me; "might be a little damp."

Then he would leave a couple of cats, "just for company like," he would say, and then go softly away.

I did not realise it was so near when that terrible time came and I followed my poor mother to her grave, seeing everything about me in a strange, unnatural manner. One minute it seemed to be real; then again as if it were all a dream. There were people about me in black, and I was in black, but I was half stunned, listening to the words that were said; and at last I was left almost alone, for those who were with me stepped back a yard or two.

I was gazing down with my eyes dimmed and a strange aching feeling at my heart, when I felt someone touch my elbow, and turning round to follow whoever it was, I found old Brownsmith there, in his black clothes and white neckerchief, holding an enormous bunch of white roses in his arms.

"Thought you'd like it, my lad," he said in a low husky voice. "She used to be very fond o' my white roses, poor soul!"

As he spoke he nodded and took his great pruning-knife from his coat pocket, opened it with his teeth, and cut the strip of sweet-scented Russia mat. Then holding them ready in his arms he stood there while I slowly scattered the beautiful flowers down more and more, more and more, till the coffin was nearly covered, and instead of the black cloth I saw beneath me the fragrant heap of flowers, and the dear, loving face that had gazed so tenderly in mine seemed once more to be looking in my eyes.

I held the last two roses in my hand for a moment or two, hesitating, but I let them fall at last; and then the tears I had kept back so long came with a rush, and I sank down on my knees sobbing as if my heart would break.

It was one of my uncles who laid his hand upon my shoulder and made me start as he bent over me, and said in a low, chilling voice:

"Get up, my boy; we are going back. Come!—be a man!"

I did get up in a weary, wretched way, and as I did so I looked round after old Brownsmith, and there he was a little distance off, watching me, it seemed. Then we went back, my relatives who were there taking very little notice of me; and I was made the more wretched by hearing one cousin, whom I had never seen before, say angrily that he did not approve of that last scene being made—"such an exhibition with those flowers."

It was about a month after that sad scene that I went over to see old Brownsmith. I was very young, but my life with my invalid mother had, I suppose, made me thoughtful; and though I used to sit a great deal at the window I felt as if I had not the heart to go into the great garden, where every path and bed would seem to bring up one of the days when somebody used to be sitting there, watching the flowers and listening to the birds.

I used to fancy that if I went down any of her favourite walks I should burst out crying; and I had a horror of doing that, for the knowledge was beginning to dawn upon me that a great change was coming over my life, and that I must begin to think of acting like a man.

As I turned in at the gate I saw Shock at the door of one of the lofts over the big packing-sheds. He had evidently gone up there after some baskets, and as soon as I saw him I walked quickly in his direction; but he darted out of sight in the loft; and if I had any idea of scaling the ladder and going up to him to take him by storm, it was checked at once, for a half-sieve basket— one of those flat, round affairs in which fruit is packed—came flying out of the door, and then another and another, one after the other, at a tremendous rate, quite sufficient to have knocked me backwards before I was half-way up.

"A brute!" I said angrily to myself. "I'll treat him with contempt;" and striding away I went down the garden, with the creaking, banging of the falling baskets going on. And when I turned to look, some fifty yards away, there was a big heap of the round wicker-work flats at the foot of the ladder, and others kept on flying out of the door.

I had not gone far before I saw old Brownsmith busy as usual amongst his cats; and as he rose from stooping to tie up a plant he caught sight of me, and immediately turned down the path where I was.

He held out his great rough hand, took mine, and shook it up and down gently for quite a minute, just as if it had been the handle of a pump.

"Seen my new pansies?" he said.

I shook my head.

"No, of course you haven't," he said. "Well, how are you?"

I said I was pretty well, and hoped he was. "Middling," he replied. "Want more sun. Can't get my pears to market without more sun."

"It has been dull," I said.

"Splendid for planting out, my lad, but bad for ripening off. Well, how are you?"

I said again that I was very well; and he looked at me thoughtfully, put one end of a bit of matting between his teeth, and drew it out tightly with his left hand. Then he began to twang it thoughtfully, and made it give out a dull musical note.

"Seen my new pansies?" he said—"no, of course not," he added quickly; "and I asked you before. Come and look at them."

He led me to a bed which was full of beautifully rounded, velvety-petalled flowers.

"What do you think of them?" he said—"eh? There's a fine one, *Mulberry Superb*; rich colour—eh?"

"They are lovely," I said warmly.

"Hah! yes!" he said, looking at me thoughtfully; "she liked white roses, though—yes, white roses—and they are all over."

My lip began to quiver, but I mastered the emotion and he went on:

"Thought I should have seen you before, my lad. Didn't think I should see you for some time. Thought perhaps I should never see you again. Thought you'd be sure to come and say 'Good-bye!' before you went. Contradictions—eh?"

"I always meant to come over and see you, Mr Brownsmith," I said.

"Of course you did, my lad. Been damp and cold. Want more sun badly."

I said I hoped the weather would soon change, and I began to feel uncomfortable and was just thinking I would go, when he thrust the piece of matting in his pocket, and took up and began stroking one of the cats.

"Ah! it's a bad job, my lad!" he said softly—"a terrible job!"

I nodded.

"A sad job, my lad!—a very sad job!"

I nodded again, and waited till a choking sensation had gone off.

"Boys don't think enough about their mothers—some boys don't," he went on. "I didn't, till she was took away. You did—stopped with her a deal."

"I'm afraid,"—I began.

"I'm not," he said, interrupting me hastily. "I notice a deal—weather, and people, and children, and boys, and things growing. Want sun badly—don't we?"

"Yes, sir," I said; and I looked up in his florid face, with its bushy white whiskers; and then I looked at his great bulging pockets, and next down lower at his black legs, which the cats were turning into rubbing-posts; and as they served me the same in the most friendly manner I began wondering whether he ever brushed his black trousers, and thought of what a job I should have to get all the cats' hairs off mine.

For there they all were, quite a little troop, arching their backs and purring, sticking their tails straight up, and every now and then giving their ends a flick.

They were so friendly in their rubbings against me that I did not like to refuse to accept their salutes; but it seemed to me as if only the light-coloured hairs came off, and in a short time I was furry from the knees of my black trousers down to my boots.

There was something, too, of welcome in their ways that was pleasant to me in my desolate position, for just then I seemed as if I had not one friend in the world; and even Mr Brownsmith seemed strange and cold, and as if he would be very glad when I was gone and he could get along with his work.

"There, there," he cried suddenly, "we mustn't fret about it, you know. It's what we must all come to, and I don't hold with people making it out dreadful. It's very sad, boy, so it is. Dull weather too. When all my trees and plants die off for the winter, we don't call that dreadful, because we know they'll all bud and leaf and blossom again after their long sleep; and so it is with them as has gone away. There, there, there, you must try to be a man."

"Yes, sir," I said; "I am trying very hard."

"That's the way," he cried; "that's the way;" and he clapped me on the shoulder. "To be sure it is hard work, though, when you are on'y twelve or thirteen years old."

"Yes, sir."

"But look here, boy, there's a tremendous deal done by a lad who makes up his mind to try; do you see?"

"Yes sir, I see," I said, looking at him wonderingly, for he did not seem to want to get rid of me now, as he was holding me tightly by the arm.

"'Member coming for the strawberries?" he said drily.

"Yes, sir."

"Thought me a disagreeable old fellow, didn't you then?"

I hesitated, but he looked at me sharply.

"Yes, sir, I did then," I said. "I did not know how kind you could be."

"That's just what I am," he said gruffly; "very disagreeable."

I shook my head.

"I am," he said. "Ask any of my men and women. Here—what's going to become of you, my lad—what are you going to be—soldier like your father?"

"Oh no!" I said.

"What then?"

"I don't know, sir. I believe I am to wait till my uncles and my father's cousin have settled."

"How many of them are to settle it, boy?"

"Four, sir."

"Four, eh, my boy! Ah, then I suppose it will take a lot of settling! You'll have to wait."

"Yes, sir, I've got to wait," I said.

"But have you no prospects?"

"Oh yes, sir!" I said. "I believe I have."

"Well, what?"

"My uncle Frederick said that I must make up my mind to go somewhere and earn my own living."

"That's a nice prospect."

"Yes, sir."

He was silent for a moment or two, and then smiled.

"Well, you're right," he said. "It is a nice prospect, though you and I were thinking different things. I like a boy to make up his mind to earn his living when he is called upon to do it. Makes him busy and self-reliant—makes a man of him. Did he say how?"

"Who, sir—my uncle Frederick?"

"Yes."

"No, sir, he only said that I must wait."

"Like I have to wait for the sun to ripen my fruit, eh? Ah, but I don't like that. If the sun don't come I pick it, and store it under cover to ripen as well as it will."

I looked at him wonderingly.

"That waiting," he went on, "puts me in mind of the farmer and his corn in the fable—get out, cats!—he waited till he found that the proper thing to do was to get his sons to work and cut the corn themselves."

"Yes, sir," I said smiling; "and then the lark thought it was time to take her young ones away."

"Good, lad; right!" he cried. "That fable contains the finest lesson a boy can learn. Don't you wait for others to help you: help yourself."

"I'll try, sir."

"That's right. Ah! I wish I had always been as wise as that lark."

"Then you would not wait if you were me, sir?" I said, looking up at him wonderingly.

"Not a week, my lad, if you can get anything to do. Fact is, I've been looking into it, and your relations are all waiting for each other to take you in hand. There isn't one of them wants the job."

I sighed, and said:

"I'm afraid I shall be a great deal of trouble to them, sir, and an enormous expense."

"Oh, you think so, do you!" he said, stooping down and lifting up first one cat and then another, stroking them gently the while. Then one of them, as usual, leaped upon his back. "Well, look here, my boy," he said thoughtfully, "that's all nonsense about expense! I—"

He stopped short and went on stroking one cat's back, as it rubbed against his leg, and he seemed to be thinking very deeply.

"Yes, all nonsense. See here; wait for a week or two, perhaps one of your uncles may find you something to do, or send you to a good school, eh?"

"No, sir," I said; "my uncle Frederick said I must not expect to be sent to a school."

"Oh he did, did he?"

"Yes, sir."

"Well, then, if nothing better turns up—if they don't find you a good place, you might come and help me."

"Help you, sir!" I said wonderingly; "what, learn to be a market-gardener?"

"Yes, there's nothing so very dreadful in that, is there?"

"Oh no, sir! but what could I do?"

"Heaps of things. Tally the bunches and check the sieves, learn to bud and graft, and how to cut young trees, and—oh, I could find you enough to do."

I looked at him aghast, and began to see in my mind's eye rough, dirty Shock, crawling about on his hands and knees, and digging out the weeds from among the onions with his fingers.

"Oh, there's lots of things you could do!" he continued. "Why, of a night you might use your pen and help me do the booking, and read and improve yourself while I sat and smoked my pipe. Cats don't come into the house."

"Do you mean that I should come and live with you, sir?" I said.

"That's it, my boy, always supposing you couldn't do any better. Could you?"

I shook my head. "I don't think so, sir," I said dismally.

"Not such a good life for a boy in winter when things are bare, as in summer when the flowers are out and the fruit comes on. Like fruit, don't you?"

"Yes, sir, but you don't let your boys eat the fruit."

"Tchah! I should never miss what you would eat," he said with a laugh, "and you would soon get tired of the apples and pears and gooseberries. Think you'd like to come, eh–em? You don't know; of course you don't. Wouldn't make a gentleman of you. I never heard of a gentleman gardener; plenty of gentlemen farmers, though."

"Yes, sir," I said, with my heart beating fast, "I've heard of gentlemen farmers."

"But not of gentlemen market-gardeners, eh? No, my boy, they don't call us gentlemen, and I never professed to be one; but a man may be a gentleman at heart whatever his business, and that's better than being a gentleman in name."

I looked up in his fresh red face, and there was such a kindly look in it that I felt happier than I had been for weeks, and I don't know what moved me to do it, but I laid my hand upon his arm.

He looked down at me thoughtfully as he went on.

"People are rather strange about these things. Gentleman farmer cultivates a hundred acres of land that he pays a hundred and fifty pounds a year for say: market-gardener cultivates twenty acres that he pays two or three hundred for; and they call the one a gentleman, the other a gardener. But it don't matter, Master Dennison, a bit. Does it?"

"No, sir," I said, "I don't think so."

"Old business, gardening," he went on, with a dry look at me—"very old. Let me see. There was a man named Adam took to it first, wasn't there? Cultivated a garden, didn't he?"

I nodded and smiled.

"Ah, yes," he said; "but that was a long time ago, and you've not been brought up for such a business. You wouldn't like it."

"Indeed, but I should, sir," I cried enthusiastically.

"No, no," he said, deliberately. "Don't be in a hurry to choose, my boy. I knew a lad once who said he would like to be a sailor, and he went to sea and had such a taste of it from London to Plymouth that he would not go any farther, and they had to set him ashore."

"He must have been a great coward," I said.

"To be sure he was; but then you might be if you pricked your finger with the thorns of a rose, or had to do something in the garden when it was freezing hard, eh?"

"I don't think I should be," I replied.

"But you must think," he said. "It's very nice to see flowers blooming and fruit fit to pick with the sun shining and the sky blue; but life is not all summer, my boy, is it? There are wet days and storms, and rough times, and the flowers you see blossoming have been got ready in the cold wintry weather, when they were only seeds, or bare shabby-looking roots."

"Yes, I know that," I said.

"And you think you would like to come?"

"Yes, sir."

"What for? to play in the garden, and look on while the work is done?"

"I think I should be ashamed to do that," I said; "it would be so lazy. If you please, Mr Brownsmith, I've got to work and do something, and if you will have me, I should like to come."

"Well, well," he said, "mine's a good business and profitable and healthy, and there are times when, in spite of bad crops, bad weather, and market losses, I thank God that I took to such a pleasant and instructive way of getting a living."

"It is instructive then, sir?" I said.

"Instructive, my lad!" he cried with energy. "I don't know any business that is more full of teaching. I've been at it all my life, and the older I grow the more I find there is to learn."

"I like that," I said, for it opened out a vista of adventure to me that seemed full of bright flowers and sunshine.

"A man who has brains may go on learning and making discoveries, not discoveries of countries and wonders, but of little things that may make matters better for the people who are to come after him. Then he may turn a bit of the England where he works into a tropical country, by covering it over with glass, and having a stove; then some day, if he goes on trying, he may find himself able to write FRHS at the end of his name."

"And did you, sir?"

"No," he said, "I never did. I was content with plodding. I'm a regular plodder, you see; so's Samuel."

"Is he, sir?" I said, for he evidently wanted me to speak.

"Yes, a regular plodder. Well, there, my boy, we'll see. Don't you be in a hurry; wait and see if your relatives are going to do anything better for you. If they are not, don't you be in a hurry."

But I was in a hurry, for the idea of coming to that garden, living there, and learning all about the flowers and fruit, excited me, longing as I was for some change.

"Yes, yes," he said, "wait, wait;" and he looked at me, and then about him in the slow meditative manner peculiar to gardeners; "we'll see, we'll see, wait till you know whether your people are going to do anything for you."

"But, indeed, sir," I began.

"Yes, yes, I know, boy," he replied; but we must wait. "Perhaps they've planted a business bulb for you, and we must wait and see whether it is going to shoot and blossom. You're impatient; you want to pull up the bulb and see if it has any roots yet."

I looked at him in a disappointed way, and he smiled.

"Come, come," he said; "at your age you can afford to wait a few days, if it is for your good. There, wait and see, and I'll be plain with you; if they do not find you something better to do, I'll take you on here at once, and do the best I can for you, as far as teaching you to be a gardener goes."

"O, thank you, sir!" I cried.

"Wait a bit," he said quietly, "wait a bit. There I'm going to be very busy; I've got a cart to load. So now suppose you be off."

I shook hands with him and walked away surprised and pleased, but at the same time disappointed, and as I neared the end of the big loft I heard two or three more baskets come rattling down.

Chapter Six
I Decide and go to Work

I felt that I ought to write to my uncles and cousins, and I consulted Mrs Beeton about it.

Mrs Beeton put her head on one side and tried how far she could get her arm down the black worsted stocking she was darning, looking at me meditatively the while.

"Well, do you know," she said, "if I were you, my dear, I would write; for it do seem strange to leave you here, as I may say, all alone."

"Then I will write," I said. "I want to know what I am going to be."

"Oh! I should be a soldier, like your dear pa was, if I were you," she said; "and I'd go into a regiment where they wore blue and silver-blue and silver always looks so well."

"I don't want to be a soldier," I said rather sadly, for my fancy did at one time go strongly in that direction; but it did not seem so very long since the news came that my poor father had been killed in a skirmish with the Indians; and I remembered how my poor mother had thrown her arms round my neck and sobbed, and made me promise that I would never think of being a soldier. And then it seemed as if after that news she had gradually drooped and faded, just as a flower might upon its stalk, till two years had gone by, and then all happened as I have related to you, and I was left pretty well alone in the world.

"I'm sorry you don't want to be a soldier," said Mrs Beeton, looking at me through her glasses, with her head a little more on one side. "If I had been a young gentleman I should have been a horse-soldier. I wouldn't be a sailor if I was you, sir."

"Why not?" I said.

"Because they do smell so of tar, and they're so rough and boisterous."

"I think I shall be a gardener," I said.

"A what?"

"A gardener."

"My dear boy!" she cried in horror, "whatever put that in your head? Why, you couldn't be anything worse. There!—I do declare you startled me so I've stuck the needle right into my finger, and it bleeds!"

We had many arguments about the matter while I was waiting for answers to my letters, for no one came down to see me.

Uncle Thomas said he was going to see about my being put in a good public school, but there was no hurry; and perhaps it would be better to wait and see what Uncle Johnson meant to do, for he should not like to offend him, as he was much better off, and it might be doing me harm.

Uncle Johnson wrote a very short letter, saying that I had better write to my Uncle Frederick.

Second-cousin Willis did not reply for a week, and he said it was the duty of one of my uncles to provide for me; and he should make a point of bringing them both to book if they did not see about something for me before long.

One or two other relatives wrote to me that they were not in circumstances to help me, and that if they were strong, stout boys such as I was, they would try and get a situation, for it was no disgrace to earn my living; and they wished me well.

I took all these letters over to Mr Brownsmith, and he read them day after day as they came; but he did not say a word, and it made my heart sink, as it seemed to me that he was repenting of his offer.

And so a month slipped by; and when I was not reading or writing I found myself gazing out of the window at the pleasant old garden, where the fruit was being gathered day after day. The time was passing, and the chances of my going over to Brownsmith's seemed to me growing remote, while I never seemed to have seen so much of Shock.

It appeared to me that he must know of my disappointment; for whenever he saw me at the window, and could do so unseen, he threw dabs of clay, or indulged in derisive gestures more extravagant than ever.

I affected to take no heed of these antics, but they annoyed me all the same; and I found myself wishing at times that Mr Brownsmith would take me, if only to give me a chance of some day thrashing that objectionable boy.

I was sitting very disconsolately at the window one day, with a table on which I had been writing drawn up very close to the bay, when I heard a footstep below, and looking down there was Old Brownsmith, who nodded to me familiarly and came up.

"Well," he said, "how are you? Nice weather for my work."

He sat down, pursed up his lips, and looked about him for some minutes without speaking.

"News," he said, "any news?"

"No, sir," I replied.

"Humph! Not going to make you manager of the Bank of England or Master of the Mint—eh?"

"No, sir. I have had no more news."

"I was afraid you wouldn't," he continued. "Well, I told you the other day not to be rash, for there was plenty of time."

"Yes, sir."

"Now I'm going to change my tune."

I jumped up excitedly.

"Yes, change my tune," he said. "You're wasting time now. What do you say after thinking it over?—like to come?"

"May I, sir?" I cried joyfully.

"I'm a man of my word, my boy," he replied drily.

"Oh! thank you, sir!" I cried. "I shall always be grateful to you for this, and—"

"Gently, gently," he said, interrupting me. "Never promise too much. Acts are better than words, my boy. There!—good-bye! See you soon, I suppose?"

I would have gone with him then, but he told me to take things coolly and get what I wanted packed up.

"Why, Grant, my boy," he said, laughing, "you'll have to look over the loading of some of my carts when I'm not there; and if you do them in that hurried fashion how will it be done?"

I felt the rebuke and hung my head.

"There!—I'm not finding fault," he said kindly; "I only want you to be business-like, for I have to teach you to be a business man."

He then went away and left me to settle up matters with Mrs Beeton, who began to cry when I told her I was going, and where.

"It seems too dreadful," she sobbed, "and you so nicely brought up. What am I to say to your friends when they come?"

"Tell them where I am," I said, smiling.

"Ah, my dear! you may laugh," she cried; "but it's a very dreadful life you are going to, and I expect I shall see you back before the week's out."

My clothes did not fill the small school-box, but I had a good many odds, and ends and books that weighed up and made it too heavy to carry, as I had intended; so I had to go over to the garden, meaning to ask for help.

I fully expected to meet Shock about the sheds or in one of the carts or wagons, but the first person I set eyes on was Old Brownsmith himself—I say *Old* Brownsmith, for everybody called him so.

He was wearing a long blue serge apron, as he came towards me with his open knife in his teeth and a quantity of Russia matting in his hands, tearing and cutting it into narrow lengths.

"Well, young fellow?" he said as coolly as if no conversation had passed between us.

"I've come, sir, for good," I said sharply.

"I hope you have," he replied drily; "but is that all of you? Where's your tooth-brush and comb, and clean stockings?"

"I wanted to bring my box, sir," I said, "but it was too heavy. Would any of the men come and fetch it?"

"Ask 'em," he said abruptly, and he turned away. This seemed cold and strange; but I knew him to be rather curious and eccentric in his ways, so I walked to one of the cart-sheds and looked about for a man to help me.

I thought I saw some one enter the shed; but when I got inside no one was there, as far as I could see—only piles of great baskets reaching from floor to ceiling.

Disappointed, I was coming away, when in the gloom at the other end there seemed to be something that was not basket; and taking a few steps forward I made out that it was the boy Shock standing close up against the baskets, with his face away from me.

I stood thinking what I should do. I was to be in the same garden with this lad, who was always sneering at me; and I felt that if I let him have the upper hand he would make my life very much more miserable than it had been lately.

My mind was made up in a moment, and with a decision for which I had not given myself credit I went right in and stood behind him.

"Shock!" I cried; but the boy only gave himself a twitch as if a spasm had run through him, and did not move.

"Do you hear, sir?" I said sharply. "Come here; I want you to help carry my box."

Still he did not move, and I felt that if I did not master him he would me.

"Do you hear what I say, sir?" I cried in my most angry tones; "come with me and fetch my box."

He leaped round so quickly that he made me start, and stood glaring at me as if about to strike.

"You must come and fetch my box," I said, feeling all the while a good deal of dread of the rough, fierce-looking boy.

I was between him and the wide door; and he stooped and looked first one side of me and then the other, as if about to dart by. But, growing bolder, I took a step forward and laid my hand upon his shoulder.

Up flew his arms as if about to strike mine away, but he caught my eye and understood it wrongly. He must have thought I was gazing resolutely at him, but I really was not. To my great satisfaction, though, he stepped forward, drooping his arms and hanging his head, walking beside me out into the open yard, where we came suddenly upon Old Brownsmith, who looked at me sharply, nodded his head, and then went on.

I led the way, and Shock half-followed, half-walked beside me, and we had just reached the gate when Old Brownsmith shouted:

"Take the barrow."

Shock trotted back like a dog; and as I watched him, thinking what a curious half-savage lad he was, and how much bigger and stronger than I was, he came back with the light basket barrow, trundling it along.

We went in silence as far as my old home, where Mrs Beeton held up her hands as she saw my companion, and drew back, holding the door open for us to get the corded box which stood in the floor-clothed hall.

Shock put down the barrow; and then his mischief-loving disposition got the better of his sulkiness, and stooping down he astonished me and made Mrs Beeton shriek by taking a leap up the two steps, like a dog, and going on all-fours to the box.

"Pray, pray, take him away, Master Dennison!" the poor woman cried in real alarm; "and do, pray, mind yourself—the boy's mad!"

"Oh, no; he won't hurt you," I said, taking one end of the box. But Shock growled, shook it free, lifted it from the floor, and before I could stop him, bumped it down the steps on to the barrow with a bang, laid it fairly across, and then seizing the handles went off at a trot.

"I can't stop," I said quickly; "I must go and look after him."

"Yes, but pray take care, my dear. He bites. He bit a boy once very badly, and he isn't safe."

Not very pleasant news, but I could not stay to hear more, and, running after the barrow, I caught up to it and laid my hand upon one side of the box as if to keep it steady.

I did not speak for a minute, and Shock subsided into a walk; then, turning to him and looking in his morose, ill-used face:

"I've never thanked you yet for getting me out of the river."

The box gave a bump and a bound, for the handles of the barrow were raised very high and Shock began to run.

At the end of a minute I stopped him, and as soon as we were going on steadily I made the same remark.

But up went the barrow and box again and off we trotted. When, after stopping him for the second time, I made an attempt to get into conversation and to thank him, Shock banged down the legs of the barrow, looking as stolid and heavy as if he were perfectly deaf, threw open the gate, and ran the barrow up to the house-door.

"Oh! here's your baggage, then!" said Old Brownsmith. "Bring it in, Shock; set it on end there in the passage. We'll take it up after tea. Come along."

Shock lifted in the box before I could help him; and then seizing the barrow-handles, with his back to me, he let out a kick like a mule and caught me in the calf, nearly sending me down.

"Hallo! hold on, my lad," said Old Brownsmith, who had not seen the cause; and of course I would not tell tales; but I made up my mind to repay Mr Shock for that kick and for his insolent obstinacy the first time the opportunity served.

I followed my master into a great shed that struck cool as we descended to the floor, which was six or seven feet below the surface, being like a cellar opened and then roofed in with wood. Here some seven or eight women were busy tying up rosebuds in market bunches, while a couple of men went and came with baskets which they brought in full and took out empty.

The scent was delicious; and as we went past the women, whose busy fingers were all hard at work, Old Brownsmith stopped where another man kept taking up so many bunches of the roses in each hand and then diving his head and shoulders into a great oblong basket, leaving the roses at the bottom as he came out, and seized a piece of chalk and made a mark upon a slate.

"Give him the slate, Ike," said Old Brownsmith. "He'll tally 'em off for you now. Look here, Grant, you keep account on the slate how many bunches are put in each barge, and how many barges are filled."

"Yes, sir," I said, taking the slate and chalk with trembling fingers, for I felt flushed and excited.

"This is the way—you put down a stroke like that for every dozen, and one like that for a barge. Do you see?"

"Yes, sir," I said, "I can do that; but when am I to put down a barge?"

"When it's full, of course, and covered in—lidded up."

"But shall we fill a barge to-night, sir?"

"Well, I hope so—a good many," said Old Brownsmith. "Will he go down to the river with me to show me where, sir?"

"River!—show you what, my boy?"

"The barges we are to fill, sir."

"Whoo–oop!"

It was Ike made this peculiar noise. It answered in him for a laugh. Then he dived down into the great oblong basket and stopped there.

"You don't know what a barge is," said Old Brownsmith kindly.

"Oh yes, sir, I do!" I replied.

"Not one of our barges, my lad," he said, laying his hand upon my shoulder. "We call these large baskets barges. You'll soon pick up the names. There, go on."

I at once began to keep count of the bunches, Old Brownsmith seeming to take no farther notice of me, while Ike the packer kept on laying in dozen after dozen, once or twice pretending to lay them in and bringing the bunches out again, as if to balk me, but all in a grim serious way, as if it was part of his work.

I was so busy and excited that I hardly had time to enjoy the sweet scent of the flowers in that cool, soft pit; but in a short time I was so far accustomed that I had an eye for the men bringing in fresh supplies, just cut, and for the women who, working at rough benches, were so cleverly laying the buds in a half-moon shape between their fingers and thumbs, the flowers being laid flat upon the bench. Then a second row was laid upon the first, a piece of wet matting was rapidly twisted round, tied, and the stalks cut off regularly with one pressure of the knife.

It seemed to me as if enough of the beautiful pink buds nestling in their delicate green leaves were being tied up to supply all London, but I was exceedingly ignorant then.

Mine was not a hard task; and as I attended to it, whenever Ike, who was packing, had his eyes averted from me, I had a good look at him. I had often seen him before, but only at a distance, and at a distance Ike certainly looked best.

I know he could not help it, but decidedly Ike, Old Brownsmith's chief packer and carter, was one of the strongest and ugliest men I ever saw. He was a brawny, broad-shouldered fellow of about fifty, with iron-grey hair; and standing out of his brown-red face, half-way between fierce, stiff, bushy whiskers, was a tremendous aquiline nose. When his hat was off, as he removed it from time to time to give it a rub, you saw that he had a very shiny bald head—in consequence, as I suppose, of so much polishing. His eyes were deeply set but very keen-looking, and his mouth when shut had one aspect, when open another. When open it seemed as if it was the place where a few very black teeth were kept. When closed it seemed as if made to match his enormous nose; the line formed by the closed lips, being continued right down on either side in a half-moon or parenthesis curve to the chin, which was always in motion.

A closer examination showed that Ike had only a mouth of the ordinary dimensions, the appearance of size being caused by two marks of caked tobacco-juice, a piece of that herb being always between his teeth.

This habit he afterwards told me he had learned when he was a soldier, and he still found it useful and comforting in the long night watches he had to take.

I have said that his eyes were piercing, and so it seemed to me at first; but in a short time, as I grew more accustomed to him, I found that they were only piercing one at a time, for as if nature had intended to make him as ugly as possible, Ike's eyes acted independently one of the other, and I often found him looking at me with one, and down into the barge basket with the other.

Old Brownsmith had no sooner left the pit than Ike seized a couple of handsful of roses, plunged with them into the basket, bobbed up, and looked at me with one eye, just as he caught me noticing him intently.

"Rum un, ain't I?" he said, gruffly, and taking me terribly aback. "Not much to look at, eh?"

"You look very strong," I said, evasively.

"Strong, eh? Yes, and so I am, my lad. Good un to go."

Then he plunged into the barge again and uttered a low growl, came up again and uttered another. I have not the least idea what he meant by it, though I suppose he expected me to answer, for to my great confusion he rose up suddenly and stared at me.

"Eh?" he said.

"I didn't speak, sir," I said.

"No, but I did. Got 'em all down? Go on then, one barge, fresh un this is: you didn't put down the other."

I hastened to rectify my error, and then we went steadily on with the task, the women being remarkably silent, as if it took all their energy to keep their fingers going so fast, till all at once Old Brownsmith appeared at the door and beckoned me to him.

"Tea's ready, my lad," he said; "let's have it and get out again, for there's a lot to do this evening."

I followed him into a snug old-fashioned room that seemed as if it had been furnished by a cook with genteel ideas, or else by a lady who was fond of a good kitchen, for this room was neither one nor the other; it had old-fashioned dining-room chairs and a carpet, but the floor was brick, and the fireplace had an oven and boiler. Then there was a dresser on one side, but it was mahogany, and in place of ordinary plates and dishes, and jugs swinging from hooks, this dresser was ornamented with old china and three big punch-bowls were turned up on the broad part upside down.

There was a comfortable meal spread, with a fresh loaf and butter, and a nice large piece of ham. There was fruit, too, on the table, and a crisp lettuce, all in my honour as I afterwards found, for my employer or guardian, or whatever I am to style him, rarely touched any of the produce of his own grounds excepting potatoes, and these he absolutely loved, a cold potato for breakfast or tea being with him a thorough relish.

"Make yourself at home, Grant, my boy," he said kindly. "I want you to settle down quickly. We shall have to work hard, but you'll enjoy your meals and sleep all the better."

I thanked him, and tried to do as he suggested, and to eat as if I enjoyed my meal; but I did not in the least, and I certainly did not feel in the slightest degree at home.

"What time did you go to bed over yonder, Grant?" said the old gentleman.

"Ten o'clock, sir."

"And what time did you get up?"

"Eight, sir."

"Ugh, you extravagant young dog!" he cried. "Ten hours' sleep! You'll have to turn over a new leaf. Nine o'clock's my bedtime, if we are not busy, and I like to be out in the garden again by four or five. What do you say to that?"

I did not know what to say, so I said nothing.

We did not sit very long over our tea, for there was the cart to load up with flowers for the morning's market, and soon after I was watching Ike carefully packing in the great baskets along the bottom of the cart, and then right over the shafts upon the broad projecting ladder, and also upon that which was fitted in at the back.

"You keep account, Grant," said Old Brownsmith to me, and I entered the number of baskets and their contents upon my slate, the old gentleman going away and leaving me to transact this part of the business myself, as I believe now, to give me confidence, for he carefully counted all the baskets and checked them off when he came back.

Ike squinted at me fiercely several times as he helped to hoist in several baskets, and for some time he did not speak, but at last he stopped, took off his hat, drew a piece of cabbage leaf from the crown, and carefully wiped his bald head with it, looking comically at me the while.

"Green silk," he said gruffly, as he replaced the leaf. "Nature's own growth. Never send 'em to the wash. Throw 'em away and use another."

I laughed at the idea, and this pleased Ike, who looked at me from top to toe.

"You couldn't load a cart," he said at last.

"Couldn't I?" I replied. "Why not? It seems easy enough."

"Seems easy! of course it does, youngster. Seems easy to take a spade and dig all day, but you try, and I'm sorry for your back and jyntes."

"But you've only got to put the baskets in the cart," I argued.

"Only got to put the baskets in the cart!" grumbled Ike. "Hark at him!"

"That's what you've been doing," I continued.

"What I've been doing!" he said. "I'm sorry for the poor horse if you had the loading up. A cart ain't a wagon."

"Well, I know that," I said, "a wagon has four wheels, and a cart two."

"Send I may live," cried Ike. "Why, he is a clever boy. He knows a cart's got two wheels and a wagon four."

He said this in a low serious voice, as if talking to himself, and admiring my wisdom; but of course I could see that it was his way of laughing at me, and I hastened to add:

"Oh, you know what I mean!"

"Yes, I know what you mean, but you don't know what I mean, and if you're so offle clever you'd best teach me, for I can't teach you."

"But I want you to teach me," I cried. "I've come here to learn. What is there in particular in loading a cart?"

"Oh, you're ever so much more clever than I am," he grumbled. "Here, len's a hand with that barge."

This was to the man who was helping him, and who now seized hold of another basket, which was hoisted into its place.

Then more baskets were piled up, the light flower barges being put at the top, till the cart began to look like a mountain as it stood there with the shafts and hind portion supported by pieces of wood.

"Look ye here," said Ike, waving his arms about from the top of the pile of baskets, and addressing me as if from a rostrum. "When you loads a cart, reck'lect as all your weight's to come on your axle-tree. Your load's to be all ballancy ballancy, you see, so as you could move it up or down with a finger."

"Oh yes, I see!" I cried.

"Oh yes, you see—now I've telled you," said Ike. "People as don't know how to load a cart spyles their hosses by loading for'ard, and getting all the weight on the hoss's back, or loading back'ards, and getting all the pull on the hoss's belly-band."

"Yes, I see clearly now," I said.

"Of course you do! Now you see my load here's so reg'lated that when I take them props away after the horse is in, all that weight'll swing on the axle-tree, and won't hurt the horse at all. That's what I call loading up to rights."

"You've got too much weight behind, Ike," said Old Brownsmith, who came up just then, and was looking on from opposite one wheel of the cart.

"No, no, she's 'bout right," growled Ike to himself.

"You had better put another barge on in front. Lay it flat," cried Old Brownsmith, whose eye was educated by years of experience, and I stood back behind the cart, listening curiously to the conversation. "Yes, you're too heavy behind."

"No, no, she's 'bout right, master," growled Ike, "right as can be. Just you look here."

He took a step back over the baskets, and I heard the prop that supported the cart fall, as Ike yelled out—"Run, boy, run!"

I did not run, for two reasons. Firstly, I was too much confused to understand my danger. Secondly, I had not time, for in spite of Ike's insistence that the balance was correct the shafts flew up; Ike threw himself down on the baskets, and the top layer of flat round sieves that had not yet been tied like the barges, came gliding off like a landslip, and before I knew where I was, I felt myself stricken down, half buried by the wicker avalanche, and all was blank.

Chapter Seven
I Make a Friend

I began to understand and see and hear again an angry voice was saying:

"You clumsy scoundrel! I believe you did it on purpose to injure the poor boy."

"Not I," growled another voice. "I aren't no spite agen him. Now if it had been young Shock—"

"Don't stand arguing," cried the first voice, which seemed to be coming from somewhere out of a mist. "Run up the road and ask the doctor to come down directly."

"All right, master! I'll go."

"Poor lad! poor boy!" the other voice in the mist seemed to say. "Nice beginning for him!—nice beginning! Tut—tut—tut!"

It sounded very indistinct and dreamy. Somehow it seemed to have something to do with my first attempt to swim, and I thought I was being pulled out of the water, which kept splashing about and making my face and hair wet.

I knew I was safe, but my forehead hurt me just as if it had been scratched by the thorns on one of the hedges close to the water-side. My head ached too, and I was drowsy. I wanted to go to sleep, but people kept talking, and the water splashed so about my face and trickled back with a musical noise into the river, I thought, but really into a basin.

For all at once I was wide awake again, looking at the geraniums in the window, as I lay on my back upon the sofa.

I did not understand it for a few minutes; for though my eyes were wide open, the aching and giddiness in my head troubled me so, that though I wanted to speak I did not know what to say.

Then, as I turned my eyes from the geraniums in the window and they rested on the grey hair and florid face of Old Brownsmith, who was busily bathing my forehead with a sponge and water, the scene in the yard came back like a flash, and I caught the hand that held the sponge.

"Has it hurt the baskets of flowers?" I cried excitedly.

"Never mind the baskets of flowers," said Old Brownsmith warmly; "has it hurt you?"

"I don't know; not much," I said quickly. "But won't it be a great deal of trouble and expense?"

He smiled, and patted my shoulder.

"Never mind that," he said good-humouredly. "All people who keep horses and carts, and blundering obstinate fellows for servants, have accidents to contend against. There!—never mind, I say, so long as you have no bones broken; and I don't think you have. Here, stretch out your arms."

I did so.

"That's right," he said. "Now, kick out your legs as if you were swimming."

I looked up at him sharply, for it seemed so strange for him to say that just after I had been thinking of being nearly drowned. I kicked out, though, as he told me.

"No bones broken there," he said; and he proceeded then to feel my ribs.

"Capital!" he said after a few moments. "Why, there's nothing the matter but a little bark off your forehead, and I'm afraid you'll have a black eye. A bit of sticking-plaster will set you right after all, and we sha'n't want the doctor."

"Doctor! Oh! no," I said. "My head aches a bit, and that place smarts, but it will soon be better."

"To be sure it will," he said, nodding pleasantly.—"Well, is he coming?"

This was to Ike, who came up to the open door. "He's out," said Ike gruffly. "Won't be home for two hours, and he'll come on when he gets home."

"That will do," said Old Brownsmith.

"Shall I see 'bout loading up again?"

"Oh, no!" said Old Brownsmith sarcastically. "Let the baskets lie where they are. It doesn't matter about sending to market to sell the things. You never want any wages!"

"What's the good o' talking to a man like that, master?" growled Ike. "You know you don't mean it, no more'n I meant to send the sieves atop o' young Grant here. I'm werry sorry; and a man can't say fairer than that."

"Go and load up then," said Old Brownsmith. "We must risk the damaged goods."

Ike looked hard at me and went away.

"Had you said anything to offend him, my lad?" said the old man as soon as we were alone.

"Oh! no, sir," I cried; "we were capital friends, and he was telling me the best way to load."

"A capital teacher!" cried the old gentleman sarcastically. "No; I don't think he did it intentionally. If I did I'd send him about his business this very night. There!—lie down and go to sleep; it will take off the giddiness."

I lay quite still, and as I did so Old Brownsmith seemed to swell up like the genii who came out of the sealed jar the fisherman caught instead of fish. Then he grew cloudy and filled the room, and then there was the creaking of baskets, and I saw things clearly again. Old Brownsmith was gone, and the soft evening air came through the open window by the pots of geraniums.

My eyes were half-closed and I saw things rather dimly, particularly one pot on the window-sill, which, instead of being red and regular pot-shaped, seemed to be rounder and light-coloured, and to have a couple of eyes, and grinning white teeth. There were no leaves above it nor scarlet blossoms, but a straw hat upside-down, with fuzzy hair standing up out of it; and the eyes kept on staring at me till it seemed to be Shock! Then it grew dark and I must have fallen asleep, wondering what that boy could have to do with my accident.

Perhaps I came to again—I don't know; for it may have been a dream that the old gentleman came softly back and dabbed my head gently with a towel, and that the towel was stained with blood.

Of course it was a dream that I was out in the East with my father, who was not hurt in the skirmish, but it was I who received the wound, which bled a good deal; and somehow I seemed to have been hurt in the shoulder, which ached and felt strained and wrenched. But all became blank again and I lay some time asleep.

When I opened my eyes again I found that I was being hurt a good deal by the doctor, who was seeing to my injuries. Old Brownsmith and Ike were both in the room, and I could see Shock peeping round the big *arbor vitae* outside the window to see what was going on.

The doctor was holding a glass to my lips, while Old Brownsmith raised me up.

"Drink that, my boy," said the doctor. "That's the way!—capital! isn't it?"

I shuddered and looked up at him reproachfully, for the stuff he had given me to drink tasted like a mixture of soap and smelling-salts; and I said so.

"Good description of the volatile alkali, my lad," he said, laughing. "There!—you'll soon be all right. I've strapped up your wound."

"My wound, sir!" I said, wonderingly.

"To be sure; didn't you know that you had a cut upon your forehead?"

I shook my head, but stopped, for it made the room seem to turn round.

"You need not mind," he continued, taking my hand. "It isn't so deep as a well nor so wide as a church-door, as somebody once said. You don't know who it was?"

"Shakespeare, sir," I said, rather drowsily.

"Bravo, young market-gardener!" he cried, laughing. "Oh! you're not very bad. Now, then, what are you going to do—lie still here and be nursed by Mr Brownsmith's maid, or get up and bear it like a man—try the fresh air?"

"I'm going to get up, sir," I said quickly; and throwing my legs off the sofa I stood up; but I had to stretch out my arms, for the room-walls seemed to run by me, the floor to rise up, and I should have fallen if the doctor had not taken my arm, giving me such pain that I cried out, and the giddiness passed off, but only came back with more intensity.

He pressed me back gently and laid me upon the sofa.

"Where did I hurt you, my boy?" he said.

"My shoulder," I replied faintly.

"Ah! another injury!" he exclaimed. "I did not know of this. Tendon a bit wrenched," he muttered as he felt me firmly but gently, giving me a good deal of pain, which I tried hard to bear without showing it, though the twitching of my face betrayed me. "You had better lie still a little while, my man. You'll soon be better."

I obeyed his orders very willingly and lay still in a good deal of pain; but I must soon have dropped off asleep for a while, waking to find it growing dusk. The window was still open; and through it I could hear the creaking of baskets as they were moved, and Old Brownsmith's voice in loud altercation with Ike.

"Well, there," said the latter, "'tain't no use for me to keep on saying I didn't, master, if you says I did."

"Not a bit, Ike; and I'll make you pay for the damage as sure as I stand here."

"Oh! all right! I'm a rich man, master—lots o' money, and land, and stock, and implements. Make me pay! I've saved a fortin on the eighteen shillings a week. Here, what should I want to hurt the boy for, master? Come, tell me that."

"Afraid he'd find out some of your tricks, I suppose."

"That's it: go it, master! Hark at that, now, after sarving him faithful all these years!"

"Get on with your work and don't talk," cried Old Brownsmith sharply. "Catch that rope. Mind you don't miss that handle."

"I sha'n't miss no handles," growled Ike; and as I lay listening to the sawing noise made by the rope being dragged through basket-handles and under hooks in the cart, I felt so much better that I got up and went out into the yard, to find that the cart had been carefully reloaded. Ike was standing on one of the wheels passing a cart-rope in and out, so as to secure the baskets, and dragging it tight to fasten off here and there.

He caught sight of me coming out of the house, feeling dull and low-spirited, for this did not seem a very pleasant beginning of my new career.

"Hah!" he ejaculated, letting himself down in a lumbering way from the wheel, and then rubbing his right hand up and down his trouser-leg to get it clean; "hah! now we'll have it out!"

He came right up to me, spreading out his open hand.

"Here, young un!" he cried; "the master says I did that thar a-purpose to hurt you, out of jealous feeling like. What do you say?"

"It was an accident," I cried, eagerly.

"Hear that, master," cried Ike; "and that's a fact; so here's my hand, and here's my heart. Why, I'd be ashamed o' mysen to hurt a bit of a boy like you. It war an accident, lad, and that's honest. So now what's it to be—shake hands or leave it alone?"

"Shake hands," I said, lifting mine with difficulty. "I don't think you could have done such a cowardly thing."

I looked round sharply at Mr Brownsmith, for I felt as if I had said something that would offend him, since I was taking sides against him.

"Be careful, please," I added quickly; "my arm's very bad, and you'll hurt me."

"Careful!" cried Ike; "I'll shake it as easy as if it was a young shoot o' sea-kale, boy. There, hear him, master! Hear what this here boy says!"

He shook hands with me, I dare say thinking he was treating me very gently, but he hurt me very much. The grip of his hard brown hand alone was bad enough, but I bore it all as well as I could, and tried to smile in the rough fellow's face.

"That's the sort as I like," he said in a good-humoured growl. "Put that down on the slate. That's being a trump, that is; and we two's shipmates after this here."

Old Brownsmith did not speak, and Ike went on:

"I say, master, what a bad un you do think me! I'd ha' hated myself as long as I lived, and never forgive myself, if I'd done such a thing. Look ye here—my monkey's up now, master—did yer ever know me ill-use the 'orses?"

"No, Ike," said Old Brownsmith shortly.

"Never once. There's the white, and I give it a crack now and then; but ask either Capen or Starlit, and see if ever they've got anything agen me. And here's a man as never ill-used a 'orse, and on'y kicked young Shock now and then when he'd been extry owdacious, and you say as I tried to upset the load on young un here. Why, master, I'm ashamed on yer. I wouldn't even ha' done it to you."

I felt sorry for Ike, and my sympathies were against Old Brownsmith, who seemed to be treating him rather hardly, especially when he said shortly:

"Did you fasten off that hind rope?"

"Yes, master, I did fasten off that hind rope," growled Ike.

"Then, now you're out o' breath with talking, go and get your sleep. Don't start later than twelve."

Ike uttered a low grunt, and went off with his hands in his pockets, and Old Brownsmith came and laid his hand upon my shoulder.

"Pretty well bed-time, Grant, my boy. Let's go in."

I followed him in, feeling rather low-spirited, but when he had lit a candle he turned to me with a grim smile.

"Ike didn't like what I said to him, but it won't do him any harm."

I looked at him, wondering how he could treat it all so coolly, but he turned off the conversation to something else, and soon after he showed me my bedroom—a neat clean chamber at the back, and as I opened the window to look out at the moon I found that there was a vine growing up a thick trellis right up to and round it, the leaves regularly framing it in.

There was a comfortable-looking bed, and my box just at the foot, and I was so weary and low-spirited that I was not long before I was lying down on my left side, for I could not lie on my right on account of my shoulder being bad.

As I lay there I could look out on the moon shining among the vine leaves, and it seemed to me that I ought to get out and draw down the blind; but while I was still thinking about it I suppose I must have dropped asleep, for the next thing that seemed to occur was that I was looking at the window, and it was morning, and as I lay trying to think where I was I saw something move gently just outside.

At first I thought it was fancy, and that the soft morning light had deceived me, or that one of the vine leaves had been moved by the wind; but no, there was something moving just as Shock's head used to come among the young shoots of the plum-trees above the wall, and, sure enough, directly after there was that boy's head with his eyes above the sill, staring right in upon me as I lay in bed.

Chapter Eight
Shock's Breakfast

I lay as if fascinated for a minute or two, staring, and he stared at me. Then without further hesitation I leaped out of bed and indignantly rushed to the window, but only on opening it to find him gone.

There was no mistake about it though, for the trellis was still quivering, and as I looked out it seemed to me that he must have dropped part of the way and darted round the house.

It was very early, but the sun was shining brightly over the dew-wet trees and plants, and a fresh, delicious scent came in at the open window. My headache and giddiness had gone, taking with them my low-spirited feeling, and dressing quickly I thought I would have a run round the garden and a look at Shock before Old Brownsmith came down.

"I wonder where Shock sleeps and lives," I said to myself as I walked round peering about the place, finding the cart gone, for I had not heard the opening gate, and crushing and bumping of the wheels as it went out at midnight.

The great sheds and pits seemed to be empty, and as I went down one of the long paths the garden was quite deserted, the men and women not having come.

"They must be late," I thought, when I heard the old clock at Isleworth Church begin to strike, and listening I counted five.

It was an hour earlier than I thought for, and turning down a path to the left I walked towards a sort of toolshed right in the centre of the garden, and, to my surprise, saw that the little roughly-built chimney in one corner of the building was sending out a column of pale-blue smoke.

"I wonder who has lit a fire so early!" I said to myself, and walking slowly on I expected to see one of the garden women boiling her kettle and getting ready for her breakfast—some of the work-people I knew having their meals in the sheds.

I stopped short as I reached the door, for before a fire of wood and rubbish burnt down into embers, and sending out a pretty good heat, there knelt Shock; and as I had approached quietly he had not heard me.

I stared with wonder at him, and soon my wonder turned into disgust, for what he was doing seemed to be so cruel.

The fire was burning on a big slab of stone, and the embers being swept away from one part the boy had there about a score of large garden snails, which he was pushing on to the hot stone, where they hissed and sent out a lot of foam and steam. Then he changed them about with a bit of stick into hotter or cooler parts, and all with his back half-turned to me.

"The nasty, cruel brute!" I said to myself, for it seemed as if he were doing this out of wantonness, and I was blaming myself for not interfering to save the poor things from their painful death, when a thought flashed across my mind, and I stood there silently watching him.

I had not long to watch for proof.

Taking a scrap of paper from his pocket, Shock opened it, and I saw what it contained. Then taking a monstrous pin from out of the edge of his jacket, he picked up one of the snails with his left hand, used the pin cleverly, and dragged out one of the creatures from its shell, reduced to about half its original size, blew it, dipped it in the paper of salt, and, to my horror and disgust, ate it.

Before I had recovered from my surprise he had eaten another and another, and he was busy over the sixth when an ejaculation I uttered made him turn and see me.

He stared at me, pin in one hand, snail-shell in the other, for a moment in mute astonishment; then, turning more away from me, he went on with his repast, and began insultingly to throw the shells at me over his head.

I bore it all for a few minutes in silence; then, feeling qualmish at the half-savage boy's meal, I caught one of the shells as it came, and tossed it back with such good aim that it hit him a smart rap on the head.

He turned sharply round with a vicious look, and seemed as if about to fly at me.

"What are you doing?" I cried.

He had never spoken to me before, and he seemed to hesitate now, staring at me as if reluctant to use his tongue, but he did speak in a quick angry way.

"Eatin'; can't you see?"

I had questioned him, but I was quite as much surprised at hearing an answer, as at the repast of which he was partaking.

I stared hard at him, and he gave me a sidelong look, after which he gave three or four of the snails a thrust with a bit of stick to where they would cook better, took up another, and wriggled it out with the pin.

I was disgusted and half nauseated, but I could not help noticing that the cooked snail did not smell badly, and that instead of being the wet, foaming, slimy thing I was accustomed to see, it looked dried up and firm.

At last, with a horrified look at the young savage, I exclaimed:

"Do you know those are snails?"

"Yes. Have one?"

He answered quite sharply, and I took a step back, for I had not had my breakfast. I was rather disposed to be faint from the effects of my last night's accident, and the sight of what was going on made me ready to flee, for all at once, after letting his dirty fingers hover for a few moments over the hot stone, he picked up the largest snail, blew it as he threw it from hand to hand because it was hot, and ended by holding it out to me with:

"Got a big pin?"

I shrank away from him with my lip curling, and I uttered a peculiar "Ugh!"

"All right!" he said gruffly. "They're stunning."

To prove his assertion he went on eating rapidly without paying any further heed to me, throwing the shells over his head, and ending by screwing the paper up tightly that contained the salt.

Then he sprang up and faced me; took two or three steps in my direction, and made a spring as if to jump right on to me.

Naturally enough I gave way, and he darted out of the shed and dashed down between two rows of trees, to be out of sight directly, for I did not give chase.

"He can talk," I said to myself as I went on down the garden thinking of the snails, and that Shock was something like the wild boy of whom I had once read.

But soon the various objects in the great garden made me forget Shock, for the men were at work, hoeing, digging, and planting, and I was beginning to feel uncomfortable and to think that Old Brownsmith would be annoyed if he found me idle, when he came down one of the walks, followed by his cats, and laid his hand upon my shoulder.

"Better?" he said abruptly. "That's right. What you're to do? Oh wait a bit, we'll see! Get used to the place first."

He gave me a short nod, and began pointing out different tasks that he wished his men to carry out, while I watched attentively, feeling as if I should like to run off and look at the ripening fruit, but not caring to go away, for fear Mr Brownsmith might want me.

One thing was quite evident, and that was that the cats were disposed to be very friendly. They did not take any notice of the men, but one after the other came and had a rub up against my leg, purring softly, and looking up at me with their slits of eyes closed up in the bright sunshine, till all at once Old Brownsmith laid his hand upon my shoulder again, and said one word:

"Breakfast!"

I walked with him up to the house, and noticed that instead of following us in, the cats ran up a flight of steps into a narrow loft which seemed to be their home, two of them seating themselves at once in the doorway to blink at the sunshine.

"Like cats?" said the old gentleman.

"Oh yes!" I said.

"Ah! I see you've made friends."

"Yes, I replied; but I haven't made friends with that boy Shock."

"Well, that does not matter," said Old Brownsmith. "Come, sit down; bread and milk morning."

I sat down opposite to him, to find that a big basin of bread and milk stood before each of us, and at which, after a short grace, Old Brownsmith at once began.

I hesitated for a moment, feeling a little awkward and strange, but I was soon after as busy as he.

"Not going to be ill, I see," he said suddenly. "You must be on the look-out another time. Accident—Ike didn't mean it."

I was going to say I was sure of that, when he went on:

"So you haven't made friends with Shock?"

"No, sir."

"Well, don't."

"I will not if you don't wish it, sir," I said eagerly.

"Be kind to him, and keep him in his place. Hasn't been rough to you, has he?"

"Oh no!" I said. "He only seems disposed to play tricks."

"Yes, like a monkey. Rum fellow, isn't he?"

"Yes, sir. He isn't—"

"Bit of an idiot, eh? Oh no! he's sharp enough. I let him do as he likes for the present. Awkward boy to manage."

"Is he, sir?"

"Yes, my lad. Ike found him under the horses' hoofs one night, going up to market. Little fellow had crawled out into the road. Left in the ditch by some one or another. Ike put him in a half-sieve basket with some hay, and fixed him in with some sticks same as we cover fruit, and he curled up and went to sleep till Ike brought him in to me in the yard."

"But where were his father and mother?" I cried.

"Who knows!" said Old Brownsmith, poking at a bit of brown crust in his basin of milk. "Ike brought him to me grinning, and he said, 'Here's another cat for you, master.'

"I was very angry," said the old gentleman after a pause; "but just then the little fellow—he was about a year old—put his head up through the wooden bars and looked at me, and I told one of the women to give him something to eat. After that I sent him to the workhouse, where they took care of him, and one day when he got bigger I gave him a treat, and had him here for a day's holiday. Then after a twelvemonth, I gave him another holiday, and I should have given him two a year, only he was such a young rascal. The workhouse master said he could do nothing with him. He couldn't make him learn anything—even his letters. The only thing he would do well was work in the garden."

"Same as he does now, sir?" I said, for I was deeply interested.

"Same as he does now," assented Old Brownsmith. "Then one day after I had given him his treat, I suppose when he was about ten years old, I found him in the garden. He had run away from the workhouse school."

"And did he stay here, sir?"

"No, I sent him back, Grant, and he ran away again. I sent him back once more, but he came back; and at last I got to be tired of it, for the more I sent him back the more he came."

The old gentleman chuckled and finished his bread and milk, while I waited to hear more.

"I say I got tired of it at last, for I knew they flogged and locked up the boy, and kept him on bread and water; but it did him no good; he would run away. He used to come here, through the gate if it was open, over the wall when it was shut, and he never said a word, only hung about like a dog.

"I talked to him, coaxed him, and told him that if he would be a good lad, and learn, I would have him to work some day, and he stared at me just as if he were some dumb animal, and when I had done and sent him off, what do you think happened, Grant?"

"He came back again, sir."

"Yes: came back again as soon as he could get away, and at last, being a very foolish sort of old man, I let him stop, and he has been here ever since."

"And never goes to school?"

"Never, Grant, I tried to send him, but I could only get him there by blows, and I gave that up. I don't like beating boys."

I felt a curious shiver run through me as he said this, and I saw him smile, but he made no allusion to me, and went on talking about Shock.

"Then I tried making a decent boy of him, giving him clothes, had a bed put for him in the attic, and his meals provided for him here in the kitchen."

"And wasn't he glad?" I said.

"Perhaps he was," said Old Brownsmith, quietly, "but he didn't show it, for I couldn't get him to sleep in the bed, and he would not sit down to his meals in the kitchen; so at last I grew tired, and took to paying him wages, and made arrangements for one of the women who comes to work, to find him a lodging, and he goes there to sleep sometimes."

I noticed that he said *sometimes*, in a peculiar manner, looking at me the while. Then he went on:

"I've tried several times since, Grant, my lad, but the young savage is apparently irreclaimable. Perhaps when he gets older something may be done."

"I hope so," I said. "It seems so dreadful to see a boy so—"

"So dirty and lost, as the north-country people call it, boy. Ah, well, let him have his way for a bit, and we'll see by and by! You say he has not annoyed you?"

"No, no," I said; "I don't think he likes me though."

"That does not matter," said the old gentleman, rising. "There, now, I'm going to shave."

I looked at him in wonder, as he took a tin pot from out of a cupboard, and brought forth his razors, soap, and brush.

"Give me that looking-glass that hangs on the wall, my lad; that's it."

I fetched the glass from the nail on which it hung, and then he set it upright, propped by a little support behind, and then I sat still as he placed his razor in boiling water, soaped his chin all round, and scraped it well, removing the grey stubble, and leaving it perfectly clean.

It seemed to me a curious thing to do on a breakfast-table, but it was the old man's custom, and it was not likely that he would change his habits for me.

"There," he said smiling, "that's a job you won't want to do just yet awhile. Now hang up the glass, and you can go out in the garden. I shall be there by and by. Head hurt you?"

"Oh no, sir!" I said.

"Shoulder?"

"Only a little stiff, sir."

Then I don't think we need have the doctor any more.

I laughed, for the idea seemed ridiculous.

"Well, then, we won't waste his time. Put on your hat and go and see him. You know where he lives?"

I said that I did; and I went up to his house, saw him, and he sent me away again, patting me on the shoulder that was not stiff.

"Yes, you're all right," he said. "Now take care and don't get into my clutches again."

Chapter Nine
Gathering Pippins

I did not understand it at the time, but that accident made me a very excellent friend in the shape of Ike, the big ugly carter and packer, for after his fashion he took me regularly under his wing, and watched over me during the time I was at Old Brownsmith's.

I'm obliged to stop again over that way of speaking of the market-gardener, but whenever I write "Mr Brownsmith," or "the old gentleman," it does not seem natural. Old Brownsmith it always was, and I should not have been surprised to have seen his letters come by the postman directed *Old Brownsmith*.

Ike used to look quite pleasant when I was busy near him, and while he taught me all he knew, nothing pleased him better than for me to call him from his digging, or hoeing, or planting, to move a ladder, or lift a basket, or perform some other act that was beyond my strength.

All the same, though, he had a way of not showing it.

I had been at the garden about a week when Old Brownsmith began talking about picking some of his pippins to send to market.

"I hear they are making a good price," he said, "and I shall try a few sieves to-morrow morning, Grant."

"Yes, sir," I said, for the sound of apple-picking was pleasant.

"I suppose if I were to send you up one of the apple trees with a basket, you would throw yourself out and break one of your limbs."

"Oh no, sir!" I said. "I could climb one of the trees and pick the apples without doing that."

"Thank you," he replied; "that's not the way to pick my apples. Why, don't you know that the fruit does not grow in the middle of a tree, but round the outside, where the sun and wind can get at the blossom?"

"I didn't know it," I said rather ruefully. "I seem to be very ignorant. I wish I had been more to school."

"They wouldn't have taught you that at school, my lad," he said smiling. "Why, of course you did not know it. I didn't know such things when I was your age. Look here. You must have a ladder put for you against a tree, and take a basket with a hook to the handle. There, I'll show you; but you are sure you will not tumble?"

"I'll take care, sir," I said. "I'll be very careful."

It was a sunny morning, and leading the way, Old Brownsmith went out to where Ike was busy putting in plants with a dibber, striding over a stretched-out line, making holes, thrusting in one of the plants he held in his left hand, and with one thrust or two of the dibber surrounding it with the soft moist earth.

He raised himself unwillingly, and went off to obey orders; one of the work-women was sent to fetch some flat sieves; while from one of the sheds I brought a couple of deep cross-handled baskets to each of which a wooden hook was attached.

By the time we had walked to where the king-pippin trees stood with their tall straight branches, Ike was before us with a ladder, with the lower rounds made of great length, so as to give width to the bottom.

I had noticed this before when I had seen the ladders hanging up in the long shed, and now asked the reason why they were so made.

"To keep them from tilting over when you are up there," said Old Brownsmith. "Gently, Ike, don't bruise them. Ah! there they go."

For, as Ike thumped down the bottom of the ladder, and then let the top lean against the tree, a couple of apples were knocked off, to come down, one with a thud on the soft soil, the other to strike in the fork of the tree and bound to my feet.

"Some on 'em's sure to get knocked off," growled Ike. "Who's agoin' to pick?"

"He is," said Mr Brownsmith shortly.

"Then you don't want me no more?"

"Not at present."

"Then I may go on with my planting?"

"Yes."

"Ho!"

I could not help feeling amused at the way in which this conversation was carried on, and the heavy clumsy manner adopted by Ike in going away.

"There you are, Grant," said Old Brownsmith, "plenty of apples. What do you say—can you go up the ladder safely and pick them?"

"Oh yes, sir!" I cried.

"And you will not fall?"

"Oh! I shall not fall, sir," I cried laughing.

"Very well. Up you go then. Take your basket and hook it on to the round of the ladder where you are picking, then take each apple carefully, raise it, and it will come off at a point on the stalk where it joins the twig. Don't tear them out and break the stalks, or they become unsaleable."

"I'll mind, sir," I said. "I know the big Marie Louise pears at home used to come off like that at a joint."

"Good!" he cried smiling, and tapping my shoulder. "When you've picked an apple of course you'll throw it into the basket?"

"Yes, sir."

"You'd better not," he cried sharply. "Lay it in as tenderly as you can. If you throw it in, the apple will be bruised—bruised apples are worth very little in the market, and soon decay."

"I'll mind them, sir," I said, and eagerly mounting the ladder I began to pick the beautiful little apples that hung about me, Old Brownsmith watching me the while.

"That's right," he said encouragingly. "When you get your basket nearly full, bring it down and empty it very gently in one of the sieves—gently, mind."

I promised, and he went away, leaving me as busy as could be in the warm sunshine, thoroughly enjoying my task, picking away carefully at the apples, beginning low down, and then getting higher and higher till I felt the ladder bend and the branch give, and I had to hold on tightly by one hand.

I had to go down three times to empty my basket, pouring out the apples very gently so as not to bruise them, and at last I had picked all the pippins I could reach from the ladder.

I got down and proceeded to move it, so as to get to another part of the tree.

It was easy enough, after I had got it free of the twigs, to pull the ladder upright, and this done I looked at the place where I meant to put it next, and getting hold of it tightly, began to lift it by the spokes just as I had seen Ike manage it.

The fact did not occur to me that I was a mere boy and he a muscular man, for I'm afraid I had plenty of conceit, and, drawing in a long breath, I lifted the ladder straight up easily enough, took a couple of steps in the right direction, and then felt to my horror that the strength of my arms was as nothing as soon as the balance ceased to be preserved, for in spite of my efforts the top of the ladder began to go over slowly, then faster and faster, then there was a sharp whishing crash as the bough of a pear-tree was literally cut off and a bump and a sharp crack.

The top of the ladder had struck the ground, breaking several feet right off, and I was clinging to the bottom.

One minute I was happy and in the highest of spirits; now I was plunged into a state of hopeless despair as I wondered what Old Brownsmith would say, and how much it would cost to repair that ladder.

I was so prostrated by my accident that for a minute or so I stood holding on to the broken ladder, ruefully gazing at my work, and once I actually found myself looking towards the wall where the trained plum-trees formed a ladder easy of ascent for Shock, and just as easy for me to get over and run for it—anywhere so as not to have to meet Old Brownsmith after destroying his property.

"Well, you've been and gone and done it now, young 'un, and no mistake," said a gruff voice; and I found that Ike had come softly up behind me. "I thought it was you tumbling and breaking of yourself again; but the ladder. Oh my!"

"I couldn't help it," I cried piteously; "the top was so heavy, it seemed to pull it over when I tried to move it. Please how much will a new one cost?"

"Cost!" said Ike grimly, as he stood looking with one eye at the ladder, with the other at me—"hundred—hundred and twenty—say a hundred pound at the very outside."

"A hundred pounds!" I cried aghast.

"Well, not more'n that," said Ike. "Trying to move it, was you? and—why, you've smashed that branch off the pear-tree. I say, hadn't you better cut and run?"

"I don't know, Ike," I said hopelessly; "had I?"

"Well, I don't think I would this time. The ganger perhaps'll let you off if you pay for it out of your wage."

"But I don't have any wages," I said in despair.

"You don't!" he cried. "Well, then, you're in for it. My word, I wouldn't be you for a crown."

I stood gazing helplessly from the ladder to Ike and back, half feeling that he was imposing upon me, but in too much trouble to resent it, and as I stared about a robin came and sat upon the broken branch, and seemed to be examining how much damage I had done.

"Well, what shall we do, young 'un?" said Ike.

"I suppose I must go on picking with the broken ladder," I said gloomily.

"You ain't going to cut then?"

"No," I said firmly.

"Then look here," said Ike; "suppose I take the broken ladder up into the shed, and hang it up, and bring another. When the ganger finds it he'll think it was Shock broke it, and then you'll be all right, eh? What do you say to that?"

"That I wouldn't be such a coward," I said stoutly. "I shall tell Mr Brownsmith myself."

"Oh, very well!" said Ike, stooping and picking up the broken ladder. "Here, give me that bit. I'll soon be back. Don't much matter. On'y four foot gone, and we wanted a shorter one. This'll just do."

"Then it won't cost a hundred pounds?" I cried.

"No; nor a hundred pennies, boy. It was only my gammon. I'll soon be back."

I felt as if a load had been lifted off my breast as Ike came back at a heavy trot with a fresh ladder and planted it for me against the apple-tree.

"That's about safe," he cried. "If you feel yourself falling, hook one of your ears over a bough and hang on. Never mind the ladder: let that go."

"That's nonsense!" I said sharply, and Ike chuckled.

"Look ye here, boy," he said, as I thanked him and ran up the ladder with my empty basket, "I'll take that bough as you broke in among the gooseberries, where he never hardly comes, and I'll tell him that I broke the ladder moving it. You've had plenty of trouble already, and my shoulders is bigger than yours."

"But it wouldn't be true," I said.

"Wouldn't it?" he replied, with a queer look. "Well, I suppose it wouldn't; but I'll tell him all the same."

"No," I cried, after a fight with a very cowardly feeling within me that seemed to be pulling me towards the creep-hole of escape, "I shall tell him myself."

Ike turned off sharply, and walked straight to where the broken pear bough lay, jumped up and pulled down the place where it had snapped off, opened his knife, and trimmed the ragged place off clean, and then went back to his work.

"Now he's offended," I said to myself with a sigh; and I went on picking apples in terribly low spirits.

Chapter Ten
My First Apple

I had been working for about half an hour longer when I found I could get no more, and this time I went a little way and called Ike from where he was at work to move the ladder for me.

He came in a surly way, and then stared at me.

"Want me to move the ladder? Why can't yer move it yerself?" he grumbled.

"You know I'm not strong enough," I said.

"Ho! that's it, is it? I thought you were such a great big cock-a-hoop sort of a chap that you could do anything. Well, where's it to be?"

"Round the other side, I think," I said.

"No; this here's best," he cried, and whisking up the ladder I stood admiring his great brown arms and the play of the muscles as he carried the ladder as if it had been a straw, and planted it, after thrusting the intervening boughs aside with the top to get it against a stout limb.

"There you are, my lad," he said. "Now, are you satisfied?"

"Yes; and thank you, Ike," I said quickly. "And I'm very much obliged to you about wanting to take the blame upon yourself about the broken ladder and—"

"Here, I can't stand listening to speeches with my plants a-shrivelling up in the sun. Call me if you wants me agen."

He gave me a curious look and went away, leaving me with the impression that I had thoroughly offended him now, and that I was a most unlucky boy.

I climbed the ladder again, picking as fast as I could to make up for lost time; and as the sun shone so hotly and I kept on picking the beautiful fruit with the bough giving and swaying so easily, I began to feel more at ease once more. While I picked and filled and emptied my basket I began to reason with myself and to think that after all Mr Brownsmith would not be so very angry with me if I went to him boldly and told the truth.

This thought cheered me wonderfully, and I was busily working away when I heard the whistling and scratching noise made by somebody walking sharply through the gooseberry bushes, and, looking round, there was Ike carrying another ladder, and Shock coming along loaded with baskets, evidently to go on picking apples from one of the neighbouring trees.

They neither of them spoke. Ike planted the ladder ready, and Shock took a basket and ran up, and was hard at work by the time Ike was out of sight.

I had hardly spoken to the boy since I had found him eating snails; and as I went on picking with my back to him, and thinking of the poor child being found crawling in the road and brought in a basket, and of his always running away from the workhouse, I felt a kind of pity for him, and determined to try if I could not help him, when all at once I felt a sharp pain accompanying a severe blow on the leg, as if some one had thrown a stone at me.

I turned sharply round, holding tightly with one hand; but Shock's back was turned to me, and he was picking apples most diligently.

I looked about, and there was no one else near, the trees being too small for anyone to hide behind their trunks. Shock did not look in my direction, but worked away, and I at last, as the sting grew less, went on with mine.

"I know it was him," I said to myself angrily. "If I catch him at it—"

I made some kind of mental vow about what I would do, finished filling my basket, went down and emptied it, and ascended the ladder again just as he was doing the same, but I might have been a hundred miles away for all the notice he took of me.

I had just begun picking again, and was glancing over my shoulder to see if he was going to play any antics, when he began to ascend his ladder, and I went on.

Thump!

A big lump of earth struck me right in the back, and as I looked angrily round I saw Shock fall from the top to the bottom of his ladder, and I felt that horrible sensation that people call your heart in your mouth.

He rose to a sitting position, put his hand to his head, and shouted out:

"Who's that throwing lumps?"

Nobody answered; and as I saw him run up the ladder again it occurred to me that it was more a slip down than a fall from the ladder, and I had just come to this conclusion when, seeing that I was watching him, he made me start and cling tightly, for he suddenly fell again.

It was like lightning almost. One moment he was high up on the ladder, the next he was at the foot; but this time I was able to make out that he guided himself with his arms and his legs, and that it was really more a slide down than a fall.

I turned from him in disgust, annoyed with myself for letting him cheat me into the belief that he had met with an accident, and went on picking apples.

"He's no better than a monkey," I said to myself.

Whiz!

An apple came so close to my ear, thrown with great violence, that I felt it almost brush me, and I turned so sharply round that I swung myself off the ladder, and had I not clung tightly by my hands I must have fallen.

As it was, the ladder turned right round, in spite of its broadly set foot, and I hung beneath it, while my half-filled basket was in my place at the top.

The distance was not great, but I felt startled as I hung there, when, to my utter astonishment, Shock threw himself round, twisted his ladder, and hung beneath just as I did, and then went down by his hands from round to round of the ladder, turned it back, ran up again, and went on picking apples as if nothing was wrong.

I could not do as he did; I had not muscle enough in my arms, but I threw my legs round the tottering ladder, and slid down, turned it back to its old place, went up quickly, and again picked away.

For the next quarter of an hour all was very quiet, and I had just finished getting all I could when Ike came along.

I started guiltily, for I thought it was Old Brownsmith, but the voice reassured me, and I felt reprieved for the moment as Ike said:

"Want the ladder moved?"

I carried my basket down, and emptied it while Ike changed the position of the ladder.

"There you are," he said. "There's plenty for you up yonder. Come, you're getting on. Yes; and clean picked, too," he continued, giving the basket a shake. "Now you, Shock, come down, and I'll move yourn."

The boy got down sullenly, and turned his back to me while the ladder was moved, so that this time we were working at different trees, but nearly facing each other.

Ike gave me a nod, and went off again to his work; and as I turned my head to gaze after him, *whack* came a little apple, and struck me on the side of the ear.

I was so much annoyed that I picked a big one out of my basket and threw it at Shock with all my might, disturbing my balance so that I had to hold on tightly with one hand.

My shot did not go anywhere near the boy, but he fell from the ladder, hanging by one leg in a horrible way, his head down, and his hands feeling about and stretching here and there, as if to get hold of something to draw him up. He swung about and uttered a low animal-like moan of distress that horrified me, and sliding down my ladder, unwilling to call for aid, I ran to help him myself.

He was squinting frightfully, and lay back head downwards, and arms outstretched on the ladder as I began to ascend. His face was flushed, his mouth open, and his tongue out. In fact, he looked as if he were being strangled by his position, and, trembling with eagerness, I went up four rounds, when *smack! crack!* I received a blow on each ear that sent me down.

When I recovered myself, my cheeks tingling, and my heart throbbing with wrath, Shock had thrown himself up again, and, with his back to me, was picking away at the apples as if nothing had been wrong.

"You see if I trust you again, my fine fellow," I cried in a rage; and, picking up a lot of clods, I began to pelt him as hard as I could, missing him half the time, but giving him several sharp blows on the back and head.

It was the last shot that hit him on the head, and the clod was big and cakey, hitting him so hard that it flew to pieces like a shell.

It must have hurt him, for he slid down and came at me fiercely with his mouth open, and showing his teeth like a dog.

I daresay at another time, as he was much bigger and stronger than I was, I should have turned and fled; but just then I was so hot and excited that I went at him with my doubled fists, and for the next five minutes we were fighting furiously, every now and then engaged in a struggle, and going down to continue it upon the ground.

I fell heavily several times, and was getting the worst of it when, all at once, I managed to get one hand free, and in my despair struck him as hard as I could.

The blow must have been a hard one, for Shock staggered back, caught his foot in one of the gooseberry bushes, and fell with a crash into one of them, splitting the bush open.

I was half blind with rage, and smarting with blows; and as he seemed to be coming at me again, I made another dash at him, striking out right and left with my arms going like a windmill, till I was checked suddenly by being lifted from the ground, and a hoarse voice uttered a tremendous— "Haw, haw, haw!"

I had felt this last time that Shock was very big and strong, hence it took me some moments to realise that the boy had crept out of the gooseberry bush and had shuffled away, while it was Ike whom I was belabouring and drumming with all my might.

"Well done, little one," he cried. "There, cool down. Shock's give in. You've whacked him. Here's the ganger coming. Get on with your work."

Shock ran by us with a rush, mounted his ladder, and I hurried up mine, to go on picking as well, while, panting and hot, smarting with blows and anger, I wondered what Old Brownsmith would say to me for what I had done.

He only went along the path, however, with his cats, as he saw that Ike was there, and the apple-picking went on till he was out of sight.

"Ah! you're only a bit dirty," said Ike to me rather less roughly than usual. "Come down and I'll give you a brush."

"There you are," he said, after performing the task for me. "Was he up to his larks with you?"

"Yes," I said; "he has been pelting me, and he pretended to fall; and when I went to help him he struck me, and I couldn't stand that."

"So you licked him well? That's right, boy. He won't do it again. If he does, give it him, and teach him better. I don't like fighting till you're obliged; but when you are obliged—hit hard's my motter, and that's what you've done by him."

Of course I knew that *that* was what I had done by him, but I felt very sorry all the same, for I knew I had hurt Shock a good deal, and I had hurt myself; and somehow, as Ike went away chuckling and rubbing his big hands down his sides, it seemed very cruel of him to laugh.

Everything seemed to have gone so wrong, and I was in such trouble, that neither the sunshine nor the beauty of the apples gave me the least satisfaction.

I kept on picking, expecting every moment that Shock would begin again, and I kept a watchful eye upon him; but he threw no more lumps of earth or apples, and only went on picking as quickly as he could, and I noticed that he always had his face turned from me.

"I do nothing but offend people," I thought, as I worked away, and I felt as sure as could be that this boy would contrive pitfalls for me and play me tricks, making my life quite a burden. In fact, I became very imaginative, as boys of my age often will, and instead of trying to take things in the manly English spirit that should be the aim of every lad, I grew more and more depressed.

Just when I was at my worst, and I was thinking what an unlucky boy I was, I heard a sound, followed by another. The nearest representation of the sounds are these—*Quack—craunche.*

"Why, he's eating apples," I said to myself, as I went down my ladder, emptied my basket, and went up again.

Now some who read this will think it a strange thing, but, though I had been busy all that morning handling beautiful little pippins, long, rosy, and flat-topped, I had never even thought of tasting one.

Like fruit? I loved it; but I was so intent upon my work, so eager to do it well, and I had had so much to think about, that it seemed to come upon me like a surprise that the apples were good to eat.

Now that Shock had begun, and was crunching away famously as he worked, I suddenly found that, though I was not so hot as I was after my encounter, my mouth felt dry. I was very thirsty, and those apples seemed to be the most tempting of any I had ever seen in my life.

But I would not touch one. I went higher up the ladder and picked; then higher and higher till I was close to the top, holding on by the tall stem of the tree picking some of the ripest apples I had yet gathered, and swaying with a pleasant motion every time I reached here or there to pick one at the end of a twig.

What beauties they seemed, and how, while those that grew in the shady parts under the leaves, were of a delicate green, the ones I had picked from out in the full sunshine were dark and ruddy and bronzed! How they clustered together too, out here in the top of the tree, so thickly that it seemed as if I should never get them all.

But by degrees I reached up and up where I could not take the basket, and thrust the apples into my breast and pockets. One I had a tremendous job to reach, after going a little lower to where my basket hung to empty my pockets before climbing again. It was a splendid fellow, the biggest yet, and growing right at the top of a twig.

It seemed dangerous to get up there, for it meant holding on by the branch, and standing on the very top round of the ladder, and I hesitated. Still I did not like to be beaten, and with the branch bending I held on and went up and up, till I stood right at the top of the ladder, and then cautiously raising my hand I was about to reach up at and try to pick the apple, when something induced me to turn my head and look in the direction of Shock's tree.

Sure enough he was watching me. I saw his face right up in the top; but he turned it quickly, and there was a rustle and a crack as if he had nearly fallen.

For a few moments this unsteadied me, and for the first time I began to think that I was running great risks, and that I should fall. So peculiar was the feeling that I clung tightly to the swaying bending branch and shut my eyes.

The feeling went off as quickly as it came, for I set my teeth, and, knowing that Shock was watching me, determined that he should not see I was afraid.

The next moment I was reaching up cautiously, and by degrees got my hand just under the apple, but could get no higher. My head was thrown back, the branch bending towards me, and my feet on the top round, so that I was leaning back far out of the perpendicular, and the more I tried to get that pippin, and could not reach, the more bright and beautiful it looked.

I forgot all about the danger, for Shock was watching me, and I would have it; and as I strained up I at last was able to touch it with the tips of my fingers, for my feet were pressing the branch one way, my hands drawing it the other, till it came lower, lower, lower, my fingers grasped the apple— more and more, and at last, when I felt that I could bear the strain no longer, the stalk gave way, and the apple dropped between the twig and my hand.

Then for a moment, as I grasped it, I felt as if I was going to lose my footing, and hang off the ladder. If I did, the bough was so thin that I knew it would break, and it was only by exerting all my strength that I held on.

At last, lowering hand below hand, I got to be a little more upright. My feet were firmer on the ladder, and I was able to take a step down.

Another few moments and, with a sigh of relief at my escape from a heavy fall—for it really was an escape—I thrust the beautiful apple in my breast and descended to my basket, gave a final glance round to see if there was any more fruit within reach, found there was not, and so I went to the foot of the ladder, emptied my basket, took out the apple from my breast, and found that it was as beautiful as it had seemed up there.

"I must have you," I thought, and, turning the rosy side towards me, I took a tremendous bite out of it, a rich sweet juicy bite, and then stood staring stupidly, for Old Brownsmith was standing there with his cats, looking at me in a quiet serious way.

Chapter Eleven
Making Things Right

Just at that moment I fancied that I heard a sort of laugh from up in the other tree, but my eyes were fixed upon Old Brownsmith, and I had a large piece of apple in my mouth that I dared not begin to chew.

He stood looking at me as I stood there, feeling three of his cats come and begin rubbing themselves up against my legs in the most friendly way, while I felt as if my misfortunes were being piled up one on the top of the other.

From previous conversations I had gathered that he expected the boys to now and then eat a little fruit, and there was no harm in it; but it seemed so hard that the very first time I tasted an apple he should be standing there watching me.

"Dinner's ready," he said suddenly; "come along."

"Shall I leave the baskets here, sir?" I said.

"Yes; just as they are."

He stooped down and examined the apples, turning them over a little.

"Hah! yes," he said; "nicely picked. That will do. You've got on too."

He went on, and I was following behind the cats, but he drew on one side to let me walk by him.

"Eat your apple," he said smiling, as he looked sidewise at me. "Only we always pick out the ugliest fruit and vegetables for home use, and send the best-looking to market."

"I'll remember that, sir," I said.

"Do, Grant, my lad. You will not lose by it, for I'll tell you something. The shabbiest-looking, awkwardly-grown apples, pears, and plums are generally the finest flavoured."

"Are they, sir?" I said.

"That they are, my boy. If you want a delicious pear don't pick out the great shapely ones, but those that are screwed all on one side and covered with rusty spots. The same with the plums and apples. They are almost always to be depended upon."

I had finished my mouthful of apple, and thrust the fruit in my jacket pocket.

"It is often the same with people in this life, my boy. Many of the plain-looking, shabby folks are very beautiful everywhere but outside. There's a moral lesson for you. Save it up."

I said I would, and looked at him sidewise, hesitating, for I wanted to speak to him. I was wondering, too, whether he knew that I had been fighting with Shock, for my hands were very dirty and my knuckles were cut.

He did not speak any more, but stooped and took up one of the cats, to stroke it and let it get up on his shoulder, and we had nearly reached the house before I burst out desperately:

"If you please, Mr Brownsmith—"

Then I stopped short and stared at him helplessly, for the words seemed to stick in my throat.

"Well," he said, "what is it? Want to speak to me?"

"Yes, sir," I burst out; "I want to tell you that I—that I broke—"

"The ladder, eh?" he said smiling. "That's right, Grant; always speak out when you have had an accident of any kind. Nothing like being frank. It's honest and gives people confidence in you. Yes, I know all about the ladder. I was coming to see if you wanted it moved when I saw you overcome by it. Did Ike trim off that branch?"

"Yes, sir," I cried hastily. "I'm very sorry, sir. I did not know that—"

"It was so heavy, Grant. Leverage, my boy. A strong man can hardly hold a ladder if he gets it off the balance."

"Will it cost much to—"

"It was an old ladder, Grant, and I'm not sorry it is broken; for there was a bad crack there, I see, covered over by the paint. We might have had a nasty accident. It will do now for the low trees. Look here."

He led me into the shed where the ladders hung, and showed me the broken ladder, neatly sawn off at the top, and thinned down a little, and trimmed off with a spokeshave, while a pot of lead-coloured paint and a brush stood by with which the old gentleman had been going over the freshly-cut wood.

"My job," he said quietly. "Dry by to-morrow. You were quite right to tell me."

Then there was a pause.

"How many apples does that make you've had to-day?" he said, suddenly.

"Apples, sir? Oh! that was the first."

"Humph!" he ejaculated, looking at me sharply. "And so you've been having a set-to with Shock, eh?"

"Yes, sir," I said in an aggrieved tone; "he—"

"Don't tell tales out of school, Grant," he said. "You've had your fight, and have come off better than I expected. Don't let's have any more of it, if you can help it. There, have a wash; make haste. Dinner's waiting."

The relief I felt was something tremendous, and though five minutes or so before I had not wanted any dinner, I had no sooner had a good wash in the tin bowl with the clean cold water from the pump, and a good rub with the round towel behind the kitchen door, than I felt outrageously hungry; and it was quite a happy, flushed face, with a strapped-up wound on the forehead and a rather swollen and cut lip, that looked out at me from the little square shaving glass on the wall.

That morning I had been despondently thinking that I was making no end of enemies in my new home. That afternoon I began to find that things were not so very bad after all. Shock was sulky, and seemed to delight in showing me the roots of his hair in the nape of his neck, always turning his back; but he did not throw any more apples and he played no more pranks, but went on steadily picking.

I did the same, making no further advances to him, though, as I recalled how I hammered his body and head, and how he must have been pricked by falling into the gooseberry bush, I felt sorry, and if he had offered to shake hands I should have forgotten how grubby his always were, and held out mine at once.

As the afternoon wore on we filled our baskets, and more had to be fetched. Then, later on, I wanted my ladder moved to another tree, and came down and called Ike, but he was not there, so I asked one of the other men, who came and did it for me, and then moved Shock's.

I was just mounting again when Ike came up, taking long strides and scowling angrily.

"S'pose you couldn't ha' waited a moment, could you?" he growled. "I didn't move the ladder just as you wanted, I suppose. You're precious partickler, you are. Now, look here, my fine gentleman, next time you want a ladder moved you may move it yourself."

"But I did call you, Ike," I said; "and you weren't there."

"I hadn't gone to get another two hundred o' plarnts, I suppose, and was comin' back as fast as I could, I s'pose. No, o' course not. I ought to ha' been clost to your elber, ready when you called. Never mind; next time you wants the ladder moved get some one else, for I sha'n't do it;" and he strode away.

Half an hour later he was back to see if I wanted it moved, and waited till I had finished gathering a few more apples, when, smiling quite good-humouredly, he shifted the ladder into a good place.

"There," he said, "you'll get a basketful up there.

"Shock, shall I shift yours 'fore I go? That's your sort. Well, you two chaps have picked a lot."

I soon grew quite at home at Old Brownsmith's, and found him very kind. Ike, too, in his rough way, quite took to me—at least if anything had to be done he was offended if I asked another of the men. I worked hard at the fruit-picking, and kept account when Ike laid straw or fern over the tops of the bushel and half-bushel baskets, and placed sticks across, lattice fashion, to keep the apples and pears in. Then of a night I used to transfer the writing on the slate to a book, and tell Old Brownsmith what I had put down, reading the items over and summing up the quantities and the amounts they fetched when the salesmen's accounts came from Covent Garden.

The men and women about the place—all very quiet, thoughtful people—generally had a smile for me when I said good-morning, and I went on capitally, my old troubles being distant and the memories less painful day by day.

But somehow I never got on with Shock. I didn't want to make a companion of him, but I did not want him to be an enemy, and that he always seemed to be.

He never threw lumps of soil or apples or potatoes at me now; but he would often make-believe to be about to hurl something, and if he could not get away because of his work he always turned his back.

"He doesn't like me, Ike," I said to the big gardener one day.

"No, he don't, that's sartain," said Ike. "He's jealous of you, like, because the ganger makes so much of you."

"Mr Brownsmith would make as much of him if he would be smart and clean, and act like other boys," I said.

"Yes, but that's just what he won't do, won't Shock. You see, young 'un, he's a 'riginal—a reg'lar 'riginal, and you can't alter him. Ain't tried to lick you again, has he?"

"Oh, no!" I said; "and he does not throw at me."

"Don't shy at you now! Well, I wonder at that," said Ike. "He's a wunner at shying. He can hit anything with a stone. I've seen him knock over a bird afore now, and when he gets off in the fields of an evening I've often knowed him bring back a rabbit."

"What does he do with it?"

"Do with it! Come, there's a good 'un. Cook it down in the shed, and eat it. He'd eat a'most anything. But don't you mind him. It don't matter whether he's pleased or whether he ain't. If he's too hard on you, hit him again, and don't be afraid."

In fact the more I saw of Shock, the more distant he grew; and though I tried to make friends with him by putting slices of bread and butter and bits of cold pudding in the shed down the garden that he used to like to make his home at meal-time and of an evening, he used to eat them, and we were as bad friends as ever.

One morning, when there was rather a bigger fire than usual down in the old tool-shed, I walked to the door, and found Shock on his knees apparently making a pudding of soft clay, which he was kneading and beating about on the end of the hearthstone.

I looked round for the twig, for I felt sure that he was going to use the clay for pellets to sling at me, but there was no stick visible.

As I came to the doorway he just glanced over his shoulder; and then, seeing who it was, he shuffled round a little more and went on.

"What are you doing, Shock?" I asked.

He made no reply, but rapidly pinched off pieces of the clay and roughly formed them into the head, body, legs, and arms of a human being, which he set up against the wall, and then with a hoarse laugh knocked into a shapeless mass with one punch of his clay-coated fist.

"He meant that for me," I said to myself; and I was going to turn away when I caught sight of something lying in the shadow beneath the little old four-paned window.

It was something I had never seen before except in pictures; and I was so interested that I stepped in and was about to pick up the object, but Shock snatched it away.

"Where did you get it?" I said eagerly.

He did not answer for a few moments, and then said gruffly, "Fields."

"It's a hedgehog, isn't it?" I said. "Here, let me look." He slowly laid the little prickly animal down on the earthen floor and pushed it towards me—a concession of civility that was wonderful for Shock; and I eagerly examined the curious little creature, pricking my fingers a good deal in the efforts to get a good look at the little black-faced animal with its pointed snout.

"What are you going to do with it?" I said.

Shock looked up at me in a curious half-cunning way, as he beat out his clay into a broad sheet; and then, as if about to make a pudding, he made the hedgehog into a long ball, laid it on the clay, and covered it up, rolling it over and over till there was nothing visible but a clay ball.

"What a baby you are, Shock, playing at making mud puddings!" I said.

He did not reply, only smiled in a half-pitying way, took an old broomstick that he used for a poker, and scraping the ashes of the fire aside rolled the clay pig-pudding into the middle of the fire, and then covered it over with the burning ashes, and piled on some bits of wood and dry cabbage-stumps, making up a good fire, which he set himself to watch.

It was a wet day, and there was nothing particular to do in the garden; so I stood looking at Shock's cookery for a time, and then grew tired and was coming away when for a wonder he spoke.

"Be done soon," he said.

Just then I heard my name called, and running through the rain I found that Old Brownsmith wanted me for a while about some entries that he could not find in the book, and which he thought had not been made.

I was able, however, to show him that the entries had been made; and as soon as I was at liberty I ran down the garden again to see how the cookery was going on.

As I reached the door the little shed was all of a glow, for Shock was raking the fire aside, but, apparently not satisfied, he raked it all back again, and for the next half hour he amused himself piling up scraps of wood and refuse to make the fire burn, ending at last by raking all away, leaving the lump of clay baked hard and red.

I had been standing by the door watching him all the time; and now he just turned his head and looked at me over his shoulder as he rose and took a little old battered tin plate from where it stuck beneath the rough thatch, giving it a rub on the tail of his jacket.

"Like hedgehog?" he said grimly.

"No," I cried with a look of disgust.

"You ain't tasted it," he said, growing wonderfully conversational as he took a hand-bill from a nail where it hung.

Then, kneeling down before the fire, he gave the hard clay ball a sharp blow with the hand-bill, making it crack right across and fall open, showing the little animal steaming hot and evidently done, the bristly skin adhering to the clay shell that had just been broken, so that there was no difficulty in turning it out upon the tin plate, the shell in two halves being cast upon the fire, where the interior began to burn.

It seemed very horrible!

It seemed very nice!

I thought in opposite directions in the following moments, and all the time my nose was being assailed by a very savoury odour, for the cookery smelt very good.

"You won't have none—will you?" said Shock, without looking at me.

"No," I said shortly; "it isn't good to eat. You might as well eat rats."

"I like rats," he replied, coolly taking out his knife from one pocket, a piece of bread from the other; and to my horror he rapidly ate up the hedgehog, throwing the bones on the fire as he picked them, and ending by rubbing the tin plate over with a bit of old gardener's apron which he took from the wall.

"Well," I said sarcastically, "was it nice?"

"Bewfle!" he said, giving his lips a smack and then sighing.

"Did you say you eat rats?" I continued.

"Yes."

"And mice too?"

"No; there ain't nuffin' on 'em—they're all bones."

"Do you eat anything else?"

"Snails."

"Yes, I've seen you eat the nasty slimy things."

"They ain't nasty slimy things; they're good."

"Do you eat anything else?"

"Birds."

"What?" I said.

"Birds—blackbirds, and thrushes, and sparrers, and starlings. Ketches 'em in traps like I do the rats."

"But do you really eat rats?"

"Yes—them as comes after the apples in the loft and after the corn. They are good."

"But don't you get enough to eat at home?" I asked him.

"Home!—what, here?"

"No, I mean your home."

"What, where I sleeps? Sometimes."

"But you're not obliged to eat these things. Does Mr Brownsmith know?"

"Oh! yes, he knows. I like 'em. I eat frogs once. Ain't fish good? I ketch 'em in the medders."

"Where you saved me when I was drowning?" I said hastily.

Shock turned his face away from me and knelt there, throwing scraps of wood, cinder, and dirt into the fire, with his head bent down; and though I tried in all kinds of ways to get him to speak again, not a single word would he say.

I gave him up as a bad job at last and left him.

That night, just before going to bed, Old Brownsmith sent me out to one of the packing-sheds to fetch the slate, which had been forgotten. It was dark and starlight, for the wind had risen and the rain had been swept away.

I found the slate after fumbling a little about the bench, and was on my way back to the door of the long packing-shed when I heard a curious rustling in the loft overhead, followed by a thump on the board as if something had fallen, and then a heavy breathing could be heard—a regular heavy breathing that was almost a snore.

For a few moments I stood listening, and then, feeling very uncomfortable, I stole out, ran into the house, and stood before Old Brownsmith with the slate.

"Anything the matter?" he said.

"There's someone up in the loft over the packing-shed—asleep," I said hoarsely.

"In the loft!" he said quickly. "Oh! it is only Shock. He often sleeps there. You'll find his nest in amongst the Russia mats."

Surely enough, when I had the curiosity next morning to go up the ladder and look in the loft, there was Shock's nest deep down amongst the mats that were used to cover the frames in the frosty spring, and some of these were evidently used to cover him up.

I came down, thinking that if I were Old Brownsmith I should make Master Shock go to his lodging and sleep of a night, and try whether I could not make him live like a Christian, and not go about feeding on snails and hedgehogs and other odds and ends that he picked up in the fields.

Chapter Twelve
An Awkward Predicament

For the next fortnight we were all very busy picking and packing fruit, and Ike was off every night about eleven or twelve with his load, coming back after market in the morning, and only doing a little work in the garden of an afternoon, and seeing to the packing ready for a fresh start in the night.

The weather was glorious, and the pears came on so fast that Shock and I were always picking so that they might not be too ripe.

It was a delightful time, for the novelty having gone off I was able to do my work with ease. I did not try to move the ladder any more, so I had no accident of that kind; and though I slipped once or twice, I was able to save myself, and began to feel quite at home up in the trees.

Every now and then if Shock was anywhere near he played some monkey trick or another. His idea evidently was to frighten me by seeming to fall or by hanging by hand or leg. But he never succeeded now, for I knew him too well; and though I admired his daring at times, when he threw himself backwards on the ladder and slid down head foremost clinging with his legs, I did not run to his help.

In spite of the conversation I had had with him in the shed, we were no better friends next time we met, or rather when we nearly met, for whenever he saw me coming he turned his back and went off in another direction.

As I said, a fortnight had passed, and the fruit-picking was at its height as far as pears and apples went, when one night, after a very hot day, when the cart was waiting in the yard, loaded up high with bushel and half-bushel baskets, and the horse was enjoying his corn, and rattling his chain by the manger, I left Old Brownsmith smoking his pipe and reading a seed-list, and strolled out into the garden.

It was a starlight night, and very cool and pleasant, as I went down one of the paths and then back along another, trying to make out the blossoms of the nasturtiums that grew so thickly along the borders just where I was.

The air smelt so sweet and fresh that it seemed to do me good, but I was thinking that I must be getting back into the house and up to my bed, when the fancy took me that I should like to go down the path as far as Mrs

Beeton's house, and look at the window where I used to sit when Shock pelted me with clay.

The path was made with ashes, so that my footsteps were very quiet, and as I walked in the shadow of a large row of pear-trees I was almost invisible. In fact I could hardly see my own hand.

All at once I stopped short, for I heard a peculiar scratching noise and a whispering, and, though I could hardly distinguish anything, I was perfectly sure that somebody had climbed to the top of the wall, and was sitting there with a leg over our side, for I heard it rustling amongst the plum boughs.

"It's all right," was whispered; and then there was more scuffling, and it seemed to me that some one else had climbed up.

Then another and another, and then they seemed to pull up another one, so that I believed there were five people on the wall.

Then came some whispering, and I felt sure that they were boys, for one said:

"Now, then, all together!" in a boyish voice, when there was a lot of rustling and scratching, and I could hear the plum-tree branches trained to the wall torn down, one breaking right off, as the intruders dropped over into our garden.

For the moment I was puzzled. Then I knew what it meant, and a flush of angry indignation came into my cheeks.

"Boys after our pears!" I said to myself as my fists clenched. For I had become so thoroughly at home at Old Brownsmith's that everything seemed to belong to me, and I felt it was my duty to defend it.

I listened to make sure, and heard a lot of whispering going on as the marauders crossed the path I was on, rustled by amongst the gooseberry bushes, and went farther into the garden.

"They're after the *Marie Louise* pears," I thought; and I was about to run and shout at them, for I knew that would startle them away; but on second thoughts I felt as if I should like to catch some of them, and turning, I ran softly back up the path, meaning to tell Mr Brownsmith.

But before I had reached the end of the path another idea had occurred to me. Old Brownsmith would not be able to catch one of the boys, but Shock would if he was up in the loft, and in the hope that he was sleeping there I ran to the foot of the steps, scrambled up, and pushing back the door, which was only secured with a big wooden latch, I crept in as cautiously as I could.

"Shock!" I whispered. "Shock! Are you here?"

I listened, but there was not a sound.

"Shock!" I whispered again. "Shock!"

"If yer don't go I'll heave the hay-fork at yer," came in a low angry voice.

"No, no: don't," I said. "I want you. Come on, and bring a big stick: there's some boys stealing the pears."

There was a rustle and a scramble, and Shock was by my side, more full of life and excitement than I had ever noticed him before.

"Pears?" he whispered hoarsely; "arter the pears? Where? Where are they?"

He kept on the move, making for the door and coming back, and behaving altogether like a dog full of expectation of a rush after some wild creature in a hunt.

"Be quiet or we sha'n't catch them," I whispered. "Some boys have climbed over the wall, and are after the *Marie Louise* pears."

He stopped short suddenly.

"Yah!" he cried, "they ain't. It's your larks."

"You stupid fellow! I tell you they are."

"Mary Louisas ain't ripe," he cried.

"Don't care; they've gone after them. Come, and bring a stick."

"Fain larks," he said dubiously.

"Just as if I would play tricks with you!" I cried impatiently.

"No, you wouldn't, would yer?" he said hoarsely. "Wouldn't be hard on a chap. Stop a minute."

He rustled off amongst the straw, and I heard a rattling noise and then a chuckle, and Shock was back to hand me a stick as thick as my finger.

"Hezzles," he whispered—"nut hezzle. Come along. You go first."

Though I had roused Shock out of bed he had no dressing to do, and following me down the ladder he walked quickly after me down one of the paths, then to the right along another till we came to a corner, when we both stopped and listened.

Shock began to hiss very softly, as if he were a steam-engine with the vapour escaping from the safety-valve, as we heard, about fifty yards from us, the rustling of the pear-trees, the heavy shake of a bough, and then through the pitchy darkness *whop! whop! whop! whop!* as the pears fell on to the soft ground.

"You go this way," I whispered to Shock, "and I'll go that way, and then we'll rush in and catch them."

"Yes," he said back. "Hit hard, and mind and get hold o' the bag."

We were separating when he caught hold of my arm.

"'Old 'ard," he whispered. "Let's rush 'em together."

In the darkness perhaps his was the better plan. At all events we adopted it, and taking hold of hands we advanced on tiptoe trembling with expectation, our sticks grasped, and every now and then the pendent branches of some tree rustling in and sweeping our faces. And all the time, just in front, we could hear the hurried shaking of boughs, the fall of the pears, and tittering and whispering as the party seemed to be picking up the spoil.

"We shall have too many," whispered a voice just before us.

"Never mind; let's fill the bag. Go it, boys."

"Hush! Some one'll hear."

"Not they. Go on. Here's a bough loaded. Oh, I say!" Shock gave my hand a nip to which I responded, and then all at once from under the tree where we stood we made a rush at the indistinct figures we could sometimes make out a few yards away.

Whish, rush, whack!

"I say what are you doing of?"

"Oh!"

"Run! run!"

"Oh!"

These ejaculations were mingled with the blows dealt by our sticks, several of which fell upon heads, backs, legs, and arms, anywhere, though more struck the trees; and in the excitement one I delivered did no end of mischief to a young pear-tree, and brought down a shower of fruit upon my head.

It was all the work of a few moments. At the first the marauding party thought it was some trick of a companion; directly after they scattered and ran, under the impression that Old Brownsmith and all his men were in pursuit.

As for me, I felt red-hot with excitement, and found myself after a dash through some gooseberry bushes, whose pricking only seemed to give me fresh energy, running along a path after one boy at whom I kept cutting with my hazel stick.

At every stroke there was a howl from the boy, who kept on shouting as he ran:

"Oh! please, sir—oh! sir—don't, sir—oh! pray, sir!"

In my hard-heartedness and excitement I showed no mercy, but every time I got near enough as we panted on I gave him a sharp cut, and he would have been punished far worse if all at once I had not run right into a hanging bough of one of the pears, and gone down backwards, while when I scrambled up again my stick was gone.

I felt that if I waited to search for it I should lose the boy I meant to make a prisoner, and ran on in the direction where I could hear his steps.

Knowing the garden as I did I was able to make a cut so as to recover the lost ground, for I realised that he was making for the wall, and I was just in time to catch him as he scrambled up one of the trained trees, and had his chest on the top.

He would have been over in another second or two had I not made a jump at his legs, one of which I caught, and, twisting my arms round it, I held on with all my might.

"Oh! oh!" he yelled pitifully. "Pray let me go, sir. I'll never come no more, sir. Help! oh my! help!"

"Come down," I panted as well as I could for want of breath, "come down!" and I gave the leg I held a tremendous shake.

"Oh!—oh! Pray let me go this time, sir."

"Come down," I cried again fiercely, and I nearly dragged him from the wall, as I held on with all my might.

"No, sir! oh, sir! It wasn't me, sir. It was—oh, please let me go!"

The voice sounded as if it were on the outside of the wall, as my captive hung by his elbows and chest, while I could feel the leg I held quiver and tremble as I tugged hard to get its owner down into the garden; but distant and muffled as that voice was, it seemed familiar when it yelled again:

"Oh I pray let me go this time, sir."

"No," I shouted, as I gave the leg a snatch and hung on, "Come down, you thieving rascal, come down."

"Why, it's you, is it?" came from the top of the wall, a little plainer now.

"What! George Day!" I exclaimed, but without relaxing my hold.

"Oh, you sneak!" he cried. "Let go, will you."

"No," I cried stoutly. "Come down."

"Sha'n't. It ain't your place. Let go, you sneak."

"I sha'n't," I cried angrily. "Come down, you thief."

"If you call me a thief I'll come down and half smash you. Let go!"

His courage returned as he found out who was his captor, and he kicked out savagely, but I held on.

"Do you hear?" he cried. "Here, let go, and I'll give you a fourpenny piece out of my next pocket-money."

"You come down to Mr Brownsmith," I cried.

"Get out! You know who I am: George Day."

"I know you're a thief, and I shall take you up to Mr Brownsmith," I said, "and here he comes."

"If you don't let go," he cried with a sudden access of fury, "I'll just come down and I'll—"

He did not finish his threat. I daresay it would have been something very dreadful, but I was not in the least frightened as I held on; but as he clung to the big quaint coping of the wall he suddenly gave two or three such tremendous kicks that one of them, aided by his getting his free foot on my shoulder, was given with such force that I was driven backwards, and after staggering a few steps, caught my heel and came down in a sitting position upon the path.

I leaped to my feet again, but only just in time to hear a scuffling noise on the top of the wall, the sound of some one dropping on the other side, and then *pat, pat, pat*, steps fast repeated, as my prisoner ran away.

"Ah!" I exclaimed, with a stamp of the foot in my disappointment.

"Chiv-ee! Why, ho! Where are yer?"

"Here, Shock!" I cried in answer to the shout on my right, and the boy came running up.

"Got him?"

"No," I replied. "He climbed up the wall and kicked me backwards. Didn't you catch one?"

"No. They skiddled off like rabbuts, and the one I tried to run down dodged me in the dark, and when I heerd him he was close up to the fence t'other side, and got away. Didn't I give it some of 'em though!"

"Oh! I do wish we had caught one," I exclaimed; and then I felt as if I did not wish so, especially as the boy I had chased was George Day.

"They didn't get the pears," said Shock suddenly; and now it struck me that we had suddenly grown to be wonderfully talkative, and the best of friends.

"No," I replied, "I don't think they got the pears. Let's go and see."

We trudged off, I for my part feeling very stiff, and as if all the excitement had gone out of the adventure; and in a minute we were feeling about under the pear-trees, and kicking against fallen fruit.

"Here she is," said Shock suddenly. "Big bag. Stodge full."

I ran to him, and was in the act of passing my hands over the bulging bag when I uttered a faint cry of horror, for something soft seemed to have dropped upon my back, and a voice from out of the darkness exclaimed:

"What are you boys doing here?"

At the same moment I knew that it was one of the cats that had leaped upon my back, and Old Brownsmith who was speaking.

"We have been after some boys who were stealing the pears, sir," I said.

"Were they?" cried the old man sternly; "and I've come and caught them. You, Shock, bring that bag up to the door."

Shock seized and shouldered the bag, and we followed the old gentleman to the house; but though I spoke two or three times he made no reply, and I felt too much hurt by his suspicions to say more.

There was a large house lantern alight in the kitchen, as if the old gentleman had been about to bring it down the garden with him and had altered his mind, and the first thing he did was to open the lantern, take out the candle in his fingers, and hold it up so as to look at each of us in turn, frowning and suspicious, while we shrank and half-closed our eyes, dazzled by the light.

Then he turned his attention to the big bag which Shock had placed upon the table, the top of which opened out, and a pear or two rolled upon the floor as soon as it was released.

"Humph! Pillow-case, eh?" said the old man, and his face brightened as if the suspicion was being cleared away. "Who heard 'em?"

"I did, sir," I cried; and I told him how I had wakened up Shock, and of our fight; but I did not mention George Day's name, and I did not mean to do so unless I was asked, for it seemed to be so shocking for a boy like that to be charged with stealing fruit.

"Humph! Ought to have caught some of the dogs! but I say, did you hit 'em hard?"

"As hard as I could, sir," I replied innocently.

"Hah! aha! That's right. Young scoundrels. Spoilt a basket of pears that were not ripe. Young dogs! I'll put glass bottles all along the walls, and see how they like that. There, be off to bed."

I hesitated.

"Well," he said, "what is it?"

"You don't think it was I who went to steal the pears, sir?" I said uneasily.

"My good boy, no!" he said. "Pooh! nonsense! Looked like it at first. Caught you dirty-handed. Good night!"

He turned away, and I ran into the yard, where Shock was slowly going back to his hole in the straw.

"Good night, Shock!" I said.

He stopped without turning round, and did not reply. It was as if the sulky morose fit had come over him again, but it did not last, for he half turned his head and said:

"I hit one on 'em such a crack on the nut."

Then he went to the ladder and climbed up into the loft, and I stood listening to him as he nestled down in amongst the straw. Then Old Brownsmith came to the back-door with the lantern and called me in to go up to my room.

Chapter Thirteen
Learning my Lessons

Next morning the old gentleman talked at breakfast-time about the police, and having the young scoundrels sent to prison. Directly after, he went down the garden with me and nine cats, to inspect the damages, and when he saw the trampling and breaking of boughs he stroked a tom-cat and made it purr, while he declared fiercely that he would not let an hour pass without having the young dogs punished.

"They shall be caught and sent to prison," he cried.

"Poor old Sammy then.—I'll have 'em severely punished, the young depredators.—Grant, you'd better get a sharp knife and a light ladder, and cut off those broken boughs—the young villains—and tell Ike to bring a big rake and smooth out these footmarks. No; I'll tell him. You get the knife. I shall go to the police at once."

I cut out the broken boughs, and Ike brought down the ladder for me and smoothed over the footmarks, chatting about the events of the past night the while.

"He won't get no police to work, my lad, not he. Forget all about it directly. Makes him a bit raw, o' course," said Ike, smoothing away with the rake. "Haw! haw! haw! Think o' you two leathering of 'em. I wish I'd been here, 'stead of on the road to London. Did you hit 'em hard?"

"Hard as I could," I said. "I think Shock and I punished them enough."

"So do I. So do he. Rare and frightened they *was* too. Why, o' course boys will steal apples. I dunno how it is, but they always would, and will."

"But these were pears," I said.

"All the same, only one's longer than t'other. Apples and pears. He won't do nothing."

Ike was right, for the matter was soon forgotten, and Mrs Dodley his housekeeper used the pillow-case as a bag for clothes-pegs.

Those were bright and pleasant days, for though now and then some trouble came like a cloud over my life there was more often plenty of sunshine to clear that cloud away.

My uncles came to see me, first one and then the other, and they had very long talks with Mr Brownsmith.

One of them told me I was a very noble boy, and that he was proud of me. He said he was quite sure I should turn out a man.

"Talks to the boy as if he felt he might turn out a woman," Old Brownsmith grumbled after he was gone.

It was some time after before the other came, and he looked me all over as if he were trying to find a hump or a crooked rib. Then he said it was all right, and that I could not do better.

One of them said when he went away that he should not lose sight of me, but remember me now and then; and when he had gone Old Brownsmith said, half aloud:

"Thank goodness, I never had no uncles!" Then he gave me a comical look, but turned serious directly.

"Look here, Grant," he said. "Some folk start life with their gardens already dug up and planted, some begin with their bit of ground all rough, and some begin without any land at all. Which do you belong to?"

"The last, sir," I said.

"Right! Well, I suppose you are not going to wait for one uncle to take a garden for you and the other to dig it up?"

"No," I said sturdily; "I shall work for myself."

"Right! I don't like boys to be cocky and impudent but I like a little self-dependence."

As the time went on, Old Brownsmith taught me how to bud roses and prune, and, later on, to graft. He used to encourage me to ask questions, and I must have pestered him sometimes, but he never seemed weary.

"It's quite right," he used to say; "the boy who asks questions learns far more than the one who is simply taught."

"Why, sir?" I said.

"Well, I'll tell you. He has got his bit of ground ready, and is waiting for the seed or young plant to be popped in. Then it begins to grow at once. Don't you see this; he has half-learned what he wants to know in the desire he feels. That desire is satisfied when he is told, and the chances are that he never forgets. Now you say to me—What is the good of pruning or cutting this plum-tree? I'll tell you."

We were standing in front of the big red brick wall one bright winter's day, for the time had gone by very quickly. Old Brownsmith had a sharp knife in his hand, and I was holding the whetstone and a thin-bladed saw that he used to cut through the thicker branches.

"Now look here, Grant. Here's this plum-tree, and if you look at it you will see that there are two kinds of wood in it."

"Two kinds of wood, sir?"

"Yes. Can't you tell the difference?"

"No, sir; only that some of the shoots are big and strong, and some are little and twiggy."

"Exactly: that is the difference, my lad. Well, can you see any more difference in the shoots?"

I looked for some moments, and then replied:

"Yes; these big shoots are long and smooth and straight, and the little twiggy ones are all over sharp points."

"Then as there is too much wood there, which had we better cut out. What should you do?"

"Cut out the scrubby little twigs, and nail up these nice long shoots."

"That's the way, Grant! Now you'll know more about pruning after this than Shock has learned in two years. Look here, my lad; you've fallen into everybody's mistake, as a matter of course. Those fine long shoots will grow into big branches; those little twigs with the points, as you call them, are fruit spurs, covered with blossom buds. If I cut them out I should have no plums next year, but a bigger and a more barren tree. No, my boy, I don't want to grow wood, but fruit. Look here."

I looked, and he cut out with clean, sharp strokes all those long shoots but one, carefully leaving the wood and bark smooth, while to me it seemed as if he were cutting half the tree away.

"You've left one, sir," I said.

"Yes, Grant, I've left one; and I'll show you why. Do you see this old hard bough?"

I nodded.

"Well, this one has done its work, so I'm going to cut it out, and let this young shoot take its place."

"But it has no fruit buds on it," I said quickly.

"No, Grant; but it will have next year; and that's one thing we gardeners always have to do with stone-fruit trees—keep cutting out the old wood and letting the young shoots take the old branches' place."

"Why, sir?" I asked.

"Because old branches bear small fruit, young branches bear large, and large fruit is worth more than twice as much as small. Give me the saw."

I handed him the thin-bladed saw, and he rapidly cut out the old hard bough, close down to the place where it branched from the dumpy trunk, and then, handing me the tool, he knelt down on a pad of carpet he carried in his tremendous pocket.

"Now look here," he said; and taking his sharp pruning-knife he cut off every mark of the saw, and trimmed the bark.

I looked on attentively till he had ended.

"Well," he said, "ain't you going to ask why I did that?"

"I know, sir," I said. "To make it neat."

"Only partly right, Grant. I've cut that off smoothly so that no rain may lodge and rot the place before the wound has had time to heal."

"And will it heal, sir?"

"Yes, Grant. In time Nature will spread a ring of bark round that, which will thicken and close in till the place is healed completely over."

Then he busily showed me the use of the saw and knife among the big standard trees, using them liberally to get rid of all the scrubby, crowded, useless branches that lived upon the strength of the tree and did no work, only kept out the light, air, and sunshine from those that did work and bear fruit.

"Why it almost seems, sir," I said one day, "as if Nature had made the trees so badly that man was obliged to improve them."

"Ah, I'm glad to hear you say that, my lad," he said; "but you are not right. I'm only a gardener, but I've noticed these things a great deal. Nature is not a bungler. She gives us apple and plum trees, and they grow and bear fruit in a natural and sufficient way. It is because man wants them to bear more and bigger fruit, and for more to grow on a small piece of ground than Nature would plant, that man has to cut and prune."

"But suppose Nature planted a lot of trees on a small piece of ground," I said, "what then?"

"What then, Grant? Why, for a time they'd grow up thin and poor and spindly, till one of them made a start and overtopped the others. Then it would go on growing, and the others would dwindle and die away."

The time glided on, and I kept learning the many little things about the place pretty fast. As the months went on I became of some use to my employer over his accounts, and by degrees pretty well knew his position.

It seemed that he had been a widower for many years, and Mrs Dodley, the housekeeper and general servant all in one, confided to me one day that "Missus's" bonnets and shawls and gowns were all hanging up in their places just as they had been left by Mrs Brownsmith.

"Which it's a dead waste, Master Grant," she used to finish by saying, "as there's several as I know would be glad to have 'em; but as to that—Lor' bless yer!"

It was not often that Mrs Dodley spoke, but when she did it was to inveigh against some oppression or trouble.

Candles were a great burden to the scrupulously clean woman.

"Tens I says," she confided to me one day, "but he will have eights, and what's the consequence? If I want to do a bit of extry needle-work I might light up two tens, but I should never have the heart to burn two eights at once, for extravagance I can't abear. Ah! he's a hard master, and I'm sorry for you, my dear."

"Why?" I said.

"Ah! you'll find out some day," she said, shaking her head and then bustling off to her work.

I had not much companionship, for Ike was generally too busy to say a word, and though after the pear adventure Shock did nothing more annoying to me than to stand now and then upon his head, look at me upside down, and point and spar at me with his toes, we seemed to get to be no better friends.

He took to that trick all at once one day in a soft bit of newly dug earth. He was picking up stones, and I was sticking fresh labels at the ends of some rows of plants, when all at once he uttered a peculiar monkey-like noise, down went his head, up went his heels, and I stared in astonishment at first and then turned my back.

This always annoyed Shock; but one day when he stood up after his quaint fashion I was out of temper and had a bad headache, so I ran to him, and he struck at me with his feet, just as if they had been hands, only he could not have doubled them up. I was too quick for him though, and with a push drove him down.

He jumped up again directly and repeated the performance.

I knocked him down angrily.

He stood up again.

I knocked him down again.

And so on, again and again, when he turned and ran off laughing, and I went on with my work, vexed with myself for having shown temper.

Every now and then a fit of low spirits used to attack me. It was generally on washing-days, when Mrs Dodley filled the place with steam early in the morning by lighting the copper fire, and then seeming to be making calico puddings to boil and send an unpleasant soapy odour through the house.

Doors and chair backs were so damp and steamy then that I used to be glad to go out and see Shock, whom I often used to find right away in the little shed indulging in a bit of cookery of his own.

If Shock's hands had been clean I could often have joined him in his feasts, but I never could fancy turnips boiled in a dirty old sauce-pan, nor tender bits of cabbage stump. I made up my mind that I would some day try snails, but when I did join Shock on a soaking wet morning when there was no gardening, and he invited me in his sulky way to dinner, the only times I partook of his fare were on chat days.

What are chat days? Why, the days when he used to have a good fire of wood and stumps, and roast the chats, as they called the little refuse potatoes too small for seed, in the ashes.

They were very nice, though there was not much in one. Still they were hot and floury, and not bad with a bit of salt.

Wet days, though, were always a trouble to me, and I used to feel a kind of natural sympathy with Mr Brownsmith as he set his men jobs in the sheds, and kept walking to the doors to see if the rain had ceased.

"That's one thing I should like to have altered in nature," he said to me with one of his dry comical looks. "I should like the rain to come down in the night, my boy, so as to leave the day free for work. Always work."

"I like it, sir," I said.

"No, you don't, you young impostor!" he cried. "You want to be playing with tops or marbles, or at football or something."

I shook my head.

"You do, you dog!" he cried.

I shook my head again.

"No, sir," I said; "I like learning all about the plants and the pruning. Ike showed me on some dead wood the other day how to graft."

"Ah, I'll show you how to do it on live wood some day. There's a lot more things I should like to show you, but I've no glass."

"No," I said; "I've often wished we had a microscope."

"A what, Grant?"

"Microscope, sir, to look at the blight and the veins in the plants' leaves."

"No, no; I mean greenhouses and forcing-houses, where fruit and vegetables and flowers are brought on early: but wait a bit."

I did wait a bit, and went on learning, getting imperceptibly to know a good deal about gardening, and so a couple of years slipped away, when one day I was superintending the loading of the cart after seeing that it was properly supported with trestles. Ike was seated astride one of the large baskets as if it were a saddle, and taking off his old hat he began to indulge in a good scratch at his head.

"Lookye here," he exclaimed suddenly, "why don't you go to market?"

"Too young," I said, with a feeling of eagerness flashing through me.

"Not you," he said slowly, as he looked down at me and seemed to measure me with his eye as one of my uncles did. "There's a much littler boy than you goes with one of the carts, and I see him cutting about the market with a book under his arm, looking as chuff as a pea on a shovel. He ain't nothing to you. Come along o' me. I'll take an old coat for wrapper, and you'll be as right as the mail. You ask him. He'll let you come."

Ike was wrong, for when I asked Old Brownsmith's leave he shook his head.

"No, no, boy. You're too young yet. Best in bed."

"Too partickler by half," Ike growled when I let him know the result of my asking. "He's jealous, that's what he is. Wants to keep you all to hisself. Not as I wants you. 'Tain't to please me. You're young and wants eddicating; well, you wants night eddication as well as day eddication. What do you know about the road to London of a night?"

"Nothing at all, Ike?" I said with a sigh.

"Scholard as you are too," growled Ike. "Why, my figgering and writing ain't even worth talking about with a pen, though I am good with chalk, but even I know the road to London."

"He'll let me go some day," I said.

"Some day!" cried Ike in a tone of disgust. "Any one could go by day. It's some night's the time. Ah! it is a pity, much as you've got to learn too. There's the riding up with the stars over your heads, and the bumping of the cart, and the bumping and rattle of other carts, as you can hear a mile away on a still night before and behind you, and then the getting on to the stones."

"On to the stones, Ike?" I said.

"Yes, of course, on to the paving-stones, and the getting into the market and finding a good pitch, and the selling off in the morning. Ah! it would be a treat for you, my lad. I'm sorry for yer."

Ike's sorrow lasted, and I grew quite uneasy at last through being looked down upon with so much contempt; but, as is often the case, I had leave when I least expected it.

We had been very busy cutting, bunching, and packing flowers one day, when all at once Old Brownsmith came and looked at my slate with the total of the flower baskets set down side by side with the tale of the strawberry baskets, for it was in the height of the season.

"Big load to-night, Grant," the old gentleman said.

"Yes, sir; largest load you've sent up this year," I replied, in all my newly-fledged importance as a young clerk.

"You had better go up with Ike to-night, Grant," said the old man suddenly. "You are big enough now, and a night out won't hurt you. Here, Ike!"

"Yes, master."

"You'll want a little help to-morrow morning to stand by you in the market. Will you have Shock?"

"Yes, master, he's the very thing, if you'll send some one to hold him, or lend me a dog-collar and chain."

"Don't be an idiot, Ike," said Old Brownsmith sharply.

"No, master."

"Would you rather have this boy?"

"Would I rather? Just hark at him!"

Ike looked round at me as if this was an excellent joke, but Old Brownsmith took it as being perfectly serious, and gave Ike a series of instructions about taking care of me.

"Of course you will not go to a public-house on the road."

"'Tain't likely," growled Ike, "'less he gets leading me astray and takes me there."

"There's a coffee-shop in Great Russell Street where you can get your breakfasts."

"Lookye here, master," growled Ike in an ill-humoured voice, "ain't I been to market afore?"

"I shall leave him in your charge, Ike, and expect you to take care of him."

"Oh, all right, master!" said Ike, and then the old gentleman gave me a nod and walked away.

"At last, Ike!" I cried. "Hurrah! Why, what's the matter?"

"What's the matter?" said Ike in tones of disgust; "why, everything's the matter. Here, let's have a look at you, boy. Yes," he continued, turning me round, and as if talking to himself, "it is a boy. Any one to hear him would have thought it was a sugar-stick."

Chapter Fourteen
A Night Journey

It seemed to me as if starting-time would never come, and I fidgeted in and out from the kitchen to the stable to see if Ike had come back, while Mrs Dodley kept on shaking her at me in a pitying way.

"Hadn't you better give it, up, my dear?" she said dolefully. "Out all night! It'll be a trying time."

"What nonsense!" I said. "Why, sailors have to keep watch of a night regularly."

"When the stormy wynds do blow," said Mrs Dodley with something between a sniff and a sob. "Does Mrs Beeton know you are going?"

"No," I said stoutly.

"My poor orphan bye," she said with a real sob. "Don't—don't go."

"Why, Mrs Dodley," I cried, "any one would think I was a baby."

"Here, Grant," cried Mr Brownsmith, "hadn't you better lie down for an hour or two. You've plenty of time."

"No, sir," I said stoutly; "I couldn't sleep if I did."

"Well, then, come and have some supper."

That I was quite willing to have, and I sat there, with the old gentleman looking at me every now and then with a smile.

"You will not feel so eager as this next time, Master Grant."

At last I heard the big latch rattle on the gate, and started up in the greatest excitement. Old Brownsmith gave me a nod, and as I passed through the kitchen Mrs Dodley looked at me with such piteous eyes and so wrinkled a forehead that I stopped.

"Why, what's the matter?" I asked.

"Oh, don't ask me, my dear, don't ask me. What could master be a-thinking!"

Her words filled me with so much dread that I hurried out into the yard, hardly knowing which I feared most—to go, or to be forced to stay at home, for the adventure through the dark hours of the night began to seem to be something far more full of peril than I had thought a ride up to market on the cart would prove.

The sight of Ike, however, made me forget the looks of Mrs Dodley, and I was soon busy with him in the stable—that is to say, I held the lantern while he harnessed "Basket," the great gaunt old horse whom I had so nicknamed on account of the way in which his ribs stuck out through his skin.

"You don't give him enough to eat, Ike," I said.

"Not give him enough to eat!" he replied. "Wo ho, Bonyparty, shove yer head through. That's the way. Not give him enough to eat, my lad! Lor' bless you, the more he eats the thinner he gets. He finds the work too hard for him grinding his oats, for he's got hardly any teeth worth anything."

"Is he so old, then?" I asked, as I saw collar and hames and the rest of the heavy harness adjusted.

"Old! I should just think he is, my lad. Close upon two hunderd I should say's his age."

"Nonsense!" I said; "horses are very old indeed at twenty!"

"Some horses; but he was only a baby then. He's the oldest horse as ever was, and about the best; ain't you, Basket? Come along, old chap."

The horse gave a bit of a snort and followed the man in a slow deliberate way, born of custom, right out into the yard to where the trestle-supported cart stood. Then as I held the lantern the great bony creature turned and backed itself clumsily in between the shafts, and under the great framework ladder piled up with baskets till its tail touched the front of the cart, when it heaved a long sigh as if of satisfaction.

"Look at that!" said Ike; "no young horse couldn't have done that, my lad;" and as if to deny the assertion, Basket gave himself a shake which made the chains of his harness rattle. "Steady, old man," cried Ike as he hooked on the chains to the shaft, and then going to the other side he started. "Hullo! what are you doing here?" he cried, and the light fell upon Shock, who had busily fastened the chains on the other side.

He did not speak, but backed off into the darkness.

"Got your coat, squire?" cried Ike. "That's well. Open the gates, Shock. That's your sort. Now, then, 'Basket,' steady."

The horse made the chains rattle as he stuck the edges of his hoofs into the gravel, the wheels turned, the great axle-tree rattled; there was a swing of the load to left and another to right, a bump or two, and we were out in the lane, going steadily along upon a lovely starlight night.

As soon as we were clear of the yard, and Shock could be heard closing the gates and rattling up the bar, Ike gave his long cart-whip three tremendous cracks, and I expected to see "Basket" start off in a lumbering trot; but he paid not the slightest heed to the sharp reports, and it was evidently only a matter of habit, for Ike stuck the whip directly after in an iron loop close by where the horse's great well-filled nose-bag was strapped to the front-ladder, beneath which there was a sack fairly filled with good old hay.

"Yes," said Ike, seeing the direction of my eyes, "we don't starve the old hoss; do we, Bonyparty?"

He slapped the horse's haunch affectionately, and Basket wagged his tail, while the cart jolted on.

The clock was striking eleven, and sounded mellow and sweet on the night air as we made for the main road, having just ten miles to go to reach the market, only a short journey in these railway times, but one which it took the bony old horse exactly five hours to compass.

"It seems a deal," I said. "I could walk it in much less time."

"Well, yes, Master Grant," said Ike, rubbing his nose; "it do seem a deal, five hours—two mile an hour; but a horse is a boss, and you can't make nothing else out of him till he's dead. I've been to market with him hunderds upon hunderds of times, and he says it's five hours' work, and he takes five hours to do it in; no more, and no less. P'r'a'ps I might get him up sooner if I used the whip; but how would you like any one to use a whip on you when you was picking apples or counting baskets of strawbys into a wan?"

"Not at all," I said, laughing.

"Well, then, what call is there to use it on a boss? He knows what he can do, and he doos it."

"Has Mr Brownsmith had him long?"

"Has *Old* Brownsmith had him long?" he said correctively. "Oh, yes! ages. I don't know how long. He had him and he was a old boss when I come, and that's years ago. He's done nothing but go uppards and down'ards all his life, and he must know how long it takes by now, mustn't he?"

"Yes, I suppose so," I said.

"Of course he do, my lad. He knows just where his orf forefoot ought to be at one o'clock, and his near hind-foot at two. Why, he goes like clockwork.

I just winds him up once with a bit o' corn and a drink o' water, starts him, and there's his old legs go tick-tack, tick-tack, and his head swinging like a pendulow. Use 'is secon' natur', and all I've got to do is to tie up the reins to the fore ladder and go to sleep if I like, for he knows his way as well as a Christian. 'Leven o'clock I starts; four o'clock he gets to the market; and if it wasn't for thieves, and some one to look after the baskets, that old hoss could go and do the marketing all hisself."

It was all wonderfully fresh and enjoyable to me, that ride along the quiet country road, with another market cart jolting on about a hundred yards ahead, and another one as far behind, while no doubt there were plenty more, but they did not get any closer together, and no one seemed to hurry or trouble in the least.

We trudged on together for some distance, and then Ike made a couple of seats for us under the ladder by folding up sacks, on one of which I sat, on the other he. Very uncomfortable seats I should call them now; most enjoyable I thought them then, and with no other drawback than a switch now and then from the horse's long tail, an attention perfectly unnecessary, for at that time of night there were no flies.

There was not much to see but hedgerows and houses and fields as we jolted slowly on. Once we met what Ike called the "padrole," and the mounted policeman, in his long cloak and with the scabbard of his sabre peeping from beneath, looked to me a very formidable personage; but he was not too important to wish Ike a friendly good-night.

We had passed the horse-patrol about a quarter of a mile, when all at once we heard some one singing, or rather howling:

"I've been to Paris and I've been to Dover."

This was repeated over and over again, and seemed as we sat there under our basket canopy to come from some one driving behind us; but the jolting of the cart and the grinding of wheels and the horse's trampling drowned the sound of the following vehicle, and there it went on:

"I've been to Paris and I've been to Dover."

But the singer pronounced it *Do-ho-ver*; and then it went on over and over again.

"Yes," said Ike, as if he had been talking about something; "them padroles put a stop to that game."

"What game?" I said.

"Highwaymen's. This used to be one of their fav'rite spots, from here away to Hounslow Heath. There was plenty of 'em in the old days, with their spanking horses and their pistols, and their 'stand and deliver' to the coach passengers. Now you couldn't find a highwayman for love or money, even if you wanted him to stuff and putt in a glass case."

"I've been to Paris and I've been to Dover."

"I wish you'd stopped there," said Ike, in a grumbling voice. "Ah, those used to be days. That's where Dick Turpin used to go, you know— Hounslow Heath."

"But there are none now?" I said, with some little feeling of trepidation.

"Didn't I tell you, no," said Ike, "unless that there's one coming on behind. How much money have you got, lad?"

"Two shillings and sixpence and some halfpence."

"And I've got five and two, lad. Wouldn't pay to keep a blood-horse to rob us, would it?"

"No," I said. "Didn't they hang the highwaymen in chains, Ike?"

"To be sure they did. I see one myself swinging about on Hounslow Heath."

"Wasn't it very horrible?"

"I dunno. Dessay it was. Just look how reg'lar old Bonyparty goes along, don't he—just in the same part of the road? I dessay he's a-counting all the steps he takes, and checking of 'em off to see how many more he's got to go through."

"I've been to Paris and I've been to Dover."

"I say, I wish that chap would pass us—it worries me," cried Ike pettishly. Then he went on: "Roads warn't at all safe in those days, my lad. There was footpads too—chaps as couldn't afford to have horses, and they used to hang under the hedges, just like that there dark one yonder, and run out and lay holt of the reins, and hold a pistol to a man's head."

"I've been to Paris and I've been to Dover."

"Go agen then, and stop," growled Ike irritably. "Swep' all away, my lad, by the road-police, and now—"

"There's a man standing in the dark here under this hedge, Ike," I whispered. "Is—is he likely to be a foot-pad?"

"Either a footpad or a policeman. Which does he look like?" said Ike.

"Policeman," I whispered. "I think I saw the top of his hat shine."

"Right, lad. You needn't be scared about them sort o' gentlemen now. As Old Brownsmith says, gas and steam-engines and police have done away with them, and the road's safe enough, night or day."

We jolted on past the policeman, who turned his bull's-eye lantern upon us for a moment, so that I could see Basket's ribs and the profile of Ike's great nose as he bent forward with his arms resting on his legs. There was a friendly "good-night," and we had left him about a couple of hundred yards behind, when, amidst the jolting of the cart and the creaking of the baskets overhead, ike said suddenly:

"Seem to have left that chap behind, or else he's gone to—"

"I've been to Paris and I've been to Dover."

"Why, if he ar'n't there agen!" cried Ike savagely. "Look here, it worries me. I'd rayther have a dog behind barking than a chap singing like that. I hates singing."

"I've been to Paris and I've been to Dover."

"Look here," said Ike; "I shall just draw to one side and wait till he've gone by. Steady, Bony; woa, lad! Now he may go on, and sing all the way to Dover if he likes."

Suiting the action to the word Ike pulled one rein; but Basket kept steadily on, and Ike pulled harder. But though Ike pulled till he drew the horse's head round so that he could look at us, the legs went on in the same track, and we did not even get near the side of the road.

"He knows it ain't right to stop here," growled Ike. "Woa, will yer! What a obstin't hammer-headed old buffler it is! Woa!"

Basket paid not the slightest heed for a few minutes. Then, as if he suddenly comprehended, he stopped short.

"Thankye," said Ike drily; "much obliged. It's my belief, though, that the wicked old walking scaffold was fast asleep, and has on'y just woke up."

"Why, he couldn't go on walking in his sleep, Ike," I exclaimed.

"Not go on walking in his sleep, mate! That there hoss couldn't! Bless your 'art, he'd do a deal more wonderful things than that. Well, that there chap's a long time going by. I can't wait."

Ike looked back, holding on by the iron support of the ladder.

"I carnt see nothing. Just you look, mate, your side." I looked back too, but could see nothing, and said so. "It's strange," growled Ike. "Go on,

Bony." The horse started again, the baskets creaked, the wheels ground the gravel, and the cart jolted and jerked in its own particular springless way, and then all of a sudden:

"I've been to Paris and I've been to Dover."

Ike looked sharply round at me, as if he half suspected me of ventriloquism, and it seemed so comical that I began to laugh.

"Look here," he said in a hoarse whisper, "don't you laugh. There's something wrong about this here."

He turned the other way, and holding tightly by the ladder looked out behind, leaning a good way from the side of the cart.

"I can't see nothinct," he grumbled, as he drew back and bent forward to pat the horse. "Seems rum."

"I've been to Paris and I've been to Dover." There was the song or rather howl again, sounding curiously distant, and yet, odd as it may seem, curiously near, and Ike leant towards me.

"I say," he whispered, "did you ever hear of anything being harnted?"

"Yes," I said, "I've heard of haunted houses."

"But you never heerd of a harnted market cart, did yer?"

"No," I said laughing; "never."

"That's right," he whispered.

"I've been to Paris and I've been to Dover."

I burst out laughing, though the next moment I felt a little queer, for Ike laid his hand on my shoulder.

"Don't laugh, my lad," he whispered; "there's some'at queer 'bout this here."

"Why, nonsense, Ike!" I said.

"Ah! you may say it's nonsense; but I don't like it."

"I've been to Paris and I've been to Dover."

This came very softly now, and it had such an effect on Ike that he jumped down from the shaft into the road, and taking his whip from the staple in which it was stuck, he let the cart pass him, and came round the back to my side.

"Well?" I said; "is there a cart behind?"

"I can't hear one, and I can't see one," he whispered; "and I says it's very queer. I don't like it, my lad, so there."

He let the cart pass him, went back behind it again, reached his own seat, and climbed in under the ladder.

Bump, jolt, creak, on we went, and all at once Basket kicked a flint stone, and there was a tiny flash of fire.

"I've been to Paris and I've been to Dover."

There it was again, so loud that Ike seized the reins, and by main force tried to stop the horse, which resisted with all its might, and then stopped short with the baskets giving a jerk that threatened to send them over the front ladder, on to the horse's back.

Ike jumped down on one side and I jumped down on the other. I was not afraid, but the big fellow's uneasiness had its effect upon me, and I certainly felt uncomfortable. There was something strange about riding along that dark road in the middle of the night, and this being my first experience of sitting up till morning the slightest thing was enough to put me off my balance.

The horse went on, and Ike and I met at the back, looked about us, and then silently returned to our seats, climbing up without stopping the horse; but we had not been there a minute before Ike bounded off again, for there once more, buzzing curiously in the air, came that curious howling song:

"I've been to Paris and I've been to Dover."

I slipped off too, and Ike ran round, whip in hand, and gripped my arm.

"It was your larks," he growled savagely, as I burst into a fit of laughing.

"It wasn't," I cried, as soon as I could speak. "Give me the whip," I whispered.

"What for?" he growled.

"You give me the whip," I whispered; and I took it from his hand, trotted on to the side of the cart, and then reaching up, gave a cut over the top of the load.

"Stash that!" shouted a voice; and then, as I lashed again, "You leave off, will yer? You'll get something you don't like."

"Woa, Bony!" roared Ike with such vehemence that the horse stopped short, and there, kneeling on the top of the high load of baskets, we could dimly see a well-known figure, straw-hat and all.

"You want me to come down, an' 'it you?" he cried, writhing.

"Here, give me that whip," cried Ike fiercely. "How did you come there?"

"Got up," said Shock sulkily.

"Who told you to come?"

"No one. He's come, ain't he?"

"That's no reason why you should come. Get down, you young dog!"

"Sha'n't!"

"You give's holt o' that whip, and I'll flick him down like I would a fly."

"No, no; don't hurt him, Ike," I said, laughing. "What were you making that noise for, Shock?"

"He calls that singing," cried Ike, spitting on the ground in his disgust. "He calls that singing. He's been lying on his back, howling up at the sky like a sick dog, and he calls that singing. Here, give us that whip."

"No, no, Ike; let him be."

"Yes; he'd better," cried Shock defiantly.

"Yes; I had better," cried Ike, snatching the whip from me, and giving it a crack like the report of a gun, with the result that Basket started off, and would not stop any more.

"Come down," roared Ike.

"Sha'n't!" cried Shock. "You 'it me, and I'll cut the rope and let the baskets down."

"Come down then."

"Sha'n't! I ain't doing nothing to you."

Crack! went the whip again, and I saw Shock bend down.

"I'm a-cutting the cart rope," he shouted.

"Come down." *Crack*! went the whip.

Shock did not speak.

"Will he cut the rope?" I whispered.

"If he do we shall be two hours loading up again, and a lot o' things smashed," growled Ike. Then aloud:

"Are you a coming down? Get down and go home."

"Sha'n't!" came from above us; and, like a good general, Ike accepted his defeat, and climbed back to his place on the left shaft, while I took mine on the right.

"It's no good," he said in a low grumbling tone. "When he says he won't, he won't, and them ropes is the noo 'uns. He'll have to go on with us now; and I'm blest if I don't think we've lost a good ten minutes over him and his noise."

"I've been to Paris and I've been to Dover," came from over our heads.

"Think o' me letting that scare me!" said Ike, giving his whip a vicious *whisk* through the air.

"But it seemed so strange," I said.

"Ay, it did. Look yonder," he said. "That's the norrard. It looks light, don't it?"

"Yes," I said.

"Ah! it never gets no darker than that all night. You'll see that get more round to the nor-east as we gets nigher to London."

So it proved, for by degrees I saw the stars in the north-east pale; and by the time we reached Hyde Park Corner a man was busy with a light ladder putting out the lamps, and it seemed all so strange that it should be broad daylight, while, as we jolted over the paving-stones as we went farther, the light had got well round now to the east, and the daylight affected Ike, for as, after a long silence, we suddenly heard once more from the top of the baskets:

"I've been to Paris and I've been to Dover!"

Ike took up the old song, and in a rough, but not unmusical voice roared out the second line:

"I've been a-travelling all the world over."

Or, as he gave it to match Do-ho-ver—"O-ho-ver." And it seemed to me that I had become a great traveller, for that was London all before me, with a long golden line above it in the sky.

Chapter Fifteen
In the Market

I could almost have fancied that there was some truth in Ike's declaration about old Basket or Bonyparty, as he called him, for certainly he seemed to quicken his pace as we drew nearer; and so it was that, as we turned into the busy market, and the horse made its way to one particular spot at the south-east corner, Ike triumphantly pointed to the church clock we had just passed.

"What did I tell yer?" he exclaimed with a grim smile of satisfaction on his countenance; "he picked up them lost ten minutes, and here we are— just four."

What a scene it seemed to me. The whole place packed with laden cart, wagon, and light van. Noise, confusion, and shouting, pleasant smells and evil smells—flowers and crushed cabbage; here it was peas and mint, there it was strawberries; then a whole wagon announced through the sides of its piled-up baskets that the load was cauliflowers.

For a time I could do nothing but gape and stare around at the bustling crowd and the number of men busily carrying great baskets on the top of porters' knots. Women, too, in caps, ready to put the same great pad round forehead and make it rest upon their shoulders, and bear off great boxes of fruit or baskets of vegetable.

Here I saw a complete stack of bushel baskets being regularly built up from the unloading of a wagon, to know by the scent they were early peas; a little farther on, some men seemed to be making a bastion for the defence of the market by means of gabions, which, to add to the fancy, were not filled with sand, but with large round gravel of a pale whitish-yellow, only a closer inspection showed that the contents were new potatoes.

The strawberries took my attention, though, most, for I felt quite a feeling of sorrow for Old Brownsmith as I saw what seemed to me to be such a glut of the rich red fruit that I was sure those which we had brought up would not sell.

How delicious they smelt in the old-fashioned pottles which we never see now—long narrow cones, with a cross-handle, over which, when filled, or supposed to be filled, for a big strawberry would block up the narrow part of the cone at times, a few leaves were placed, and then a piece of white paper was tied over with a bit of bast. Nowadays deep and shallow punnets are the order of the day, and a good thing too.

Flowers! There seemed to me enough to last London for a month; and I was going, after a look round, to tell Ike that I was afraid we should have to take our load back, when I felt a heavy thump on the back of my head, which knocked off my cap.

Nothing annoyed me more as a boy than for my cap to be knocked off. Shock knew that, and it had been one of his favourite tricks, so that I knew, as I thought, whence this piece of annoyance had come, and, picking up the small hard cabbage that had been thrown, I determined to avenge myself by sending it back with a good aim.

True enough there was Master Shock, lying flat on his chest with his chin resting in his hands, and his feet kicking up behind, now going up and down, now patting together, for he had taken off his boots.

Shock was having a good stare over the market from his elevated position on the top of the baskets; and, taking a good aim as I thought, I threw the little hard stale cabbage, and then dodged round the side of the cart. I stood aghast directly after, beside a pile of baskets, and watch a quarrel that had just begun a dozen yards away, where a big red-faced man was holding a very fluffy white hat in his hand and brushing it with his arm, and bandying angry words with a rough-looking young market porter, who, with a great flat basket under one arm and his other through a knot, was speaking menacingly—

"Don't you hit me again."

"Yes, I will, and knock your ugly head off if you do that again," said the man with the white hat.

"Do what again?"

"Do what again!—why, throw rotten cabbages at my hat."

"I didn't."

"Yes, you did."

"No, I didn't."

"Why, half-a-dozen here saw you do it. You've got hold of the wrong man, my lad, for larks; so now, then!"

I saw him stick on his white hat all on one side, and he looked very fierce and severe; while I felt covered with shame and confusion, for I knew that it was my cabbage that had done the mischief.

Whop!

That was another right in my ear, and I turned angrily upon Shock, forgetting all about the man with the white hat and the half-conceived idea of going up to him and telling the truth. But there was Shock staring about him from a dozen feet above my head, and singing softly, "I've been to Paris and I've been to Dover;" and the cabbage had struck me on the other side, so that unless Shock had learned how to project decayed cabbage after the fashion of boomerangs it could not have been he.

There was a group of bare-legged boys, though, away to my left—a set of ragged objects who might have passed for Shock's brothers and cousins, only that they were thin and unwholesomely pale, and extremely dirty, while although Shock was often quite as dirty, his seemed to be the wholesome dirt of country earth, and he looked brown, and healthy, and strong.

Then I became aware of the presence of Ike, who said with a grim smile:

"Don't you heed them, my lad. I see one of 'em chuck it and then turn round. Wait a bit and I shall get a charnce, and I'll drar my whip round one of 'em in a way as'll be a startler."

A quick busy-looking man came bustling up just then, had a chat with Ike, and hurried off, carrying away my companion; and as soon as he had gone a bruised potato struck the side of the cart, and as I changed my position a damaged stump of a cauliflower struck Basket on the flank, making him start and give himself a shake that rattled all the chains of the harness before resetting down to the task of picking the corn out of the chaff in his well-filled nose-bag.

My first idea was to call Shock down from where he was see-sawing his legs to and fro till his feet looked like two tilt-hammers beating a piece of iron, and then with his help attack the young vagabonds who were amusing themselves by making me a target for all the market refuse they could find.

Second thoughts are said to be best, and I had sense enough to know that nothing would be gained by a struggle with the young roughs. So, gaining knowledge from my previous experience, I changed my position so as to get in the front of some sturdy-looking men who were all standing with their hands in their pockets chinking their money. I had yet to learn that they were costermongers waiting for prices to come down.

Directly after *whiz*! came something close by my head and struck one of the men in the face, with the result that he made a dash at the boys, who darted away in and out among the baskets, whooping and yelling defiance; but one ran right into the arms of a man in uniform, who gave him three or four sharp cuts with a cane and sent him howling away.

This episode was hardly over before Ike was back, and he nodded as he said:

"He's coming direckly to sell us off."

"Shall you be able to sell the things, then, this morning?"

"Sell 'em! I should just think we shall; well too. There's precious little in the market to-day."

"Little!" I exclaimed. "Why, I thought there would be too much for ours to be wanted."

"Bless your young innocence! this is nothing. Bad times for the costers, my boy; they'll get nothing cheap. Here you, Shock, as you are come, help with these here ropes; and mind, you two, you look after these new ropes and the sacks."

"Look after them!" I said innocently.

"Yes," said Ike with a queer look; "they gets wild and into bad habits in London—walks away, they does—and when you go and look for 'em, there you finds 'em in marine store-shops in the dirty alleys."

Shock and I set to work helping to unfasten the ropes, which were laced in and out of the basket-handles, and through the iron stays, and beneath the hooks placed on purpose about the cart, after which the ropes were made into neat bunches by Ike, who passed them from hand to elbow over and over and tied them in the middle, and then in a row to the ladder of the cart.

The baskets were just set free when the busy-looking man came back along with a tall red-nosed fellow. I noticed his red nose because it was the same colour as a book he held, whose leather cover was like a bad strawberry. He had a little ink-bottle hanging at his buttonhole and a pen in his mouth, and was followed by quite a crowd of keen-looking men.

"Now, Jacob," said the little man, and clapping his hand upon the thin man's shoulder he stepped up on to the top of a pile of barge-baskets, whose lids were tied down with tarred string over the cauliflowers with which they were gorged.

Then, as I stared at him, he put his hands on either side of his mouth and seemed to go mad with satisfaction, dancing his body up and down and slowly turning round as he yelled out:

"Strawby's! strawby's! strawby's!" over and over again.

I looked up at Ike, whose face was as if cut out of mahogany, it was so solid; then I looked round at the people, but there wasn't a smile. Nobody laughed but Shock, who grinned silently till he saw me watching him, and then he looked sulky and turned his back.

Just then Ike, who seemed as solemn as a judge, climbed up the wheel and on to the cart with another man following him; and as the crowd increased about our cart I realised that everything was being sold by auction, for the busy man kept shouting prices quickly higher and higher, and then giving a tap with a pencil on a basket, entering something in a memorandum-book, while his red-nosed clerk did the same.

I stared to see how quickly it was all done, Ike and the strange man handing down the baskets, which were seized and carried away by porters to carts standing at a distance; and I wondered how they would ever find out afterwards who had taken them, and get the money paid.

But Ike seemed to be quite satisfied as he trampled about over the baskets, which were handed rapidly down till from being high up he was getting low down, before the busy-looking man began to shout what sounded to me like, "Flow—wow—wow—wow!" as if he were trying to imitate barking like a dog.

Half the crowd went away now, but a fresh lot of men came up, and first of all baskets full of flowers were sold, then half-baskets, then so many bunches, as fast as could be.

Again I found myself wondering how the money would be obtained, and I thought that Old Brownsmith would be sure to be cheated; but Ike looked quite easy, and instead of there being so many things in the market that ours would not sell, I found that the men around bought them up eagerly, and the baskets grew less in number than ever.

I glanced round once or twice on that busy summer morning, to see the street as far as I could grasp packed with carts, and to these a regular throng of men were carrying baskets, while every here and there barrows were being piled up with flowers.

All about us too, as far as I could see by climbing up to the ladder over Basket's back, men were shouting away as they sold the contents of other carts, whose baskets were being handed down to the hungry crowds, who were pushing and struggling and making way for the porters with the heavy baskets on their heads.

By degrees I began to understand that all this enormous quantity of garden produce was being bought up by the greengrocers and barrow-dealers from all over London, and that they would soon be driving off east, west, north, and south, to their shops and places of business.

I should have liked to sit perched up there and watching all that went on, but I had to move to let Ike drag back the baskets; then I had to help handing out bunches, till at last the crowd melted away, and the busy man closed his book with a snap.

"Very good this morning," he shouted to Ike; and then climbing down he went off with his red-nosed clerk, and the people who were about followed him.

"Getting warm, mate?" said Ike, grinning at me.

"Yes," I said; "the sun's so hot, and there's no wind here."

"No, my lad; they builds houses to shut it out. Soon be done now. You and Shock get down and hand up them baskets."

He pointed to a pile that some men had been making, and these I found all had "Brownsmith, Isleworth," painted upon them, and it dawned upon me now that those which had been carried away would not be returned till next journey.

"That's it," said Ike. "Market-gardeners has to give a lot o' trust that way."

"But do they get the baskets all back again, Ike?" I said.

"To be sure they do, my lad—Oh yes, pretty well."

"But shall we get paid the money for all that's been sold this morning?"

"Why, of course, my lad. That gentleman as sold for us, he's our salesman; and he pays for it all, and they pay him. Don't you see?"

I said "Yes," but my mind was not very clear about it.

"We're all right there. Work away, Shock, and let's finish loading up, and then we'll have our breakfast. Nice sort o' looking party you are, to take anywhere to feed," he grumbled, as he glanced at Shock, whose appearance was certainly not much in his favour.

It was much easier work loading with empty baskets, and besides there was not a full load, so that it was not very long before Ike had them all piled up to his satisfaction and the ropes undone and thrown over and over and laced in and out and hooked and tied and strained to the sides of the cart.

"That's the way we does it, squire," cried Ike; "haul away, Shock, my lad. You've worked well. Old Bonyparty's had the best of it; this is his rest and feeding time. You might leave him there hours; but as soon as it's time to go home, away he starts, and there's no stopping him.

"That's about it," he said, as he fastened off a rope. "That'll do. We sha'n't want no more for this lot. Now don't you two leave the cart. I'm going up to Mr Blackton, our salesman, you know, just to see if he's anything to say, and then we'll go and have our braxfass. Don't you chaps leave the cart."

"I sha'n't go," I said, and I glanced at Shock, who climbed up to the top of the baskets, and lay down flat on his face, so as to be away from me as it seemed, but I could see him watching me out of one eye from time to time.

"I wonder whether he will ever be different," I thought to myself, as I watched the selling of a huge load of beautifully white bunches of turnips, as regular and clean as could be, when all at once I felt a blow in my back, and looking sharply round, there were several of the ragged boys who haunted the market grinning at me.

There was no handy place for me to post myself again so as to stop the throwing, and I had to content myself with looking at them angrily; but that did no good, for they separated, getting behind baskets and stacks of baskets, like so many sharpshooters, and from thence laid siege to me, firing shots with bits of market refuse, and anything they could find.

I generally managed to dodge the missiles, but the boys were clever enough to hit me several times, and with my blood boiling, and fingers tingling to pull their ears or punch their dirty heads, I had to stand fast and bear it all.

Barelegged, barefooted, and as active as cats, I felt sure that if I chased one he would dodge in and out and escape me, and as to throwing back at them, I was not going to stoop to do that.

"Dirty young vagabonds!" I said to myself, and I looked at them contemptuously with as much effect as if I had directed my severe looks at a market basket; and then I went and leaned against the end of the cart, determined to take no notice of them, and wishing that Ike would come back.

The young rascals only grew more impudent though, and came nearer, two in particular, and one of them, quite a little fellow with a big head and two small dark shiny eyes, over which his shock head of hair kept falling, ran right in, making charges at me, and striking at me with a muddy little fist, while his companion made pokes with a stick.

This was getting beyond bearing, for I was not a wild beast in a cage unable to get away; but still I determined not to be led into any disgraceful struggle with the dirty little blackguards.

I was not afraid of them, for I was too angry for that, and nothing would have given me greater satisfaction than to have come to blows. But that would not do, I knew.

I glanced round and saw that there were plenty of people about, but they were all too busy with their own affairs to take much notice of me, so that if I wanted to free myself from the pack of young ruffians I must act for myself.

The attack went on, and I should have fared worse, only that it soon became evident that ammunition was running short; and failing this, the boys began to throw words, while the two most daring kept making rushes at me and then shrank back ready to throw themselves down if I should strike at them.

All at once I thought of Ike's great cart-whip, and in the full confidence that I could make it crack as loudly and as well as its master I determined to give it a good whish or two in the air.

It was stuck high up in one of the staples in the front of the cart, and, determined to climb up and reach it down, I turned and raised one foot to a spoke of the great wheel, when the two foremost boys uttered a yell and made a furious onslaught upon me.

They were too late, for in an instant I had seen the object of their advance. There was no doubt about it. They were keeping my attention from what was going on upon the other side, where one of their companions had been stealing along under cover of some baskets, and was just in the act of untying one of the coils of nearly new rope, which had not been required and hung from the ladder.

The young thief had that moment finished, and slipped his arm through, catching sight of me at the same time, and darting off.

I did not stop to think. In one flash I realised that I had been left in charge of the cart, and had been so poor a sentry that I had allowed the enemy to get possession of something that I ought to have protected, and thinking of what Ike would say, and later on of Old Brownsmith, I ran off after the thief.

Chapter Sixteen
An Exciting Chase

But not without shouting to Shock, whom I suddenly remembered.

"Shock—Shock!" I cried; "look out for the cart." Not that I supposed that the boys I left behind would run off with it and the old horse; but there were more coils of rope swinging from the ladder, and there were the sacks and Ike's old coat and whip.

I thought of all this in an instant as I ran, followed by the yells of the young plunderer's companions.

I was not far behind, but he was barefoot, used to the place, knew every inch of the ground, and while I slipped and nearly went down twice over, he ran easily and well, pad—pad—pad—pad over the stones. He doubled here and went in and out of the carts and wagons, dodged round a stack of baskets there, threaded his way easily among the people, while I tried to imitate him, and only blundered against them and got thrust aside. Then I nearly knocked over a basket of peas built up on the top of other baskets like a pillar, and at last nearly lost my quarry, for he darted in at the door of a herbalist's shop; and as I went panting up, sure now of catching him, I suddenly awakened to the fact that there was a door on the other side out by which he had passed.

As luck had it, when I darted round I just caught sight of him disappearing behind a cabbage wagon.

This time, as he disappeared, I tried to bring a little strategy to bear, and running round another way by which I felt sure he would go, I was able to make up all my lost ground, for I came plump upon him.

"Stop, you young thief!" I panted as I made a snatch at the rope and his arm.

It was like catching at an eel. Just as I thought I had him he dodged aside, dived under a horse, and as I ran round the back of the cart, not caring to imitate his example, he was a dozen yards away, going in and out of stalls and piles of vegetables.

I lost sight of him then, and the next minute saw him watching me round a corner, when I again gave chase, hot, panting, and with a curious aching pain in my legs; but when I reached the corner he had gone, and I felt that I had lost him, and, thoroughly disheartened, did not know which way to turn. I was about to go despondently back to the cart, when, giving a final glance round, I saw him stealing away beyond some columns.

He had not seen me, and he was walking; so, keeping as much out of sight as I could, and rejoicing in the fact that I had recovered my breath, I hurried on.

All at once I heard a shrill warning cry, and looking to my right saw the two young ruffians who had been the most obnoxious, while at the same moment I saw that the warning had taken effect, the boy I chased having started off afresh.

"I will catch you," I muttered through my teeth; and, determined not to lose sight of him again, I ran on, in and out among carts and vans, jostling and being jostled, running blindly now, for my sole thought was to keep that boy in view, and this I did the more easily now, that feeling at last that he could not escape me in the market, he suddenly crossed the road, ran in and out for a minute in what seemed like an archway, and then ran as hard as he could along a wide street and I after him.

Suddenly he turned to the right into a narrow street, and along by a great building. At the end of this he turned to the right again, past the front and nearly to the bottom of the street, when he turned to the left and followed a wide street till it became suddenly narrow, and instead of being full of people it was quite empty.

Here he darted into a covered way with columns all along the side, running very fast still, and I suppose I was too, and gradually overtaking him, but he reached the end of the street before I could come up with him, and as he turned the corner I felt quite despairing once more at seeing him pass out of sight.

It was only a matter of moments before I too turned the corner, and found myself in the dirtiest busiest street I had ever seen, with unpleasant-looking people about, and throngs of children playing over the foul pavement and in the road.

My boy seemed quite at home there and as if he belonged to the place. I noticed that as I ran after him, wondering whether it would be of any use to call to them to stop him, though if I had determined that it would be I had not the breath, as I panted on at a much slower rate now, and with the perspiration streaming down my face.

I kept losing sight of him, there were so many people grouped about the pavement along which he ran, while I kept to the road, but he went in and out among them as easily as a dog might have run, till all at once I saw him dive in amongst a number of men talking at the entrance of a narrow archway with a public-house on one side, and as I ran up I found that it was a court, down which I caught a glimpse of the boy with the rope still over his arm.

I stopped for nothing but dashed in after him, the men giving way at first, but as I blundered in my haste against one rough-looking fellow, he roared out savagely:

"Now, then, where are you running to?" and made a snatch at my collar.

I eluded him by making quite a bound in my alarm, and nearly falling over the leg of another, who thrust it out to trip me up. I escaped a fall, however, and entered the court, which seemed to be half full of children, just in time to see my boy slip into a house nearly at the bottom, on the left.

He stopped for a moment to look back to see if I was coming, and then he disappeared, and my heart gave a bound, for in my excitement I felt that I had succeeded, and that I had traced the young thief to his lair.

I did not think about anything else, only that the children all stopped their games and set up a kind of yell, while it seemed to me that the men who were at the entrance of the court were all following me slowly with their hands thrust down low in their pockets, and it struck me for the moment that they were all coming down to see the capture of the thief.

I was in happy ignorance just then that I had followed the boy into one of the vilest and most dangerous parts of London in those days,—to wit a Drury Lane court, one of the refuges of some of the worst characters in that district.

In this ignorance I was still observant, and noticed that the doors on each side of the dirty court stood wide open, while the yell set up by the children brought people to some of the open windows.

That was all seen in a glance, as I made for the open door at the end, before which a boy of my own size ran as if to stop me; but even if I had wished to stop just then I could not, and I gave him a sharp push, the weight of my body driving him back into a sitting position as I stumbled in from the pavement, up a couple of stone steps, and on to the boards of the narrow passage, which seemed, by contrast to the bright sunshine outside, quite dark.

I did not stop, but went on as if by instinct to the end, passed a flight of steps leading down to the cellar kitchen, up which came a noisome odour that turned me sick, and began to ascend the stairs before me.

Then I paused for a moment with my hand on a sticky balustrade and listened.

Yes! I was quite right, for up above me I could hear the stairs creaking as if some one was going up; and to make me the more sure that the boy had not entered a room I could hear his hoarse panting, accompanied by a faint whimpering cry, as if every moment or two he kept saying softly, "Oh!"

That satisfied me, and as fast as I could I went up one flight and then another of dirty creaking stairs and found myself on the first floor. Then up another flight, dirtier, more creaking, and with the woodwork broken away here and there.

Up another flight worse still, and by the light of a staircase window I could see that the plaster ceiling was down here and there, showing the laths, while the wall was blackened by hands passing over it. On the handrail side the balusters were broken out entirely in the most dangerous way; but all this seemed of no consequence whatever, for there was the boy still going on, evidently to the very top of the house.

All at once there was silence above me, and I thought he must have gone, but he was only listening, and as he heard me coming he uttered a faint cry, and went on up whimpering, evidently so much exhausted by the long chase that he could hardly drag himself up higher.

By this time I was up to the second floor, where there were a couple of battered doors and another staircase window nearly without glass, the broken panes being covered with paper pasted on, or else, fortunately for the inhabitants of the noisome place, left open for the air to blow through.

I ought to have stopped; in fact I ought never to have gone; but I was too much excited by my chase to think of anything but getting hold of that boy and shaking him till he dropped our new rope; and now as I began to toil breathlessly up the last flight I knew that my task was done, for my young enemy could hardly crawl, and had begun to sob and whine, and I could just make out:

"You'd best let me be—I—I—ain't—I ain't done—done—"

I heard no more, only that doors were being thrown open, and there was a buzz of voices below, with heavy footsteps in the passage.

Still that did not seem to have anything to do with me, so intent was I on my pursuit up those last two flights of stairs, which seemed to be steeper, more broken, and more difficult to climb than those which had gone before. In fact the boy above me was dragging himself up, and I had settled down into a walk, helping myself on by the dirty hand-rail, and panting so hoarsely that each breath came to be a snore. My heart, too, throbbed heavily, and seemed to be beating right up into my throat.

I had gained on my quarry, so that we were on the last flight together, and this gave me the requisite strength for the last climb, for I knew that he could go no further.

Half-way up and there was a sloping ceiling above, in which was a blackened skylight, across which was a string and some dirty white garments hanging to dry, while to right and to left there were doors that had been painted black for reasons full of wisdom; and as my head rose higher I saw the boy who had literally crawled up on to the landing, rise up, with the rope still upon his arm, and fling himself against the farthest of these two doors.

It flew open with a crash, and then seemed to be banged to heavily, but it was against me, for, summoning up all my remaining strength, I reached the top, and imitating the boy's action, the door came back upon my hands, and was dashed open again.

I almost tumbled in, staggering forward, and hardly able to keep upon my legs, so that I nearly reached the middle of the room before I was aware that the boy was cowering down in a corner upon our rope, and that a big scowling stubble-chinned man had just risen dressed from a bed on which he had lain, to catch me by the shoulders in a tremendous grip, and hold me backwards panting like some newly captured bird.

I noticed that the man wore a great sleeved waistcoat, breeches, and heavy boots, and that his low forehead was puckered up into an ugly scowl, with one great wrinkle across it that seemed like another mouth as he forced me right back against the wall, and held me shivering there.

"Here, shet that there door, Polly," he said in a low harsh growl, like the snarl of a wild beast. Then to me:

"Here, what d'yer mean a-comin' in here, eh?"

He accompanied his words with a fierce shake that made the back of my head tap against the wall.

For a few moments the man's savage look seemed to fascinate me, and I felt horribly alarmed, as I could think for the moment about nothing but the Ogre and Hop-o'-my-thumb, and wonder whether he was going to take out a big knife and threaten me. I was still panting and breathless with my exertions, and there was a curious pain in my legs, mingled with a sensation as if they were going to double up under me, but I made an effort to be brave as the great heavy-browed scoundrel gave me another shake, and said:—

"D'yer hear? What d'yer mean by banging into my room like that 'ere?"

I glanced at a sad-faced dull-eyed slatternly woman who had closed the door, and then at the boy, who still crouched close up under the window, whimpering like a whipped dog, but keenly watching all that was going on with his sharp restless dark eyes; then, making a determined attempt to be braver than I looked, I said as stoutly as I could:

"I want our new rope. He stole our new rope."

"Who stole yer noo rope!" cried the fellow, giving me another shake; "what d'yer mean?"

"He took our rope off the cart in Covent Garden this morning," I cried, feeling angry now.

"Why, he ain't been out o' the court this morning," said the fellow sharply; "have yer, Micky?"

"No, father," said the boy.

"Jest up, ain't he, missus?" continued my captor, turning to the heavy-eyed woman.

"Yes, just up," said the woman in a low mechanical voice, and then with more animation, "Let him go, Ned."

"You mind yer own business," said the fellow savagely; then to me, "Now, then, d'yer hear that?"

"I don't care; he did," I said firmly. "He stole our rope—that's it, you give it me directly."

"What! that?" he cried. "You're a nice un, you are. Why, that's my rope, as 'longs to my donnerkey-cart. Don't you come lying here."

"I tell you that's our rope, and I saw him steal it," I cried, growing stronger now. "You let me go, and give me my rope, or I'll tell the police."

"Why, you never had no rope, yer young liar!" he cried.

"It's my master's rope," I said, struggling to get free. "I will have it."

"What! yer'd steal it, would yer? Yer'd tell the polliss, would yer!" growled the fellow, tightening his grip; "I'll soon see about that. Here you, Micky, bring that there rope here."

The boy struggled to his feet, and came slowly to us with the rope, which the man scanned eagerly.

"I don't want to make no mistakes," he growled. "Let's see it. If it's your rope, you shall have it, but—now then! d'yer hear?"

This was to the boy, who took advantage of my helpless position to give me a couple of savage kicks in the leg as he stood there; but as he had no shoes on, the kicks did not do much harm.

"Why, o' course it is our rope," growled the fellow. "Gahn with you, what d'yer mean by coming here with a tale like that?"

He gave me a shake, and the woman interfered.

"Let him go, Ned," she said, "or ther'll be a row."

The man took one hand from my shoulder, and doubled his great fist, which he held close to the woman's face in a menacing way. Then turning sharply he made believe to strike me with all his might right in the mouth, when, as I flinched, he growled out with a savage grin:

"Ah! yer know'd yer deserved it. Now I dunno whether I'm going to keep yer here, or whether I shall let yer go; but whichever I does, don't you go a sweering that this here's your rope, a cause it's mine. D'yer hear, mine?"

The door was kicked open at that moment, and a couple of the rough-looking fellows I had seen at the entrance to the court stood half inside, leaning against the door-posts and looking stolidly on.

I was about to appeal to them for help, but my instinct told me that such an application would be in vain, while their first words told me how right I was.

"Give it him, Ned. What's he a-doin' here?" said one.

"See if he's got any tin," said the other.

"Ah! make him pay up," said the first.

"'Ow much have yer got, eh?" said my captor, giving me a shake, which was the signal for the boy to kick at me again with all his might.

"Gahn, will yer," cried the man, "or I'll wrap that rope's end round yer."

The woman just then made a step forward and struck at the boy, who dodged the blow, and retreated to the far end of the room, the woman shrinking away too as the man growled:

"Let him alone; will yer?"

I seized the opportunity to wrench myself partly away, and to catch hold of the rope, which the man had now beneath one of his feet.

"Ah, would yer!" he shouted, tearing the rope away from me. "Comes up here, mates, bold as brass, and says it's his'n."

I felt more enraged and mortified now than alarmed, and I cried out:

"It is our rope, and that boy stole it; and I'll tell the police."

"Oh! yer will, will yer?" cried my captor. "We'll see about that. Here, what money have yer got?"

"I've only enough for my breakfast," I cried defiantly. "Give me my rope and let me go."

"Oh yes, I'll let yer go," he cried, as I wrestled to get away, fighting with all my might, and striving to reach the rope at the same moment.

"Look out, Ned," said one of the men at the door, grinning. "He'll be too much for yer;" and the other uttered a hoarse laugh.

"Ah, that he will!" cried the big fellow, letting me get hold of the rope, and, tightening his grasp upon my collar, he kicked my legs from under me, so that I fell heavily half across the coil, while he went down on one knee and held me panting and quivering there, perfectly helpless.

The boy made another dart forward, and I saw the woman catch at him by the head, but his shortly-cropped hair glided through her hands, and he would have reached me had not the man kicked out at him and made him stop suddenly and watch for another chance.

"Who's got a knife?" growled the man now savagely as he turned towards the two fellows at the door; "I'll soon show him what it is to come here a-wanting to steal our cart-ropes. Chuck that there knife here."

He rose as he spoke, and planted one foot upon my chest. Then catching the pocket-knife thrown to him by one of the men at the door, he opened it with a great deal of show and menace, bending down to stare savagely in my eyes as he whetted the blade upon the boot resting on my chest.

Of course I was a good deal alarmed, but I knew all the while that this was all show and that the great ruffian was trying to frighten me. I was in a desperately bad state, in an evil place, but it was broad daylight, and people had seen me come in, so that I did not for a moment think he would dare to kill me. All the same, though, I could not help feeling a curious nervous kind of tremor run through my frame as he flourished the knife about and glared at me as if pondering as to what he should do next.

"I wish Ike were here," I thought; and as I did so I could not help thinking how big and strong he was, and how little he would make of seizing this great cowardly ruffian by the throat and making him let me go.

"Now, then," he cried, "out wi' that there money." For answer, I foolishly showed him where it was by clapping my hand upon my pocket, when, with a grin of satisfaction, he tore my hand away, thrust in his great fingers, and dragged it out, spat on the various coins, and thrust them in his own pocket.

"What d'yer say?" he cried, bending down again towards me.

"The police shall make you give that up," I panted.

"Says we're to spend this here in beer, mates," he said, grinning, while the woman stood with her eyes half shut and her arms folded, looking on.

The two men at the door laughed.

"Now, then," said the big fellow, "since he's come out genteel-like with his money, I don't think I'll give him the knife this time. Get up with yer, and be off while your shoes are good."

He took his great boot off my chest, and I started up.

"I wouldn't give much for yer," he growled, "if yer showed yer face here agen."

He accompanied this with such a menacing look that I involuntarily shrank away, but recovering myself directly I seized the coil of rope and made for the door.

"What!" roared the great ruffian, snatching the rope, and, as I held on to it, dragging me back. "Trying to steal, are you?"

"It's mine—it's ours," I cried passionately.

"Oh! I'll soon let yer know about that," he cried. "Look here, mates; this is our rope, ain't it?"

"Yes," said one of them: "I'll swear to it."

"It's mine," I cried, tugging at it angrily.

"Let go, will yer—d'yer hear; let go."

He tugged and snatched at it savagely, and just then the boy leaped upon me, butting at me, and striking with all his might, infuriating me so by his cowardly attack, that, holding on to the rope with one hand, I swung round my doubled fist with the other and struck him with all my might.

It must have been a heavy blow right in the face, for he staggered back, caught against a chair, and then fell with a crash, howling dismally.

"Look at that, now," cried the big ruffian. "Now he shall have it."

"Serves him right!" said the woman passionately.

"Let the boy go, Ned, or you'll get into trouble."

"I'll get into trouble for something then," cried the fellow savagely, as he hurt me terribly by jerking the rope out of my hand and catching me by the collar, when I saw the two men at the open door look round, and I heard a familiar growl on the stairs that made my heart leap with joy.

"Ike!—Here!—Ike!" I shouted with all my might.

"Hold yer row," hissed the great ruffian in a hoarse whisper, and clapping one hand behind my head he placed the other upon my mouth.

He dragged me round, half-choked and helpless, and then he said something over his shoulder to the woman, while I fought and struggled, and tried hard to shout again to Ike, whose heavy feet I could hear in the midst of a good deal of altercation on the stairs.

As I struggled to get free I saw that the window was opened and the rope thrown out. Then the window was quickly shut, and I was dragged towards the door.

"Here, you be off outer this," whispered the great ruffian, with his lips close to my ear. "You cut; and don't you—"

He stopped short, holding me tightly, and seemed to hesitate, his eyes glaring round as if in search of some place where he could hide me, not knowing what to do for the best.

"Shut the door, mates," he said quickly; and the two men dragged the door to after them as they stood outside.

"Just you make half a sound, and—"

He put his lips close to my ear as he said this, and closed the great clasp-knife with a sharp click which made me start; while his eyes seemed to fascinate me as he bent down and glared at me.

It was only for a moment, though, and then I managed to slip my face aside and shouted aloud:

"Ike!"

There was a rush and a scuffle outside, and the woman said in an ill-used tone:

"I told yer how it would be."

"You hold—"

He did not finish, for just then one of the men outside growled—plainly heard through the thin door:

"Now, then, where are yer shovin' to?"

"In here," roared a voice that sent a thrill of joy through me.

"Now, then, what d'yer want?" cried the big fellow, thrusting me behind him as Ike kicked open the door and strode into the room.

"What do I want?" he roared. "I want him and our cart-rope. Now, then, where is it?"

There was a fierce muttering among the men, and they drew together while the boy and the woman cowered into one corner of the attic.

"Oh! you're not going to scare me," cried Ike fiercely. "There's the police just at hand if I wants help. Now then, where's that rope?"

"What rope?" growled the ruffian. "I don't know about no ropes."

"They threw it out of the window, Ike," I cried.

"That's a lie," snarled the man. "There ain't never been no ropes here."

"There has been one," I cried, feeling bold now; "but they threw it out of the window."

"Well, of all—" began one of the men, who had crossed the room with his companion to the big ruffian's side.

"You go on down, my lad," whispered Ike in a low deep voice. "Go on, now."

"But are you coming?" I whispered back.

"You may depend on that," he said, as if to himself, "if they'll let me. Go on."

I moved towards the open door, when one of the men made a dash to stop me; but Ike threw put one leg, and he fell sprawling. At the same moment my enemy made a rush at Ike, who stepped back, and then I saw his great fist fly out straight. There was a dull, heavy sound, and the big ruffian stopped short, reeled, and then dropped down upon his hands and knees.

"Quick, boy, quick! You go first," whispered Ike, as I stopped as if paralysed; "I'll foller."

His words roused me, and I ran out of the room.

Chapter Seventeen
What Became of the Rope

I nearly fell headlong down as I reached the stairs, for my foot went through a hole in the boards, but I recovered myself and began to run down as fast as I dared, on account of the rickety state of the steps, while Ike came clumping down after me, and we could hear the big ruffian's voice saying something loudly as we hurried from flight to flight.

There were knots of women on the different landings and at the bottom of the stairs, and they were all talking excitedly; but only to cease and look curiously at us as we went by.

There was quite a crowd, too, of men, women, and children in the court below as we left the doorway; but Ike's bold manner and the decided way in which he strode out with me, looking sharply from one to the other, put a stop to all opposition, even if it had been intended.

There were plenty of scowling, menacing looks, and there was a little hooting from the men, but they gave way, and in another minute we were out of the court and in the dirty street, with a troop of children following us and the people on either side looking on.

"But, Ike," I said in a despairing tone, "we haven't got the rope after all."

"No," he said; "but I've got you out o' that place safe, and I haven't got much hurt myself, and that's saying a deal. Talk about savages and wild beasts abroad! why, they're nothing."

"I didn't see any policemen, Ike," I said, as I thought of their power.

"More didn't I," he replied with a grim smile. "They don't care much about going down these sort o' places; no more don't I. We're well out of that job, my lad. You didn't ought to have gone."

"But that boy was running off with the best cart rope, Ike," I said despondently, "and I was trying to get it back, and now it's gone. What will Mr Brownsmith say?"

"Old Brownsmith won't say never a word," said Ike, as we trudged on along a more respectable street.

"Oh, but he will," I cried. "He is so particular about the ropes."

"So he be, my lad. Here, let's brush you down; you're a bit dirty."

"But he will," I said, as I submitted to the operation.

"Not he," said Ike. "Them police is in the right of it. I'm all of a shiver, now that bit of a burst's over;" and he wiped his brow.

"You are, Ike?" I said wonderingly.

"To be sure I am, my lad. I was all right there, and ready to fight; but now it's over and we're well out of it, I feel just as I did when the cart tipped up and all the baskets come down atop of you."

"I am glad you feel like that," I said.

"Why?" he cried sharply.

"Because it makes me feel that I was not such a terrible coward after all."

"But you were," he said, giving me a curious look. "Oh, yes: about as big a coward as ever I see."

I did not understand why I was so very great a coward, but he did not explain, and I trudged on by him.

"I say, what would you have done if I hadn't come?"

"I don't know," I said. "I suppose they would have let me go at last. They got all my money."

"They did?"

"Yes," I said dolefully; "and then there's the rope. What will Mr Brownsmith say?"

"Nothin' at all," said Ike.

"But he will," I cried again.

"No he won't, because we'll buy a new one 'fore we goes back."

"I thought of that," I said, "but I've no money now."

"Oh, all right! I have," he said. "We may think ourselves well out of a bad mess, my lad; and I don't know as we oughtn't to go to the police, but we haven't no time for that. There'll be another load o' strawb'ys ready by the time we get back, and I shall have to come up again to-night. Strawb'ys sold well to-day. No: we've no time for the police."

"They deserve to be taken up," I said.

"Ay, they do, my boy; but folks don't get all they deserve."

"Or I should be punished for letting that boy steal the rope."

"Hang the rope!" he said crustily. "I mean, hang the boy or his father, and that's what some of 'em'll come to," he cried grimly, "if they don't mind. They're a bad lot down that court. Lor' a mussy me! I'd sooner live in one of our sheds on some straw, with a sack for a pillow, than be shut up along o' these folk in them courts."

"But they wouldn't have hurt me, Ike?" I said.

"I dunno, my lad. P'r'aps they would, p'r'aps they wouldn't. They might have kept you and made a bad un of yer. Frightened you into it like."

I shook my head.

"Ah! you don't know, my lad. How much did they get?"

"Two shillings and ninepence halfpenny," I said dolefully.

"And a nearly new rope. Ah, it's a bad morning's work for your first journey."

"It is, Ike," I said; "but I didn't know any better. How did you know where I was?"

"How did I know? Why, Shock saw you and followed you, and come back and fetched me, when I was staring at the cart and wondering what had gone of you two."

"Where is he now?" I asked.

"What, Shock? Oh, I don't know. He's a queer chap. P'r'aps they've got him instead of you."

I stopped short and looked at him, but saw directly that he was only joking, and went on again:

"You don't think that," I said quickly; "for if you did you would not have come away. Do you think he has gone back to the cart?"

"Oh, there's no knowing," he replied. "P'r'aps when we get back there won't be any cart; some one will have run away with it. They're rum uns here in London."

"Why, you haven't left the cart alone, Ike," I cried.

"That's a good one, that is," he exclaimed. "You haven't left the cart alone! Why, you and Shock did."

"Yes," I said; "but—"

"There, come and let's see," he said gruffly. "We should look well, we two, going back home without a cart, and old Bonyparty took away and cut up for goodness knows what and his skin made into leather. Come along."

We walked quickly, for it seemed as if this was going to be a day all misfortunes; but as we reached the market again I found that Ike had not left the cart untended, for a man was there by the horse, and the big whip curved over in safety from where it was stuck.

"Seen anything of our other boy?" said Ike as we reached the cart.

"No," was the reply.

"Hadn't we better go back and look for him?" I said anxiously.

"Well, I don't know," said Ike, rubbing one ear; "he ain't so much consequence as you."

"I've been to Paris and I've been to Do-ho-ver."

"Why, there he is," I cried; and, climbing up the wheel, there lay Shock on his back right on the top of the baskets, and as soon as he saw my face he grinned and then turned his back.

"He's all right," I said as I descended; and just then there was a creaking noise among the baskets, and Shock's head appeared over the edge.

"Here y'are," he cried. "That there tumbled out o' window, and I ketched it and brought it here."

As he spoke he threw down the coil of nearly new rope, and I felt so delighted that I could have gone up to him and shaken hands.

"Well, that's a good un, that is," said Ike with a chuckle. "I am 'bout fine and glad o' that."

He took the rope and tied it up to the ladder again, and then turned to me.

"Come along and get some breakfast, my lad," he said. "I dessay you're fine and hungry."

"But how about Shock?"

"Oh, we'll send him out some. Here, you, Shock, look after the cart and horse. Don't you leave 'em," Ike added to the man; and then we made our way to a coffee-house, where Ike's first act, to my great satisfaction, was to procure a great mug of coffee and a couple of rolls, which he opened as if they had been oysters, dabbed a lump of butter in each, and then put under his arm.

"He don't deserve 'em," he growled, "for coming; but he did show me where you was."

"And he saved the rope," I said.

Ike nodded.

"You sit down till I come back, my lad," he said; and then he went off, to return in a few minutes to face me at a table where we were regaled with steaming coffee and grilled haddocks.

"This is the best part of the coming to market, my lad," he said, "only it's a mistake."

"What is?" I asked.

"Haddocks, my lad. They're a trickier kind o' meat than bloaters. I ordered this here for us 'cause it seemed more respectable like, as I'd got company, than herrin'; but it's a mistake."

"But this is very nice," I said, beginning very hungrily upon the hot roll and fish, but with a qualm in my mind as to how it was to be paid for.

"Ye–es," said Ike, after saying "soup" very loudly as he took a long sip of his coffee; "tidyish, my lad, tidyish, but you see one gets eddicated to a herring, and knows exactly where every bone will be. These things seems as if the bones is all nowhere and yet they're everywhere all the time, and so sure as you feel safe and take a bite you find a sharp pynte, just like a trap laid o' purpose to ketch yer."

"Well, there are a good many little bones, certainly," I said.

"Good many! Thick as slugs after a shower. There's one again, sharp as a needle. Wish I'd a red herrin', that I do."

"I say, Ike," I said suddenly, as I was in the middle of my breakfast, "I wish I could make haste and grow into a man."

"Do you, now?" he said with a derisive laugh. "Ah! I shouldn't wonder. If you'd been a man I s'pose you'd have pitched all those rough uns out o' window, eh?"

"I should have liked to be able to take care of myself," I said.

"Without old Ike, eh, my lad?"

"I don't mean that," I said; "only I should like to be a man."

"Instead o' being very glad you're a boy with everything fresh and bright about you. Red cheeks and clean skin and all your teeth, and all the time to come before you, instead of having to look back and think you're like an old spade—most wore out."

"Oh, but you're so strong, Ike! I should like to be a man."

"Like to be a boy, my lad, and thank God you are one," said old Ike, speaking as I had never heard him speak before. "It's natur', I s'pose. All boys wishes they was men, and when they're men they look back on that happiest time of their lives when they was boys and wishes it could come over again."

"Do they, Ike?" I said.

"I never knew a man who didn't," said Ike, making the cups dance on the table by giving it a thump with his fist. "Why, Master Grant, I was kicked about and hit when I was a boy more'n ever a boy was before, but all that time seems bright and sunshiny to me."

"But do you think Shock's happy?" I said; "he's a boy, and has no one to care about him."

"Happy! I should just think he is. All boys has troubles that they feels bad at the time, but take 'em altogether they're as happy as can be. Shock's happy enough his way or he wouldn't have been singing all night atop of the load. There, you're a boy, and just you be thankful that you are, my lad; being a boy's about as good a thing as there is."

We had nearly finished our breakfast when Ike turned on me sharply.

"Why, you don't look as if you was glad to be a boy," he said.

"I was thinking about what Mr Brownsmith will say when he knows I've been in such trouble," I replied.

"Ah, he won't like it! But I suppose you ain't going to tell him?"

"Yes," I said, "I shall tell him."

Ike remained silent for a few minutes, and sat slowly filling his pipe.

At last, as we rose to go, after Ike had paid the waitress, he said to me slowly:

"Sometimes doing right ain't pleasant and doing wrong is. It's quite right to go and tell Old Brownsmith and get blowed up, and it would be quite wrong not to tell him, but much the nystest. Howsoever, you tell him as soon as we get back. He can't kill yer for that, and I don't s'pose he'll knock yer down with the kitchen poker and then kick you out. You've got to risk it."

I did tell Old Brownsmith all my trouble when we reached home, and he listened attentively and nodding his head sometimes. Then he said softly, "Ah!" and that was all.

But I heard him scold Master Shock tremendously for going off from his work without leave.

Shock had been looking on from a distance while I was telling Old Brownsmith, and this put it into his head, I suppose, that I had been speaking against him, for during the next month he turned his back whenever he met me, and every now and then, if I looked up suddenly, it was to see him shaking his fist at me, while his hair seemed to stand up more fiercely than ever out of his crownless straw hat like young rhubarb thrusting up the lid from the forcing-pot put on to draw the stalks.

Chapter Eighteen
The Gardener Surgeon

"People sneer at gardening and gardeners, Grant," said the old gentleman to me one day. "Perhaps you may take to some other occupation when you grow older; but don't you never be ashamed of having learned to be a gardener."

"I'm sure I never shall," I said.

"I hope you will not, my boy, for there's something in gardening and watching the growth of trees and plants that's good for a lad's nature; and if I was a schoolmaster I'd let every boy have a garden, and make him keep it neat. It would be as good a lesson as any he could teach."

"I like gardening more and more, sir," I said.

"That's right, my boy. I hope you do, but you've a deal to learn yet. Gardening's like learning to play the fiddle; there's always something more to get hold of than you know. I wish I had some more glass."

"I wish you had, sir," I said.

"Why, boy?—why?" he cried sharply.

"Because you seem as if you'd like it, sir," I said, feeling rather abashed by his sharp manner.

"Yes, but it was so that I should be able to teach you, sir. But wait a bit, I'll talk to my brother one of these days."

Time glided on, and as I grew bigger and stronger I used now and then to go up with Ike to the market. He would have liked me to go every time, but Mr Brownsmith shook his head, and would only hear of it in times of emergency.

"Not a good task for you, Grant," he used to say. "I want you at home."

We were down the garden one morning after a very stormy night, when the wind had been so high that a great many of the fruit-trees had had their branches broken off, and we were busy with ladder, saw, and knife, repairing damages.

I was up the ladder in a fine young apple-tree, whose branch had been broken and was hanging by a few fibres, and as soon as I had fixed myself pretty safely I began to cut, while when I glanced down to see if Old Brownsmith was taking any notice I saw that he was smiling.

"Won't do—won't do, Grant," he said. "Cutting off a branch of a tree that has been broken is like practising amputation on a man. Cut lower, boy."

"But I wanted to save all that great piece with those little boughs," I said.

"But you can't, my lad. Now just look down the side there below where you are cutting, and what can you see?"

"Only a little crack that will grow up."

"Only a little crack that won't grow up, Grant, but which will admit the rain, and the wet will decay the tree; and that bough, at the end of two or three years, instead of being sound and covered with young shoots, will be dying away. A surgeon, when he performs an amputation, cuts right below the splintered part of the bone. Cut three feet lower down, my lad, and then pare all off nice and smooth, just as I showed you over the pruning.

"That's the way," he said, as he watched me. "That's a neat smooth wound in the tree that will dry up easily after every shower, and nature will send out some of her healing gum or sap, and it will turn hard, and the bark, just as I showed you before, will come up in a new ring, and swell and swell till it covers the wood, and by and by you will hardly see where the cut was made."

I finished my task, and was going to shoulder the ladder and get on to the next tree, when the old gentleman said in his quaint dry way:

"You know what the first workman was, Grant?"

"Yes," I said, "a gardener."

"Good!" he said. "And do you know who was the first doctor and surgeon?"

"No," I said.

"A gardener, my boy, just as the men were who first began to improve the way in which men lived, and gave them fruit and corn and vegetables to eat, as well as the wild creatures they killed by hunting."

"Oh, yes!" I said, "I see all that, but I don't see how the first doctor and surgeon could have been a gardener."

"Don't you?" he said, laughing silently. "I do. Who but a gardener would find out the value of the different herbs and juices, and what they would do. You may call him a botanist, my lad, but he was a gardener. He would find out that some vegetables were good for the blood at times, and from that observation grew the whole doctrine of medicine. That's my theory, my boy. Now cut off that pear-tree branch."

I set the ladder right, and proceeded to cut and trim the injury, thinking all the while what a pity it was that the trees should have been so knocked about by the storm.

"Do you know who were the best gardeners in England in the olden times, Grant?" said the old gentleman as he stood below whetting my knife.

"No, sir,—yes, I think I do," I hastened to add—"the monks."

"Exactly. We have them to thank for introducing and improving no end of plants and fruit-trees. They were very great gardeners—famous gardeners and cultivators of herbs and strange flowers, and it was thus that they, many of them, became the doctors or teachers of their district, and I've got an idea in my head that it was on just such a morning as this that some old monk—no, he must have been a young monk, and a very bold and clever one—here, take your knife, it's as sharp as a razor now."

I stooped down and took the knife, and hanging my saw from one of the rounds of the ladder began to cut, and the old gentleman went on:

"It must have been after such a morning as this, boy, that some monk made the first bold start at surgery."

I looked down at him, and he went on:

"You may depend upon it that during the storm some poor fellow had been caught out in the forest by a falling limb of a tree, one of the boughs of which pinned him to the ground and smashed his leg."

"An oak-tree," I said, quite enjoying the fact that he was inventing a story.

"No, boy, an elm. Oak branches when they break are so full of tough fibre that they hang on by the stump. It is your elm that is the treacherous tree, and snaps short off, and comes down like thunder."

"An elm-tree, then," I said, paring away.

"Yes, a huge branch of an elm, and there the poor fellow lay till some one heard his shouts, and came to his help."

"Where he would be lying in horrible agony," I said, trimming away at the bough.

"Wrong again, Grant. Nature is kinder than that. With such an injury the poor fellow's limb would be numbed by the terrible shock, and possibly he felt but little pain. I knew an officer whose foot was taken off in a battle in India. A cannon-ball struck him just above the ankle, and he felt a terrible blow, but it did not hurt him afterwards for the time; and all he thought of was that his horse was killed, till he began to struggle away from the fallen beast, when he found that his own leg was gone."

"How horrible!" I said.

"All war is horrible, my boy," he said gravely. "Well, to go on with my story. I believe that they came and hoisted out the poor fellow under the tree, and carried him up to the old priory to have his broken leg cured by one of the monks, who would be out in his garden just the same as we are, Grant, cutting off and paring the broken boughs of his apple and pear trees. Then they laid him in one of the cells, and his leg was bound up and dressed with healing herbs, and the poor fellow was left to get well."

"And did he?" I said.

"Then the gardener monk went out into the garden again and continued to trim off the broken branches, sawing these and cutting those, and thinking all the while about his patient in the cell.

"Then the next day came, and the poor fellow's relatives ran up to see him, and he was in very great agony, and they called upon the monks to help him, and they dressed the terrible injury again, and the poor fellow was very feverish and bad in spite of all that was done. But at last he dropped off into a weary sleep, and the poor people went away thinking what a great thing it was to have so much knowledge of healing, while, as soon as they had gone the monk shook his head.

"Next day came, and the relatives and friends were delighted, for the pain was nearly all gone, and the injured man lay very still.

"'He'll soon get well now,' they said; and they went away full of hope and quite satisfied; but the monk, after he had given the patient some refreshing drink, went out into his garden among his trees, and then after walking about in the sunny walk under the old stone wall, he stopped by the mossy seat by the sun-dial, and stood looking down at the gnomon, whose shadow marked the hours, and sighed deeply as he thought how many times the shadow would point to noon before his poor patient was dead."

"Why, I thought he was getting better," I said.

"Carry your ladder to the next tree, Grant," said the old gentleman, "and you shall work while I prattle."

I obeyed him, and this time I had a great apple-tree bough to operate upon with the thin saw. I began using the saw very gently, and listening, for I seemed to see that monk in his long grey garment, and rope round his waist, looking down at the sun-dial, when Old Brownsmith went on slowly:

"He knew it could not be long first, for the man's leg was crushed and the bone splintered so terribly that it would never heal up, and that the calm sense of comfort was a bad sign, for the limb was mortifying, and unless that mortification was stopped the man must die."

"Poor fellow!" I ejaculated, for the old man told the story with such earnestness that it seemed to be real.

"Yes, poor fellow! That is what the monk said as he thought of all the herbs and decoctions he had made, and that not one of them would stop the terrible change that was going on. He felt how helpless he was, and at last, Grant, he sat down on the mossy old stone bench, and covering his face with his hands, cried like a child."

"But he was a man," I said.

"Yes, my lad; but there are times when men are so prostrated by misery and despair that they cry like women—not often—perhaps only once or twice in a man's life. My monk cried bitterly, and then he jumped up, feeling ashamed of himself, and began walking up and down. Then he went and stood by the great fish stew, where the big carp and tench were growing fatter as they fed by night and basked in the sunshine among the water weeds by day; but no thought came to him as to how he could save the poor fellow lying in the cell."

Old Brownsmith stopped to blow his nose on a brown-and-orange silk handkerchief, and stroke two or three cats, while I sawed away very slowly, waiting for what was to come.

"Then he went round by where one apple-tree, like that, had lost a bough, and whose stump he had carefully trimmed—just as you are going to trim that, Grant."

"I know," I cried, eagerly; "and then—"

"You attend to your apple-tree, sir, and let me tell my story," he said, half gruffly, half in a good-humoured way, and I sawed away with my thin saw till I was quite through, and the stump I had cut off fell with such a bang that the cats all jumped in different directions, and then stared back at the stump with dilated eyes, till, seeing that there was no danger, one big

Tom went and rubbed himself against it from end to end, and the others followed suit.

"All at once, as he stood staring at the broken tree, an idea flashed across his brain, Grant."

"Yes," I said, pruning-knife in hand.

"He knew that if he had not cut and trimmed off that branch the limb would have gone on decaying right away, and perhaps have killed the tree."

"Yes, of course," I said, still watching him.

"Isn't your knife sharp enough, my lad?" said Old Brownsmith dryly.

"Yes, sir," I said; and I went on trimming. "Well, he thought that if this saved the tree, why should it not save the life of the man?" and he grew so excited that he went in at once and had a look at the patient, and then went in to the prior, who shook his head.

"'Poor fellow,' he said; 'he will die.'

"'Yes,' said the young monk, 'unless—'

"'Unless—' said the prior.

"'Yes, unless,' said the young monk; and he horrified the prior by telling him all his ideas, while the other monks shook their heads.

"'It could not be done,' they said. 'It would be too horrible.'

"'There is no horror in performing an act like that to save a man's life,' said the young monk; 'it is a duty.'

"'But it would kill the poor fellow,' they chorused.

"'He will die as it is,' said the young monk. 'You said as much when I came in, and I am sure of it.'

"'Yes,' said the prior sadly, 'he will die.'

"'This might save his life,' said the young monk; but the old men shook their heads.

"'Such a thing has never been done,' they said. 'It is too horrible.'

"'And even if it saved his life he would only have one leg.'

"'Better have no legs at all,' said the young monk, 'than die before his time.'

"'But it would be his time,' said the old monks.

"'It would not be his time if I could save his life,' said the young monk.

"But still the old monks shook their heads, and said that no man had ever yet heard of such a thing. It was too terrible to be thought of, and they frowned very severely upon the young monk till the prior, who had been very thoughtful, exclaimed:—

"'And cutting the limb off the apple-tree made you think that?'

"The young monk said that it was so.

"'But a man is not an apple-tree,' said the oldest monk present; and all the others shook their heads again; but, oddly enough, a few minutes later they nodded their heads, for the prior suddenly exclaimed:—

"'Our brother is quite right, and he shall try.'

"There was a strange thrill ran through the monks, but what the prior said was law in those days, Grant, and in a few minutes it was known all through the priory that Brother Anselm was going to cut off the poor swineherd's leg.

"Then—I say, my boy, I wish you'd go on with your work. I can't talk if you do not," said Old Brownsmith, with a comical look at me, and I went on busily again while he continued his story.

"When Brother Anselm had obtained the prior's leave to try his experiment he felt nervous and shrank from the task. He went down the garden and looked at the trees that he had cut, and he felt more than ever that a man was, as the monks said, not an apple-tree. Then he examined the places which looked healthy and well, and he wondered whether if he performed such an operation on the poor patient he also would be healthy and well at the end of a week, and he shook his head and felt nervous."

"If you please, Mr Brownsmith," I said, "I can't go on till you've done, and I must hear the end."

He chuckled a little, and seating himself on a bushel basket which he turned upside down, a couple of cats sprang in his lap, another got on his shoulder, and he went on talking while I thrust an arm through one of the rounds of the ladder, and leaned back against it as he went on.

"Well, Grant," he said, "Brother Anselm felt sorry now that he had leave to perform his experiment, and he went slowly back to the cell and talked to the poor swineherd, a fine handsome, young man with fair curly brown hair and a skin as white as a woman's where the sun had not tanned him.

"And he talked to him about how he felt; and the poor fellow said he felt much better and much worse—that the pain had all gone, but that he did not think he should ever be well any more.

"This set the brother thinking more and more, but he felt that he could do nothing that day, and he waited till the next, lying awake all night thinking of what he would do and how he would do it, till the cold time about sunrise, when he had given up the idea in despair. But when he saw the light coming in the east, with the glorious gold and orange clouds, and then the bright sunshine of a new day, he began to think of how sad it would be for that young man, cut down as he had been in a moment, to be left to die when perhaps he might be saved. He thought, too, about trees that had been cut years before, and which had been healthy and well ever since, and that morning, feeling stronger in his determination, he went to the cell where the patient lay, to talk to him, and the first thing the poor fellow said was:—

"'Tell me the truth, please. I'm going to die, am I not?'

"The young monk was silent.

"'I know it,' said the swineherd sadly. 'I feel it now.'

"Brother Anselm looked at him sadly for a few minutes and then said to him:—

"'I must not deceive you at such a time—yes; but one thing might save your life.'

"'What is that?' cried the poor fellow eagerly; and he told him as gently as he could of the great operation, expecting to see the patient shudder and turn faint.

"'Well,' he said, when the monk had ended, 'why don't you do it?'

"'But would you rather suffer that—would you run the risk?'

"'Am I not a man?' said the poor fellow calmly. 'Yes: life is very sweet, and I would bear any pain that I might live.'

"That settled the matter, and the monk went out of the cell to shut himself up in his own and pray for the space of two hours, and the old monks said that it was all talk, and that he had given up his horrible idea; but the prior knew better, and he was not a bit surprised to see Anselm coming out of his cell looking brave, and calm, and cool.

"Then he took a bottle of plant juice that he knew helped to stop bleeding, and he got ready his bandages, and his keenest knives, and his saw, and a bowl of water, and then he thought for a bit, and ended by asking the monks which of them would help him, but they all shrank away and turned pale, all but the prior, who said he would help, and then they went into the poor fellow's cell."

Old Brownsmith stopped here, and kept on stroking one of the cats for such a long time, beginning at the tip of his nose and going right on to the end of his tail, that I grew impatient.

"And did he perform the operation?" I said eagerly.

"Yes, bravely and well, but of course very clumsily for want of experience. He cut off the leg, Grant, right above where the bone was splintered, and all the terrible irritation was going on."

"And the poor fellow died after all?" I said.

"No, he did not, my lad; it left him terribly weak and he was very low for some days, but he began to mend from the very first, and I suppose when he grew well and strong he had to make himself a wooden leg or else to go about with a crutch. About that I know nothing. There was the poor fellow dying, and there was a gardener who knew that if the broken place were cut Nature would heal it up; for Nature likes to be helped sometimes, my boy, and she is waiting for you now."

"Yes, sir, I'll do it directly," I said, glancing at the stump I had sawn off, and thinking about the swineherd's leg, and half-wondering that it did not bleed; "but tell me, please, is all that true?"

"I'm afraid not, Grant," he said smiling; "but it is my idea—my theory about how our great surgeons gained their first knowledge from a gardener; and if it is not true, it might very well be."

"Yes," I said, looking at him wonderingly as he smoothed the fur of his cats and was surrounded by them, rubbing themselves and purring loudly, "but I did not know you could tell stories like that."

"I did not know it myself, Grant, till I began, and one word coaxed out another. Seriously, though, my boy, there is nothing to be ashamed of in being a gardener."

"I'm not ashamed," I said; "I like it."

"Gardeners can propagate and bring into use plants that may prove to be of great service to man; they can improve vegetables and fruits—and when you come to think of what a number of trees and plants are useful, you see what a field there is to work in! Why, even a man who makes a better cabbage or potato grow than we have had before is one who has been of great service to his fellow-creatures. So work away; you may do something yet."

"Yes," I cried, "I'll work away and as hard as I can; but I begin to wish now that you had some glass."

"So do I," said the old gentleman.

"There!" I said, coming down the ladder, "I think that will heal up now, like the poor swineherd's leg. It's as smooth as smooth."

"Let me look," said a voice behind me; and I started with surprise to find myself face to face with a man who seemed to be Old Brownsmith when he was, if not Young Brownsmith, just about what he would have been at forty.

Chapter Nineteen
Brother Solomon

The new-comer went slowly up the ladder, looked at my work, and then took out a small knife with a flat ivory handle, came down again, stropped the knife on his boot, went up, and pared my stump just round the edge, taking off a very thin smooth piece of bark.

"Good!" he said as he wiped his knife, came down, and put the knife away; "but your knife wanted a touch on a bit o' Turkey-stone. How are you, Ezra?"

Old Brownsmith set down some cats gently, got up off the bushel basket slowly, and shook hands.

"Fairly, Solomon, fairly; and how are you?"

"Tidy," said the visitor, "tidy;" and he stared very hard at me. "This is him, is it?"

"Yes, this is he, Solomon. Grant, my lad, this is my brother Solomon."

I bowed after the old fashion taught at home.

"Shake hands. How are you?" said Mr Solomon; and I shook hands with him and said I was quite well, I thanked him; and he said, "Hah!"

"He has just come up from Hampton, Grant—from Sir Francis Linton's. He's going to take you back."

"Take me back, sir!" I said wonderingly. "Have—have I done anything you don't like?"

"No, my lad, no—only I've taught you all I can; and now you will go with him and learn gardening under glass—to grow peaches, and grapes, and mushrooms, and all kinds of choice flowers."

I looked at him in a troubled way, and he hastened to add:

"A fine opportunity for you, my boy. Brother Solomon is a very famous gardener and takes prizes at the shows."

"Oh! as to that," said Brother Solomon, "we're not much. We do the best we can."

"Horticultural medals, gold and bronze," said Old Brownsmith, smiling. "There!—you'll have to do so as well, Grant, my lad—you will have to do me credit."

I crept close to him and half-whispered:

"But must I go, sir?"

"Yes, my lad, it is for your benefit," he said rather sternly; and I suppose I gave him such a piteous look that his face softened a little and he patted my shoulder. "Come," he said, "you must be a man!"

I seemed to have something in my throat which I was obliged to swallow; but I made an effort, and after a trial or two found that I could speak more clearly.

"Shall I have to go soon, sir?"

"Yes: now," said Old Brownsmith.

"Not till I've had a look round," said Brother Solomon in a slow meditative way, as he took out a handkerchief and wiped his hands, staring about him at the trees and bushes, and then, as a cat gave a friendly rub against his leg, he stooped down after the fashion of his brother, picked it up, and held it on his arm, stroking it all the time.

I had not liked the look of Brother Solomon, for he seemed cold, and quiet, and hard. His face looked stiff, as if he never by any chance smiled; and it appeared to me as if I were going from where I had been treated like a son to a home where I should be a stranger.

"Yes," he said after looking about him, as if he were going to find fault, "I sha'n't go back just yet awhile."

"Oh no! you'll have a snap of something first, and Grant here will want a bit of time to pack up his things."

Old Brownsmith seemed to be speaking more kindly to me now, and this made me all the more miserable, for I had felt quite at home; and though Shock and I were bad friends, and Ike was not much of a companion, I did not want to leave them.

Old Brownsmith saw my looks, and he said:

"You will run over now and then to see me and tell me how you get on. Brother Solomon here never likes to leave his glass-houses, but you can get away now and then. Eh, Solomon?"

"P'r'aps," said Brother Solomon, looking right away from us. "We shall see."

My heart sank as I saw how cold and unsympathetic he seemed. I felt that I should never like him, and that he would never like me. He had hardly looked at me, but when he did there was to me the appearance in his eyes of his being a man who hated all boys as nuisances and to make matters worse, he took his eyes off a bed of onions to turn them suddenly on his brother and say:

"Hadn't he better go and make up his bundle?"

"Yes, to be sure," said Old Brownsmith. "Go and tell Mrs Dodley you want your clean clothes, my boy; and tell her my brother Solomon's going to have a bit with us."

"And see whether your boy has given my horse his oats, will you?" said Brother Solomon.

I went away, feeling very heavy-hearted, and found Shock in the stable, in the next stall to old Basket, watching a fine stoutly-built cob that had just been taken out of a light cart. The horse's head-stall had been taken off, and a halter put on; and as he munched at his oats, Shock helped him, munching away at a few that he took from one hand.

I was in so friendly a mood to every one just then that I was about to go up and shake hands with Shock; but as soon as he saw me coming he dived under the manger, and crept through into old Basket's stall, and then thrust back his doubled fist at me, and there it was being shaken menacingly, as if he were threatening to punch my head.

This exasperated me so that in an instant the honey within me was turned to vinegar, and I made a rush round at him, startling our old horse so that he snorted and plunged; but I did not catch Shock, for he dived back through the hole under the manger into the next stall. Then on under the manger where Brother Solomon's horse was feeding, making him start back and nearly break his halter, while Shock went on into the third stall, disturbing a hen from the nest she had made in the manger, and sending her cackling and screaming out into the yard, where the cock and the other hens joined in the hubbub.

As I ran round to the third stall I was just in time to see Shock's legs disappearing, as he climbed up the perpendicular ladder against the wall, and shot through the trap-door into the hay-loft.

"You shall beg my pardon before I go," I said between my teeth, as I looked up, and there was his grubby fist coming out of the hole in the ceiling, and being shaken at me.

I rushed at the ladder, and had ascended a couple of rounds, when bang went the trap-door, and there was a bump, which I knew meant that Shock had seated himself on the trap, so that I could not get it up.

"Oh, all right!" I said aloud. "I sha'n't come after you, you dirty old grub. I'm going away to-day, and you can shake your fist at somebody else."

I had satisfied myself that Brother Solomon's horse was all right, so I now strode up to the house and told Mrs Dodley to spread the table for a visitor, and said that I should want my clean things as I was going away.

"What! for a holiday?" she said.

"No; I'm going away altogether," I said.

"I know'd it," she cried angrily; "I know'd it. I always said it would come to that with you mixing yourself up with that bye. A nasty dirty hay-and-straw-sleeping young rascal, as is more like a monkey than a bye. And now you're to be sent away."

"Yes," I said grimly; "now I'm to be sent away."

She stood frowning at me for a minute, and then took off her dirty apron and put on a clean one, with a good deal of angry snatching.

"I shall just go and give Mr Brownsmith a bit of my mind," she said. "I won't have you sent away like that, and all on account of that bye."

"No, no," I said. "I'm going away with Mr Brownsmith's brother, to learn all about hothouses I suppose."

"Oh, my dear bye!" she exclaimed. "You mustn't do that. You'll have to be stoking and poking all night long, and ketch your death o' cold, and be laid up, and be ill-used, and be away from everybody who cares for you, and and I don't want you to go."

The tears began to run down the poor homely-looking woman's face, and affected me, so that I was obliged to run out, or I should have caught her complaint.

"I must be a man over it," I said. "I suppose it's right;" and I went off down the garden to say "Good-bye" to the men and women, and have a few last words with Ike.

As I went down the garden I suddenly began to feel that for a long time past it had been my home, and that every tree I passed was an old friend. I had not known it before, but it struck me now that I had been very happy there leading a calm peaceable life; and now I was going away to fresh troubles and cares amongst strangers, and it seemed as if I should never be so happy again.

To make matters worse I was going down the path that I had traversed that day so long ago, when I first went to buy some fruit and flowers for my mother, and this brought back her illness, and the terrible trouble that had followed. Then I seemed to see myself up at the window over the wall there, at Mrs Beeton's, watching the garden, and Shock throwing dabs of clay at me with the stick.

"Poor old Shock!" I said. "I wonder whether he'll be glad when I'm gone. I suppose he will."

I was thinking about how funny it was that we had never become a bit nearer to being friendly, and then I turned miserable and choking, for I came upon half a dozen of the women pulling and bunching onions for market.

"I've come to say good-bye," I cried huskily. "I'm going away."

"Oh! are you?" said one of them just looking up. "Good luck to you!"

The coolness of the rough woman seemed to act as a check on my sentimentality, and I went on feeling quite hurt; and a few minutes later I was quite angry, for I came to where the men were digging, and told them I was going away, and one of them stopped, and stared, and said:

"All right! will yer leave us a lock of yer hair?"

I went on, and they shouted after me:

"I say, stand a gallon o' beer afore you go."

"There's nobody cares for me but poor Mrs Dodley," I said to myself in a choking voice, and then my pride gave me strength.

"Very well," I exclaimed aloud; "if they don't care, I don't, and I'm glad I'm going, and I shall be very glad when I'm gone."

That was not true, for, as I went on, I saw this tree whose pears I had picked, and that apple-tree whose beautiful rosy fruit I had put so carefully into baskets. There were the plum-trees I had learned how to prune and nail, and whose violet and golden fruit I had so often watched ripening. That was where George Day had scrambled over, and I had hung on to his legs, and there—No; I turned away from that path, for there were the two brothers slowly walking along with the cats, looking at the different crops, and I did not want to be seen then by one who was so ready to throw me over, and by the other, who seemed so cold and hard, and was, I felt, going to be a regular tyrant.

"And I'm all alone, and not even a cat to care about me," I said to myself; and, weak and miserable, the tears came into my eyes as I stopped in one of the cross paths.

I started, and dashed away a tear or two that made me feel like a girl, for just then there was a rustle, and looking round, there was one of Old Brownsmith's cats coming along the path with curved back, and tail drooped sidewise, and every hair upon it erect till it looked like a drooping plume.

The cat suddenly rushed at me, stopped short, tore round me, and then ran a little way, and crouched, as if about to make a spring upon me, ending by walking up in a very stately way to rub himself against my leg.

"Why, Ginger, old fellow," I said, "are you come to say good-bye?"

I don't think the cat understood me, but he looked up, blinked, and uttered a pathetic kind of *mew* that went to my heart, as I stooped down and lifted him up in my arms to hug him to my breast, where he nestled, purring loudly, and inserting his claws gently into my jacket, and tearing them out, as if the act was satisfactory.

He was an ugly great sandy Tom, with stripes down his sides, but he seemed to me just then to be the handsomest cat I had ever seen, and the best friend I had in the world, and I made a vow that I would ask Old Brownsmith to let me have him to take with me, if his brother would allow me to include him in my belongings.

"Will you come with me, Ginger?" I said, stroking him. The cat purred and went on, climbing up to my shoulder, where there was not much room for him, but he set his fore-paws on my shoulder, drove them into my jacket, and let his hind-legs go well down my back before he hooked on there, crouching close to me, and seeming perfectly happy as I walked on wondering where Ike was at work.

I found him at last, busy trenching some ground at the back of Shock's kitchen, as I called the shed where he cooked his potatoes and snails.

As I came up to the old fellow he glanced at me surlily, stopped digging, and began to scrape his big shining spade.

"Hullo!" he said gruffly; and the faint hope that he would be sorry died away.

"Ike," I said, "I'm going away."

"What?" he shouted.

"I'm going to leave here," I said.

"Get out, you discontented warmint!" he cried savagely, "you don't know when you're well off."

"Yes, I do," I said; "but Mr Brownsmith's going to send me away."

"What!" he roared, driving in his spade, and beginning to dig with all his might.

"Mr Brownsmith's going to send me away."

"Old Brownsmith's going to send you away?"

"Yes."

"Why, what have you been a-doin' of?" he cried more fiercely than ever, as he drove his spade into the earth.

"Nothing at all."

"He wouldn't send you away for doing nothing at all," cried Ike, giving an obstinate clod that he had turned up a tremendous blow with his spade, and turning it into soft mould.

"I'm to go to Hampton with Mr Brownsmith's brother," I said, "to learn all about glass-houses."

"What, Old Brownsmith's brother Sol?"

"Yes," I said sadly, as I petted and caressed the cat.

"He's a tartar and a tyrant, that's what he is," said Ike fiercely, and he drove in his spade as if he meant to reach Australia.

"But he understands glass," I said.

"Smash his glass!" growled Ike, digging away like a machine.

"I'm going to-day," I said after a pause, and with all a boy's longing for a sympathetic word or two.

"Oh! are you?" he said sulkily.

"Yes, and I don't know when I shall get over here again."

"Course you don't," growled Ike, smashing another clod. I stood patting the cat, hoping that Ike would stretch out his great rough hand to me to say "Good-bye;" but he went on digging, as if he were very cross.

"I didn't know it till to-day, Ike," I said.

"Ho!" said Ike with a snap, and he bent down to chop an enormous earthworm in two, but instead of doing so he gave it a flip with the corner of his spade, and sent it flying up into a pear-tree, where I saw it hanging across a twig till it writhed itself over, when, one end of its long body being heavier than the other, it dropped back on to the soft earth with a slight pat.

Still Ike did not speak, and all at once I heard Old Brownsmith's voice calling.

"I must go now, Ike," I said, "I'll come back and say 'Good-bye.'"

"And after the way as I've tried to make a man of yer," he said as if talking to his mother earth, which he was chopping so remorselessly.

"It isn't my fault, Ike," I said. "I'll come over and see you again as soon as I can."

"Who said it war your fault?"

"No one, Ike," I said humbly. "Don't be cross with me."

"Who is cross with yer?" cried Ike, cleaning his spade.

"You seemed to be."

"Hah!"

"I will come and see you again as soon as I can," I repeated.

"Nobody don't want you," he growled.

"Grant!"

"Coming, sir," I shouted back, and then I turned to Ike, who dug away as hard as ever he could, without looking at me, and with a sigh I hurried off, feeling that I must have been behaving very ungratefully to him. Then there was a sense as of resentment as I thought of how calmly everybody seemed to take my departure, making me think that I had done nothing to win people's liking, and that I must be a very unpleasant, disagreeable kind of lad, since, with the exception of Mrs Dodley and the cat, nobody seemed to care whether I went away or stayed.

Chapter Twenty
A Cold Start in a New Life

Brother Solomon loitered about the garden with Old Brownsmith, and it was not until we had had an early tea that I had to fetch down my little box to put in the cart, which was standing in the yard with Shock holding the horse, and teasing it by thrusting a barley straw in its nostrils and ears.

As I came down with the box, Mrs Dodley said "Good-bye" very warmly and wetly on my face, giving as she said:

"Mind you send me all your stockings and shirts and I'll always put them right for you, my dear, and Goodbye."

She hurried away, and as soon as my box was in the cart I ran down the garden to say "Good-bye" to Ike; but he had gone home, so I was told, and I came back disappointed.

"Good-bye, Shock!" I said, holding out my hand; but he did not take it, only stared at me stolidly, just as if he hated me and was glad I was going; and this nettled me so that I did not mind his sulkiness, and drawing myself up, I tried hard to smile and look as if I didn't care a bit.

Brother Solomon came slowly towards the cart, rolling the stalk of a rosebud in his mouth, and as he took the reins he said to one of the chimneys at the top of the house:

"If I was you, Ez, I'd plant a good big bit with that winter lettuce. You'll find 'em go off well."

I knew now that he was talking to his brother, but he certainly seemed to be addressing himself to the chimney-pot.

"I will, Sol, a whole rood of 'em," said Old Brownsmith, "and thank ye for the advice."

"Quite welkim," said Brother Solomon to the horse's ears. "Jump up."

He seemed to say this to Shock, who stared at him, wrinkled up his face, and shook his head.

"Yes, jump up, Grant, my lad," said Old Brownsmith. "Fine evening for your drive."

"Yes, sir," I said, "good-bye; and say good-bye to Ike for me, will you, please?"

"Yes, to be sure, good-bye; God bless you, lad; and do your best."

And I was so firm and hard just before, thinking no one cared for me, that I was ready to smile as I went away.

That "God bless you!" did it, and that firm pressure of the hand. He did like me, then, and was sorry I was going; and though I tried to speak, not a word would come. I could only pinch my lips together and give him an agonised look—the look of an orphan boy going off into what was to him an unknown world.

I was so blinded by a kind of mist in my eyes that I could not distinctly see that all the men and women were gathered together close to the cart, it being near leaving time; but I did see that Brother Solomon nodded at one of the gate-posts, as he said:

"Tlck! go on."

And then, as the wheels turned and we were going out of the gate, there was a hoarse "*Hooroar!*" from the men, and a shrill "*Hurray!*" from the women; and then—*whack!*

A great stone had hit the panel at the back of the cart, and I knew without telling that it was Shock who had thrown that stone.

Then we were fairly off, with Brother Solomon sitting straight up in the cart beside me, and the horse throwing out his legs in a great swinging trot that soon carried us past the walls of Old Brownsmith's garden, and past the hedges into the main road, on a glorious evening that had succeeded the storm of the previous night; but, fast as the horse went, Brother Solomon did not seem satisfied, for he kept on screwing up his lips and making a noise, like a young thrush just out of the nest, to hurry the horse on, but it had not the slightest effect, for the animal had its own pace—a very quick one, and kept to it.

I never remember the lane to have looked so beautiful before. The great elm-trees in the hedgerow seemed gilded by the sinking sun, and the fields were of a glorious green, while a flock of rooks, startled by the horse's hoofs, flew off with a loud cawing noise, and I could see the purply black feathers on their backs glisten as they caught the light.

The wheels spun round and seemed to form a kind of tune that had something to do with my going away, while as the horse trotted on and on, uttering a snort at times as if glad to be homeward bound, my heart seemed to sink lower and lower, and I looked in vain for a sympathetic glance or a word of encouragement and comfort from the silent stolid man at my side.

"But some of them were sorry I was going!" I thought with a flash of joy, which went away at once as I recalled the behaviour of Ike and Shock, towards whom I felt something like resentment, till I thought again that I was for the second time going away from home, and this time among people who were all as strange as strange could be.

At any other time it would have been a pleasant evening drive, but certainly one wanted a different driver, for whether it was our crops at Old Brownsmith's, or the idea that he had undertaken a great responsibility in taking charge of me, or whether at any moment he anticipated meeting with an accident, I don't know. All I do know is that Mr Solomon did not speak to me once, but sat rolling the flower-stalk in his mouth, and staring right before him, aiming straight at some place or another that was going to be my prison, and all the while the sturdy horse trotted fast, the wheels spun round, and there was a disposition on the part of my box to hop and slide about on the great knot in the centre made by the cord.

Fields and hedgerows, and gentlemen's residences with lawns and gardens, first on one side and then on another, but they only suggested hiding-places to me as I sat there wondering what would be the consequences if I were to slip over the back of the seat on to my box when Mr Solomon was not looking, and then over the back of the cart and escape.

The idea was too childish, but it kept coming again and again all through that dismal journey.

All at once, after an hour's drive, I caught sight of a great white house among some trees, and as we passed it Mr Solomon slowly turned round to me and gave his head a jerk, which nearly shook off his hat. Then he poked it back straight with the handle of his whip, and I wondered what he meant; but realised directly after that he wished to draw my attention to that house as being probably the one to which we were bound, for a few minutes later, after driving some distance by a high blank wall, he stuck the whip behind him, and the horse stopped of its own accord with its nose close to some great closed gates.

On either side of these was a brick pillar, with what looked like an enormous stone egg in an egg-cup on the top, while on the right-hand pillar there was painted a square white patch, in the centre of which was a black knob looking out of it like an eye.

I quite started, so wrapped was I in thought, when Mr Solomon spoke for the first time in a sharp decided way.

"Pop out and pull that bell," he said, looking at it as if he wondered whether it would ring without being touched.

I hurriedly got down and pulled the knob, feeling ashamed the next moment for my act seemed to have awakened the sleepy place. There was a tremendous jangling of a great angry-voiced bell which sounded hollow and echoing all over the place; there was the rattling of chains, as half a dozen dogs seemed to have rushed out of their kennels, and they began baying furiously, with the result that the horse threw up his head and uttered a loud neigh. Then there was a trampling, as of some one in very heavy nailed boots over a paved yard, and after the rattling of bolts, the clang of a great iron bar, and the sharp click of a big lock, a sour-looking man drew back first one gate and then the other, each fold uttering a dissatisfied creak as if disliking to be disturbed.

The horse wanted no driving, but walked right into the yard and across to a large open shed, while five dogs—there were not six—barked and bayed at me, tugging at their chains. There was a large Newfoundland— this was before the days of Saint Bernards—a couple of spotted coach-dogs, a great hound of some kind with shortly cropped ears, and looking like a terrier grown out of knowledge, and a curly black retriever, each of which had a great green kennel, and they tugged so furiously at their chains that it seemed as if they would drag their houses across the yard in an attack upon the stranger.

"Get out!" shouted Mr Solomon as the sour-looking man closed and fastened the doors; but the dogs barked the more furiously. "Here, come along," said Mr Solomon to me, and he took me up to the great furious-looking hound on whose neck, as I approached, I could see a brass collar studded with spikes, while as we closed up, his white teeth glistened, and I could see right into his great red mouth with its black gums.

"Hi, Nero!" cried Mr Solomon, as I began to feel extremely nervous. "Steady, boy. This is Grant. Now, Grant, make friends."

There was a tremendous chorus of barks here, just as if Nero was out of patience, and the other four dogs were savage because he was going to be fed with the new boy before them; but as Mr Solomon laid his hand on the great fierce-looking beast's head it ceased barking, and the others stopped as well.

"He won't hurt you now," said Mr Solomon. "Come close."

I did not like the task, for I was doubtful of the gardener's knowledge, but I did go close up, and the great dog began to smell me from my toes upwards, and subsided into a low growl that sounded like disappointment that he was not to eat me.

"Pat him now," said Mr Solomon.

I obeyed rather nervously, and the great dog threw up his head and began striking at me with one great paw, which I found meant that it was to be taken, and I gave it a friendly shake.

Hereupon there was a chorus of short sharp whining barks and snaps from the other dogs, all of which began to strain at their chains with renewed vigour.

"Go and pat 'em all," said Mr Solomon; "they'll make friends now."

I went to the great shaggy Newfoundland, who smelt me, and then threw himself up on his hind legs, and hanging against his chain put out his tongue in the most rollicking fashion, and offered me both his hands—I mean paws—in token of friendship. Then the retriever literally danced, and yelped, and jumped over his chain, favouring me with a lick or two on the hand, while the two spotted coach-dogs cowered down, licked my boots, and yelped as I patted them in turn.

Only so many dogs, who barked again as I left them, but it seemed to do me good, and I felt better and readier to help Mr Solomon when he called me to aid in unharnessing the horse, which trotted of its own free-will into its stable, while we ran the cart back into the shed, and lifted my box out on to the stones.

"That'll be all right till we fetch it," said Mr Solomon in his quiet dry way, and he led the way into the stable, where, as I was thinking how hard and unfriendly he seemed, he went up to the horse, patted it kindly, and ended by going to a bin, filling a large measure with oats; and taking them to the horse, which gave a snort of satisfaction as they were turned into its manger.

"Shall I get a pail of water for him, sir?" I said.

He looked at me and nodded, and I went out to a great pump in the middle of the yard with a hook on its spout, upon which I was able to hang the stable pail as I worked hard to throw the long handle up and down.

"Wages!" said Mr Solomon, taking the pail from me and holding it for the horse to drink.

For the moment I felt confused, not knowing whether he meant that as a question about what wages I required, but he turned his back, and by degrees I found that he meant that the corn and water were the horse's wages.

He busied himself about the horse for some minutes in a quiet punctilious way, for the sour-looking man had gone, and as I waited about, the great yard seemed with its big wall and gates, and dog-kennels, such a cold cheerless place that the trees had all turned the shabby parts of their backs to it and were looking the other way. Everything was very prim and clean and freshly painted, and only in one place could I see some short grass peeping between the stones. There was a patch of moss, too, like a dark green velvet pin-cushion on the top of the little penthouse where the big bell lived on the end of a great curly spring, otherwise everything was carefully painted, and the row of stabling buildings with rooms over looked like prisons for horses and their warders, who must, I felt, live very unhappy lives.

There was one door up in a corner of the great yard, right in the wall, and down towards this, from where it had grown on the other side, there hung a few strands of ivy in a very untidy fashion, and it struck me that this ivy did not belong to the yard, or else it would have been clipped or cut away.

In summer, with the warm glow of the setting sun in the sky, the place looked shivery and depressing, and as I waited for Mr Solomon I found myself thinking what a place it must be in the winter when the snow had fallen and drifted into the corners, and how miserable the poor dogs must be.

Then as I stood looking at my box and wondering what Shock was doing, and whether he had gone to his home or was sleeping in the loft, and why Ike was so surly to me, and what a miserable piece of business it was that I should have to leave that pleasant old garden and Old Brownsmith, I suddenly felt a hand laid upon my shoulder.

I started and stared as I saw Mr Solomon's cold, stern face.

"Come along," he said; and he led the way to that door in the corner that seemed to me as if it led into an inner prison.

I shivered and felt depressed and cold as we went towards the door, and, to make matters worse, the dogs rattled their chains and howled in chorus as if, having made friends, they were very sorry for me. The big hound, Nero, seemed the most sorrowful of all, and putting his head as high as he could reach he uttered a deep hollow howl, that to my excited fancy sounded like "Poooooor boooooy!" just as Mr Solomon, with a face as stern as an executioner's might have been as he led someone to the Tower block, threw open the great door in the wall and said shortly:

"Go on!"

I went on before him, passed through in a wretched, despairing way, wishing I had been a boy like Shock, who was not ashamed to run away, and then, as I took a few steps forward, I uttered a loud "Oh!"

Chapter Twenty One
I Look Round

My ejaculation made Mr Solomon look completely changed, for, as I glanced back at him, I could see that there was a twinkle in his eyes and a little dent or two about the corners of his lips, but as he saw me looking wonderingly at him he became cold and stern of aspect again.

"Well," he said shortly, "will that do?"

"Do, sir!" I cried excitedly; "is this your garden?"

"Master's," he said, shortly.

"Your master's garden?"

"And your master's, too," he said. "Well, will it do?"

"Do!" I cried; "it's lovely. I never saw such a beautiful garden in my life. What a lawn! what paths! what flowers!"

"What a lot o' work, eh? What a lot to do?"

"Yes," I said; "but what a place!"

After that cold cheerless yard I seemed to have stepped into a perfect paradise of flowers and ornamental evergreens. A lawn like green velvet led up to a vast, closely-clipped yew hedge, and down to a glistening pool, full of great broad lily leaves, and with the silver cups floating on the golden surface, for the water reflected the tints in the skies. Here and there were grey-looking statues in nooks among the evergreens, and the great beauty of all to me was that there was no regularity about the place; it was all up and down, and fresh beauties struck the eye at every glance. Paths wandered here and there, great clumps of ornamental trees hid other clumps, and patches of soft velvet turf were everywhere showing up beds in which were masses of flowers of every hue. There were cedars, too, that seemed to be laying their great broad boughs upon the grass in utter weariness—they were so heavy and thick; slopes that were masses of rhododendrons, and when I had feasted my eyes for a time on one part Mr Solomon led me on in his serious way to another, where fresh points of beauty struck the eye.

"It's lovely," I cried. "Oh! Mr Solomon, what a garden!"

"Mr Brownsmith, not Mr Solomon," he said rather gruffly; and I apologised and remembered; but I must go on calling him Mr Solomon to distinguish him from my older friend.

"I never saw such a place," I added; "and it's kept so well."

"Tidyish—pretty tidy," he said coldly. "Not enough hands. Only nine and me—and you—but we do our best."

"Why, it's perfection!" I cried.

"No it ain't," he said gruffly. "Too much glass. Takes a deal o' time. I shall make you a glass boy mostly."

"Make me—a what, sir?"

"Glass boy. You'll see."

I said "Oh," and began to understand.

"Was it like this when you came?" I said.

I was very glad I said it, for Mr Solomon's mouth twitched, then his eyes closed, and there were pleasant wrinkles all over his face, while he shook himself all over, and made a sound, or series of sounds, as if he were trying to bray like a donkey. I thought he was at first, but it was his way of laughing, and he pulled himself up short directly and looked quite severe as he smoothed the wrinkles out of his face as if it were a bed, and he had been using a rake.

"Not a bit," he said. "Twenty years ago. Bit of garden to the house with the big trees and cedars. All the rest fields and a great up-and-down gravel pit."

"And you made it like this?" I cried with animation.

He nodded.

"Like it?" he asked.

"Like it!" I cried. "Oh!"

"Come along," he said. "This is the ornamental. Useful along here."

I followed him down a curving path, and at a turn he gave his head a jerk over his right shoulder.

"House!" he said.

I looked in the indicated direction, and could see the very handsome long, low, white house, with a broad green verandah in the front, and a great range of conservatories at one end, whose glass glistened in the evening light. The house stood on a kind of terrace, and lawn, and patches of flowers and shrubs sloped away from it down into quite a dell.

"Old gravel, pits," said Mr Solomon, noticing the way I gazed about the place. "Come along."

He walked up to a great thick yew hedge with an archway of deep green in it, and as soon as we were through he said shortly:

"Useful."

I stared with wonder, for though I was now in a fruit and vegetable garden it was wonderfully different to Old Brownsmith's, for here, in addition to exquisite neatness, there was some attempt at ornamentation. As soon as we had passed under the green arch we were on a great grass walk, beautifully soft and velvety, with here and there stone seats, and a group of stone figures at the farther end. Right and left were abundance of old-fashioned flowers, but in addition there were neatly trained and trimmed fruit-trees by the hundred, not allowed to grow high like ours, but tied down as espaliers, and full of the promise of fruit.

Away right and left I could see great red brick walls covered with more fruit-trees spread out like fans, or with one big stem going straight up and the branches trained right and left in straight lines.

Everywhere the garden was a scene of abundance: great asparagus beds, trim and well-kept rows of peas laden with pods, scarlet-runners running at a tremendous rate up sticks; and lower down, quite an orchard of big pyramid pear and apple trees.

"Like it?" said Mr Solomon, watching me narrowly.

"I can't tell you how much, sir!" I cried excitedly. "I never thought to see such a garden as this."

"Ain't half seen it yet," he replied. "Come and see the glass."

He led me towards where I could see ranges of glass houses, looking white and shining amongst the trees, and as we went on he pointed to different plots of vegetables and other objects of interest.

"Pump and well," he said. "Deep. 'Nother at the bottom. Dry in summer; plenty in the pools. Frames and pits yonder. Nobody at home but the young gents. Wish they weren't," he added in a growl. "Limbs, both of them. Like to know where you are to live?" he said.

"Yes, sir. Is it at the house?"

"No. Yonder."

He pointed to a low cottage covered with a large wisteria, and built almost in the middle of the great fruit and vegetable garden, while between it and the great yew hedge lay the range of glass houses.

"You can find your way?"

"Yes, sir," I said, feeling damped again by his cold manner. "Are you going?"

"Yes, now."

"Shall I fetch my box, sir?"

"No; I told Tom to take it to the cottage. You would like to look round and see where you'll work? Don't want to begin to-night, eh?"

"Yes, sir, I'm ready, if you like," I said.

"Humph!" he ejaculated. "Well, perhaps we'll go and look at the fires by and by. You're my apprentice now, you know."

"Am I, sir?"

"Yes; didn't Brother Ezra tell you?"

I shook my head.

"Don't matter. Come to learn glass. There's the houses; go and look round. I'll call you when supper's ready."

I don't know whether I felt in good spirits or bad; but soon ceased to think of everything but what I was seeing, as, being about to become a glass boy, I entered one of the great hothouses belonging to the large range of glass buildings.

A warm sweet-scented puff of air saluted me as I raised the copper latch of the door, and found myself in a great red-tiled vinery, with long canes trained from the rich soil at the roots straight up to the very ridge, while, with wonderful regularity, large bunches like inverted cones of great black grapes hung suspended from the tied-in twigs. There were rows of black iron pipes along the sides from which rose a soft heat, and the effect of this was visible in the rich juicy-looking berries covered with a pearly bloom, while from succulent shoot, leaf, and tendril rose the delicious scent that had saluted me as soon as I entered the place.

From this glass palace of a house, as it seemed to me, I went down into a far hotter place, where the walls were whitewashed and the glass roof very low. There was a peculiar odour of tan here, and as I closed the door after me the atmosphere felt hot and steamy.

But the sight that greeted my eyes made me forget all other sensations, for there all along the centre were what seemed to be beautiful, luxuriant aloes; and as I thought of the old story that they bloomed only once in a hundred years, I began to wonder how long it was since one of these spiky-leaved plants had blossomed, and then I cried excitedly:

"Pine-apples!"

True enough they were, for I had entered a large pinery where fruits were ripening and others coming on in the most beautiful manner, while what struck me most was the perfection and neatness of all the place.

Then I found myself in another grape-house where the vines bore oval white grapes, with a label to tell that they were Muscats. Then I went on into a long low house full of figs—small dumpy fig-trees in pots, with a peculiar odour rising from them through the hot moist air.

Again I was in a long low place something like the pinery, and here I was amongst melons—large netted-skinned melons of all sizes, some being quite huge, and apparently ready to cut.

I could have stayed in these various houses for hours, but I was anxious to see all I could, and I passed on over the red-tiled floor to a door which opened at once into the largest and most spacious house I had seen.

Here the air was comparatively cool, and there was quite a soft breeze from the open windows as I walked along between little trees that formed a complete grove, with cross paths and side walks, and every long leaf looking dark and clear and healthy.

I could not keep back an exclamation of delight as I stopped in one of the paths of this beautiful little grove; for all about me the trees were laden with fruit in a way that set me thinking of the garden traversed by Aladdin when in search of the wonderful lamp.

I was in no magic cave, it is true, but I was in a sort of crystal palace of great extent, with here and there beautiful creepers running along rods up the sides and across close to the roof, while my trees were not laden with what looked like bits of coloured glass, but the loveliest of fruit, some smooth and of rich, deep, fiery crimson; others yellowish or with russet gold on their smooth skins, while others again were larger and covered with a fine down, upon which lay a rich soft carmine flush.

I had seen peaches and nectarines growing before, trained up against walls; but here they were studded about beautiful little unsupported trees, and their numbers and the novelty of the sight were to me delightful.

I began to understand now why Old Brownsmith had arranged with his brother for me to come; and, full of visions of the future and of how I was going to learn how to grow fruit in this perfection, I stopped, gazing here and there at the ripe and ripening peaches, that looked so beautiful that I thought it would be a sin for them to be picked.

In fact, I had been so long amongst fruit that, though I liked it, I found so much pleasure in its production that I rarely thought of eating any, and though this sounds a strange thing for a boy to say, it is none the less perfectly true. In fact, as a rule, gardeners rather grudge themselves a taste of their own delicacies.

I must have been in this house a full quarter of an hour, and had only seen one end, and I had turned into a cross walk of red tiles looking to right and left, when, just beyond the stem of one peach-tree whose fruit was ripening and had ripened fast, I saw just as it had fallen one great juicy peach with a bruise on its side, and a crack through which its delicious essence was escaping. Pale creamy was the downy skin, with a bloom of softest crimson on the side beyond the bruise and crack, and making a soft hissing noise as I drew in my breath—a noise that I meant to express, "Oh, what a pity!"—I stooped down and reached over to pick up the damaged fruit, and to lay it upon one of the open shelves where I had seen a couple more already placed.

I heard no step, had seen no one in the place, but just as I leaned over to get the fruit there was a swishing sound as of something parting the air with great swiftness, and I uttered a cry of pain, for I felt a sensation as if a sharp knife had suddenly fallen upon my back, and that knife was red hot, and, after it had divided it, had seared the flesh.

I had taken the peach in my hand when the pain made me involuntarily crush it before it fell from my fingers upon the rich earth; and, grinding my teeth with rage and agony, I started round to face whoever it was that had struck me so cruel a blow.

Chapter Twenty Two
Master Philip

"What! I caught you then, did I?" cried a sharp unpleasant voice. "Just dropped upon you, did I, my fine fellow? You scoundrel, how dare you steal our peaches!"

The speaker was a boy of somewhere about my own age, and as I faced him I saw that he was thin, and had black hair, a yellowish skin, and dark eyes. He was showing his rather irregular teeth in a sneering smile that made his hooked nose seem to hang over his mouth, while his high-pitched, harsh, girlish voice rang and buzzed in my ears in a discordant way.

I did not answer; I felt as if I could not speak. All I wanted to do was to fly at him and strike out wildly, while something seemed to hold me back as he stood vapouring before me, swishing about the thin, black, silver-handled cane he carried, and at every swish he cut some leaf or twig.

"How dare you strike me?" I cried at last furiously, and I advanced with my teeth set and my lists clenched, forgetting my position there, and not even troubling myself in my hot passion to wonder who or what this boy might be.

"How dare I, you ugly-looking dog!" he cried, retreating before me a step or two. "I'll soon let you know that. Who are you, you thief?"

"I'm not a thief," I shouted, wincing still with the pain.

"Yes, you are," he cried. "How did you get in here? I've caught you, though, and we shall know now where our fruit goes when we get the blame. Here, out you come."

The boy caught me by the collar, and I seized him by the arms with a fierce, vindictive feeling coming over me; but he was very light and active, and, wresting himself partly free, he gave the cane a swing in the air, raised it above his head, and struck at me with all his might.

I hardly know how it all occurred in the hurry and excitement, but I know that I gave myself a wrench round, driving him back as I did so, and making a grasp at the cane with the full intention of getting it from him and thrashing him as hard as I could in return for his blow.

He missed his aim: I missed mine. My hand did not go near the cane; the cane did not come down as he intended upon my back, but with a fierce swish struck the branch of one of the peaches, breaking it so that it hung by the bark and a few fibres, while three or four of the ripe fruit fell with heavy thuds upon the ground.

"There, now you've done it, you young rough!" he cried viciously. "Come out."

His dark eyes glowed, and he showed his white teeth as he struck at me again and again; but I avoided the blows as I wrestled with him, and at last my sturdy strength, helped by the work I had had in Old Brownsmith's garden, told, and I got hold of the cane, forced open his hand, and wrested it away.

I remember very well the triumphant feeling that came over me as I raised the cane and was in the act of bringing it down with all my might, when there was a strong hand from behind upon my shoulder, and another caught my arm, ran down it to the wrist and hand, wrested the cane away, and swung me round.

It was Mr Solomon, looking very red in the face, and frowning at me severely.

"What are you doing?" he cried. "Do you know who that is?"

"He struck me with the cane."

"He was stealing peaches."

"I was not; I was picking one up."

"He was stealing them. Just look what he has done."

"I did not do it, Mr Solomon," I cried. "It was he."

"Oh, what a cracker, Brownie! I came and caught him at it; and because I said he was a thief he hit at me with that cane."

"How did he get the cane? Why, it's yours," said Mr Solomon; "and I believe you broke that young peach."

"Get out! It was he. Take him to the police. I caught him at it."

Mr Solomon stooped and picked up the bruised and fallen peaches, laid them on a shelf, and then took out his knife and cut away the broken bough neatly.

Then he stood and looked at it for a moment, and the sight of the damage roused up a feeling of anger in him, for he turned sharply.

"Here, you be off!" he said, advancing on the boy with the cane under his arm.

For answer the boy snatched the cane away. "What do you say?" he cried haughtily.

"I say you be off out of my glass-houses, Master Philip. I won't have you here, and so I tell you."

"How dare you talk to me like that?" cried the boy.

"Dare! I'll dare a deal more than that, young fellow, if you are not off," cried Mr Solomon, who was a great deal more excited and animated than I should have imagined possible. "I'm not going to have my fruit spoiled like this."

"Your fruit indeed! I like that," cried the boy. "Yours?"

"See what you've done to my Royal George!"

"See what I've done to your Royal George!"—mockingly.

"Now be off," cried Mr Solomon. "Serves me right for not keeping the houses locked up. Now, then, you be off out."

"Sha'n't," said the boy. "I shall stop here as long as I like. You touch me if you dare. If you do I'll tell papa."

"I shall tell him myself, my lad," cried Mr Solomon.

"You forget who I am," cried the boy.

"I don't know anything about who you are when my show of fruit's being spoiled," replied Mr Solomon. "A mischievous boy's a boy doing mischief to me when I catch him, and I won't have him here."

"Turn him out, then," cried the boy; "turn out that rough young blackguard. I came in and caught him picking and stealing, and I gave him such a one."

He switched his cane as he spoke, and looked at me so maliciously that I took a step forward, but Mr Solomon caught me sharply by the shoulder and uttered a low warning growl.

"I don't believe he was stealing the fruit," said Mr Solomon slowly. "He has got a good character, Master Philip, and that's what you haven't been able to show."

"If you talk to me like that I'll tell papa everything, and have you discharged."

"Do!" said Mr Solomon.

"And I'll tell papa that you are always having in your friends, and showing 'em round the garden. What's that beggar doing in our hothouses?"

"I'm not a beggar," I cried hotly.

"Hold your tongue, Grant," said Mr Solomon in a low growl as he trimmed off a broken twig that had escaped him at first.

"It was lucky I came in," continued the boy, looking at me tauntingly. "If I hadn't come I don't know how many he wouldn't have had."

"Mr Brownsmith," I said, as I smarted with pain, rage, and the desire to get hold of that cane once more, and use it, "I found a peach lying on the ground, and I was going to pick it up."

"And eat it?" said the gardener without looking at me.

"Eat it! No," I said hotly, "I can go amongst fruit without wanting to eat it like a little child."

I looked at him indignantly, for he seemed to be suspecting me, he was so cold and hard, and distant in his manner.

"Mr Brownsmith always trusted me amongst his fruit," I said angrily.

"Humph!" said Mr Solomon, "and so you weren't going to eat the peach?"

"He was; I saw him. It was close up to his mouth."

"It is not true," I cried.

"He isn't fit to be trusted in here, and I shall tell papa how I saved the peaches. He won't like it when he hears."

"I won't stop a day in the place," I said to myself in the heat of my indignation, for Mr Solomon seemed to be doubting me, and I felt as if I couldn't bear to be suspected of being a thief.

My attention was taken from myself to the boy and Mr Solomon the next moment, for there was a scene.

"Now," said Mr Solomon, "I want to lock up this house, young gentleman, so out you go."

"You can come when I've done," said the boy, poking at first one fruit and then another with the cane, as he strutted about. "I'm not going yet."

He was in the act of touching a ripe nectarine when Mr Solomon looked as if he could bear it no longer, and he snatched the cane away.

"Here, you give me my cane," cried the boy. "You be off out, sir."

"Sha'n't!"

"Will you go?"

"No. Don't you push me!"

"Walk out then."

"Sha'n't. It's our place, and I sha'n't go for you."

"Will you go out quietly?"

"No, I shall stop as long as I like."

"Once more, Master Philip, will you go?"

"No!" yelled the boy; "and you give me back my cane."

"Will you go, sir? Once more."

"Send that beggar away, and not me," cried the boy.

"I shall stop till I choose to go, and I shall pick the peaches if I like."

Mr Solomon looked down at him aghast for a few moments, and then, as the boy made a snatch at his cane, he caught him up, tucked him under his arm, and carried him out, kicking and struggling with all his might.

I followed close behind, thoroughly enjoying the discomfiture of my enemy, and was the better satisfied for seeing the boy thrown down pretty heavily upon a heap of mowings of the lawn.

"I'll pay you for this," cried the boy, who had recovered his cane; and, giving it a swish through the air, he raised it as if about to strike Mr Solomon across the face.

I saw Mr Solomon colour up of a deeper red as he looked at the boy very hard; and then he said softly, but in a curious hissing way:

"I shouldn't advise you to do that, young sir. If you did I might forget you were Sir Francis' boy, and take and pitch you into the gold-fish pond. I feel just as if I should like to do it without."

The boy quailed before his stern look, and uttered a nasty sniggering laugh.

"I can get in any of the houses when I like, and I can take the fruit when I like, and I'll let papa know about your beggars of friends meddling with the peaches."

"There, you be off," said the gardener. "I'll tell Sir Francis too, as sure as my name's Brownsmith."

"Ha—ha—ha! There's a name!" cried the boy jeeringly. "Brownsmith. What a name for a cabbage-builder, who pretends to be a gardener, and is only an old woman about the place! Roberts's gardener is worth a hundred

Sol Brownsmiths. He grows finer fruit and better flowers, and you'll soon be kicked out. Perhaps papa will send you away now."

Mr Solomon bit his lips as he locked the door, for he was touched in a tender place, for, as I found out afterwards, he was very jealous of the success of General Roberts's gardener.

His back was turned, and, taking advantage of this, the boy made a dash at me with his cane.

This was too much in my frame of mind, and I went at him, when the head gardener turned sharply and stood between us.

"That'll do," he cried sternly to us both.

"All right!" said the boy in a cool disdainful manner. "I'll watch for him, and if ever he comes in our garden again I'll let him know. I'll pay the beggar out. He is a beggar, isn't he, old Solomon?"

"Well, if I was asked which of you was the young gentleman, and which the ill-bred young beggar, I should be able to say pretty right," replied the gardener slowly.

"Oh! should you? Well, don't you bring him here again, or I'll let him know."

"You'd better let him know now, boy, for he's going to stop."

"What's he, the new boy?" said the lad, as if asking a very innocent question. "Where did you get him, Brownsmith? Is he out of the workhouse?"

Mr Solomon smiled at the boy's malice, but he saw me wince, and he drew me to his side in an instant. I had been thinking what a cold, hard man he was, and how different to his brother, who had been quite fatherly to me of late; but I found out now that he was, under his stern outward seeming, as good-hearted as Old Brownsmith himself.

He did not speak, but he laid one hand upon my shoulder and pressed it, and that hand seemed to say to me:

"Don't take any notice of the little-minded, contemptible, spoiled cub;" and I drew a deep breath and began to feel that perhaps after all I should not want to go away.

"I thought so," cried the boy with a snigger—"he's a pauper then. Ha, ha, ha! a pauper! I'll tell Courtenay. We'll call him pauper if he stops here."

"And that's just what he is going to do, Master Philip," said the head gardener, who seemed to have recovered his temper; "and that's what, thank goodness, you are not going to do. And the sooner you are off back to school to be licked into shape the better for you, that is if ever you expect to grow into a man. Come along, my lad, it's getting late."

"Yes, take him away," shouted the boy as I went off with Mr Solomon, my blood seeming to tingle in my veins as I heard a jeering burst of laughter behind me, and directly after the boy shouted:

"Here, hi! Courtenay. Here's a game. We've got a new pauper in the place."

Mr Solomon heard it, but he said nothing as we went on, while I felt very low-spirited again, and was thinking whether I had not better give up learning how to grow fruit and go back to Old Brownsmith, and Ike, and Shock, and Mrs Dodley, when my new guide said to me kindly:

"Don't you take any notice of them, my lad."

"Them?" I said in dismay.

"Yes, there's a pair of 'em—nice pair too. But they're often away at school, and Sir Francis is a thorough gentleman. They're not his boys, but her ladyship's, and she has spoiled 'em, I suppose. Let 'em grow wild, Grant. I say, my lad," he continued, looking at me with a droll twinkle in his eye, "they want us to train them, and prune them, and take off some of their straggling growths, eh? I think we could make a difference in them, don't you?"

I smiled and nodded.

"Only schoolboys. Say anything, but it won't hurt us. Here we are. Come in."

He led the way into a plainly furnished room, where everything seemed to have been scoured till it glistened or turned white; and standing by a table, over which the supper cloth had been spread, was a tall, quiet-looking, elderly woman, with her greyish hair very smoothly stroked down on either side of her rather severe face.

"This is young Grant," said Mr Solomon.

The woman nodded, and looked me all over, and it seemed as if she took more notice of my shirt and collar than she did of me.

"Sit down, Grant, you must be hungry," said Mr Solomon; and as soon as we were seated the woman, who, I supposed, was Mrs Solomon, began to cut us both some cold bacon and some bread.

"Master Philip been at you long?" said Mr Solomon, with his mouth full.

"No, sir," I said; "it all happened in a moment or two."

"I'm glad you didn't hit him," he said. "Eat away, my lad."

The woman kept on cutting bread, but she was evidently listening intently.

"I'm glad now, sir," I said; "but he hurt me so, and I was in such a passion that I didn't think. I didn't know who he was."

"Of course not. Go on with your supper."

"I hope, sir, you don't think I was going to eat that peach," I said, for the thought of the affair made my supper seem to choke me.

"If I thought you were the sort of boy who couldn't be trusted, my lad, you wouldn't be here," said Mr Solomon quietly. "Bit more fat, mother."

I brightened up, and he saw it.

"Why, of course not, my lad. Didn't I trust you, and send you in among my choice grapes, and ripe figs, and things. There, say no more about it. Gardeners don't grow fruit to satisfy their mouths, but their eyes, and their minds, my lad. Eat away. Don't let a squabble with a schoolboy who hasn't learned manners spoil your supper. We've never had any children; but if we had, Grant, I don't think they would be like that."

"They make me miserable when they are at home," said Mrs Solomon, speaking almost for the first time.

"Don't see why they should," said Mr Solomon, with his voice sounding as if his tongue were a little mixed up with his supper. "Why, they don't come here."

"They might be made such different boys if properly trained."

"They'll come right by and by, but for the present, Grant, you steer clear of them. They're just like a couple of young slugs, or so much blight in the garden now."

The supper was ended, and Mrs Solomon, in a very quiet, quick way, cleared the cloth, and after she had done, placed a Bible on the table, out of which Mr Solomon read a short chapter, and then shook hands with me and sent me away happy.

"Good night, my lad!" he said. "It's all strange to you now, and we're not noisy jolly sort of people, but you're welcome here, and we shall get on."

"Yes," said Mrs Solomon in a very cold stern way that did not seem at all inviting or kind. "Come along and I'll show you your bed-room."

I followed her upstairs and into a little room with a sloping ceiling and a window looking out upon the garden; and at the sight of the neat little place, smelling of lavender, and with some flowers in a jug upon the drawers, the depression which kept haunting me was driven away.

Everything looked attractive—the clean white bed and its dainty hangings, the blue ewer and basin on the washstand, the picture or two on the wall, and the strips of light-coloured carpet on the white floor, all made the place cheerful and did something to recompense me for the trouble of having to leave what seemed to be my regular home, and come from one who had of late been most fatherly and kind, to people who were not likely to care for me at all.

"I think there's everything you want," said Mrs Solomon, looking at me curiously. "Soap and towel, and of course you've got your hair-brush and things in your box there."

She pointed at the corded box which stood in front of the table.

"If there's anything you want you can ask. I hope you'll be very clean."

"I'll try to be, ma'am," I said, feeling quite uncomfortable, she looked at me so coldly.

"You can use those drawers, and your box can go in the back room. Good-night!"

She went away and shut the door, looking wonderfully clean and prim, but depressing instead of cheering me; and as soon as she was gone I uncorded my box, wondering whether I should be able to stay, and wishing myself back at Isleworth.

I had taken out my clothes and had reached the bottom of my box, anxious to see whether the treasures I had there in a flat case, consisting of pinned-out moths and butterflies, were all right and had not been shaken out of place by the jolting of the cart, when there was a sharp tap at the door and Mr Solomon came in.

"Hullo!" he said; "butterflies and moths!—eh?"

He spoke quite angrily, as it seemed to me, and chilled me, as I felt that he would not like me to do such a thing as collect.

"Hah!" he said. "I used to do that when I was a boy. There's lots here; but don't go after them when you're at work."

"No, sir," I said.

"Thought I'd come up, my lad, as it's all strange to you. I haven't much to say to you, only keep away from those boys. Let 'em talk, but never you mind."

"I'll try, sir."

"That's right. Work to-morrow morning at six. You may begin sooner if you like. I often, do. Breakfast at eight; dinner at twelve; tea at five, and then work's supposed to be done. I generally go in the houses then. Always something wants doing there."

He stood thinking and looking as cold and hard as could be while I waited for him to speak again; but he did not for quite five minutes, during which time he stood picking up my comb and dropping it back into the hair-brush.

"Yes," he said suddenly, "I should go in for those late lettuces if I was Ezra. He'd find a good sale for them when salads were getting scarce. Celery's very good, but people don't like to be always tied down to celery and endives—a tough kind of meat at the best of times. If you write home—no, this is home now—if you write to Brother Ezra, you say I hope he'll keep his word about the lettuces. Good-night!"

I felt puzzled as soon as he had gone, and had not the slightest idea how I felt towards the people with whom I was to pass months—perhaps years.

"I shall never like Mrs Solomon," I said to myself dolefully; "and I shall only like him half and half—liking him sometimes and not caring for him at others."

I was very tired, and soon after I was lying in the cool sweet sheets thinking about my new home, and watching the dimly-seen window; and then it seemed to be all light and to look over Old Brownsmith's garden, where Shock was pelting at me with pellets of clay thrown from the end of a switch. And all the time he came nearer and nearer till the pellets went right over my shoulder, and they grew bigger till they were peaches that he kept sticking on the end of the switch, and as he threw them they broke with a noise that was like the word *Push*!

I wanted to stop him, but I could not till he threw one peach with all his might, and the switch caught me across the back, and I retaliated by taking it away and thrashing him.

Then I woke with a start, and found I had been dreaming. I lay for a few minutes after that in the darkness thinking that I would learn all I could about fruit-growing as fast as possible, so as to know everything, and get back to Old Brownsmith; and then all at once I found myself sitting up in bed listening, with the sun shining in at one side of my blind, while I was wondering where I was and how I had come there.

Chapter Twenty Three
I Begin Work

Boys like sleep in the morning, but the desire to cuddle up for a few minutes more and to go back to dreamland is not there on the first morning at a new home or at a fresh school.

On that particular morning I did not feel in the least sleepy, only uncomfortably nervous; and, hearing voices through the wall, I jumped up and dressed quickly, to find on going down that Mr Solomon was in the kitchen putting on his thick boots.

"Just coming to call you," he said, nodding. "Harpus five. Hah! change coming," he cried, stamping his feet in his boots; "rain—rain. Come along."

He unbolted the door and I followed him out, drawing a breath of the sweetly fragrant air as we stepped at once into the bright sunshine, where the flowers were blooming and the trees were putting forth their strength.

But I had no opportunity for looking about the garden, for Mr Solomon led the way at once to the stoke-holes down behind the glass-houses, rattled open the doors, and gave a stoke here with a great iron rod, and a poke there where the fires were caked together; while, without waiting to be asked, I seized upon the shovel I saw handy and threw on some coke.

"Far back as you can, my lad," said Mr Solomon. "Seems a rum time of year to be having fires; but we're obliged to keep up a little, specially on cloudy days."

This done, he led the way into one of the sunken pits where the melons were growing, and after reaching in among them and snipping off a runner or two he routed out a slug and killed it.

Then turning to me:

"First thing in gardening, Grant, is to look out for your enemies. You'll never beat them; all you can do is to keep 'em down. Now look here," he said, picking off a melon leaf and holding it before me, "What's the matter with that?"

"I don't see much the matter," I said, "only that the leaf looks specked a little with yellow, as if it was unhealthy."

"Turn it over," he said.

I did, and looked at it well.

"There are a few red specks on it—very small ones," I said.

"Good eyes," he said approvingly. "That's what's the matter, my lad. You've seen the greatest enemy we have under glass. Those red specks, so small that you can hardly see them, cover the lower parts of the leaves with tiny cobwebs and choke the growth while they suck all the goodness out, and make the yellow specks on the top by sucking all the sap from the leaves."

"What, those tiny specks!"

"Yes, those little specks would spoil all our melon plants if we did not destroy them—melons, cucumbers, vines, peaches, and nectarines— anything almost under glass. But there's your gun and ammunition; load up and shoot 'em. Never give them any rest."

I looked at him wonderingly, for he was pointing at a syringe standing in a pail of soapy-looking water.

"Yes," he continued, "that's right—kill 'em when you can. If you leave them, and greenfly, and those sort of things, alone till to-morrow, by that time they're turned into great-grandfathers, and have got such a family of little ones about 'em that your leaves are ten times worse."

"But what are those red specks?" I said.

"Red spider, boy. Now I'll show you. This is my plan to keep my plants healthy: have a bucket of soap and water in every house, and a syringe in it. Then you take it up as soon as you see the mischief and kill it at once. It's all handy for you, same as it is to have a bit of matting hanging up on a nail, ready to tie up the stem that wants it. Somebody said, Grant, 'A stitch in time saves nine,' it ought to have been, 'A washed leaf keeps off grief.' See here."

He took the syringe, filled it, and sent a fine shower beneath the leaves of the melons, where they were trained over a trellis, thoroughly washing them all over.

"Now you try," he said, and taking off my jacket I syringed away vigorously, while with matting and knife he tied in some loose strands and cut off others, so as to leave the vines neat.

"That'll do for the present," he said; "but mind this, Grant, if ever you see an enemy, shoot him while he's a single man if you can. Wait till to-morrow, you'll have to shoot all his relations too."

He led the way out of the pit, and round by the grounds, where different men were at work mowing and sweeping, the short cut grass smelling delicious in the morning air. He spoke to first one and then another in a short business-like way, and then went on with me to one of the great conservatories up by the house.

"I might put you to that sort of work, Grant," he said, giving his head a backward jerk; "but that wants no brains. Work under glass does. You want to work with your hands and your head. Now we'll have a tidy up in here. Sir Francis likes plenty of bright flowers."

I should have liked to stop looking about as soon as we were in the large glass building, which was one mass of bloom; but following Mr Solomon's example I was soon busily snipping off dead flowers and leaves, so as to make the various plants tidy; and I was extremely busy in one corner over this when I suddenly found that Mr Solomon was watching me, and that a big bell was ringing somewhere.

"That's right," he said, nodding his head in a satisfied way. "That's what I want. You don't know much yet, but you will. If I was to set one of those men to do that he'd have knocked off half the buds, and—what have you been doing there?"

"I tied up those two flower-stems," I said. "Wasn't it right, sir?"

"Right and wrong, my lad," he said, whipping out his knife and cutting them free. "Look here."

He took a piece of wet matting—a mere strip—and tied them up again, with his big fingers moving so quickly and cleverly that I wondered.

"There, that's the way. Looks the same as you did it, eh?"

"Yes," I said, smiling.

"No, it isn't. You tied yours in front of the stem, with an ugly knot to rub and fret it, and make a sore place when the windows were open. I've put a neat band round mine, and the knot rests on the stick."

"Oh, I see!" I cried.

"Yes, Grant, there's a right way and a wrong way, and somehow the natural way is generally the wrong. Never saw one tried, but I believe if you took a savage black and told him to get up on a horse, he would go on the wrong side, put his left foot in the stirrup, and throw his right leg over, and come down sitting with his face to the tail. Breakfast."

"What! so soon?" I said.

"Soon! Why, it's past eight."

I was astounded, the time had gone so quickly; and soon after I was saying "good morning" to Mrs Solomon, and partaking of the plain meal.

"Well?" said Mrs Solomon in her cold impassive way.

Mr Solomon was so busy with a piece of cold bacon and some bread that he did not look up, and Mrs Solomon waited patiently till he raised his head and gave her a nod.

"I am glad," she said, giving a sigh as if she were relieved; and then she turned to me and looked quite pleasantly at me, and taking my cup, refilled it with coffee, and actually smiled.

"Notice the missus?" said Mr Solomon, as, after a glance at his big silver watch, he had suddenly said "Harpusate," and led the way to the vineries.

"Notice Mrs Brownsmith?" I said.

"Yes; see anything about her?"

"I thought she looked better this morning than she did last night. Was she ill?"

"Yes," he said shortly. "Get them steps."

I fetched *them* steps, and thought that a gardener might just as well be grammatical.

He opened them out, and opening his knife, cut a few strands of matting ready, stuck them under one of his braces, after taking off his coat, and then climbed up to the top to tie in a long green cane of the grape-vine.

"Hold the steps steady," he said; and then with his head in amongst the leaves he went on talking.

"Bit queer in the head," he said slowly, and with his face averted. "Shied at you."

I stared. His wife was not a horse, and I thought they were the only things that shied; but I found I was wrong, for Mr Solomon went on:

"I did, too. Ezra said a lot about you. Fine young shoot this, ain't it?"

I said it was, for it was about ten feet long and as thick as my finger, and it seemed wonderful that it should have grown like that in a few months; but all the time my cheeks were tingling as I wondered what Old Brownsmith had said about me.

"Sounded all right, but it's risky to take a boy into your house when you are comfortable without, you see."

I felt ashamed and hurt that I should have been talked of so, and remained silent.

"The missus said you might be dirty and awkward in the house. This cane will be loaded next year if we get it well ripened this year, Grant. That's why I'm tying it in here close to the glass, where it'll get plenty of sun and air."

"What! will that bear grapes next year, sir?" I said, for I felt obliged to say something.

"Yes; and when the leaves are off you shall cut this one right out down at the bottom yonder."

He tapped a beautiful branch or cane from the main stem, which was bearing about a dozen fine bunches of grapes, and it seemed a pity; but of course he knew best, and he began cutting and snapping out shoots and big leaves between the new green cane and the glass.

"She was afraid you'd be a nuisance to me, and said you'd be playing with tops, and throwing stones, and breaking the glass. I told her that Brother Ezra wouldn't send me such a boy as that; but she only shook her head. 'I know what boys are,' she said. 'Look at her ladyship's two.' But I said that you wouldn't be like them, and you won't, will you?"

I laughed, for it seemed such a comical idea for me to be behaving as Mrs Solomon had supposed.

"What are you laughing at?" he said, looking down at me.

"I was thinking about what Mrs Brownsmith said," I replied.

"Oh yes! To be sure," he continued. "You'll like her. She's a very nice woman. A very good woman. I've known her thirty years."

"Have you had any children, sir?" I said.

"No," he replied, looking at me with a twinkle in his eye; "and yet I've always been looking after nurseries—all my life."

In about an hour he finished his morning work in the vinery, and I went out with him in the garden, where he left me to tidy up a great bed of geraniums with a basket and a pair of scissors.

"I've got to see to the men now," he said. "By-and-by we'll go and have a turn at the cucumbers."

The bed I was employed upon was right away from the house in a sort of nook where the lawn ran up amongst some great Portugal laurels. It was a mass of green and scarlet, surrounded by shortly cropped grass, and I was very busy in the hot sunshine, enjoying my task, and now and then watching the thrushes that kept hopping out on to the lawn and then back under the shelter of the evergreens, when I suddenly saw a shadow, and, turning sharply, found that my friend of the peach-house had come softly up over the grass with another lad very much like him, but a little taller, and probably a couple of years older.

"Hullo, pauper!" said the first.

I felt my cheeks tingle, and my tongue wanted to say something very sharp, but I kept my teeth closed for a moment and then said:

"Good morning, sir!"

He took no notice of this, but turned to his brother and whispered something, when they both laughed together; and as I bent down over my work I felt as if I must have looked very much like one of the scarlet geraniums whose dead blossom stems I was taking out.

Of course, a boy with a well-balanced brain and plenty of sound, honest, English stuff in him ought to be able to treat with contempt the jeering and laughter of those who are teasing him; but somehow I'm afraid that there are very few boys who can bear being laughed at with equanimity. I know, to be frank, I could not, for as those two lads stared at me and then looked at each other and whispered, and then laughed heartily—well, no; not heartily, but in a forced way, I felt my face burn and my fingers tingle. My mouth seemed to get a little dry, too, and the thought came upon me in the midst of my sensations that I wanted to get up and fight.

The circumstances were rather exceptional, for I was suffering from two sore places. One started from my shoulder and went down my back, where there must have been the mark of the cane; the other was a mental sore, caused by the word *pauper*, which seemed to rankle and sting more than the cut from the cane.

Of course I ought to have treated it as beneath my notice, but whoever reads this will have found out before now that I was very far from perfect; and as those two lads evidently saw my annoyance, and went on trying to increase it, I bent over my work in a vicious way, and kept on taking out the dead leaves and stems as if they were some of the enemies Mr Solomon had been talking about in the pits.

All at once, as I was bending down, I heard Courtenay, the elder boy, say:

"What did he say—back to school and be flogged?"

"Yes," said Philip aloud; "but he didn't know. They only flog workhouse boys and paupers."

"I say, though," said Courtenay, "who is that chap grubbing out the slugs and snails?"

My back was turned, and I went on with my work. "What! that chap I spoke to?" said Philip; "why, I told you. He's a pauper."

"Is he?"

"Yes, and Browny fetched him from the workhouse. Brought him home in the cart. He's going to be a caterpillar crusher."

I felt as if I should have liked to be a boy crusher, and have run at him with my fists clenched, and drubbed him till he roared for mercy, but I did not stir.

"Then what's he doing here?" said Courtenay in a sour, morose tone of voice. "He ought to be among the cabbages, and not here."

This was as if they were talking to themselves, but meant for me to hear.

"Old Browny was afraid to put him there for fear he'd begin wolfing them. I caught him as soon as he came. He got loose, and I found him in the peach-house eating the peaches, but I dropped on to him with the cane and made the beggar howl."

"Old Browny ought to look after him," said Courtenay.

"Don't I tell you he ran away. I expect Browny will have to put a dog-collar and chain on him, and drive a stake down in the kitchen-garden to keep him from eating the cabbages when he's caterpillaring. These workhouse boys are such hungry beggars."

"Put a muzzle on him like they do on a ferret," said Courtenay; and then they laughed together.

"Hasn't he got a rum phiz?" said Philip, who, I soon found, was the quicker with his tongue.

"Yes; don't talk so loud: he'll hear you. Just like a monkey," said Courtenay; and they laughed again.

"I say, is he going to stop?" said Courtenay.

"I suppose so. They want a boy to scrape the shovels and light the fires, and go up the hothouse chimneys to clear out the soot. He's just the sort for that."

"He'll have to polish Old Browny's boots, too."

"Yes; and wash Mother Browny's stockings. I say, Court, don't he look a hungry one?"

"Regular wolf," said Courtenay; and there was another laugh.

"I say," said Courtenay, "I don't believe he's a workhouse."

"He is, I tell you; Browny went and bought him yesterday. They sell 'em cheap. You can have as many as you like almost for nothing. They're glad to get rid of 'em."

"I wonder what they'd say to poor old Shock!" I thought to myself. "I'm glad he isn't here."

"I don't care," said Courtenay; "I think he's a London street boy. He looks like it from the cut of his jib."

I paid not the slightest heed, but my heart beat fast and I could feel the perspiration standing all over my face.

"I don't care; he's a pauper. I wonder what Old Browny will feed him on."

"Skilly," said Courtenay; and the boys laughed again. All at once I felt a push with a foot, and if I had not suddenly stiffened my arms I should have gone down and broken some of the geraniums, but they escaped, and I leaped to my feet and faced them angrily.

"Here, what's your name?" said Courtenay haughtily.

I swallowed my annoyance, and answered:

"Grant."

"What a name for a boy!" said Courtenay. "I say, Phil, isn't his hair cut short. He ought to have his ears trimmed too. Here, where are your father and mother?"

I felt a catch in my throat as I tried to answer steadily:

"Dead."

"There, I told you so," cried Philip. "He hasn't got any father or mother. Didn't you come out of the workhouse, pauper?"

"No," I said steadily, as my fingers itched to strike him.

"Here, what was your father?" said Courtenay.

I did not answer.

"Do you hear? And say 'sir' when you speak," cried Courtenay with a brutal insolent manner that seemed to fit with his dark thin face. "I say, do you hear, boy?"

"Yes," I replied.

"Yes, *sir*, you beggar," cried Courtenay. "What was your father?"

"He don't know," cried Philip grinning. "Pauper boys don't know. They're all mixed up together, and they call 'em Sunday, Monday, Tuesday, or names of streets or places, anything. He doesn't know what his father was. He was mixed up with a lot more."

"I'll make him answer," said Courtenay. "Here, what was your father?"

"An officer and a gentleman," I said proudly.

"Ha! ha! ha!" laughed Philip, dancing about with delight, and hanging on to his brother, who laughed too. "Here's a game—a gardener's boy a gentleman! Oh my!"

I was sorry I had said those words, but they slipped out, and I stood there angry and mortified before my tormentors.

"I say, Court, don't he look like a gentleman? Look at the knees of his trousers, and his fists."

"Never mind," said Courtenay, "I want to bat. Look here, you, sir, can you play cricket?"

"Yes," I said, "a little."

"Yes, *sir*, you beggar; how many more times am I to tell you! Come out in the field. You've got to bowl for us. Here, catch!"

He threw a cricket-ball he had in his hand at me with all his might, and in a nasty spiteful way, but I caught it, and in a jeering way Philip shouted:

"Well fielded. Here, come on, Court. We'll make the beggar run."

I hesitated, for I wanted to go on with my work, but these were my master's sons, and I felt that I ought to obey.

"What are you standing staring like that for, pauper?" cried Philip. "Didn't you hear Mr Courtenay say you were to come on and bowl?"

"What do you want, young gentleman?" said a voice that was very welcome to me; and Mr Solomon came from behind the great laurels.

"What's that to you, Browny? He's coming to bowl for us in the field," said Courtenay.

"No, he is not," said Mr Solomon coolly. "He's coming to help me in the cucumber house."

"No, he isn't," said Philip; "he's coming to bowl for us. Come along, pauper."

I threw the ball towards him and it fell on the lawn, for neither of the boys tried to catch it.

"Here, you, sir," cried Courtenay furiously, "come and pick up this ball."

I glanced at Mr Solomon and did not stir.

"Do you hear, you, sir! come and pick up this ball," said Courtenay.

"Now, pauper, look alive," said Philip.

I turned and stooped down over my work.

"I say, Court, we're not going to stand this, are we?"

"Go into the field and play, boys," said Mr Solomon coldly; "we've got to work."

"Yes, paupers have to work," said Courtenay with a sneer.

"If I thought that worth notice, young fellow, I'd make you take that word back," said Mr Solomon sternly.

"Yes, it's all right, Courtenay; the boy isn't a pauper."

"You said he was."

"Yes, but it was a mistake," sneered Philip; "he says he's a gentleman."

The two boys roared with laughter, and Mr Solomon looked red.

"Look here, Grant," he said quietly, "if being a gentleman is to be like these two here, don't you be one, but keep to being a gardener."

"Ha, ha, ha!—ho, ho, ho!" they both laughed. "A gentleman! Pretty sort of a gentleman."

"Pauper gentleman," cried Philip maliciously. "Yes, I daresay he has got a title," said Courtenay, who looked viciously angry at being thwarted; and he was the more enraged because Mr Solomon bent down and helped me at the bed, taking no notice whatever of the orders for me to go.

"Yes," said Philip; "he's a barrow-net—a wheelbarrow-net. Ha, ha, ha!"

"With a potato-fork for his crest."

"And ragged coat without any arms," said Philip.

"And his motto is 'Oh the poor workhouse boy!'" cried Courtenay.

"There, that will do, Grant," said Mr Solomon. "Let these little boys amuse themselves. It won't hurt us. Bring your basket."

"Yes, take him away, Browny," cried Philip.

"Ah, young fellows, your father will find out some day what nice boys you are! Come along, Grant and let these young *gentlemen* talk till they're tired."

"Yes, go on," cried Philip; while I saw Courtenay turn yellow with rage at the cold bitter words Mr Solomon used. "Take away your pauper—take care of your gentleman—go and chain him up, and give him his skilly. Go on! take him to his kennel. Oh, I say, Courtenay—a gentleman! What a game!"

I followed Mr Solomon with my face wrinkled and lips tightened up, till he turned round and looked at me and then clapped his hand on my shoulder.

"Bah!" he said laughing; "you are not going to mind that, my lad. It isn't worth a snap of the fingers. I wish, though, you hadn't said anything about being a gentleman."

"So do I, sir," I said. "It slipped out, though, and I was sorry when it was too late."

"Never mind; and don't you leave your work for them. Now come and have a look at my cucumber house, and then—ha, ha, ha! there's something better than skilly for dinner, my boy."

I found out that Mr Solomon had another nature beside the one that seemed cold.

Chapter Twenty Four
Sir Francis and a Friend

The next few days passed pleasantly enough, for I saw very little of the two young gentlemen, who spent a good deal of their time in a meadow beyond the garden, playing cricket and quarrelling. Once there seemed to have been a fight, for I came upon Philip kneeling down by a watering-pot busy with his handkerchief bathing his face, and the state of the water told tales of what had happened to his nose.

As he seemed in trouble I was about to offer him my services, but he turned upon me so viciously with, "Hullo! pauper, what do you want?" that I went away.

The weather was lovely, and while it was so hot Mr Solomon used to do the principal part of his work in the glass houses at early morn and in the evening.

"Makes us work later, Grant," he used to say apologetically; "but as it's for our own convenience we ought not to grumble."

"I'm not going to grumble, sir," I said laughing; "all that training and tying in is so interesting, I like it."

"That's right," he said, patting me on the shoulder; "always try and like your work; take a pride in it, my man, and it will turn up trumps some time or another. It means taking prizes."

I had not seen Sir Francis yet, for he had been away, and I could not help feeling a little nervous about our first meeting. Still I was pretty happy there, and I felt that in spite of a few strong sensations of longing to be back at the old garden with Ike and Shock, I was getting to like my new life very much indeed, and that as soon as the two boys had gone back to their school I should be as happy as could be.

I was gradually getting to like Mr Solomon, and Mrs Solomon grew more kind to me every day. The men about the garden, too, were all very civil to me, and beyond a little bit of good-humoured banter from them now and then I had no cause for complaint.

My great fear was that they would catch up the name young Philip had bestowed upon me. That they knew of it I had pretty good evidence, for one day when I was busy over one of the verbena beds—busy at a task Mr Solomon had set me after the sun had made the peach-house too hot, a big bluff gardener came and worked close by me, mowing the grass in a shady part under some trees.

"It's dry, and cuts like wire," he said, stopping to wipe his scythe and give it a touch with the stone, making the blade ring and send forth what always sounded to be pleasant music to me.

"Oughtn't you to cut it when the dew is on?" I said.

"Yes, squire, if you can," he replied; "but there is so much grass we can't get over it all in the early morning."

He went on mowing, and I continued my task of pegging down the long shoots of the beautiful scarlet, crimson, and white flowers, just as Mr Solomon had instructed me, when all at once he came and looked on, making me feel very nervous; but he nodded and went away, so I supposed he was satisfied, and I worked on again as cheerfully as could be, till all at once I felt the blood flush up in my face, for the voice of young Philip Dalton came unpleasantly grating on my ear, as he said:

"Hullo, Bunce, mowing again?"

"Yes, Master Philup, mowin' again."

"Why, you've got the pauper there!" cried Philip. "I say, did you know he was a pauper?"

"No," said Bunce, "I didn't know. Do you want your legs ampytated?"

"No, stoopid, of course I don't."

"Then get outer the way or I shall take 'em off like carrots."

"Get out!" said Philip, as I saw that he was watching me. "I say, though, did you know that he was a pauper, and lived on skilly?"

"No," said the gardener quietly; and I felt as if I must get up and go away, for now I knew I should be a mark of contempt for the whole staff who worked in the garden.

"He was," said Philip.

"Pauper, was he?" said Bunce, making his scythe glide round in a half circle. "I shouldn't ha' thought it."

"Oh but he was or is, and always will be," said the boy maliciously. "Once a pauper always a pauper. Look at him."

"I've been a looking at him," said Bunce slowly, for he was a big meditative man, and he stood upright, took a piece of flannel from the strap that supported his whetstone sheath, and wiped the blade of the scythe.

"Well, can't you see?" cried my tormentor, watching me as I worked away and assumed ignorance of his presence.

"No," said Bunce sturdily; "and seeing what a long, yellow, lizardly-looking wisp you are, Master Phil, if you two changed clothing I should pick you out as the pauper."

"How dare you!" cried the boy fiercely.

"Mind the scythe," shouted Bunce; "d'yer want to get cut?"

"You insolent old worm chopper, how dare you call me a pauper?"

"I didn't call you a pauper," said Bunce chuckling; "did I, Grant?"

"No," I said.

"You're a liar, you pauper!" cried the boy, who was furious. "I'll tell papa—I'll tell Sir Francis, and you shall both be discharged, you blackguards."

"I'm just going to mow there, squire," said Bunce, sharpening away at his scythe.

"Then you'll wait till I choose to move."

"If you don't get out of the way I shall take the soles off your boots," said Bunce, putting back his rubber.

"I'll speak to papa about your insolence," cried the boy, with his eyes flashing and his fists clenched; and I thought he was going to strike Bunce.

"Well," said a sharp ringing voice, "speak to him then. What is it?"

I started to my feet, and Bunce touched his cap to a tall elderly gentleman with closely-cut grey hair and a very fierce-looking white moustache, whose keen eyes seemed to look me through and through.

"I said, what is it, Phil?" cried the newcomer, whom I felt to be Sir Francis before Philip spoke.

"This fellow called me a pauper, pa!"

Sir Francis turned sharply on Bunce, who did not seem in the slightest degree alarmed.

"How dare you call my son a pauper, sir?" he said sternly.

"I—"

"Stop!" cried Sir Francis. "Here, you boy, go away and wait till I call you. Not far."

"Yes, sir," I said; and I walked away thinking what a fierce quick man he seemed, and not knowing then that he was one of the magistrates.

A minute later he called to me to go back, and as soon as I had reached him, with Philip by his side and Bunce before him, Philip stepped back and held up his fist at me menacingly.

He thought the movement was unobserved by his stepfather; but Sir Francis, who was an old Indian officer, noted the act, as he showed us directly after.

"Now, boy," he said, "what's your name?"

"Grant, Sir Francis."

"Well, Grant, did this under-gardener call Master Philip a pauper?"

I told him exactly what had occurred, and Sir Francis turned sharply on his step-son.

"You were already self-condemned, Philip," he said sternly. "I saw you threaten this boy with your fist. The way to win respect from those beneath you in station is to treat them with respect."

"But, papa—"

"Hold your tongue, sir," said Sir Francis sternly.

"I had eight hundred men in my regiment, and all the band came from one of the unions, and better fellows could not be found. My lad," he continued, "I dare say you know that pauper only means poor. It is no disgrace to be poor. Philip, go indoors."

"That's a flea in his ear," said Bunce chuckling, as Sir Francis went one way, Philip the other. "What do you think of the master?"

"He seems very sharp and angry," I said, returning to my work.

"He's all that," said the man; "but he's a reg'lar gentleman. He always drops on to them two if he catches 'em up to their larks. Nice boys both of 'em."

That word *pauper* rankled a good deal in my breast, for it was quite evident to me that Sir Francis thought I was from one of the unions, and I had had no opportunity of showing him that I was not.

"But I will show him," I said to myself angrily. "He sha'n't see anything in me to make him believe it. It's too bad."

I was busy, as I said that, arranging a barrowful of plants in rows, where they were to be surrounded with earth, "plunged," as we called it, under the shelter of a wall, where they would get warmth and sunshine and grow hardy and strong, ready for taking in to the shelter of the greenhouse when the weather turned cold.

It was some days since I had seen Philip; but, weakly enough, I let the memory of that word rankle still.

To carry out my task I had to fetch a pot at a time from the large wide barrow, and set them down in the trench that had been cut for them. This necessitated stooping, and as I was setting one down a lump of something caught me so smartly on the back that I nearly dropped the flower-pot and started upright, looking round for the thrower of the piece of clay, for there it was at my feet.

I could not see, but I guessed at once that it was Philip, though it might have been Courtenay hiding behind some gooseberry bushes or the low hornbeam hedge, about twenty yards away.

"I won't take any notice of the ill-bred young cubs," I said to myself angrily; and I stooped and arranged the pot in its place and went back for another, when *whack*! came another well-aimed piece, and hit me on the side of the cap.

"You—"

I stopped myself, as I banged down the pot in a rage—stopped words and act, for I was going to run towards the spot whence the clay seemed to have come.

"It's only play after all," I said to myself. "I'll show them, pauper or no, that I'm above being annoyed by such a trifle as that."

I moved a couple more pots, when something whizzed by my ear, and then I was hit on the shoulder by a little raw potato.

I wanted to run round to the back of the hornbeam hedge, which had been planted to shelter plants and not sharpshooters, but I restrained myself.

"Playing cricket makes them take such good aim," I thought to myself, as a piece of clay hit me on the back again; and I worked hard to finish my task so as to get to the pit from which I was fetching the pots down to the grass walk where I was; and I had got to the last pot, when, in stooping to put it in its place, *plop* came a soft lump of clay on the nape of my neck, and began to slip under my collar.

Down went the pot, and my cap on to the plant, and I turned sharp round, certain now that the missiles had been sent, not from the shelter hedge nor the gooseberry bushes, but from the wall, and there, sure enough, with his head and shoulders above the top, was my assailant.

My angry look changed to a bland smile as I saw the ragged straw hat with the hair standing out of the top, and the grubby face of Shock looking at me with his eyes twinkling and the skin all round wrinkled, while the rest of his face was sour.

"Why, Shock!" I cried; "who'd have thought of seeing you? How did you get there?"

"Clum up."

"Did Mr Brownsmith send you?"

He shook his head.

"How is it you are here, then?"

"Hooked it."

"Why, you haven't run away?"

"I jest have, though."

"But you are going back?"

He shook his head with all his might.

"I've sin you lots o' times," he said.

"When?"

"Yes'day. Day afore, and day afore that."

"What! have you been here three days?" Shock nodded.

"Where have you slept, then?"

"Haystack."

"And what have you had to eat?"

"Bread. Lots o' things I fun' in the fields. Rabbud."

"Who's that boy?" said a sharp voice that well knew; and Shock's head disappeared.

"Mr Ezra Brownsmith's boy, Sir Francis," I said. "He used to work with me."

"Was he from the workhouse?"

"Yes, Sir Francis."

"Tell him not to do that again, and don't you encourage him. I don't approve of it. Go on with your work."

I took the barrow handles and wheeled it away, biting my lips, for it had suddenly struck me that Sir Francis thought that I was talking to a boy who was my companion in the workhouse, and it seemed as if fate was fixing the term pauper upon me so tightly that I should not be able to get it removed.

Plenty of little annoyances occurred, but I put up with them; and not the least was the appearance of Shock at the top of first one wall and then another, but never near enough to speak to me.

He showed himself so often here and there that I used to go about the garden feeling sure that he was watching me; and at last I found, to my horror, that he had grown more bold, and used to get into the garden, for one day I caught sight of him creeping on hands and knees among the gooseberry bushes.

I started in pursuit, but stopped directly, feeling sure that if I did so the act would result in trouble to us both, and determined to write to Mr Ezra about him. I was glad I did so the next minute, for Courtenay and Philip came down the garden to amuse themselves picking gooseberries and eating them.

I was busy watering some celery that had been planted in trenches and shaded from the hot sun.

To do this I had a barrel fitted on wheels in a sort of barrow. From this I filled my can by dipping it, and when I had finished I had to go down to the bottom of the garden to a good-sized pond and reverse the process, dipping a bucket at some steps and filling the barrel.

I had filled my barrel once, and was busy dipping my can and thinking about Shock and what would be the consequences if he were seen by the two boys, when I suddenly found them by me, each with his cap full of ripe gooseberries, which they were eating as they watched me; and after giving his brother a look, Philip opened the annoyance by saying:

"Come, pauper, work away."

I took no notice, when a half-sucked gooseberry struck me on the arm.

It was a disgusting act on the young coward's part, but though in a moment I felt on fire, I only wiped it off, when Courtenay threw one and hit me on the face.

I wiped that away too, and raising my can stepped off the path on to the bed to go to the trench, but not in time to avoid a large over-ripe gooseberry which smashed as it struck me in the ear and began to trickle down.

I was in such a rage that the roar of laughter from my two tyrants half maddened me, and I watered that celery in a way that washed some of the roots quite bare.

They were waiting for me when I got back to the tub, and, emboldened by the patient way in which I bore their insults, they kept on pelting me with the over-ripe fruit till I had it in my hair, my eyes, and down within the collar of my shirt.

I ground my teeth with rage, and felt that I could bear it no longer, but I made no sign.

Then they pelted me with words too, inventing ridiculous names, asking me about the workhouse food, and at last I determined to bear it no longer, but go straight up to the house and show Sir Francis the state I was in and beg him to put a stop to this annoyance.

But just then it flashed upon my mind that Sir Francis and her ladyship had gone out the day before to stay somewhere for a fortnight, and this explained the boldness of the two young ruffians, who had never behaved so outrageously before.

"If I go and tell Mr Solomon," I thought, "he will only tell me I was foolish to take any notice;" and at last, writhing with annoyance, I emptied the barrel and trundled it down to the pond, hoping to leave my tormentors behind.

But no; they followed me and continued their assaults as soon as they had replenished their caps with the gooseberries that were abundant on the bushes, over-ripe many of them, and of monstrous size.

"Did you ever see such a coward?" said Philip.

"Like all these paupers," cried Courtenay. "Ha! ha! ha! right in the ear."

I stamped with rage for his words were true about his aim, though I did not feel cowardly, for I was working hard to do my duty and keep my hands from my assailants.

"Give him one in the eye," said Philip. "Bet you twopence, Court, I hit him first in the eye."

They went on pelting and I went on filling my barrel, dipping with the bucket and pouring it in, and a dozen times over it was all I could do to keep from discharging the contents of the pail in Courtenay's face.

Full at last, and I was ready to go up the garden again.

I glanced round in the hope of seeing Mr Solomon or Bunce or one of the other gardeners; but they were all busy in the upper gardens, while I was quite shut in here with my tormentors.

"Here, let's get some more shot, Court," cried Philip. "I'll serve the sneaking coward out for getting me in that row with pa."

"Wait a bit," said his brother; "look at him. He goes down just like a monkey. He's going to wash his gooseberry face."

He was quite right, for I had laid my cap aside and stooped down at the dipping place to wash off some of the seedy, sticky pulp before going back.

"Dirty brute!" said Philip. "I never saw such a coward in my life."

I ought to have been on my guard and not have given them the opportunity which I did, for as I stooped down there, crouching on my heels, I placed a great temptation in Courtenay Dalton's way. For as I stooped right down, scooping up the water with one hand to bathe my face, I suddenly felt a sharp thrust from a foot on my back, and before I could save myself I was head over heels in the deep water.

It was not so deep but that I got my footing directly, and seizing the post at the side tried to struggle out, when amidst shouts of laughter Philip cried:

"Give him another dowse. That's the way to wash a pauper clean."

I was half-blind with the water, as Courtenay thrust my hand from the post, and in I went again, to come up red hot instead of cold.

He thrust me in again and I went right under; but my rage was not quenched, and, taught by my experience, I made a rush as if to spring out on to the dipping-place but instead of doing so I caught at a branch of a willow by the side and sprang out.

"Shake yourself, dog!" cried Courtenay, roaring with laughter.

"Fetch him a towel," cried Philip. "A towel for the clean pauper. Give him another ducking, Courtenay."

He ran at me, but in those moments I had forgotten everything in my thirst to be revenged on my cowardly persecutors.

Philip only seemed to be something in my way as I made at his brother, and throwing out one fist, he went down amongst the willows, while the next minute I was striking at Courtenay with all my might.

He was a bigger boy than I. Taller and older, and he had had many a good fight at school no doubt; but my onslaught staggered him, and I drove him before me, striking at him as he reached the handles of my water-barrow, and he fell over them heavily.

This only enraged him, and he sprang up and received my next blow right in the face, to be staggered for the moment.

Then I don't know what happened, only that my arms were going like windmills, that I was battering Courtenay, and that he was battering me; that we were down, and then up, and then down again, over and over, and fighting fiercely as a couple of dogs.

I think I was getting the best of it, when I began to feel weak, and that my adversary was hitting me back and front at once.

Then I realised that Philip had attacked me too, and that I was getting very much the worst of it in a sort of thunderstorm which rained blows.

Then the blows only came from one side, for there was a hoarse panting and the sound of heavy blows and scuffling away from me, while I was hitting out again with all my might at one boy instead of two.

All at once there was a crash and the rattle of an iron handle, and Courtenay went down. He had caught against the pail and fallen.

This gave me time to glance round and see in a half-blinded way that Philip was fighting with some other boy, who closed with him, and down they went together.

"Yah! yah! Cowards! cowards!" cried a voice that I well knew; and I saw giddily that Courtenay and Philip were running up the path, and that Shock was standing beside me.

"Well done!" cried another voice. "What a licking you two give 'em!"

Shock started, and ran, darting among the bushes, while I sat down on a barrow-handle, feeling rather thick and dizzy.

"I was coming to stop it. Two to one's too bad; but that ragged chap come out at young Phil, and my word, he did give it him well. Are you much hurt, my lad?"

"No, not much, Mr Bunce," I said, staring at him in rather a confused way.

"Here, I'll get some water," he said; and he went and dipped a pailful. "Bathe your face in that."

I did so, and felt clearer and refreshed directly.

"Go on," he said; "keep it up. It will stop the bleeding. What! have you been in the pond?"

"Yes," I said; "they've been pelting me this last half hour, and then they pushed me in."

"The young rips!" cried Bunce. "Never mind. I'm as pleased as if some one had given me a sovereign."

"Yes," I said dismally; "and they'll tell Sir Francis, and I shall have to go."

"Not you," said Bunce. "They're awful curs, but they're beaten, and they won't tell."

"Hallo! what's all this?" said Mr Solomon, coming up.

Bunce told him.

"And did he thrash 'em well?" said Mr Solomon, looking rather angry, "the pair of them?"

"No. They were too strong both at once, but that Ragged Jack of a chap that's been hanging about—him as I told you of this morning—he come out and tackled young Phil when he was on Grant's back, and my word those two have gone off with their tails between their legs. Licked, sir, licked out and out."

"I suppose I shall be sent away, sir," I said, wringing the water out of my shirt-sleeves.

"I suppose you won't," said Mr Solomon sharply. "I've seen a deal, my lad, and I wondered you didn't have a turn at them before. I didn't think you'd got the stuff in you, to tell you the truth."

"Oh, but he had!" said Bunce. "I wish you'd ha' seen."

"Well, I'm sorry," said Mr Solomon. "No, I'm not; I'm glad. They'll leave you alone now. There, go and change your things. It was time you did strike. Here, I'll go with you, or you'll frighten the missus into fits. I say," he shouted back, "keep a sharp look-out for that boy, and catch him if you can. I must have him stopped."

"Poor old Shock!" I thought, as I felt grateful to him for what he had done.

The next minute I was at the gardener's cottage, being scolded and wiped by Mrs Solomon, who said she had never seen such a sight in her life, and who was not happy till she had me down-stairs in dry things, bathing one of my eyes, putting a leech on the other, and carefully strapping up a cut on the back of my head.

Chapter Twenty Five
I Have a Difficult Task

The gardener was right. The fight was a lesson for the boys, who kept at a distance from me, during the next few days, while our scratches and bruises grew faint and began to heal.

We had expected they would have been off to school; but for some reason, illness I believe, the holidays were extended for a month, and so they stayed, but I was pretty well left in peace.

My first hint of Sir Francis' return was given by that gentleman himself, who came upon me suddenly as I was busy in the peach-house. I was painting away at the branches that had become infected with a tiresome kind of blight, when I heard a sharp quick step behind me, and my heart quailed, for I felt that it was Sir Francis about to take me to task for my encounter with his sons.

I kept busily on with my work, in the faint, hope that he might pass me and say nothing, but he stopped short, and looked on as I busied myself with my brush and the poisonous decoction that was to kill the insects.

I was in agony, for I felt that he was looking me through and through, and when he did speak at last I gave quite a jump.

"Hah!" he exclaimed, "rather hard upon the insects. Well, Grant, how are you getting on?"

"Very well, Sir Francis, I think," I said.

"Seen any more of that boy?"

"Yes, Sir Francis," I said, colouring.

"Climbed up the wall, has he?"

"I don't know, Sir Francis," I replied; "but he has got into the garden lately."

"That's right, my lad, be frank," he said. "I know he has got into the garden. I caught my young gentleman and took him to task. He says he came because you were here."

"I'm afraid that is why he did come, Sir Francis," I said.

"Did you tell him to come?"

"No, Sir Francis. We were never very friendly."

"Ho!" he said, and he walked on looking at the peaches for a few minutes, and then went away, leaving me to wipe the cold perspiration off my forehead, for I had fully expected a severe scolding.

I finished my task in the peach-house, and then went to see how the celery was getting on, for I found that when Mr Solomon gave me a task he expected me to continue to watch, whatever it was.

"So that I may feel that when I have put anything in your hands it will be properly done," he said more than once; so, feeling that I was responsible for the success of the celery plants, I was on my way to the bottom garden by the pond, thinking of the encounter I had when I was busy watering there that day, when, as I turned down one of the alleys of the garden, I saw a man in the distance digging up a piece of ground with a broad spade, and turning over the soil in that easy regular way, levelling it as he went, that experienced gardeners acquire.

There was something in his way of digging that seemed familiar, and I stopped and stared. The man stopped too, and glanced in my direction; but he only scraped his spade and went on, while, as soon as I had seen his profile I ran up to him and held out my hand.

"Why, Ike!" I cried, "is that you?"

He paused for a few moments, ran his hand over his nose, involuntarily, I'm sure, glanced down at first one leg, and then the other, after which he went on digging.

"Yes," he said; "it's me."

"Why, what are you doing here?"

"Digging," he said gruffly, and, turning up a spadeful of earth, he gave it a blow with the spade, as if he were boxing its ears, and levelled it smoothly.

"I know that," I cried; "but how is it you're here?"

"Got took on."

"Oh! I am glad," I cried.

He looked up at me sidewise, and drove his spade in again.

"No, you ain't," he said gruffly.

"Indeed I am, Ike," I cried, "though you wouldn't say good-bye."

"Now—now—now—now!" he cried; "don't go on that how."

"Did you come this morning?" I said.

"Been here 'most a week."

"And I didn't know! But why did you leave Mr Brownsmith?"

"I left Old Brownsmith because I wanted to leave him."

"Did you have a quarrel, Ike?"

"Quarrel? No! What should I want to quarrel for?"

"But why did you leave?"

"'Cause I liked. Man ain't a slave, is he?"

"I am glad you're here, though, Ike," I cried.

"Not you," he said sourly, as he thrust and chopped and levelled the soil.

"Indeed but I am," I cried. "Yes, sir, coming," I shouted, for I heard Mr Solomon asking for me.

I went to him, and he set me to water the pots that had been plunged under the big wall; but on going to the pump in the middle of the big walk, where the well was that we used for this garden, I found the handle swing loosely up and down.

I went and told Mr Solomon that there was no water to be had there.

"I thought as much!" he cried angrily. "I saw those boys jerking the handle about yesterday. Here, Bunce!"

Bunce was sent off with a message, and I went about some other task, glad to find that Ike was there at work, for somehow I liked him, though I did not know why, since he was always very gruff and snappish with me. But still it seemed as if he had come to Hampton because I was there.

The next morning, after breakfast, as I went down the garden I found that Mr Solomon was by the well talking to a man who carried a basket of tools.

As I approached he put them down, Mr Solomon helped him, and together they lifted up a great stone in the pathway, which covered the mouth of the well.

There is something very attractive and yet repellent about a well, at least to me. I always want to look down it and listen to the peculiar echoing noise, and the whispers that seem to creep about its green wet sides.

It was so here, and while the man stood talking to Mr Solomon I went down on one knee and peered into the well, to see, far down, a glistening round of what looked like a mirror with my face in it, but in a blurred indistinct way, for there was a musical splashing of water falling from the sides, and as I bent lower the air seemed cold and dank, while above it was sunny and warm.

I started up suddenly, for just then I heard a laugh, and recalling the way in which I had been thrust into the pond I did not care to risk a kick from him who laughed, or from his companion.

For, attracted by Bunce, who was carrying a long ladder, they asked him if he was going to gather fruit, and on learning that the well was being opened they, to use their own words, came to see the fun.

Bunce laid the ladder along the path and went off again to his work, while the two boys seemed to ignore my presence, and stood talking to one another and waiting, Philip throwing stones, while Courtenay amused himself by kicking a coil of rope that lay upon the path.

"Here, Grant," cried Mr Solomon, turning upon me suddenly. "Run to the cottage and get a candle and a box of matches."

"Yes, sir," I said, going.

"Yes sir, certainly sir, yes sir," said Philip in a mocking tone.

"And, Grant," shouted Mr Solomon, "bring one of the men with you."

"Bunce?" I said.

"No, he's busy. Bring that new man, Isaac."

I ran off to the cottage for the candle and matches, and Mrs Solomon asked what they were for.

"To see down in the well, I think," I said.

"Oh yes, to be sure! the pump is broken. Tell master to be very careful. Wells are very dangerous places. I once knew of a well where four men tumbled down and never came up again."

"We'll take care not to tumble," I cried laughing; and I ran off to find Ike, who was digging away near where I had seen him before.

"Eh! Good mornin'!" he said sourly. "Is it? I didn't know. Mornin's seems always all alike to a man as has to dig."

"But how well you're doing it, Ike! It's better dug than our men generally dig it."

"Be it?" he said dubiously: "Well, I have punished it pretty well. Ground's very foul and full o' bear-bine."

"Put down your spade and come along with me," I cried; "they're doing something to the well."

"All right, I'll come!" said Ike sourly. "Pay me my wage and I'm ready. Night work or day work, it's all the same to me, and such is life. 'Tis a rum set out."

"Don't grumble, Ike," I said, "on a morning like this."

"Grumble! That ain't grumbling. But I say, young 'un, are you glad I come?"

"Why, of course I am, Ike."

"So am I then. I s'pose I come o' purpose to work along o' you; but I miss my hoss a deal. I say, Old Brownsmith didn't like it a bit; but here I am; and did you know about young Shock?"

"No: what about him? Have they caught him and sent him away?"

"No: they've caught him and give him a decent suit of clothes, so stiff he can't hardly move in 'em, and he's took on."

"Shock is?"

"To be sure he is; and if he behaves decent his fortun's made."

"Oh, look here, my man," said Mr Solomon as we came up, "you had better stop here and help. Lower down that ladder."

Ike took hold of the ladder as if it were an enemy, gave me a nod, and I went and stood at the foot, so as to hold it down, while Ike raised it erect, and then, taking it by the rounds with his strong brown hands, he lifted it as if it had been a feather, and, walking to the mouth of the well, let the ladder glide softly down till he held the top in his hands; then, swinging it about, he found a resting-place for the bottom upon a piece of wood such as were fixed across the well every ten or a dozen feet to support the pipe and other gear of the pump.

"That do, master?" said Ike.

"Yes," said Mr Solomon. "Now, Mr Grinling, you had better try her. Here, stop, what are you going to do?"

"Going down," said Courtenay.

"Do you know that well is perhaps very foul?" cried Mr Solomon.

"Then it's your place to keep it clean," said Philip sharply. "Go on down, Court, or else I shall."

"You won't, neither of you, go down while I'm here," said Mr Solomon stoutly.

"What right have you to interfere?" cried Courtenay:

"Same right as any man has to interfere when he sees a young goose going to throw away his life."

"Oh rubbish!" said Courtenay. "Just as if I couldn't go down a ladder. Here, stand aside."

Mr Solomon did not stand aside, and he looked so very sturdy and firm that Courtenay gave up and drew back with his brother, whispering and waiting his opportunity.

During this time the plumber had been rattling his tools in his basket, and Mr Solomon turned to him again.

"Ain't you going to try her?" he said. "That well hasn't been open these two years."

"Oh! she's right enough," said the plumber sourly. "It ain't the first time I've been down a well."

"But I don't think it's safe," said Mr Solomon. "What do you say?" he continued, turning to Ike.

"Looks right enough," said Ike, kneeling down and looking into the well. Then rising, "but I wouldn't go down unless I didn't want to come up no more."

"Tchah!" ejaculated the plumber; and I knelt down once more to look for the danger, but could see nothing but the dark whispering hole, with, at a great depth below, the round disc of light representing the mouth of the well.

Just then something passed my head and fell down with, after a while, a strange hollow *plash* from below.

"That'll do," said Mr Solomon angrily. "No more of that, please."

"You mind your own business, Browny. Anyone would think you were the master here."

"Master or no, here's Sir Francis coming. Let's see whether he likes you to be throwing stones down the well."

Mr Solomon uttered a sigh of relief, for, as Sir Francis came along a neighbouring path, the two lads slowly walked away.

"That's a blessing," he said. "Now we can work in peace. You'll try her first—won't you, plumber?"

"All right, gardener. What are you scared about?"

Mr Solomon looked at him angrily and then said:

"I don't know that I'm scared about you, my man; but I don't want to risk my life, or to send down one of my men to fetch you out."

The plumber grunted, and I looked on wondering what the danger was, for I knew nothing then about chemistry or foul gases; and I stared all the more when the plumber took a ball of thin string from his jacket pocket, tied the candle with a couple of half hitches, and then struck a match and lit the wick. Then as soon as it was burning brightly, sheltered by his hands from the breeze, he stooped down and held it in the well and then lowered it down.

We stood round watching the candle swing gently and the flame dance as the plumber slowly unrolled the ball of string.

At first the light looked very pale; but it grew brighter as it left the sunshine near the mouth of the well and lit up the dark slimy-looking old bricks, the rusty iron pipe, and the cross pieces of timber, while far down I could now and then catch sight of the cylinder of the pump as the candle began to swing now like a pendulum. It was very indistinct, just gleaming now and then, while the walls glistened, and I realised more and more what a horrible place it would be for anyone to fall into.

I was full of imaginings of horror, and I fancied the fearful splash, the darkness, the rising to the surface, and then the poor wretch—myself perhaps—striving to get my fingers in between the slippery bricks, and getting no hold, and then—"There!—what did I tell you?" said Mr Solomon.

"She's a foul un, and no mistake," growled Ike.

"Oh! that's nothing," said the plumber. "I've been down worse wells than that."

I was puzzled, for it seemed to me that the candle must be bad. As I had watched it the flame grew brighter and brighter as it reached the darkness, and then it burned more palely, grew smaller, and then all at once it turned blue and went out.

He drew it up, lit it again, and lowered it once more, and it seemed to go down a little lower before it went out.

He drew it up again, relit it, and once more sent it down; and this time it went as far as the cylinder of the pump—which was fixed, I saw, on a sort of scaffold or framework where the foot of the ladder rested.

I was able to see all this before the light went out and was drawn up again.

"All right in a few minutes," said the plumber; and he unfastened the candle, lowered down his basket of tools by means of the string, and made it lodge on a bit of a platform close by the works of the pump.

It was all very interesting to me to see how low down the pump was fixed, and that the handle worked an iron rod up and down—a rod of great length.

The plumber took off his jacket and rolled up his sleeves, after sticking the candle in his waist and the matches in his pocket, and prepared to descend.

"Why, you are not going down like that—are you?" said Mr Solomon.

"I always do go down like that," said the man with a laugh. "How should you go down-head first?"

"No," cried Mr Solomon angrily; "but with a rope fastened to my waist, and a couple of men to hold it."

"D'yer think I'm a baby?" said the plumber, "or a little child?"

"Worse," said Mr Solomon shortly. "You can make them do what's right."

"Tchah! I know what I'm about, just as well as you know how to bud roses."

"I dare say you do," said Mr Solomon sternly; "but that well's got a lot of foul gas in it, and you're not going down without a rope to hold you."

"Rubbish!" said the plumber, laughing; "I am."

"And who's going to use the water agen if you're drowned in it?" said Ike seriously. "It'll be all full o' white-lead and putty, and kill the plarnts!"

"You're very clever," said the plumber sharply; "but just mind your own business."

As he spoke he sat down with his legs in the well, but Mr Solomon seized him by the collar.

"You stop," he cried; "I won't have it. You don't go down that well without a rope round you. Fetch Bunce," he said, addressing Ike.

"If I can't do my work my own way," said the plumber sharply, "I sha'n't do it at all."

He started up, threw on his jacket, and went off after Ike, while Mr Solomon stood thinking.

"Such idiocy!" he exclaimed. "The well isn't safe, and he wants to run unnecessary risks. I suppose he'll come back," he muttered. "Perhaps I shall have to fetch him. Here, Grant, you stop here and don't leave the mouth of the well for fear anyone should go near."

He went after the men, and I lay down gazing into the dark hollow place, wondering what the foul gas was like, and whether I could see it down below; and I was just wishing that I had the candle and string to try experiments, and wondering how far the light would go down now, when I uttered a cry.

My heart seemed to give a great leap, for somebody gave me a rough push and it seemed as if I were going to be thrust down the well.

"There's a coward!" cried Philip jeeringly. "Did you ever see such a cur, Court? Thought he was going down."

"Perhaps I did," I replied warmly, as I glanced from one to the other, wondering whether it was to be war again; but they paid no further attention to me, and began arguing between themselves.

"You daren't!" said Philip.

"Daren't!" cried Courtenay. "Why, I went down last time hanging to a rope when it was cleaned out, and there was no water at the bottom."

"But there is water now—twenty or thirty feet, and you daren't go down."

"Yes I dare."

"Bet you sixpence you daren't."

"Done!" cried Courtenay. "Mind I shall make you pay."

"You daren't go."

"All right; you'll see!" cried Courtenay; and to my horror he went close to the mouth and looked down.

"You can't go down," I said; "the well isn't safe."

"Who spoke to you, pauper?" cried Philip sharply. And then with a sniggering laugh, "It ain't safe, Courtenay. You can't go down, and you'll have to pay me all the same."

"I'm going down," said Courtenay.

"You can't," I cried. "It's full of foul air."

"You mind your own business, pauper," cried Courtenay.

This repetition of the word pauper so enraged me that for the moment I felt tempted to let him go down, but the next moment I shuddered at the thought and cried:

"It is my business. I was to keep everyone from going near."

"Don't take any notice of the workus boy, Court. Go on down, if you dare."

"I dare," he said, laughing.

"I tell you it isn't safe," I cried.

"Do you want a punch on the head?" said Philip menacingly.

"Yes, but you daren't give it me," I cried fiercely.

"Never mind him," said Courtenay. "Look here, I'm only going to the bottom of the ladder. I'm not going to slide down the pipe to the water."

As he spoke he sat down on the edge with his legs dangling over the side.

"Ha, ha, ha!" laughed Philip, seating himself opposite to him and kicking at his brother's feet. "You daren't go."

"You say I daren't go again I'll take you by the scruff of the neck and make you go down instead. I say, let's send the pauper down to swallow the foul air."

"There, I knew you daren't go," cried Philip.

"I dare."

"You daren't."

"He shall not go," I cried; and I caught the lad by the collar.

He gave himself a twist, and as he freed himself he struck me a savage blow with his elbow right in the lower part of the chest.

The blow took away my breath and made me stagger back in agony, and gasping, while by the time I had recovered myself he had stepped on to the ladder, gone down several rounds, and his head disappeared.

"There, coward, what do you think of that?" cried Philip.

I ran to the side with my heart throbbing painfully, and I felt as if my eyes were wild and staring as I saw the lad go down about a dozen feet and stop.

"I say, Phil," he cried, with his voice echoing and sounding hollow, "come down. It is so jolly and cool."

"I'll go down when you've come up," said his brother. "That isn't far enough. I don't call that anything."

"Wait a bit. Don't be in a wax."

"Come up, sir, pray come up," I cried. "There's foul air lower down. The candle wouldn't burn."

"Pitch him down if he don't hold his tongue, Phil," cried Courtenay. "Here goes for a slide."

He grasped the sides of the ladder, took his feet off the round on which he stood, and throwing his legs round he began to slide slowly down.

"I say, it's as cool as eating ices, Phil," he cried. "Come on down."

Philip made no answer, but glanced at me, and I suppose my blanched and horrified countenance startled him, for he too suddenly turned white and exclaimed:

"There, you've won, Court. I give in. Come back now."

Too late! Courtenay slid slowly on for a few moments, then faster, and then we saw his arms relax and he fell over backwards, while as I stood on the brink gazing down I felt as if I had suddenly been turned to stone.

Chapter Twenty Six
"What shall we do?"

I seemed to be standing there some time, but Mr Solomon afterwards told me it was not a moment, before I looked up, and seeing him returning with the plumber, ran towards them swiftly, shouting for help.

The two men started running directly, and as we reached the well together there was Philip lying upon the ground beside the path, face downwards, and with his fingers thrust into his ears.

"Now, then," shouted Mr Solomon to the plumber, as Ike came running up straight across beds, bushes, everything. "Now, then, you said the well was safe; go down and fetch him up."

The plumber went upon one knee, seized the top of the ladder, and got up again shaking his head.

"I can't afford it," he said. "I've a wife and bairns at home."

"I—I daren't go down," groaned Mr Solomon. "Man, man, what shall we do?"

"It scares me," growled Ike hoarsely; "but I've got no wife and no bairns; and if Master Grant here says, 'Go,' I'll go, though," he added slowly, "it's going down into one's grave."

"Can you see him, Grant?" cried Mr Solomon.

"Yes; down on the wood," I said in a hoarse whisper; "he's lying across a beam with his head down. What shall we do?"

As I asked this piteously I raised my head, to see Philip close by me kneeling on the gravel, his eyes half closed, his face of a yellowish grey, his hands clenched, and his teeth chattering.

No one spoke, and as I looked from one man to the other every face was pale and stony-looking, for the men felt that to go down into that carbonic acid gas was to give up life.

I felt horribly frightened, and as if I were sinking somewhere. I glanced round, and there was the beautiful garden all flowers and fruit, with the glorious sunshine over all. Below me that terrible pit with the falling whispering water, and a chill seeming to rise out of its depths.

As I looked I saw Shock coming towards us at a run, as if he divined that something was the matter, and the sight of him made me think of Mr Brownsmith's garden and my happy life there, and I gave a low sob as my eyes filled with tears.

I tell you I felt horribly frightened, and all this that has taken so long to describe seemed to pass in a flash—almost as I started from gazing down the well to my feet.

"Tie the rope round me," I said huskily. "You can pull me up if I fall."

"Well done, young un!" shouted the plumber, catching up the coil of rope. "I like pluck, I do."

"You stand aside," cried Ike, snatching the rope from him and giving him a rough thrust with his elbow. "I'll do this here."

He ran the rope rapidly through his hands, and secured one end about my chest.

Then he made a running noose at the other end.

"Look here," he cried. "You take this here noose in your hand, my lad; there's plenty of rope to reach down double. When you gets to him put it over his arm or his leg, or anywhere, and pull it tight. I'll take care o' you, my boy, and have you up again like a shot."

"Shake hands, Ike," I said, all of a tremble.

"Ay, I will, boy."

"Go, and God help you!" groaned Mr Solomon; and the next instant, with the noose in my hand and just feeling the rope drag on my chest, I stepped on to the ladder, clasped it as Courtenay had done, and let myself slide down.

As I went I looked up, and it seemed dark, for there was a ring of heads round the top; but below as I looked it was still darker.

Down, down, with a curious catching of the breath, and a strange sensation of this not being real seizing me. Then I seemed to wake up and find myself where the water was dripping, and the well whispering, and still I slid down till I was on the slimy platform where the foot of the ladder rested, but young Dalton was not there, but some ten feet down, on the next crosspiece of timber.

"Lower me down," I cried, and hanging by the rope I felt myself lowered more and more, and that I was slowly spinning round; but as I swung to and fro I caught at something I could dimly see, and found it was the great slippery pipe that went down into the water, and guided myself by that.

Only about ten feet; but the distance in that curious state of dread that made me feel as if my breath was painful and difficult, seemed ten times as great. The rope seemed to be compressing the bones of my chest tighter and tighter, and twice over I felt that I was in amongst the foul air that I believed would kill me before I reached the crosspiece on which the lad hung.

The next minute I was seated astride the slippery piece of oak with the water about half a dozen feet below me, and I saw that the least touch would send Courtenay off.

I remembered my lesson though, and, forgetting my dread in the excitement, I slipped the rope over the hanging arm nearest to me, right up to the shoulder, and was in the act of drawing it tight, when, as I bent down, a curious choking sensation seized me, and all was blank.

Ike told me what took place afterwards, for I knew nothing more till I opened my eyes, and found that I was lying down, and several people whose faces looked misty and confused were about me.

I felt sick, and my head throbbed violently. There was a weight over me too, and a curious feeling of confusion, in the midst of which a cool hand was laid upon my fore-head, and I heard some one say:

"He's coming round fast."

I lay quite still for some time, and at last I exclaimed:

"What's the matter—is anyone hurt?"

"Lie still, my lad," said a strange voice.

"I know," I cried excitedly. "Did you get him out?"

"Yes, yes, he's all right, and so are you, Grant, my lad," said Mr Solomon; and just then the room seemed to be darkened, and I heard Ike's voice:

"Is he coming to?"

"Yes. He's all right."

Then I felt that I was wrong about some one else, and that it was that accident with the cart tipping up at Old Brownsmith's, and it was I who was hurt.

That all passed away like a cloud, and my full senses seemed to come back.

"Did you get Master Courtenay out?" I said.

"Yes, my lad, he is quite safe," said a quick sharp voice, which its owner seemed to me trying to make gentle, and turning my head I saw Sir Francis.

I tried to get up, but turned giddy.

"Lie still, my lad," he said kindly. "Don't disturb him, Brownsmith. Good-bye, my lad! I'll see you again."

He shook hands with me and went to the door.

"Well," he said sharply, "are you going to shake hands with the brave fellow who saved your brother's life?"

The next moment I saw young Philip at my side, and he took my hand in his, which felt cold and damp like the tail of a cod-fish.

"If he seems to change in any way," said the voice I had heard before, "send for me directly; but I think he will be all right in an hour or two. I'm going up to the house."

"Who's that?" I said sharply.

"The doctor, my lad," said Mr Solomon.

"But I'm not ill," I said. "What was it? Did I fall into the water?"

"Foul air overcame you, my lad. How do you feel?"

"Yes, how do you feel?" said Mrs Solomon gently, as she took my hand.

"I'm all right," I said, sitting up, and this time I didn't feel giddy. "Only something seems to hurt my chest."

"The rope cut you a bit, that's all. It will soon go off."

Through the open door I could see Ike standing watching me attentively, and as soon as he caught my eye he began to jerk his arm in the air as if he were crying "Hooray!"

Just then a head came slowly round the door-post, and I saw Shock staring in at me; but as soon as he saw that I was looking his head was snatched back.

"How is he now?" said the plumber, coming to the door.

"Oh, I am quite well," I said, in an irritable tone that was new to me, and I got up; "I'm going out now."

"You're well out of it, my lad," said the plumber. "I knowed a case once where five chaps went down one after the other to save him as had gone first, and they all fell to the bottom and died."

"There, for goodness' sake, man, don't talk like that to the lad after what he has gone through," said Mrs Solomon.

"All right, mum," said the plumber; "but as I was going to say, I don't think I shall have the heart to go down today, but I'll see how the air is whether or no."

"You're not going out," said Mrs Solomon.

"Yes, please; it will do me good," I said; and the air did seem to refresh me, as I followed them back to the well, where the plumber tried it again by lowering down the lighted candle, to find it burn brightly till it was down by the cross piece on which young Dalton had lain, after which it went out directly.

He tried it again and again, always with the same result.

"It's got lower and lower," he said. "By to-morrow there won't be much in. That young gent couldn't have been overcome by the bad air," he continued. "It's my belief as he fell out of being frightened, and it's lucky for him that he stopped where he did. If he'd gone a foot lower, that doctor wouldn't have brought him round."

"Well," said Mr Solomon rather impatiently, "what are you going to do?"

"Kiver up the well for to-day, and come on tomorrow."

"But we want water."

"Can't help it; I couldn't go down and work there to-day. My nerves is shook."

"Suppose we put a rope round you."

"Bless your heart, Mr Brownsmith, sir, I couldn't go down if you put two ropes round me. I'm just going to lift out this here ladder, and then p'r'aps your man will help me put on the stone."

Mr Solomon grunted, and I looked on, shivering a little in spite of the hot sunshine as I saw the ladder lifted out and laid down beside the path by Ike, after which Mr Solomon himself helped to put the stone back in its place before walking with the plumber towards the gate.

"How was it all, Ike?" I said eagerly.

"Oh, you'd better ask young Shock here."

Shock, who was in a stiff suit of corduroys, looked at him sharply, spun round, and ran off.

"Y'ever see the likes o' him?" said Ike chuckling. "Puts me in mind of a scared dog, he do, reg'lar."

"But tell me," I said; "how was it? I don't remember."

"Well, it were like this, you see," said Ike. "I were holding the rope tightly and watching of you, and I see you slip on the noose, and tightened it, and then all at once I shouted to the others, 'Hook on,' I says, 'it's got him.'

"I was on the watch for it, you see, and ready, and hauled at once. Thank goodness, I am strong in the arm if I ain't in the head. So I hauled, and they hauled, and so had you both up a few feet directly, one at each end of the rope, and you two couldn't be civil to each other even then, but must get quarrelling."

"Quarrelling! Nonsense, Ike! I was insensible, and so was he."

"I don't care; you was quarrelling and got yourselves tangled up together, and the rope twissen round and round under one of them bits o' wood as goes acrost."

"Yes, I know," I said excitedly, for the thought made me shudder.

"Well, there you was; and the more you was pulled the tighter you was, just below the bottom of the ladder."

"And what did you do, Ike?"

"Well, I was going down, and was about handing the ropes to Old Brownsmith's brother, when young Shock hops in on to the ladder like a wild monkey a'most. Down he goes chattering like anything, and it was no use to shout to him to have a rope. Afore we knowed it a'most, he was down and lying flat on his stum. 'Lower a bit,' he shouts, and we lowered, and he untwisted you two and guided you both clear, and stopped till you were both out, when he came out whistling as if nothing was the matter."

"A brave fellow!" I cried warmly.

"That's what I said," cried Ike; "but the plumber said it was because he didn't know there was any danger."

"Well, Ike, what then?"

"Oh, there's no more to tell, only that Sir Francis come and a doctor was fetched, and the guv'nor said it would be a warning to them two boys; and young shaver who went down's up at home getting all right, and you've got all right, and that's all."

That was not all, for I went down the garden—and found Shock, to thank him for what he had done, but he only turned his back on me and then walked away; while, feeling faint, I turned to go up to the cottage and lie down till the sick sensation had gone off.

I had gone about a dozen yards, when, *thump*! a worm-eaten baking pear, half-grown, hit me on the back, and I did not need telling that it was thrown by Shock.

Chapter Twenty Seven
At the Sand-Pit

The plumber came and repaired the pump next day, going down the well with a couple of men to hold the rope he had round his waist, and I heard Mr Solomon grumbling and laughing a good deal about the care he was taking.

"If he does meet with an accident, Grant," he said, "it won't be his fault this time. Why, you look poorly, my lad. Don't you feel well?"

"I don't indeed, sir," I said; "my head swims, and things look strange about me."

"Ah! yes," he said. "Well, look here; you have a good idle for a day or two."

"But there are so many things want doing in the houses, sir," I said.

"And always will be, Grant. Gardeners are never done. But let that slide. I can get on without you for a day or two."

"Have you heard how Mr Courtenay is?" I asked.

"Yes, ever so much better, young whelp! Sir Francis has been giving his brother a tremendous setting down, I hear; and I think they are going to school or somewhere else at once."

That day, as I was wandering about the kitchen-garden after a chat with Ike, who had settled down to his work just as if he belonged to the place, and after I had tried to have a few words with Shock, who puzzled me more than ever, for he always seemed to hate me, and yet he had followed me here, I heard some one shout, "Hi! halt!"

I turned and saw Sir Francis beckoning to me, and I went up to him.

"Better? Yes, of course. Boys always get better," he said. "Look here. Behaved very well yesterday. Go on. I've said a word to Brownsmith about you; but, look here: don't you tease my lads. Boys will be boys, I know; but they are not in your station of life, and you must not try to make companions of them."

I made no answer: I could not, I was so taken aback by his words; and by the time I had thought of saying that I had never teased either Courtenay or Philip, and that I had always tried to avoid them, he was a hundred yards away.

"They must have been telling lies about me," I said angrily; and I walked on to where Ike was digging, to talk to him about it and ask his advice as to whether I should go and tell Sir Francis everything.

"No," he said, stopping to scrape his spade when I had done. "I shouldn't. It's kicks, that's what it is, and we all gets kicked more or less through life, my boy; but what of it? He wouldn't think no better of you for going and telling tales. Let him find it out. Sure to, some day. Feel badly?"

"Yes," I said, rather faintly.

"Ah! sure to," said Ike, driving his spade into the ground. "But you don't want no doctor. You swallowed a lot of bad air; now you swallow a lot of good, and it'll be like lime on a bit o' newly dug ground. Load or two would do this good. There's the ganger hollering after you."

"Yes!" I cried, and I went towards where Mr Brownsmith was standing.

"Look here, Grant," he said, looking very red in the face. "Sir Francis has given me this to buy you a watch by and by. He says you're too young to have one now, but I'm to buy it and keep it for you a year or two. Five pounds."

"I'm much obliged to him," I said rather dolefully; but I did not feel at all pleased, and Mr Solomon looked disappointed, and I'm afraid he thought I was rather a queer boy.

At the end of the week I heard that Courtenay was better, but that he was to go with his brother down to the seaside, and to my great delight they went; and though I thought the lad might have said, "Thank you," to me for saving his life, I was so pleased to find he was going, that this troubled me very little, for it was as if a holiday time had just begun.

The effects of my adventure soon passed away, and the days glided on most enjoyably. There was plenty to do in the glass-houses, but it was always such interesting work that I was never tired of it; and it was delightful to me to see the fruit ripening and the progress of the glorious flowers that we grew. Mr Solomon was always ready to tell or show me anything, and I suppose he was satisfied with me, for he used to nod now and then—he never praised; and Mrs Solomon sometimes smiled at me, but not very often.

The autumn was well advanced when one day Mr Solomon told me that he had arranged for Ike, as he was a good carter, to go with the strongest horse and cart to a place he named in Surrey, to fetch a good load of a particular kind of silver sand for potting.

"It's a long journey, Grant," he said; "and you'll have to start very early, but I thought you would like to go. Be a change."

"I should like it," I said. "Does Ike know I'm going?"

"No; you can tell him."

I went down to Ike, who was as usual digging, for he was the best handler of a spade in the garden, and he liked the work.

"Hullo!" he said surlily.

"I'm to go with you for the sand, Ike," I cried.

"Think o' that now!" he replied with a grim smile. "Why, I was just a-thinking it would be like going off with the old cart and Bonyparty to market, and how you and me went."

"With Shock on the top of the load," I said laughing.

"Ay, to be sure. Well, he's a-going this time to help mind the horse. And so you are going too?"

"Yes," I said mischievously, "to look after you, and see that you do your work."

"Gahn!" he growled, beginning to dig again. Look here, though; if you ain't ready I shall go without you.

"All right, Ike!" I said. "What time do you start?"

"Twelve o'clock sees me outside the yard gates, my lad. Five arter sees me down the road."

"Do you know the way, Ike?" I said.

"Do I know the way!" cried Ike, taking his spade close up to the blade and scraping and looking at it as if addressing it. "Why, I was born close to that san'-pit, and put Old Brownsmith's brother up to getting some. I can show him where to get some real peat too, if he behaves hisself."

The trip to the sand-pit kept all other thoughts out of my head; and though I was packed off to bed at seven for a few hours' rest, Mr Solomon having promised to sit up so as to call me, I don't think I slept much, and at last, when I was off soundly, I jumped up in a fright, to find that the moon was shining full in at my window, and I felt sure that I had overslept myself and that Ike had gone.

I had not undressed, only taken off jacket, waistcoat, and boots; and I softly opened my door and stole down in my stocking feet to look at the eight-day clock, when, as I reached the mat, a peculiar odour smote on my senses, and then there was the sound of a fire being tapped gently, and Mrs Solomon said:

"I think I'll go and wake him now."

"I am awake," I said, opening the door softly, to find the table spread for breakfast, and Mr Solomon in spectacles making up his gardening accounts.

"Just coming to call you, my lad," he said. "Half-past eleven, and Ike has just gone to the stable."

"And Shock?" I said.

"The young dog! he has been sleeping up in the hay-loft again. Ike says he can't keep him at their lodgings."

I ran back upstairs and finished dressing, to come down and find that Mr Solomon had taken out two basins of hot coffee and some bread and butter for Ike and Shock, while mine was waiting.

"Put that in your pocket, Grant," said Mrs Solomon, giving me a brown paper parcel.

"What is it?" I asked.

"Sandwiches. You'll be glad of them by and by."

I took the packet unwillingly, for I was not hungry then, and I thought it a nuisance; for I had no idea then that I was providing myself with that which would save my life in the peril that was to come.

It was ten minutes to twelve when I went down to the yard, where all the dogs were standing on their hind legs and straining at their chains, eager to be patted and talked to, and strongly excited at the sight of the horse being put to in the strong, springless cart.

They howled and yelped and barked, begging in their way for a run, but they were nearly all doomed to disappointment.

"Just going to start without you," cried Ike in his surly way.

"No, you were not," I said. "It isn't time."

"'Tis by my watch," he growled as he fastened the chains of the cart harness. "I don't pay no heed to no other time."

"Bring as good a load as you can, and the coarser the better; but don't hurry the horse," said Mr Solomon. "Give him his own time, and he'll draw a very heavy load."

"All right, master. I'll take care."

"Got your shovel and pick?"

"Shovel. Shan't want no pick; the sand comes down as soon as you touch it. Now, then, Mars Grant, ready? May as well take a couple more sacks."

The sacks were put in, and we were ready for a start, when a yelp took my attention, and I said:

"I suppose you wouldn't like us to take Juno, sir?"

"Oh, I don't know. Do the dog good. Do you want to take her?"

"Yes," I said eagerly.

The handsome, black, curly-haired retriever barked furiously, for she saw that we were looking at her.

Mr Solomon nodded, and I ran and unbuckled the dog's collar, having my face licked by way of thanks.

As I threw the chain over the kennel Juno bounded up at the horse and then rushed at the gate, barking furiously. Then she rushed back, and charged at all the other dogs, barking as if saying, "Come along, lads, we're off."

But the big gates were set open, Juno rushed out, there was a final word or two from Mr Solomon, who said:

"I sha'n't be surprised if you are very late."

Then the dogs set up a dismal howl as the cart rumbled out over the stones, and in chorus they seemed to say:

"Oh what a shame!"

Then I looked back, and saw Mr Solomon in the moonlight shutting the gates, and I was trudging along beside Ike, close to the horse; and it almost seemed, in the stillness of the night, with the cart rattling by us and the horse's hoofs sounding loud and clear on the hard road, that we were bound for Covent Garden.

"But where's Shock?" I said all at once.

Ike gave his head a jerk towards the cart, and I ran and looked over the tailboard, to see a heap of sacks and some straw, but no Shock. In one corner, though, there was a strongly made boot, and I took hold of that, to find it belonged to something alive, for its owner began to kick fiercely.

"Better jump in, my lad," said Ike, and we did so, when, the seat having been set right so as to balance the weight, Ike gave a chirrup, and we went off at a good round trot.

"Let him be," said Ike as I drew his attention to the heap of straw and sacks. "He goes best when you let him have his own way. He'll go to sleep for a bit, and I dessay we can manage to get on without him. His conversation isn't so very entertaining."

I laughed, and for about an hour we trotted on, the whole affair being so novel and strange that I felt quite excited, and wondered that Ike neither looked to right nor left, but seemed to be studying the horse's ears.

The fact was his thoughts were running in one particular direction, and I soon found which, for he began in his morose way:

"Just as if I should overload or ill-use a hoss! Look at old Bonyparty."

"What do you mean?" I said.

"Why, him talking like that afore we started. I know what I'm about. You'd better lie down and cover yourself over with some sacks. Get a good sleep; I'll call you when we get there."

"What, and miss seeing the country?" I cried.

"Seeing the country! Lor', what a baby you are, Mars Grant! What is there to see in that?"

I thought a great deal; and a glorious ride it seemed through the moonlight and under the dark shadows of the trees in the country lanes. Then there was the dawn, and the sun rising, and the bright morning once more, with the dew glittering on the grassy strands and hedgerows; and I was so happy and excited that Ike said, with one of his grim smiles:

"Why, anybody'd think you was going out for a holiday 'stead of helping to load a sand cart."

"It's such a change, Ike," I said.

"Change! What sort o' change? Going to use a shovel 'stead of a spade; and sand's easy to dig but awful heavy. Here, get up; are you going to lie snoring there all day?"

He leaned over me and poked with the butt of the whip handle at Shock, but that gentleman only kicked and growled, and so he was left in peace.

Just before eight o'clock, after a glorious morning ride through a hilly country, we came to a pretty-looking village with the houses covered in with slabs of stone instead of slates or tiles or thatch, and the soft grey, and the yellow and green lichen and moss seemed to make the place quaint and wonderfully attractive to me; but I was not allowed to sit thinking about the beauty of the place, for Ike began to tell me of the plan of our campaign.

"Yon's the sand-hill," he said, pointing with his whip as he drew up at a little inn. "We'll order some braxfass here; then while they're briling the bacon we'll take the cart up to the pit and leave it, and bring the horse back to stop in the stable till we want him again."

The order was given, and then we had a slow climb up a long hill to where, right at the top, the road had been cut straight through, leaving an embankment, forty or fifty feet high, on each side, while, for generations past, the sand had been dug away till the embankments were some distance back from the road.

"Just like being on the sea-shore," said Ike. "I see the ocean once. Linkyshire cost. All sand like this. Rum place, ain't it?"

"I think it's beautiful," I said as the cart was drawn over the yielding sand, the horse's hoofs and the wheels sinking in deep, while quite a cliff, crowned with dark fir-trees, towered above our heads. The face of the sandy cliff was scored with furrows where the water had run down, and here it was reddish, there yellow or cream colour, and then dazzlingly white, while just below the top it was honey-combed with holes.

"San'-martins' nesties," said Ike, pointing with his whip. "There's clouds of 'em sometimes. There they go."

He pointed to the pretty white-breasted birds as they darted here and there, and on we still went, jolting up and down in the sandy bottom, where there was only a faint track, till we were opposite to a series of cavern-like holes and the sand cliff towered up with pine-trees here and there half-way down where the sand had given way or been undermined, and they had glided down a quarter—half—three parts of the distance. In short, it was a lovely, romantic spot, with a view over the pleasant land of Surrey on our right, and on our left a cliff of beautiful salmon-coloured sand, side by side with one that was quite white.

"You won't get better sand than that nowheres," said Ike, standing up and getting out of the cart, an example I followed. "Here we'll pitch, Mars Grant, and—"

Quickly and silently, as he gave me a comical look, he unhitched a chain or two, unbuckled the belly-band, and let the shafts fly up.

The result was that Shock's head went bang against the tail-board, and then his legs went over it, and he came out with a curious somersault, and stared about only half awake, and covered with straw and sacks.

He jumped up angrily, and as soon as he saw that we were laughing at him, turned his back, and kicked the sand at us like a pawing horse; but Ike gave the whip a flick at him, and told him to put the sacks in the cart.

"No one won't touch them. Come along, old horse," he cried; and, leading the way, the horse followed us with the reins tucked in its pad, and we waded through the sand in which Juno rolled and tried to burrow till we were out once more in the hard road, where the dog had to be whistled for, consequent upon her having started a rabbit.

We found her at last, trying to get into a hole that would have been a tight fit for a terrier, and she came reluctantly away.

The most delicious breakfast I ever tasted was ready at the little inn; but Ike saw to his horse first, and did not sit down till it was enjoying its corn, after a good rub down with a wisp of straw. Then the way in which we made bread and bacon disappear was terrible, for the journey had given us a famous appetite.

Shock would not join us, preferring the society of the horse in the stable, but he did not fare badly. I saw to that.

At last after a final look at the horse, who was to rest till evening, we walked back to the sand-pit, climbing higher and higher into the sweet fresh air, till we were once more by the cart, when Ike laid one hand upon the wheel and raised the other.

"Look here, lads," he said; "that horse must have eight hours' rest 'fore tackling her load, and a stop on the way home, so let's load up at once with the best coarse white—we can do it in half an hour or so—then you two can go rabbiting or bird-nesting, or what you like, while I have a pipe and a sleep in the sand till it's time to get something to eat and fetch the horse and go."

"Where's a shovel?" I cried; and Shock jumped into the cart for another.

"Steady, lads, steady," said Ike; "plenty of time. Only best coarse white, you know. Wait till I've propped the sharps and got her so as she can't tilt uppards. That's your sort. She's all right now. We don't want no more berryin's, Mars Grant, do we? Now, then, only the best white, mind. Load away."

He set the example, just where the beautiful white sand seemed to have trickled, down from the cliff till it formed a softly rounded slope, and attacking this vigorously we were not long before Ike cried:

"Woa!"

"But it isn't half full," I cried.

"No, my lad. If it was," said Ike, "our horse couldn't pull it. That stuff's twice as heavy as stones. There, stick in your shovels, and now be off. Don't go far. You ought with that dog to find us a rabbit for dinner."

Shock's eyes flashed, and he looked quite pleased, forgetting to turn his back, and seeming disposed for once to be friendly, as, with Juno at our heels, we started up the sandy bottom on an expedition that proved one of the most adventurous of our lives.

Chapter Twenty Eight
Lost!

Purple heath, golden gorse, and tufts of broom. Tall pines with branches like steps to tempt you to climb. Regular precipices after climbing above the sand-pit, from which you could jump into the soft sand, and then slide and roll down to the bottom. Once I jumped upon a little promontory high above the slope, and it gave way, and I slid down on about a ton of matted root and earth and sand.

Then we climbed to the sand-martins' nests, and slipped down or rolled down, and climbed again, and along ledges, and thrust in our arms, but nesting was over for the year, and the swift little birds made their nurseries beyond our reach, for we did not find the bottom of one single hole.

Shock was full of fun, and shouted and threw sand at Juno, who barked, and made believe to bite him, and rolled over and over with him down some slope, to be half buried in the sand at the bottom.

We soon forgot all about Ike, but we once smelt a whiff of tobacco, which seemed to be mingled with the sweet scent of the pines in the hot sunshine.

There were butterflies, too, red admirals, that came flitting into the sandy bottom, and settled on the face of the sandy cliff, but always sailed away before we got near. Then we went out on to the wild heathery waste to the south, and chased lizards in the dry short growth. Then Shock uttered an excited cry and drew back Juno, who was sniffing, and struck two or three rapid blows at something, ending by stooping and raising a little writhing serpent by the tail.

"Nedder," he said, and he crushed it beneath his heel.

There were grasshoppers, too, by the thousand, and furze, and stone-chats flitting from bush to bush, while sometimes a dove winged its way overheard, or uttered its deep coo from the pine-wood at the foot of the hill.

Delicious blue sky overhead; a view all about that seemed to fade into a delicious bluey pink; and the sweet warm odour of the earth rising to be breathed and drunk in and enjoyed; the place seemed to me a very paradise, and the dog appeared to enjoy it as much as I.

Shock rarely spoke to me, but he did not turn his back. The boy was as excited as the dog, going down on all-fours to push his way amongst the heath and broom, and scratch some hole bigger where it was evident that a rabbit had made his home. Then he was after a butterfly; then stalking a bird, as if he expected to catch it without the proverbial salt for its tail; and I'm afraid I was just as wild.

I don't know that I need say *afraid*, for our amusement was innocent enough, and you must remember that we were two boys, who resembled Juno, the dog, in this respect that we were let loose for a time, and enjoying the freedom of a scamper over the hills.

We had gone some distance through the pines, when, as we turned back and came to where they suddenly ended, and the earth down the slope seemed to be covered with pine needles, and was all heather and short fine furze, I sat down suddenly on the soft fir leaves, taking off my cap for the sweet fresh breeze to blow through my hair. Shock flung himself down on his chest, and the dog couched between us with her eyes sparkling, her mouth open, and her tongue out and curled up at the end, as she panted with fatigue and excitement.

"I say," cried Shock all at once, with his face flushed, and his eyes full of excitement, "don't let's go back—let's stop and live here. I'll find a cave in the sand."

"And what are we to live on?" I said.

"Rabbits, and birds, and snails, and fish—there's a big pond down there. Let's stop. There'll be nuts and blackberries, and whorts, and pig-nuts, and mushrooms. There's plenty to eat. Let's stop."

He looked up at me eagerly.

"I can make traps for birds, and ketch rabbits, and—look, there she goes."

He started to his feet, for there was a bound and a rustle just below us, as a rabbit suddenly found it was in danger, and darted away to find out a place of refuge lower down the hill.

"Hey, dog! on, dog!" cried Shock, clapping his hands; and Juno took up the scent directly, running quickly in and out amongst, the furze and heath, while Shock and I followed for about a quarter of a mile, when, panting and hot, we came upon Juno carrying a fine rabbit in her mouth, for this time she had overtaken it before one of the burrows was reached.

"Good dog!" cried Shock. "Dinner;" and, taking the rabbit by the hind legs, the dog wagged her tail as if asking whether she had not done that well, and followed us as we went back to where we had seen the holes in the sandy cliff.

We avoided the cut near which we knew that Ike would be having his nap, and, making our way to the bottom of the cliff, we selected one of the biggest of the holes, stooped and went in, and found that it widened out to some ten or a dozen feet, and then ran back, thirty or forty.

It seemed to be partly natural, partly to have been scooped out by hand, while it certainly seemed just the place for us.

"We'll stop here," cried Shock. "You go and get a lot of wood from up a-top, where there's lots lying, while I skins the rabbud."

"What are you going to do?" I said.

"Make a fire and cook him for dinner."

I was in no wise unwilling, for it seemed very good fun, and going out I climbed up through a narrow gully and into the fir-wood, where I soon found a good armful of wood, carried it to the edge of the cliff, just over the mouth of the hole, and went back and got another and another.

When I climbed down again I found Shock busy finishing his task, and as I entered Juno was making a meal of the skin peppered with sand.

Shock came out after sticking his knife in the cliff wall for a peg on which to hang the rabbit, and we soon put the wood inside the hole, where, Shock being provided with matches, we soon had a fire burning, and from the way in which it drew into the cave it seemed as if there must be a hole somewhere, and this I found in the shape of a crack in the roof, through which the smoke rose.

The novelty of the idea kept me from minding the smoke, and I entered into the fun of keeping up the fire, feeding it with bits of wood, while Shock skewered the rabbit on a neatly cut stick, and placed it where the fire was clear of smoke, so that it soon began to hiss and assume a pleasanter colour than the bluish-red that a skinned rabbit generally wears.

The fire burned freely, and Shock lay down on his chest and kicked his heels about after the fashion practised when he was on the top of the market cart.

His face was a study, as he watched the progress of his cookery; while Juno took the other side of the fire, couched, and watched the hissing sputtering rabbit too, as if calculating how much she would get for her share.

I looked at them for a few minutes, and then, finding the smoke rather too much for me, not being such an enthusiast about cooking as Shock, I began to explore the sand-cave, to find it ended about a dozen paces in from the fire, and that there was nothing more to see, while the place was very smoky and very hot.

"Here, come and watch the rabbud while I go and get some more wood," shouted Shock to me.

"No, thank you," I said. "You may watch the cooking. I'll get some wood."

I hung my jacket on a stone that stuck out of the wall and went out for the wood, glad to be away from the heat and smoke, and after climbing up among the firs I collected and brought back a good faggot, with which the fire was fed till Shock declared the rabbit done.

"Are you ready?" he said.

"Ready!" I replied, as I looked at the half-raw, half-burned delicacy. "No: I don't want any, Shock. You may have it."

"You don't want none?" he said, staring at me with astonishment.

"No: I've got some sandwiches in my pocket, and I shall eat them by and by."

"Oh, all right!" he said; and, taking his pocket-knife, he cut off the rabbit's head and held it out to the dog.

"There's your bit," he said. "Be off."

Juno took the hot delicacy rather timorously; but she seemed to give the donor a grateful look, and then trotted out into the sunshine, and lay down to crunch the bones.

The fire was nearly out, the fir-wood burning fiercely and quickly away; but though it was a nuisance to me it seemed to find favour with Shock, who set to work, like the young savage he was, tearing off and devouring the rabbit, throwing the bones together, ready for the dog when she should come back. I felt half disgusted, and yet hungry, so, going to where I had hung my jacket, I thought I would get out the sandwiches Mrs Solomon had cut for me; but as I turned round and looked at Shock I felt that I should enjoy them better if I waited till he had done.

So I leaned against the rough side of the sand-cave, watching him tear away at the bones, holding a piece in one hand, the remains of the rabbit in the other.

I remember it all so well—him sitting there with just a faint blue curl of smoke rising from the embers, and beyond him, seen as it were in a rugged frame formed by the low entrance of the hole, was the lovely picture of hill and vale, stretching far as the eye could reach, and all bright in the sunshine, and with the bare sky beyond.

I was just thinking what a rough-looking object Shock seemed as he sat there just in the entrance to the hole, and wishing that, now he had a good situation and was decently clothed, he would become like other boys, when I saw Juno come slowly towards Shock, wagging her tail and showing her teeth as if asking for more bones, but she suddenly whisked round and darted away, as, with a noise like a dull clap of thunder, something seemed to shut out the scene from the mouth of the hole, I felt a puff of heat and smoke in my face, and all was darkness.

I stood there as if petrified for a minute, I should think, quite unable to make out what was the matter, and panting for breath.

Then the thought came like a flash, that a quantity of sand had fallen, and blocked up the mouth of the cave.

For a moment or two I felt as if I should fall. Then the instinct of self-preservation moved me to act, and with my hands stretched out before me I went quietly towards the entrance.

"Shock! Shock!" I cried, but there was no reply, and it sounded as if my voice was squeezed up in a narrowed space; then I seemed to hear a rustling noise as I stepped forward, I was kicked violently in the shins and fell forward with my hands plunging into a mass of soft sand, and to my horror I found that I was lying upon my companion, who was half buried.

The perspiration stood out all over me as I leaped to my feet; and then went down again to find that Shock was kicking frantically, and a moment's investigation told me that he could not extricate himself.

Seizing one of his legs, which as I grasped by the ankle and clasped it to my side, kept giving spasmodic jerks, I dragged with all my might, and found I could not move him; but as I dragged again he seemed to give a tremendous throb, and I went backwards, followed, it seemed to me in the darkness, by a quantity of soft sand; but Shock was free, for I could feel him by me lying on his face, and as I turned him over he uttered a groan.

And now a horrible sensation of fear came over me as I thoroughly realised that I was buried alive in that sand-cave. I felt that my climbing about on the top of the cliff had loosened or cracked the compressed sand. Shock and I had jumped about over it when we threw down the wood we had gathered, and that seemed to be the explanation of the mishap.

But I had no time to think of this now, for the thought that perhaps Shock was killed, suffocated, came over me with terrible force, and I bent over him, feeling his face, his heart, and hands.

His heart was beating fast, and his hands were warm, but though I spoke to him over and over again, in the darkness, there was no answer, and with a cry of despair I threw myself on my knees, when all at once he shouted:

"Hullo!"

"Shock," I cried, "I'm here."

"What yer do that for?" he cried fiercely.

"I didn't do anything."

"Yes, yer did," he cried. "Yer threw a lump o' sand on my head. I'm half blind, and my ears is full. Just wait till I gets hold on yer, I'll pay yer for it."

Then he began panting, and spitting, and muttering about his eyes, and at last—"Here, where are yer?"

"I'm here, close by you," I said. "Don't you understand? The sand has fallen and shut us in."

There was silence for a few minutes—a terrible painful silence to me, as I felt that I was face to face with death. Then Shock seemed to have grasped the situation, for he said coolly enough:

"Like the rabbuds. Well, we shall have to get out."

"Yes, but how?" I cried.

"Same's they do. Scratch yer way, and make a hole. I don't mind, do you?"

"Mind!" I said, "it's horrible."

"Is it?" he replied quietly. "Why?"

"Don't you see—"

"No," he said sharply, "not werry well. I can a little."

"But I mean, don't you understand?" I cried in an awe-stricken choking voice, "that if we don't get out soon, we shall die."

"What, like when you kills a rabbud or a bird?"

"Yes."

"Get out!" he cried in contemptuous tones. "I hadn't finished my rabbud, and my eyes is half full of sand still."

"Never mind the rabbit," I said angrily, "let's try and dig our way out."

"Let Ikey do it," he said, "he's got the shovels."

Brownsmith's Boy | 249

"But will he find out where we are," I cried, for I must own to being terribly unnerved, and ready to marvel at Shock's coolness.

"Why, of course he will," said Shock. "I say, don't you be frightened. You don't mind the dark, do you?"

"I don't mind the dark," I replied, "but it's horrible to be shut in here."

"Why, it's only sand," he said, "only sand, mate."

"But it nearly smothered you," I cried. "It would have smothered you if I hadn't pulled you out."

"Yes, but that was because it fell atop of my head and held me down, else it wouldn't. I thought it was your games."

I had never heard Shock talk like this before. Our mutual distress seemed to have made us friends, and I felt ready to shake hands with him and hold on by his arm.

"I say," he cried, his voice sounding, like mine, more and more subdued—at least so it seemed to me—"I say, I weren't looking; it didn't go down on the dog too—did it?"

"No, Shock, I saw her run away."

There was a few moments' silence and then he said:

"Well, I am glad of that. I likes dorgs, and we was reg'lar good friends."

"Hark!" I said; "is that Ike digging?"

"No," he said; "it was some more sand tumbled down, I think."

I knew he was right, for there was a dull thud, and then another; but whether inside or outside I could not tell. It made me tremble though; for I wondered whether I should be able to struggle out if part of the roof came down upon my head.

All at once Shock began to whistle—not a tune, but something of an imitation of a blackbird; and as I was envying him his coolness in danger I heard a scratching noise and saw a line of light. Then there was another scratch and a series of little sparkles. Another scratch, and a blue flame as the brimstone on the end caught fire; and then, as the splint of wood burned up, I could see in the midst of a ring of light the face of Shock, looking very intent as he bent over the burning match, and held to it the wick of a little end of a common tallow candle.

"I allus carries a bit o' candle out of the lanthorns," he said, showing his teeth; and then he held up the light, and I could see that the opening to the cave was completely closed up, just as if the roof had all come down, and the cave we were in was not half the size it was at first, a slope of sand encroaching on the floor. I felt chilled, for I felt that it would be impossible to tunnel through that sand.

"Now, then," said Shock coolly, "that there's the way—ain't it? Well, we don't want no light to see to do that; so you put it out 'case we wants it agen, and put it in yer pocket. I'll go down on my knees and have first scratch, and when I'm tired you shall try, and we'll soon get through it. We won't wait for Ike."

I longed to keep the candle burning, but what Shock said seemed to be right; so I put it out, and as I did so I saw the boy begin to scratch away as hard as he could at the sand in the direction of the entrance, and then in the dark I could hear him panting away like some wild animal.

"I say," he cried at last.

"Yes," I said.

"It don't seem no good. More you pulls it away, more it comes down. It's like dry water, and runs all through your hands."

"Let me have a try," I said.

"All right. You go where I did, and keep straight on."

Keep straight on! It was, as he said, like grasping at water; and the more I tore at it, in the hope of making a tunnel through, the more it came pouring down, till in utter despair I gave it up and told Shock it was no good.

"Never mind," he said. "It's dry and warm. I've been in worse places than this is, where you couldn't keep the rain out. Let's sit down and talk. I say I wish I'd got the rest o' my rabbud."

I didn't answer, for, hot, weary, and despairing at our position, I was lying down on the sand with my hands covering my face.

I don't know how long a time passed, for I felt confused and strange; but I was aroused by Shock, who exclaimed suddenly:

"Here, I want to get out of this. Let's have another try at scratching a hole."

I heard him move, and then he struck a light again so as to see where to begin.

"Must know, you see," he said. "If I get scratching at the wrong side, it would take so long to get out."

In spite of my trouble I could not help feeling amused, there seemed to be something so droll in the idea of Shock burrowing his way right into the hill and expecting to get out; but the next moment I was listening to him and watching the tiny spark at the end of the burned match die out.

Rustle, rustle, rustle, he went on, and every now and then there was a loud panting such as some wild animal would make. Then I uttered a cry of fear, for I felt a quantity of sand strike me and I bounded aside, for it seemed that the top was coming down.

"What's matter?" cried Shock, stopping short.

"Nothing," I said as I realised the cause of my fright. "Some of the sand hit me."

"What! some as I chucked behind me?"

"Yes."

The scratching and tearing went on again, and I felt the sand scattered over me several times, but the fear did not attack me again.

All at once there was a soft rushing noise, and Shock uttered a yell which seemed to make my heart leap.

"Shock!" I cried, "Shock!" but there was no answer, only a scuffling noise. "Shock! where are you?"

The scuffling noise continued, and their there was a loud panting, a cry of "Oh!" and my companion staggered by me.

"Shock!" I cried.

"Oh! I say," he groaned, "I've got it all in my eyes agen. A lot come down and buried me. I sha'n't do it no more."

He uttered a series of strange gasps and cries, shaking himself, spitting, and stamping on the ground.

"I swallowed lots o' sand, I think, and it come down on my back horrid. You try now."

I hesitated, but felt that I must not be cowardly if I wished for us to escape; and so I asked him to light a match again.

He did so, and by its feeble light I saw where to work, and also that, the place seemed to be filling up with the sand, and that we had not half so much room as we had at first.

Then out went the light, and with a desperate haste I went down on my hands and knees and began to tear at and throw the sand behind me, filling up our prison more and more, but doing nothing towards our extrication, for as fast as I drew the sand away from the tunnel more came; and at last, just as I began to think that I was making a little progress, I heard a rustling, dribbling sound, some hard bits of adhesive sand fell upon my head, and I instinctively started back, as there was a rush that came over my knees, and I knew that if I had remained where I was, tunnelling, I should have been buried.

"What, did you get it?" cried Shock, laughing.

I was so startled that I did not answer.

"Oh! he's buried!" cried Shock in a wild tone; and he threw himself by me, and began to tear at the sand. "Mars Grant, Mars Grant," he cried excitedly. "Don't leave me here alone."

"I'm not there, Shock," I said. "I jumped back."

"Then what did yer go and pretend as you was buried in the sand for?" cried the boy savagely.

I did not reply, and I heard him go as far from me as he could, muttering and growling to himself, and in spite of my position I could not help thinking of what a curious and different side I was seeing of Shock's character. I had always found him so quiet and reserved, and yet it was evident that he could talk and think like the best of us, and somehow it seemed as if in spite of the way in which he turned away he had a sort of liking for me.

This idea influenced me so that I felt a kind of pity for my companion in misfortune. That was a good deal in the direction of liking him in return. I felt sorry that I had frightened him, and at last after a good deal of thinking I said to him:

"Shock!"

"Hullo!"

"I'm sorry I made you think I was buried."

"Are yer?"

"Yes. Will you shake hands?"

"What for?"

This staggered me, and I could make no reply, and so we remained silent for some time.

"Here, let's see," said Shock all at once. "Where's that there candle?"

"Here it is," I said, and as he struck a light I held the scrap of little more than an inch long to the flame, and it burned up so that we could examine our position, and we soon found that our prison was reduced to about half its size.

"It's of no use to try and dig our way out, Shock," I said despairingly, as I extinguished the candle. "We shall only bring down more sand and cover ourselves in."

"Like Old Brownsmith's toolips," said Shock, laughing. "I say, should we come up?"

"Don't talk like that," I said angrily. "Don't you understand that we are buried alive."

"Course I do," he said. "Well, what on it?"

"What of it?" I said in agony, as the perspiration stood upon my brow.

"Yes, what on it? They'll dig us out like we do the taters out of a clamp. What's the good o' being in a wax. I wish I'd some more rabbud."

I drew in a long breath, and sat down as far from the sealed-up opening as I could get, and listened to the rustling trickling noise made by the sand every now and then, as more and more seemed to be coming in, and I knew most thoroughly now that our only course was to wait till Ike missed us, and came and dug us out.

"And that can't be long," I thought, for we must have been in here two or three hours.

All at once I heard a peculiar soft beating noise, and my heart leaped, for it sounded like the quick strokes of a spade at regular intervals.

"Hear that, Shock?" I cried.

"Hear what?" he said, and the noise ceased.

"Somebody digging," I cried joyfully.

"No. It was me—my feet," he said, and the sound began again, as I realised that he must be lying in his old attitude, kicking his legs up and down.

If I had any doubt of it I was convinced the next moment, for he burst out:

"I've been to Paris, and I've been to Do-ho-ver,
I've been a travelling all the world o-ho-ver.
Over and over, and over, and o-ho-ver,
So drink up yer licker and turn the bowl o-ho-ver."

"Don't, don't, don't, Shock," I cried passionately. "I can't bear it;" and I again covered my face with my hands, and crouched lower and lower, listening to the trickling of the sand that seemed to be flowing in like water to take up all the space we had left.

Suddenly I started, for a hand touched me.

"Is that you, Shock?"

"Yes. Mind my coming and sitting along o' you? I ain't so werry dirty now."

"Mind? no," I said: "it will be company."

"Yes," he said. "It's werry dark and werry quiet like, ain't it?"

"Yes, very."

"Ain't Ike a long time?"

"Yes," I said despairingly, for I began to wonder whether we should be found.

"I'd ha' came shovelling arter him 'fore now. I say, ain't you tired?"

"Tired!" I said. "No, I never thought of feeling tired shut up in this horrible place. Let's try if we can't get out by the way the smoke went."

"I've been trying," said Shock; "but it's too high up. You can't reach it."

"Not if you stood on my shoulders?"

"No," he said. "I looked when you had hold of the candle, and if you did try you'd only pull the sand down atop of your head."

I knew it, and heaved a deep sigh.

Then there was a long silence, and I was roused out of thoughts about how we had enjoyed ourselves that morning, and how little we had imagined that we should have such a termination to our holiday, by a heavy breathing.

I listened, and there it was quite loud as if some animal were near.

"Do you hear that, Shock?" I whispered.

There was no answer.

"Shock!" I said, "do you hear that noise?"

No answer, and I understood now that in spite of our perilous position he had fallen fast asleep.

Chapter Twenty Nine
Finding a Treasure

"Can't be time to get up yet," I thought, and I turned over on my soft bed. It was too dark, and I was dozing off again when a loud snorting gasp made me start and throw off the clothes that lay so heavy on me.

Then I stopped short, trembling and puzzled. Where was I? It was very dark. That was not clothes, but something that slipped and trickled through my fingers as I grasped at it. My legs felt heavy and numbed, and this darkness was so strange that I couldn't make it out.

Was I asleep still? I must have been to sleep—heavily asleep, but I was awake now, and—what did it mean?

A curious feeling of horror was upon me, and I lay perfectly still. I could not stir for some minutes, and then it all came like a flash, and I knew that I must have lain listening for some time to Shock breathing heavily, and then insensibly have fallen asleep, and for how long?

That I could not of course tell, but so long that the sand had gone on trickling in till it had nearly covered me, as I lay nearest to the opening. It had been right over my chest, and sloped up and away from, me, so that my legs were deeply buried, and it required quite a struggle to get them free, while to my horror as I dragged them out from beneath the heavy weight more sand came down, and one hard lump rolled down and up against me sufficiently hard to give me pain.

There was the same terrible silence about me, and it seemed to grow deeper. A short time before I had heard Shock breathing hard, but now his breath came softly, and then seemed to cease.

That silence had lasted some time, when all at once it was broken by my companion as I knelt there in the soft sand.

"Mars Grant! I say. You awake?"

"Yes."

"What yer doing of?"

"I am saying my prayers."

There was another silence here, and then Shock said softly:

"What yer praying for?"

"For help and protection in this terrible place," I cried passionately; and I crouched down lower as I bowed myself and prayed that I might see the sunshine and the bright sky once again—that I might live.

Just then a hand was laid upon my shoulder, and I felt Shock's lips almost touch my ear as he whispered softly:

"I say—I want to say my prayers too."

"Well," I said sternly, "pray."

There was again that silence that seemed so painful, and then a low hoarse voice at my side said slowly:

"I can't. I 'most forgets how."

"Shock," I cried, as I caught at his hands, which closed tightly and clung to mine; and for the first time it seemed to come to me that this poor half-wild boy was only different to myself in that he had been left neglected to make his way in life almost as he pleased, and that in spite of his wilful ways and half-savage animal habits it was more the want of teaching than his fault.

I seemed to feel brighter and more cheerful as we sat together soon after, discussing whether we should light the candle again, and all at once Shock exclaimed:

"I say."

"What, Shock?"

"I won't shy nothing at you no more."

"It does not seem as if you will ever have the chance, Shock," I cried dolefully.

"Oh, I don't know, mate," he said; and at that word "mate" I seemed to feel a curious shrinking from him; but it passed off directly.

"Shall I light the candle?" he said after a pause.

"Yes, just for one look round," I said. "Perhaps we can find a way out."

The candle was lit, and I started as I saw how much the sand had crept in during the time that we had been asleep. It had regularly flowed in like water, and as we held the candle down there was one place where it trickled down a slope, just as you see it in an egg-boiler or an old-fashioned hourglass.

We looked all round; went to the spot where the hole ended in what was quite hard sandy rock. Then we looked up at the top, where we could dimly make out the crack or rift through which the smoke had gone, but there was no daylight to be seen through it, though of course it communicated with the outer air.

Then we had a look at the part where we had come in, but there the sand was loose, and we had learned by bitter experience that to touch it was only to bring down more.

"I say," said Shock, as we extinguished the scrap of candle left, part of which had run down on Shock's hand; "we're shut up."

"Shut up!" I said indignantly; "have you just found that out?"

"Well, don't hit a fellow," he cried. "I say, have a bit?"

"Bit of what?" I cried, as I realised how hungry I had grown.

"Taller," he said. "Some on it run down. There ain't much; two or three little nobbles. I'll give yer a fair whack."

"Why, you don't mean to eat that, you nasty fellow," I cried.

"Don't!" he said; "but I do. Here's your half. I've eat worse things than that."

"Why, Shock," I cried, as a flash of hope ran through me, "I forgot."

"Forgot what?" he cried. "Way out?"

"No," I said gloomily; "but my sandwiches—bread and meat Mrs Solomon cut for me."

"Bread and meat!" he shouted. "Where is it?"

"In my jacket. I hung it on a stone in the side somewhere here. Light a match."

Crick—crick—crack went the match; then there was a flash, and the sputtering bubbling blue flame of the sulphur, for matches were made differently in those days, when paraffin had not been dreamed of for soaking the wood.

Then the light burned up clearly, and Shock held the splint above his head, and we looked round.

"There ain't no jacket here," said Shock dolefully. "What did yer say bread and meat for?" he continued, as the match burned out and he threw it down. "It's made me feel so hungry. I could eat a bit o' you."

"I can't understand it, Shock," I said.

"I wish I'd got some snails or some frogs," he muttered. "I could eat 'em raw."

"Don't," I said with a shudder.

"I knowed a chap once who eat two live frogs. Put 'em on his tongue—little uns, you know—and swallowed 'em down. He said he could feel 'em hopping about inside him after. Wasn't he a brute?"

"Don't talk to me," I cried, as I went feeling about the wall, with my head in a state of confusion. "I know I had the jacket in here."

"Have you got it on?" he said.

"No—no—no! I hung it on a bit of sharp stone that stuck out of the wall somewhere, and I can't feel the place. It's so puzzling being in the dark. I don't know which is front and which is back now."

"Front's where the soft sand is," said Shock.

"Of course," I cried, feeling half stupefied all the time. "Then this is the front here. I hung it on the stone and it was just above my head."

I walked about on the soft sand, feeling about above my head, and all over the face of the cave side for a long time in vain; and then with my head swimming I sank down in despair, and leaned heavily back, to utter a cry of pain.

"What's matter?" cried Shock, coming to me.

"I've struck the back of my head against a sharp stone," I cried, turning round to feel for the projecting piece.

"Why, it's here, Shock. This is the piece I hung my jacket on, but it has sunk down. No, no," I cried; "I forgot; it is the bottom of the hole that has filled up. The sand has come up all this way. Keep back."

I had turned on my hands and knees and was tearing out the sand just below the projecting piece of sand-rock.

"What yer doing?" cried Shock. "You'll make more come down and cover us up."

"My jacket is buried down here," I cried, and I worked away feeling certain that I should find it, and at last, in spite of the sand coming down almost as fast as I tore it out, I scratched and scraped away till, to my great delight, I got hold of a part of the jacket and dragged it out.

"Hurrah!" I cried. "I've got it."

"And the bread and meat?" cried Shock. "Oh, give us a bit; I am so bad."

"No," I said despairingly.

"What! yer won't give me a bit?" he cried fiercely.

"It isn't here," I said. "It was in my pocket, but it's gone. Stop!" I cried; "it was a big packet and it must have come out."

I plunged my arms into the soft sand again, and worked away for long, though I was ready to give up again and again, and my fingers were getting painfully sore, but I worked on, and at last, to my great delight, as I dug down something slipped slowly down on to the back of my hands—I had dug down past it, and the sand had brought it out of the side down to me.

"Here it is!" I cried, standing up and shaking the sand away from the paper as I tore it open.

Shock uttered a cry like a hungry dog as he heard the paper rustle, and then I divided the sandwiches in two parts and wrapped one back in the paper.

"What yer doin'?" cried Shock.

"Saving half for next time," I said. "We mustn't eat all now."

Shock growled, but I paid no heed, and gave him half of what I had in my hands, and then putting the parcel with the rest right at the end where the sand did not fall, I sat down and we ate our gritty but welcome meal.

We tried round the place again and again, using up the candle till the wick fell over and dropped in the sand; and then first one match and then another was burned till we were compelled to give up all hope of escaping by our own efforts.

Refreshed and strengthened by the food, Shock expressed himself ready for a new trial at digging his way out.

"I can do it," he said. "I'll soon get through."

Soon after he was clinging to me, hot, panting, and trembling in every limb, after narrowly escaping suffocation, and when I wanted to take up the task where he had left off, he clung to me more tightly and would not let me go from his side.

"Yer can't do it," he said hoarsely. "Sand comes down and smothers yer. Faster yer works, faster it comes. Let Ike bring the shovels."

There was no other chance. I felt that, and sat down beside Shock and talked and tried to cheer him up; and when I broke down he roused up and tried to cheer me. Then I talked to him about stories I had read, where people had been buried alive, and where they were always dug out at last, and when I was weary he took his turn, showing me that in his rough way he could talk quickly and in an interesting way about catching birds and rats. How at times he had caught rats with his hands, and had been bitten by them.

"But," he added, with a laugh, "I served 'em out for it—I bit them after I'd skinned and cooked 'em."

"How horrible!" I said.

"Horrible! Why? They'd lived on our fruit and corn till they were fat as fat, I like rat."

Then we grew tired, and as soon as we ceased talking a curious sensation of fear came over us. I say us, for more than once I knew that Shock felt it, by his whispering to me in an awe-stricken tone:

"I never know'd as being in the dark was like this before. It's darker like, much darker, you know than being in one of the lofts under the straw."

Chapter Thirty
How we were Rescued

It is all confused at times as I try to recall it. Some of our adventure stands out clear to me, as if it took place only yesterday, while other parts seem strange and dreamy, and I know now that we both dozed a great deal in the warm close place like a pair of animals shut up for their winter sleep.

We soon finished our food, for we were in such good hope of soon being dug out that we had not the heart to save a part of it in our hungry state. Then we slept again, and woke, and slept again, till waking and sleeping were mixed up strangely. The horror seemed to wear off a great deal, only when Shock started up suddenly and began talking loudly about something I could not understand, my feeling of fear increased.

How time went—when it was night and when it was day—I could not tell; and at last almost our sole thought was about what we should eat when we got out again.

At last I felt too weak and helpless to do more than lie still and try to think of a prayer or two, which at times was only half uttered before I dropped asleep.

Then I woke to think of Mr Solomon and the garden, and fell asleep again. And then I recall trying to rouse up Shock, who seemed to be always sleeping; and while I was trying feebly to get him to speak to me again I seem to have gone to sleep once more, and everything was like being at an end.

At first I had suffered agonies of fear and horror. At last all seemed to fade, as it were, into a dreamless sleep.

"It was like this here," Ike told me afterwards. "I lay down and made myself comfortable, and then after smoking a pipe I went off asleep. When I woke up I heerd you two a chiveying about and shouting, but it was too soon to move, so I went asleep again.

"Then I woke up and looked about for you, and shouted for you to come down and have something to eat, and bring up the horse again, for I thought by that time he'd have had a good rest.

"I shouted again, but I couldn't make you hear, so I went up higher and hollered once more, and then Juno came trotting up to me and looked up in my face.

"I asked her where you two was, but she didn't say anything of course, so I began to grow rough, and I said you might find your way back, my lads; and I went down to the public, ordered some tea and some briled ham; see to my horse having another feed and some water, and then, as you hadn't come down, I had my tea all alone in a huff.

"Then I finished, and you hadn't come, so I says, 'Well, that's their fault, and they may go without.' But all the same I says to myself, 'Well, poor chaps, they don't often get a run in the country!' and that made me a bit soft like, and I pulled a half-quartern loaf in two and put all the briled ham that was left in the middle, and tied it up in a clean hankychy for you to eat going home.

"Then I pays for the eating and the horse, harnessed him up, after a good rub down his legs, and whistled to Juno, who was keeping very close to me, and we went up the hill to the sand-pit again.

"I shouted and hollered again, and then, as it was got to be quite time we started, I grew waxy, and pulls out my knife and cuts a good ash stick out of the hedge for Master Shock, for I put it down to him for having led you off.

"Still you didn't come, and though I looked all about there was nothing fresh as I could see, only sand everywhere; and at last I says to myself, 'I sha'n't wait with that load to get out of the pit here,' and so I started.

"Nice tug the hoss had, but she brought it well out on to the hard road, and there I rested just a quarter of an hour, giving a holler now and then.

"'I'm off!' I says at last, 'and they may foller. Come on, Juno,' I says; but the dog wasn't there.

"That made me more waxy, and I shouted and whistled, and she come from out of the sand-pit and kept looking back, as if she wanted to know why you two didn't come. She follered the cart, though, right enough; and feeling precious put out, I went on slowly down the hill; stopped in the village ten minutes, and then, knowing you could find out that I'd gone on, I set to for my long job, and trudged on by the hoss.

"It was a long job, hour after hour, for I couldn't hurry—that little looking load was too heavy for that. And so I went on, and eight o'clock come, and nine, and ten, and you didn't overtake me, and then it got to be twelve o'clock; and at last, reg'lar fagged out, me and hoss, we got to the yard just as it was striking four, and getting to be day.

"I put the hoss up, and saw Juno go into her kennel, but I was too tired to chain her, and I lay down in the loft on some hay and went off to sleep.

"I didn't seem to have been asleep above ten minutes, but it was eight o'clock when Old Brownsmith's brother stirs me up with his foot, and I sat up and stared at him.

"'Where's young Grant and the boy?' he says.

"'What! ain't they come?' I says, and I told him.

"'And you've left the dog behind too,' he says, quite waxy with me.

"'No,' I says; 'she come home along o' me and went into her kennel.'

"'She's not there now,' he says.

"'Then,' says I, 'she's gone back to meet 'em.'

"'Then there's something wrong,' he says sharply; 'and look here, Ike, if you've let that boy come to harm I'll never forgive you.'

"'Why, I'd sooner come to harm myself,' I says. 'It's larks, that's what it is.'

"'Well,' he says, 'I'll wait till twelve o'clock, and if they're not back then you must come along with me and find 'em, for there is something wrong.'

"I never cared a bit about you, my lad, but I couldn't sleep no more, and I couldn't touch a bit o' breakfast; and when twelve o'clock came, Mrs Old Brownsmith's brother's wife had been at me with a face as white as noo milk, and she wanted us to go off before.

"We was off at twelve, though, in the light cart and with a fresh horse; and though I expected to see you every minute along the road, we got back to the public, and asked for you, and found that you hadn't been seen.

"Then we put up the hoss and went and looked about the sand-pits, and could see nothing of you there, and we didn't see nothing of the dog. Then we went over the common and searched the wood, and there was no sign.

"Then back we was at the sand-pits, and there was the sand everywhere, but nothing seemed to say as it had fallen down. There was some holes, and we looked in all of 'em, but we couldn't tell that any of 'em had filled up. Last of all, it was getting dark, when we heard a whine, and saw Juno come out of the fir-wood on the top with a rabbit in her mouth.

"But that taught us nothing, and we coaxed her down to the public again, and drove home.

"'I've got it,' I says, as we stood in the stable-yard: 'that boy Shock's got him on to it, and they've gone off to Portsmouth to be sailors.'

"Old Brownsmith's brother looked at me and shook his head, but I stuck to it I was right; and he said he'd go down to Portsmouth and see.

"But he didn't, for next day he goes over to Isleworth, and as I was coming out of the garden next night he was back, and he stops me and takes me to the cottage.

"'Good job,' he says, 'as Sir Francis ain't at home, for he thought a deal of that boy.'

"'Warn't my fault,' I says; but he shook his head, and took me in, and there sat Old Brownsmith's brother's wife, with a white face and red eyes as if she had been crying, and Old Brownsmith himself.

"Well, he gives me a long talking to, and I told him everything about it; and when I'd done I says again as it warn't my fault, and Old Brownsmith turns to his brother and he says, as fair as a man could speak, 'It warn't his fault, Solomon; and if it's as he says, Grant's that sort o' boy as'll repent and be very sorry, and if he don't come back before, you'll get a letter begging your pardon for what he's done, or else I shall. You wait a couple of days.'

"I dunno why, but I was reg'lar uncomf'table about you, my lad, and I didn't understand Juno stopping away so, for next day she was gone again, but next night she was back. Next day she was gone again, and didn't come back, and on the fourth, when I was down the garden digging—leastwise, I wasn't digging, for I was leaning on my spade thinking, up comes Old Brownsmith's brother with his mouth open, and before he could say a word I says to him, 'Stop!' I says; 'I've got it,' for it come to me like a flash o' lightning.

"'What?' he says.

"'Them boys is in that sand-pit, covered over!' I says.

"'That's it!' he says. 'I was coming to say I thought so, and that we'd go over directly.'

"Bless your heart, my boy, I was all of a shiver as I got into the light cart alongside Old Brownsmith's brother and six shovels and four spades in the bottom of the cart as I felt we should want, and I see as Old Brownsmith's brother had got a flask o' something strong in his breast-pocket. Then I just looked and saw that Juno warn't there, and we were off.

"My hye, how that there horse did go till we got to the little public. We stopped once to give her mouth a wash out and a mouthful of hay, and then we were off again, never hardly saying a word, but as we got to the public we pulls up, and Old Brownsmith's brother shouts to the landlord, 'Send half-a-dozen men up to the sand-pit directly. Boys buried.'

"You see he felt that sure, my lad, that he said that, and then we drove on up the hill, with the horse smoking, and a lot of men after us.

"First thing we see was Juno trotting towards us, and she looked up and whined, and then trotted back to a place where it was plain enough, now we knew, a great bit of the side had caved down and made a slope, and here Juno began scratching hard, and as fast as she scratched the more sand come down.

"I looked, at Old Brownsmith's brother, and he looked at me, and we jumped out, slipped off our coats and weskits, took a shovel apiece, and began to throw the sand away.

"My head was all of a buzz, for every shovelful I threw out I seemed to see your white gal's face staring at me and asking of me to work harder, and I did work like a steam-engyne.

"Then, one by one, eight men come up, and we set 'em all at work; but Old Brownsmith's brother, the ganger, you know, stops us after a bit.

"'This is no use!' he says; 'we're only burying of 'em deeper.'

"Right he was, for the sand kept crumbling down from the top as soon as ever we made a bit of space below, and twice over some one called out 'Warning!' and we had to run back to keep from being buried, while I got in right up to the chest once.

"'There's hundreds o' tons loose,' says the old—the ganger, you know; 'and we shall never get in that way.' He stopped to think, but it made me mad, for I knowed you must be in there, and I began digging again, wondering how it was that Juno hadn't found you before, and 'sposed the sand didn't hold the scent, or else the rabbits up above 'tracted her away.

"'I can see no other way,' said the ganger at last. 'You must dig, my lads. Go on. I'll get on the top, and see how much more is loose. Take care. You,' he said to a tall, thin lad of sixteen—'you stand there; and as soon as you see any sand crumbling down, you shout.'

"The men began to dig again, and at the end of a minute the lad shouted, and we had to scuttle off, or we should have been buried, and things looked worse than ever. We'd been digging and shovelling back the sloping bank, but it grew instead of getting less, and this made me obstint as I dug away as hard as I could get my shovel down.

"All at once I hears a shout from the ganger. 'Come up here, Ike,' he says; and I shouldered my spade, and had to go a good bit round 'fore I could climb up to him, and I found him twenty or thirty foot back from the edge, among some furze.

"'Look here,' he says; 'I was hunting for cracks when I slipped down here.'

"I looked, and I saw a narrow crack, 'bout a foot wide, nearly covered with furze.

"'Now, listen,' he says, and he kneeled down and shouted, and, sure enough, there was a bit of a groan came up.

"'Echo!' I says.

"'No,' he says. 'Listen again,' and he shouted, and there was a sort of answer.

"'They're here,' he says excitedly. 'Hi! Juno, Juno!' The dog came rushing up, and we put her to the hole or crack, and she darted into it, went down snuffling, and came back again barking. We sent her down again, and then she didn't come back, and when we called we could hear her barking, but she didn't come to us, and at last we felt that she couldn't get back.

"'What's to be done?' said the ganger. 'We can't get down there.'

"'Dig down,' I says.

"'No, no,' says he. 'If we do we shall smother them.'

"'That boy, then, you sot to look out—send him down.'

"'Go and bring him,' says the ganger; 'and—oh, we have no rope. Bring the reins; they're strong and new.'

"Five minutes after, the boy was up with us, and he said he'd go down if we'd put the reins round him like a rope, and so we did, and after we'd torn some furze away he got into the hole feet first, and wriggled himself down till only his head was out.

"'Goes down all sidewise,' he says, 'and then turns round.'

"'Will you go, my lad? The dog's down there, and we'll hold on to the reins, and have you out in a minute, if you shout.'

"'And 'spose the sand falls?'

"'Why, we've got the reins to trace you by, and we'll dig you out in a jiffy,' I says.

"'All right!' he says, and he shuffled himself down and went out of sight, and he kept on saying, 'all right! all right!' and then all at once, quickly, 'I've slipped,' he says, as if frightened. 'There's no bottom. I'm over a big hole.'

"Just then, my lad, the rein had tightened, but we held on.

"'Pull me up!' he says, and we pulled hard, and strained the reins a good deal, and at last he come up, looking hot and scared.

"'I couldn't touch bottom,' he says, 'and the dog began to bark loudly.'

"'I see,' says the ganger, 'the dog slipped there, and can't get out. We must have a rope; you, Ike, take the reins, and drive down to the village and get a stout cart-rope. Bring two.'

"The landlord of the inn had just come up, and he said he'd got plenty, and he'd go with me, and so he did, and in a quarter of an hour we'd been down and driven back with two good strong new ropes.

"There was no more digging going on, it was no use; but while we'd been gone they'd chopped away the furze, cutting through it with spades, so that the hole, which was a big crack, was all clear.

"'Now, then,' says Old Brownsmith's brother, 'go down again, my boy. With this stout rope round we can take care of you,' but the boy shook his head, he'd been too much scared last time.

"'Who'll go?' says the ganger. 'A sovereign for the man who goes down and fetches them up.'

"The chaps talked together, but no one moved.

"'It'll cave in,' says one of 'em.

"'You must cut a way down, Ike,' says the ganger. 'I'm too stout, or I'd go down myself.'

"'Nay,' I says, 'if they're down there, and you get digging, you'll bury 'em. P'r'aps I could squeedge myself down. Let's try.'

"So they ties the rope round me, and I lets myself into the hole, which was all sand, and roots to hold it a bit together.

"'It's a tight fit,' I says, as I wriggled myself down with my face to the ganger, but I soon found that wouldn't do, and I dragged myself out again and took off my boots, tightened my strap, and went down the other way.

"That was better, but it was a tight job going all round a corner like a zigger-me-zag, as you calls it, or a furnace chimney; and as I scrouged down with my eyes shut, and the sand and stones scuttling down after me, I began to wonder how I was going to get up again.

"'Here!' I shouts, 'I shall want two ropes. See if you can reach down the other.'

"I put up my hand as far as I could reach, and the thin boy put a loop round his foot and come down, shutting out the light, till he could reach my hand, and I got hold of the second rope, and went scuttling farther, till all at once I found it like the boy had said—my legs was hanging and kicking about.

"'Here's in for it now,' I says to myself; and I wondered whether I should be buried; but I shouts out, 'Lower away,' and I let myself slide, and then there was a rush of falling sand and I was half smothered as I swung about, but they lowered down, and directly after I touched bottom with my feet, and Juno was jumping about me and barking like mad.

"'Found 'em?' I heard the ganger shout from up in daylight, and I began to feel about for you; and, Lor'! there has been times when I've longed for a match, when I've wanted a pipe o' tobacco; but nothing like what I longed then, so as to see where I was, for it was as black as pitch.

"But I felt about with the dog barking, and followed to where she was, and feeling about, I got hold of you two boys cuddled up together as if you was asleep, and nearly covered up with sand.

"I puts my hands to my mouth, and I yells out as loud as I could: 'I've got 'em!' and there came back a 'Hooray!' sounding hollow and strange like, and then I s'pose it was the sand had got in my eyes so as they began to water like anything.

"But I knelt down trembling all over, for I was afraid you was both dead, and I can't a-bear touching dead boys. I never did touch none, but I can't a-bear touching of 'em all the same.

"Then I felt something jump up in my throat, as if I'd swallowed a new potato, only upside down like, other way on, you know, the tater coming up and not going down for when I got feeling you about you was both warm.

"'Out o' the way, dog,' I says, for she kept licking of you both, and I feels to find out which was you, and soon found that out, because Shock had such a rough head; and then I says to myself, 'Which shall I send up first?'

"I did think o' sending Shock, so as to make him open the hole a bit more; but I thought p'raps the top'd fall in with sending the first one up, and you was more use than Shock, so I made the rope, as was loose, fast round your chest, and then I shouts to 'em as I lifted you up.

"'Haul steady,' I shouts, and as the rope tightened hoisted you more and more, till you went up and up, and I was shoving your legs, then your feet, and then you was dragged away from me, and I was knocked down flat by 'bout hunderd ton o' sand coming on my head. I didn't weigh it, so p'r'aps there warn't so much.

"I was made half stupid; but I heerd them cheering, and I knowed they'd got you out, for they shouted down the hole for the next, and I had to drag the rope I had out of the sand before I fastened it round Shock, who give a bit of a groan as soon as I touched him, and I wished I'd heerd you groan too.

"'Haul away,' I shouted, and I walked right up a heap of sand, as they hauled at Shock, and as soon as they'd dragged him away from me, and he was going up, I jumped back, expecting some more sand to fall, and so it did, as they hauled, whole barrowfuls of it.

"Then come some more shouting, and Old Brownsmith's brother roared down the hole:—

"'All right. Safe up.'

"'All right, is it?' I says, scratching the sand out o' my head, 'and how's me and the dog to come?'

"They seemed to have thought of that, for the ganger shouts down the crooked hole—'How are we to get down the rope to you?'

"'I d'know,' I says; and I stood there in the dark thinking and listening to the buzzing voices, and wondering what to do.

"'Wonder how nigh I am to the hole,' I says to myself; and I walked up quite a heap o' sand and tried if I could touch anything, but I couldn't.

"Then I thought of the dog.

"'Hi, Juno!' I says, and she whined and come to me, and I took hold of her.

"'Here, you try if you can't get out, old gal,' I says; and I believe as she understood me as I lifted her up and helped her scramble up, and somehow I got her right with her stomach on my head. Then I lifted her shoulders up as high as I could reach, as I stood on the heap o' sand, and she got her legs on my head, and my! how she did scratch, and then the sand began to come down, and I knowed she could reach the top. Next moment she'd got one of her hind paws on my hand as I reached up high, and then there was a rush and scramble, and I heard another shouting of 'Hooray!' while the sand come down so that I had to get right as far away as I could.

"'What shall we do now?' says the ganger, shouting to me:—

"'Send the dog down again with the two ropes round her.'

"'Right!' he says; and then in a minute there was a scuffling and more rushing, and Juno come down with a run, to begin barking loudly as she fell on the soft sand.

"'There you are, old gal,' I says, patting her, as I took off one rope, and felt that the other was fast round her. 'Up you go again.' I lifted her up and shouted to 'em to haul, and in half a minute she was gone, and I was alone in the dark, but with the rope made fast round my chest.

"'Are you ready?' shouts the ganger.

"'Ay!' I says. 'Pull steady, for I'm heavier than the dog.'

"They began to haul as I took tight hold of the rope above my head, and up I went slowly with the sand being cut away by the tight line, and coming thundering down on me at an awful rate, just as if some one was shooting cart loads atop of me.

"'Steady!' I yelled; and they pulled away slowly, while I wondered whether the rope would give way. But it held, and I felt my head bang against the sand, and some more fell. Then, as I kicked my legs about, I felt myself dragged more into the hole, and I tried to help myself; but all I did was to send about a ton of sand down from under me. Then very slowly I was hauled past an elbow in the hole, and I was got round towards the other when a lot more sand fell from beneath me, and then, just as I was seeing daylight, there was a sort of heave above me, and the top came down and nipped me fast just about the hips.

"'Haul! my lads, haul!' the ganger shouted, and they hauled till I felt most cut in two, and I had to holler to 'em to stop.

"'I shall want my legs,' I says. 'They ain't much o' ones, but useful!'

"There was nothing for it but to begin digging, for they could see my face now, and they began watching very carefully that the sand didn't get over my head, when, all at once, as they dug, there was a slip, and the sand, and the roots, and stones all dropped down into the hole below, and I was hauled out on to the top safe and sound, 'cept a few scratches, and only a bit of the sleeve of my shirt left.

"There, you know the rest."

Chapter Thirty One
"What's the Meaning of all this?"

I did know the rest; how Shock and I lay for a fortnight at the little country inn carefully tended before we were declared fit to go back home, for the doctor was not long in bringing us back to our senses; and, save that I used to wake with a start out of my sleep in the dark, fancying I was back in the pit, I was not much the worse. Shock was better, for he looked cleaner and fresher, but he objected a great deal to our nurse brushing his hair.

I was just back and feeling strong again, when one day Sir Francis came down into the pinery, and stopped and spoke to me. He said he had heard all about my narrow escape, and hoped it would be a warning to me never to trust myself in a sand-pit again.

He was very kind after his manner, which was generally as if he thought all the world were soldiers, and I was going up to my dinner soon, after I had stopped for a bit of a cool down in one of the other houses, when, to my great disgust, I saw Courtenay and Philip back, and I felt a kind of foreboding that there would soon be some more troubles to face.

I was quite right, for during the rest of their stay at home they seemed to have combined to make my life as wretched as they possibly could.

I was often on the point of complaining, but I did not like to do so, for it seemed to be so cowardly, and besides, I argued to myself that I could not expect all sunshine. Old Brownsmith used to have me over to spend Sundays with him, and his brother and Mrs Solomon were very kind. Ike sometimes went so far as to say "Good-morning" and "good-night," and Shock had become so friendly that he would talk, and bring me a good moth or butterfly for my case.

I went steadily on collecting, for Mr Solomon said, as long as the work was done well he would rather I did amuse myself in a sensible way.

The consequence was that I often used to go down the garden of a night, and my collection of moths was largely increased.

I noticed about this time that Sir Francis used to talk a good deal to Shock, and by and by I found from Ike that the boy was going regularly to an evening-school, and altering a great deal for the better. Unfortunately, Ike, with whom he lodged, was not improving, as I had several opportunities of observing, and one day I took him to task about it.

"I know the excuse you have, Ike," I said, "that habit you got into when going backwards and forwards to the market; but when you had settled down here in a gentleman's garden, I should have thought that you would have given it up."

"Ah, yes," he said, as he drove in his spade. "You're a gent, you see, and I'm only a workman."

"I'm going to be a workman too, Ike," I said.

"Ay, but not a digger like me. They don't set me to prune, and thin grapes, and mind chyce flowers. I'm not like you."

"It does not matter what any one is, Ike," I said. "You ought to turn over a new leaf and keep away from the public-house."

"True," he said, smashing a clod; "and I do turn over a noo leaf, but it will turn itself back."

"Nonsense!" I said. "You are sharp enough on Shock's failings, and you tell me of mine. Why don't you attend to your own?"

"Look here, young gent," he cried sharply, "do you want to quarrel just because I like a drop now and then?"

"Quarrel! No, Ike. I tell you because I don't want to see you discharged."

"Think they would start me if they knowed, lad?"

"I'm sure of it," I said earnestly. "Sir Francis is so particular."

"Then," he said, scraping his spade fiercely, "it won't do. I want to stop here. I'll turn over a noo leaf."

One day in the next autumn, as I was carefully shutting in a pill-box a moth that I had found, a gentleman who was staying at the house caught sight of me and asked to see it.

"Ah, yes!" he said. "Goat-moth, and a nice specimen. Do you sugar?"

"Do I sugar, sir?" I said vacantly. "Yes, I like sugar, sir."

"Bless the lad!" he said, laughing. "I mean sugar the trees. Smear them with thick sugar and water or treacle, and then go round at night with a lantern; that's the way to catch the best moths."

I was delighted with the idea and was not long before I tried it, and as luck would have it, there was an old bull's-eye lantern in the tool-house that Mr Solomon used when he went round to the furnaces of a night.

I remember well one evening, just at leaving-off time, taking my bottle of thick syrup and brush from the tool-house shelf, and slipping down the garden and into the pear-plantation where the choice late fruit was waiting and asking daily to be picked.

Mr Solomon was very proud of his pears, and certainly some of them grew to a magnificent size.

I was noticing how beautiful and tawny and golden some of them were growing to be as I smeared the trunk of one and then of another with my sweet stuff, and as it was a deliciously warm still evening, I was full of expectation of a good take.

I had just finished when all at once I heard a curious noise, which made me think of lying in the dark in the sand-cave listening to Shock's hard breathing; and I gave quite a shudder as I looked round, and then turned hot and angry.

I knew what the noise was, and had not to look far to find Ike lying under a large tree right away from the path fast asleep, and every now and then uttering a few words and giving a snort.

"Ike!" I said, shaking him. "Ike! wake up and go home."

But the more I tried the more stupid he seemed to grow, and I stood at last wondering what I had better do, not liking the idea of Mr Solomon hearing, for it was certain to mean a very severe reprimand. It might mean discharge.

It seemed such a pity, too, and I could not help thinking that this bad habit of Ike's was the reason why he had lived to fifty and never risen above the position of labourer.

I tried again to wake him, but it was of no use, and just then I heard Mr Solomon shout to me that tea was waiting.

I ran up the garden quickly for fear Mr Solomon should come down and see Ike, and as I went I made up my mind that I would get the key of the gate into the lane and come down after dark and smuggle him out without anyone knowing.

"Well, butterfly boy," said Mrs Solomon, smiling in her half-serious way, "we've been waiting tea these ten minutes."

I said I was very sorry, and though I felt a little guilty as I sat down I soon forgot all about Ike in my pleasant meal.

Then I felt frightened as I heard some laughing and shouting, and started and listened, for it struck me that Courtenay and Philip might be going down the garden, and if they should see poor Ike in such a state, I knew that they would begin baiting and teasing him, when he would perhaps fly in a passion such as I had seen him in once before, when he abused me, and apologised the next day, saying that it wasn't temper, but beer.

The sound died away, and then it seemed to rise again nearer to us.

"Ah!" said Mr Solomon, "I'm sorry for those who have boys."

"No, you are not, Solomon," said his wife, cutting the bread and butter.

"Well, such boys as them."

"Ah!" said Mrs Solomon. "That's better."

That seemed a long tea-time, and it appeared to be longer still before I could get away, for Mr Solomon had a lot of things to ask me about the grape-house and pit. I kept glancing at the wall where the key hung on a nail, and though another time I might easily have taken it, on this particular occasion it seemed as if I could not get near the place unobserved.

At last my time came; Mrs Solomon had gone into the back kitchen, and Mr Solomon to his desk in the parlour. I did not lose a moment, but, snatching the key from the nail, I slipped it in my pocket, caught my cap from the peg, and slipped out.

I was not going to do any wicked act, but somehow I felt as if all this was very wrong, and I found myself running along the grass borders, leaping over the gravel paths, so that my footsteps should not be heard, and in this way I reached the tool-house, where, quite at home in the darkness, and making no more noise than jingling a hanging spade against the bricks, I reached up on to the corner shelf and found my lantern and matches.

There was the little lamp inside already trimmed, and I soon had it alight and darkened by the shade, slipped it in my pocket, and then started down the long green walk by the big wall where the espaliers were trained, and the wall was covered with big pear-trees.

"I feel just like a robber," I said to myself as I stole along to find Ike and turn him out.

Then I stopped short, for there was a scrambling noise on one side.

"He is awake and trying to get over the wall," I said to myself, and setting down my lantern by one of the big trees, I went forward towards the great pear-tree, whose branches would make a ladder right to the top.

It was very dark, and the great wall made it seem blacker as I stole on over the soft green path meaning to make sure that Ike had gone over quite safely, and then go to my moth-hunting.

"It's as well not to speak to him," I thought.

Then I stopped again, for if it was Ike he was either talking to himself or had some one whispering to him.

"It can't be Ike," I thought, for after the whispering some one jumped down on the soft bed, and then some one else followed—*crash*.

There was a scuffle here, and some one uttered an ejaculation of pain as if he had hurt himself in jumping, while the other laughed, and then they whispered together.

It was not Ike going away then, but two people come over the wall to get at the great choice pears that were growing on my left.

"What a shame," I thought; and as I recalled a similar occurrence at Old Brownsmith's I wished that Shock were with me to help protect Sir Francis' choice fruit.

I ought to have slipped off back and told Mr Solomon, who would have made the gardener come from the lower cottage; but I did not think of that; I only listened and heard one of the thieves whisper to the other:

"Get up; you aren't hurt. Come along."

Then there was a rustling as they forced their way among the bushes, and went bang up against an espalier. This they skirted, coming close to me as I stood in the shadow of a pear-tree.

"Come along quick!" I heard; and then the two figures went on rustling and crashing among the black-currant bushes, so that I could smell the peculiar herbaceous medicine-scent they gave out.

I knew as well as if I had been told where they were going, and that was to a double row of beautiful great pears that were just ready to pick, and which I had noticed that morning, and again when I was sugaring the trees close by.

At first I had taken them for men, but by degrees, by the tone of their whispers and the faint sight I got of them now and then as they passed an open place, I knew that they were boys.

A few minutes before I had felt excited and nervous; then I felt less alarm. My first idea was to frighten them by shouting for the different men about the place; but as soon as I was sure that they were boys, a curiously pugnacious sensation came over me, and I determined to see if I couldn't catch one of them and drag him up to Mr Solomon, for I felt sure that I should only have one to fight with, the other would be sure to run as hard as he could go.

I stopped short again with an unpleasant thought in my mind. Surely this could not be Shock with some companion.

No, it could not be he, I felt sure, and I was rather ashamed of having thought it as I crept on after the two thieves, so that I was quite near them when, as I expected they would, they stopped by the little thick heavily-laden trees.

"Look out! hold the bag and be quick," was whispered; and then there was snapping of twigs, the rustling of leaves, and a couple of dull thuds as two pears fell.

"Never mind them," was whispered in the same tone. "There's no end of 'em about."

I crept nearer with my teeth grinding together, for it seemed to be such a shameful thing to clear those pears from the tree in that way, and then I grew furious, for one whispered something to the other, and the tree being stripped was shaken, and then *thump, thump, thump,* one after another the beautiful fruit fell.

They scuffled about, and I was so close now that I could hear the pears banged and bruised one upon another as they were thrown into a bag. Then I felt as if I could bear it no longer. The pears were as if they were my own, and making a dash at the faintly seen figure with the bag I struck him a blow with all my might, and that, the surprise, and the weight of my body combined were sufficient to send him over amongst the black currants, while I went at the other, and in a blind fury began laying on to him with my fists as hard as I could.

He tried to get away, but I held on to him, and this drove him to fight desperately, and for some minutes we were up and down, fighting, wrestling, and hanging on to each other with all the fury of bitter enemies.

I was beaten down to my knees twice over. I struggled up again though, and held on with the stubbornness of a bull-dog.

Then being stronger than I he swung me round, so that I was crushed up against the trunk of one of the trees, but the more he hurt me the more angry I grew, and held on, striking at him whenever I could get an arm free. I could hear him grinding his teeth as he struggled with me, and at last I caught my feet in a currant bush, for even then I could tell it by the smell, and down I went.

But not alone. I held on to him, and dragged him atop of me.

"Let go!" he cried hoarsely, as he struck me savagely in the face; and when the pain only made me hang on all the more tightly he called out to his companion, who had taken no farther part in the fray:

"Here, Phil, Phil. Come on, you sneak."

I felt as if I had been stunned. Not by his blow, but by his words, as for the first time I realised with whom I had been engaged.

A rustling noise on my left warned me that some one else was coming; but I let my hands fall to my side, for I had made a grievous mistake, and must strike no more.

In place now of my hanging on to Courtenay, he was holding me, and drawing in his breath he raised himself a little, raised one hand and was about to strike me, but before he could, Philip seemed to seize me by the collar, and his brother too, but in an instant I felt that it was a stronger grip, and a hoarse gruff voice that I knew well enough was that of Sir Francis shouted out, "Caught you, have I, you young scoundrels."

As he spoke he made us rise, and forced us before him—neither of us speaking—through the bushes and on to the path, a little point of light appearing above me, and puffs of pungent smoke from a cigar striking my face.

"I've got t'other one," said a rough voice that I also recognised, and I cried out involuntarily:

"Ike—Ike!"

"That's me, lad. I've got him fast."

"You let me go. You hurt me," cried Philip out of the darkness.

"Hurt yer? I should think I do hurt you. Traps always does hurt, my fine fellow. Who are you? What's your name?"

"Bring him here," cried Sir Francis; and as Ike half carried, half dragged Philip out from among the trees on to the broad green walk, Sir Francis cried fiercely:

"Now, then! What's the meaning of all this!"

I heard Philip give a gasp as I opened my lips to speak, but before I could say a word Courtenay cried out quickly:

"Phil and I heard them stealing the pears, and we came down to stop them—didn't we, Phil?"

"Yes: they pounced upon us in the dark."

"I am knocked about," cried Courtenay.

"What a wicked lie!" I exclaimed, as soon as I could get my breath.

"Lie, sir, lie!" cried Sir Francis fiercely, as he tightened his grasp upon my collar. "Why, I saw you come creeping along with that dark lantern, and watched you. You had no business down here, and yet I find you along with this fellow, who has no right to be in the garden now, assaulting my sons."

Chapter Thirty Two
Circumstantial Evidence

"Now, sir," cried Sir Francis angrily, "have the goodness to explain what you were doing there."

This was to Ike, who seemed stupid and confused. The excitement of the fight had roused him up for a few minutes; but as soon as that was over he yawned very loudly, and when Sir Francis turned fiercely upon him and asked him that question he said aloud:

"Eh?"

"Answer me, you scoundrel!" cried Sir Francis. "You heard what I said."

"Eh? Hah, yes. What had I been a-doing—heigh—ho—hum! Oh, how sleepy I am! What had I been a-doing here? What I been doing, Mars Grant?"

"You were asleep," I said on being appealed to; and I spoke angrily, for I was smarting under the accusation and suspicion of being a thief.

"Asleep!" cried Ike. "To be sure. That's it. Asleep I was under the bushes there. Dropped right off."

"You repeat your lesson well," said Sir Francis. "Pray, go up to the house—to the library, you boys—you, sir, follow me."

Courtenay and Philip went on in advance, Sir Francis followed, and we were bringing up the rear when Ike exclaimed in remonstrance:

"That ain't fair, master. You ought to sep'rate them two or a nyste bit of a tale they'll make up between them."

"You insolent scoundrel!" roared Sir Francis.

"All right, sir; scoundrel it is, just as you like. Wonder who'll tell the truth, and who won't?"

"Hold your tongue, Ike!" I said angrily.

Plop!

That strange sound was made by Ike, who struck his mouth with his hand as if to stop it up and prevent more words coming.

Meanwhile we were going up the garden, and came suddenly upon a spot of fire which kept glowing and fading, and resolved itself into Mr Solomon's evening pipe in the kitchen-garden middle walk.

"Hallo! young gentlemen!" he exclaimed; and then, seeing his master: "Anything the matter, Sir Francis?"

"Matter!" cried Sir Francis, who was in a great passion. "Why are you, my head gardener, not protecting my place with the idle scoundrels I pay? Here am I and my sons obliged to turn out of an evening to keep thieves from the fruit."

"Thieves! What thieves?" cried Mr Solomon. "Why, Isaac, what are you doing here?"

"Me!" said Ike. "Don't quite know. Thought I'd been having a nap. The master says I've been stealing o' pears."

"Silence!" cried Sir Francis. "You, Brownsmith, see that those two fellows come straight up to the library. I hold you answerable for their appearance."

Sir Francis went on first and we followed, to find ourselves, about ten minutes later, in the big library, with Sir Francis seated behind a large table, and a lamp and some silver candlesticks on table and mantel-piece, trying to make the gloomy room light.

They did not succeed, but there was light enough to show Courtenay and Philip all the better for running up to their rooms and getting a wash and brush, while I was ragged, dirty and torn, bruised and bleeding, for I could not keep my nose from giving forth tokens of the fierce fight.

Courtenay was not perfect, though, for his mouth looked puffy and his eyes were swelling up in a curious way that seemed to promise to reduce them to a couple of slits.

I glanced at Mr Solomon, and saw that he was looking very anxious, and as our eyes met his lips moved, and he seemed to be saying to me: "How could you do such a disgraceful thing?" but I smiled at him and looked him full in the eyes without flinching, and he appeared to be more cheerful directly.

"Attention!" cried Sir Francis as if he were drilling his men; but there was no more fierceness. The officer and angry master had given place to the magistrate, and he cleared his throat and proceeded to try the case.

There was a little shuffling about, and Philip whispered to Courtenay.

"Silence!" cried Sir Francis. "Now, Courtenay, you are the elder: tell me what you were doing down the garden."

"We were up by the big conservatory door, papa," said Courtenay boldly—"Phil and I—and we were talking together about getting some bait for fishing, when all at once there came a whistle from down the garden, and directly after some one seemed to answer it; and then, sir—'what's that?' said 'Phil,' and I knew directly."

"How did you know?" cried Sir Francis.

"Well, I guessed it, sir, and I said it was someone after the fruit; and I asked Phil if he'd come with me and watch and see who it was."

"And he did?"

"Yes, sir; and we went down the garden and couldn't hear or see anything, and we went right to the bottom, and as we were coming back we heard the pear-trees being shaken."

"How did you know it was the pear-trees, sir?—it was dark."

"It sounded like pear-trees, sir, and you could hear the big pears tumbling on the ground."

"Well, sir?"

Courtenay spoke out boldly and well. He did not hesitate in the least; and I could not help feeling what a ragged dejected-looking object I seemed, and how much appearances were against me.

"I said to Phil that we ought to try and catch the thieves, and he said we would, so we crept up and charged them, and I had this boy, and I suppose Phil brought that man, but it was so dark I could not see what he did."

"Well, sir?"

"Well, papa, this boy knocked me about shamefully, and called me all sorts of names."

"And you knocked him about too, I suppose?" said Sir Francis.

"Yes, I suppose I did, sir. He hurt me, and I was in a passion."

"Now, Philip, what have you to say?"

Philip looked uneasy as he glanced at his brother and then at Sir Francis.

"Well, go on, sir."

"We were up by the big con—"

"Yes, yes, we have heard all about that," cried Sir Francis.

"Yes, pa; and we heard whistles, and Courtenay said, 'What's that?'"

"I thought it was you said 'What's that?'"

"No, pa, it was Courtenay," cried the boy quickly: "he said it. And then I wanted to go down and catch the thieves, and Courtenay came too, and we could hear them shaking down the pears. Then I went one way and Courtenay went the other, and I saw that new labourer—that man—"

"Fine eyes for his age," said Ike in a low growl.

"How dare you speak, sir, till you are called upon for your defence!" cried Sir Francis.

"Oh, all right, your worship!" growled Ike. "On'y you know how dark it weer."

"Silence, man!"

Plop!

That was Ike's hand over his mouth again to enforce silence.

"Go on, Philip," said Sir Francis quietly.

"Yes, pa," cried the boy excitedly. "As soon as I saw that man shaking down the big pears I ran at him to try and catch him."

"You should ha' took off your cap, young un, and ketched me like a butterfly," growled Ike.

"Will you be silent, sir!"

Plop!

"He struck me, then, in the chest, pa, and knocked me right down in among the bushes."

"No, he did not," I exclaimed indignantly; "it was I."

"It was not; it was that man," cried Philip; and Ike burst out into a hearty laugh.

"Am I to order you out of the room, sir?" cried Sir Francis, severely.

"All right, your worship! No," cried Ike.

Plop!

"Now, Philip, go on."

"Yes, pa. I'm not very strong, and he shook me and banged me about ever so; but I was determined that I would not let him go, and held on till we heard you come; and then instead of trying to get away any more he turned round and began to drag me towards you, pretending that he had caught me, when I had caught him, you know."

"Go and sit down," said Sir Francis. "You boys talk well."

"Yes, papa, we are trying to tell you everything," said Philip.

"Thank you," said Sir Francis, and then he turned to me and looked me all over.

"Well, sir," he said, "your appearance and the evidence are very much against you."

"Yes, Sir Francis," I said; "very much indeed."

"Well, what have you to say?"

I could not answer for some moments, for my feelings of indignation got the better of me, but at last I blurted out:

"I went down the garden Sir Francis, to try and catch some moths."

"With this, eh?" said Sir Francis picking up something from the floor, and placing my old dark lantern on the table.

"Yes, Sir Francis," I said. "I am making a collection."

"Where is it, then?"

"Down at the cottage, Sir Francis."

"Humph!" ejaculated Sir Francis. "Have you seen his collection, Brownsmith?"

"Yes, Sir Francis; he has a great many—butterflies and moths."

"Humph! Sugar the trees, eh?"

"Yes, sir," I said quickly.

"And do you know that he goes down the garden of a night?"

"Yes, Sir Francis, often," said Mr Solomon.

"Isn't it enough to tempt him to take the pears?"

"No, Sir Francis," replied Mr Solomon boldly. "I might just as well say to you, 'Isn't it enough to tempt him to take the grapes or the peaches to trust him among them alone.'"

"He did steal the peaches when he first came. I caught him at it," cried Philip viciously.

"No, you did not, young gentleman," said Mr Solomon sternly; "but I saw you cut two bunches of grapes one evening—the Muscat of Alexandria—and take them away."

"Oh what a wicked story!" cried Philip, angrily.

"Call it what you like, young gentleman," said Mr Solomon; "but it's a fact. I meant to speak to Sir Francis, for I hate the choice fruit to be touched till it's wanted for the house; but I said to myself he's only a schoolboy and he was tempted, and here are the young gentleman's nail scissors, Sir Francis, that he dropped in his hurry and left behind."

As Mr Solomon spoke he handed a pair of pearl-handled scissors—a pair of those spring affairs with a tiny knife-blade in each handle—and in the midst of a dead silence laid them on the table before Sir Francis.

"Those are not mine," said Philip hastily.

"Humph!" ejaculated Sir Francis, picking them up and examining them. "I shall have to order you out of the room, man, if you make that noise," he cried, as he turned to Ike.

"I weer on'y laughin', your worship," said Ike.

"Then leave off laughing, sir," continued Sir Francis, "and have the goodness to tell me what you were doing down the garden. Were you collecting moths with a dark lantern?"

"Me, your honour! not I."

"What were you doing, then?"

"Well, your honour's worship, I was having a bit of a sleep—tired, you see."

"Oh!" exclaimed Sir Francis. "Now, look here, Grant, you knew that man was down the garden."

"Yes, Sir Francis."

"And didn't you go to join him?"

"Yes, Sir Francis."

"To get a lot of my pears?"

"No, Sir Francis."

"Then why did you go?" he thundered.

I was silent.

"Do you hear, sir?"

"Yes, Sir Francis."

"Then speak, sir."

I remained silent.

"Will you tell me why you went down the garden to join that man?"

I looked at poor Ike, and felt that if I spoke it would be to get him discharged, so I preferred to remain silent, and said not a word.

"Will you speak, sir?" cried Sir Francis, beating the table with his fist.

"I can't tell you, Sir Francis."

"You mean you won't, sir?"

"Yes, Sir Francis."

"Why not tell the whole truth, Grant?" said Mr Solomon, reproachfully.

"Because I can't, sir," I replied sadly.

"Be silent, Brownsmith," cried Sir Francis fiercely.

"He's too good a mate to tell," said Ike stoutly. "Here, I may as well make a clean breast of it, and here it is. I'm an old soldier, sir, and—well, theer, it got hold of me at dinner-time. 'Stead of having anything to eat I had a lot to drink, having had some salt herrin' for breakfast, and I suppose I took too much."

"Herring, my man?"

"No, your worship, beer; and I went to sleep down among the bushes. There, that's the honest truth, Mr Brownsmith's brother. Fact as fact."

"I believe you, Ike," said Mr Solomon. "He's a very honest workman, Sir Francis."

"Thank ye; I call that handsome, I do," said Ike.

"Stop! this is getting very irregular," cried Sir Francis. "Now, Grant, once more. Did you not go down the garden thinking you would get some of those pears?"

"No, Sir Francis."

"To meet that man, and let him take them away?"

"No, Sir Francis."

"Do you mean to tell me, sir, that you did not go down to join that man?"

"I did go down to join him, Sir Francis," I replied. "I saw him asleep and tipsy in among the black currants and I left him there, and took this key to-night to wake him up and let him out by the gate in the wall."

"Why not through the coach-yard?"

"Because I was afraid he would meet Mr Solomon Brownsmith, and get into disgrace for drinking."

"Thankye, Mars Grant, thankye kindly," said Ike.

"Silence!"

Plop!

"A nice tale?" said Sir Francis. "We are getting to the bottom of a pretty state of things."

Just then I saw Courtenay look at Philip as if he were uneasy. Then I glanced at Sir Francis and saw him gnawing at his moustache.

"Lookye here, sir," said Ike sturdily. "Is it likely as we two would take the fruit? Why, we're always amongst it, and think no more of it than if it was so much stones and dirt. We ain't thieves."

"Look here," said Sir Francis, suddenly taking a tack in another direction, "you own that you beat my son—my stepson," he added correctively, "in that way?"

"Yes, Sir Francis," I said, "I didn't know who he was in the dark."

"You couldn't see him?"

"Only just, Sir Francis; and I hit him as hard as I could."

"And you, my man, do you own that you struck my other stepson as hard as you could in the chest?"

"No!" cried Ike fiercely; and to the surprise of all he threw off his jacket and rolled up his shirt sleeve, displaying a great red-brown mass of bone and muscle, and a mighty fist. "Lookye here, your worship. See there. Why, if I'd hit that boy with that there fist as hard as ever I could, there wouldn't be no boy now, only a coroner's inquess. Bah! I wonder at you, Sir Francis! There's none of my marks on him, only where I gripped his arms. Take off your jacket, youngster, and show your pa."

"How dare you!" cried Philip indignantly.

"Take off your jacket, sir!" roared Sir Francis, and trembling and flushing, Philip did as he was told, and at a second bidding rolled up his sleeves to show the marks of Ike's fingers plainly enough.

Ike said nothing now, but uttered a low grunt.

"He did hit me," cried Philip excitedly.

"No; I hit you," I cried, "when I rushed at you first. I followed you after I'd heard you scramble over the wall."

"Oh!" cried Philip with an indignant look.

"You heard them scramble over the wall?" said Sir Francis sharply.

"Yes, Sir Francis. I think it was by the big keeping-pear that is trained horizontally—that large old tree, the last in the row."

Sir Francis sat back in his chair for a few moments in silence; and Courtenay said to his brother in a whisper, but loud enough for everyone to hear:

"Did you ever hear anyone go on like that!"

Sir Francis took no notice, but slowly rose from his seat, crossed the room, opened the French window that looked out upon the lawn, and then said:

"Hand me a candle, Brownsmith."

The candle was placed in his hands, and he walked with it right out on to the lawn and then held it above his head.

Then, walking back into the room, he took up another candlestick.

"Let everyone stay as he is till I come back."

"Do you mean us to stay here, papa—with these people?" said Courtenay haughtily.

Sir Francis stopped short and looked at him sternly without speaking, making the boy blench. Then he turned away without a word, and followed by Mr Solomon bearing a lighted candle, which hardly flickered in the still autumn evening, he went on down the garden.

"Haw—haw—haw!" laughed Ike as soon as we were alone. "You're a pair o' nice uns—you are! But you're ketched this time," he added.

"How dare you speak to us, sir!" cried Courtenay indignantly. "Hold your tongue, sir!"

"No use to hold it now," said Ike laughing. "I say, don't you feel warm?"

"Don't take any notice of the fellow, Court," cried Phil; "and as for pauper—"

"You leave him to me," said Courtenay with a vindictive look. "I'll make him remember telling his lies of me—yes, and of you too. He shall remember to-night as long as he lives, unless he asks our pardon, as soon as Sir Francis comes back and owns that it was he who was taking the pears."

I turned away from them and spoke to Ike, who was asking me about my hurts.

"Oh! they're nothing," I said—"only a few scratches and bruises. I don't mind them."

The two boys were whispering eagerly together, and I heard Philip say:

"Well, ask him; he'd do anything for money."

"Look here," said Courtenay.

I believe he was going to offer to bribe us; but just then there was the sound of voices in the garden and Sir Francis appeared directly after, candle in hand, closely followed by Mr Solomon, and both of them looking very serious, though somehow it did not have the slightest effect on me, for I was watching the faces of Courtenay and Philip.

"Shut that window, Brownsmith," said Sir Francis, as he set down his candle and went back to his chair behind the table.

Mr Solomon shut the window, and then came forward and set down his candle in turn.

"Now," said Sir Francis, "we can finish this business, I think. You say, Grant, that you heard someone climb over the wall by the big trained pear-tree?"

"I heard two people come over, sir, and one of them fell down, and, I think, broke a small tree or bush."

"Yes," said Sir Francis, "a bush is broken, and someone has climbed over by that big pear-tree."

"I digged that bit along that wall only yesterday," said Ike.

"Be silent, sir," cried Sir Francis; "stop. Come forward; set a candle down on the floor, Brownsmith."

It was done.

"You, Isaac, hold up one of your feet—there, by the candle. No, no, man; I want to see the sole."

Ike held up a foot as if he were a horse about to be shod, and growled out:

"Fifteen and six, master, and warranted water-tights."

"That will do, my man," said Sir Francis, frowning severely as if to hide a smile; and Ike put down his great boot and went softly back to his place.

"Now you, Grant," said Sir Francis.

I walked boldly to the candle and held up my heavily-nailed garden boots, so that Sir Francis could see the soles.

"That will do, my lad," he said. "Now you, Courtenay, and you, Philip."

They came forward half-puzzled, but I saw clearly enough Sir Francis' reasons, Ike's remark about the fresh digging having given me the clue.

"That will do," said Sir Francis; and as the boys passed me to go back to their places I heard Philip utter a sigh of relief.

"What time did you hear these people climb over the wall, Grant?" said Sir Francis.

"I can't tell exactly, Sir Francis," I replied. "I think it must have been about eight o'clock."

"What time is it now, Courtenay?" said Sir Francis. The lad clapped his hand to his pocket, but his watch was not there.

"I've left it in the bed-room," he said hastily; and he turned to leave the library, but stopped as if turned to stone as he heard Sir Francis thunder out:

"You left it hanging on the Easter Beurré pear-tree, sir, when you climbed down with your brother—on one of the short spurs, before you both left your foot-marks all over the newly-dug bed. Courtenay Dalton—Philip Dalton, if you were my own sons I should feel that a terrible stain had fallen upon my name."

The boys stood staring at him, looking yellow, and almost ghastly.

"And as if that proof were not enough, Courtenay, Dalton; when you fell and broke that currant bush—"

"It was Phil who fell," cried the boy with a vicious snarl.

"The truth for the first time," said Sir Francis. Then bitterly: "And I thought you were both gentlemen! Leave the room."

"It was Phil who proposed it all, papa," cried Courtenay appealingly.

"Ah, you sneak!" cried Philip. "I didn't, sir. I was as bad as he was, I suppose, and I thought it good fun, but I shouldn't have told all those lies if he hadn't made me. There, they were all lies! Now you can punish me if you like."

"Leave the room!" said Sir Francis again; and he stood pointing to the door as the brothers went out, looking miserably crestfallen.

Then the door closed, and the silence was broken by a sharp cry, a scuffle, the sound of blows, and a fall, accompanied by the smashing of some vessel on the stone floor.

Sir Francis strode out into the hall, and there was a hubbub of voices, and I heard Philip cry passionately:

"Yes; I did hit him. He began on me, and I'll do it again—a coward!"

Then there was a low murmur for a few minutes, and Sir Francis came back into the library and stood by the table, with the light shining on his great silver moustache; and I thought what a fine, handsome, fierce old fellow he looked as he stood frowning there for quite a minute without speaking. Then, turning to Mr Solomon, he said quickly:

"I beg your pardon, Brownsmith. I was excited and irritable to-night, and said what I am sorry for now."

"Then don't say any more, Sir Francis," replied Mr Solomon quietly. "I've been your servant—"

"Faithful servant, Brownsmith."

"Well, Sir Francis, 'faithful servant,'" said Mr Solomon smiling, "these twenty years, and you don't suppose I'm going to heed a word or two like that."

"Thank you, Brownsmith," said Sir Francis, and he turned to Ike and spoke sharply once more.

"What regiment were you in, sir?"

"Eighth Hoozoars, Captain," said Ike, drawing himself up and standing at attention.

"Colonel," whispered Mr Solomon.

"All right!" growled Ike.

"Well, then, Isaac Barnes, speaking as one old soldier to another, I said words to you to-night for which I am heartily sorry. I beg your pardon."

"God bless you, Colonel! If you talk to me like that arterward, you may call me what you like."

"Eh?" cried Sir Francis sharply; "then I will. How dare you then, you scoundrel, go and disgrace yourself; you, an ex-British soldier—a man who has worn the king's uniform—disgrace yourself by getting drunk? Shame on you, man, shame!"

"Go on, Colonel. Give it to me," growled Ike. "I desarve it."

"No," said Sir Francis, smiling; "not another word; but don't let it occur again."

Ike drew his right hand across one eye, and the left over the other, and gave each a flip as if to shake off a tear, as he growled something about "never no more."

I hardly heard him, though, for I was trembling with agitation as I saw Sir Francis turn to me, and I knew that my turn had come.

"Grant, my lad," he said quietly; "I can't tell you how hurt and sorry I felt to-night when I believed you to be mixed up with that contemptible bit of filching. There is an abundance of fruit grown here, and I should never grudge you sharing in that which you help to produce. I was the more sorry because I have been watching your progress, and I was more than satisfied: I beg your pardon too, for all that I have said. Those boys shall beg it too."

He held out his hand, and I caught it eagerly in mine as I said, in choking tones.

"My father was an officer and a gentleman, sir, and to be called a thief was very hard to bear."

"It was, my lad; it was," he said, shaking my hand warmly. "There, there, I'll talk to you another time."

I drew back, and we were leaving the room, I last, when, obeying an impulse, I ran back.

"Well, my lad?" he said kindly.

"I beg your pardon, Sir Francis; but you said that they should beg my pardon."

"Yes," he said hotly; "and they shall."

"If you please, Sir Francis," I said, "I would rather they did not."

"Why, sir?"

"I think they have been humbled enough."

"By their own conduct?" said Sir Francis. "Yes, you are right. I will not mention it again."